APART

APART

C. J. Pastore

Apart

By C.J. Pastore

ISBN: 978-0-9979480-2-8

Interior Design and Formatting by:

www.emtippettsbookdesigns.com

THE PAST

Chase Reardon, Afghanistan, 2006

omething's not right. The chipped landscape of barren desert glares into my eyes, blurring their lock on someone treading alongside the road carrying a wrapped bundle like it's a swathed newborn. His arms never waver, his clasp doesn't loosen; only his eyes shift as he monitors my approach. Dogs bark in the distance, lone hungry howls that mirror the cry of wolves. A nervous sweat peppers my forehead and squinting ahead, I study his stooped form. Thick bearded and wearing a white karakul cap, long white shirt, and loose-fitting trousers, he looks like any one of the hundreds of local farmers. Problem is so does the enemy, who has the tendency to surface like an army of ants ready to devour their prey. Gripping my weapon, I watch for any sudden movement as I head towards him.

My platoon of six walk behind, armed and ready to flush out Taliban insurgents. Sammy keeps a razor eye on the ground just ahead of each crunch of my footsteps. The man gives me a toothless grin and holding his parcel to his chest with one hand, he places the other over his heart then extends it for a handshake. His hand is coarse and lined, its fingernails split and caked with dirt. Definitely a farmer. I offer mine and we shake. He asks in choppy English, "You good today, my friend?" When meeting in Afghanistan, not asking about someone's well-being is rude.

I nod assent. "And you?" Eager to end the intro, I focus on his hands and the parcel they hold.

"Yes, yes, go to Kabul." His arm shifts and my finger readies for the trigger. His expression holds uncertainty blended with fright, a look that can be seen on any person at any given time in this godforsaken stretch of land. In war, enemy and friends occupy the same dimension of terror. The only difference is one is out to kill you and the other to protect you.

One fucking whopping difference.

He unwraps his bundle and raises it for me to see. My hand stills. Peeking out from the bundle, a leafy bush dons a poised, pink rose bud. Its stunning perfection is like seeing a glimmer of hope.

"Baghe Babur," he intones, grinning and bobbing his head. Sammy looks up and shakes his head. I'm just as confused, but since it doesn't seem rigged with explosives, I'm ready to move on. The man idles closer, his face crinkling with warmth as he points to the small bush. "Beautiful, yes? I bring to plant in Garden of Babur, in Kabul." It's hard to tear my gaze from the rose's flawless form. It's as if the sweet scent is softening the grit and dust trapped in my nose and mouth. He keeps the blossom unwrapped and extended, marveling at its luster, before carefully covering it again. "I go now. Live in peace, my friend."

We step aside, and he strides forward continuing his trek towards Kabul. The flowering visage vanishes on the buckled link of roadway that's littered with mismatched army and civilian vehicles ambling towards Kandahar.

Two scorpions skulk from the crevice of a rock, the first scurrying across my boot. I kick it towards Sammy as I watch the other take cover under a boulder. Damn fuckers are everywhere.

Sammy lifts his boot and kicks it aside with a grunt. "Screw you, Ivy. You won't be laughing when I wrap one around your dick tonight." His eyes fastened on the road ahead, he takes one slow step, then another. Quick and relentless, Sammy's a human IED detector.

Ivy. That's what everyone calls me since my acceptance to Yale. No bother. Scholarships and the good old GI bill just got me a free university ride. Keeping myself and my buddies alive is what matter now.

"Yeah, well, Sammy, that'd be the most action his dick has seen in a long time. Might even get off on it. Isn't that right, Ivy?" Hank smirks before gingerly stepping onto a clump of

C. J. Pastore

flattened earth. He knows death hides in unsettled sand that masks explosives.

Taking a respite from relentless scrutiny, I point to the buckling and potholed thoroughfare. "Hey, bro, how are you enjoying this new motorway? It's Highway 1, just like the route along the ocean of your home state. Look familiar?" Hank's from southern California and there must be something about that area's chronic sunshine because he's been deployed several months now and he still has that tanned surfer look.

It's hard to miss the irony the innocuous name paints of what is really a stretch of perilous highway: a peopled road that's become an easy target for insurgent suicide bombers and roadside explosives. Bureaucrats came up with the idea that a good way to improve travel and communication in a war-torn country rife with corruption was to build a road linking Kabul and Kandahar. Always trying to earn points for winning the *human war*.

Problem is, in Afghanistan there's always some group wanting to fight another. No matter if they're warlords, drug lords, Al-Qaida, Northern Alliance, or Taliban, one faction interfaces with the other, with the desire to fight a common thread. Public relations and ideology are not high on their to-do lists. To them, we're enemy combatants infringing on their right to run their land as they see fit.

It's like this cat, Slick, my sister Fiona adopted. Slick was nothing more than a striped fur ball that darted through the grass hunting birds, mice, bugs, dogs, other cats, and just about any creature that infringed on his turf. I once spotted him stalking a circling hawk. Nothing more than a small form crouched in a feline pounce position determined to keep that hawk from swooping into his territory.

Slick especially hated pigeons. Every day he tracked them until finally he caught one. Pounced and clawed at that poor bird until its wing was damaged and it couldn't fly. Fiona was devastated. She carried the bird in a box to the nearest veterinarian and insisted she help. The vet wanted nothing to do with what she referred to as a "rodent with wings," so Fiona took care of that bird herself. Nursed it back to health then set it free, but Slick continued hunting no matter what Fiona did. Placing a bell on his collar, keeping him inside for long stretches of time, wagging a finger and telling him no, nothing worked. First chance Slick got, he was back hunting and stalking animals and birds like they were some plague invading his space.

Infidels. That's what they call us here. We hear it so often, Mac had it tattooed across his upper arm, right above a dragon exhaling an AK-47. Dramatic, but not going to keep us alive. I figure, why mar my body with inked needles when I'm trying to remain unscathed by bombs and bullets. Funny how the mind thinks of someone or something that seems random until awareness reveals it has a purpose. I haven't seen Mac since special-op training ended ten months ago, but his words ring in my ears as if he's standing right here. "Trust your gut.

If it doesn't feel right, it's not right and identifying what's off is what keeps you alive."

Fuck if I know what's off here. Hank's bantering tone belies the fear his eyes speak. "Well, Ivy, I'm just waiting for the ocean views to start so I can lower the top of my convertible and cruise on down the highway with my girlfriend. Maybe pull over and make sweet love to her with the surf as an orchestra. Yep, I got romance coursing through my veins." He slants his head at me and smirks.

"Eyes forward. You want to be sure you spew love and not your guts."

His gaze reverts to the rocky banks ahead. My uneasiness is constant, like some dank, noxious cloud that spreads each time my searches reveal nothing. I hear the chug and whir of engines from the truckloads of military and medical personnel heading towards Kandahar to address the unrest and treat the population for a Polio epidemic. Our job is to see that they safely reach the next check point where other military personnel will pick up the guard.

Taliban insurgents would like nothing more than to blow up these trucks of health-care workers. Even declared a fatwa against the medics despite the fact that all they're trying to do is protect children from a crippling virus. No way I can figure out their ass-backwards politics, but I can keep myself and my platoon alive.

There's a hiss and thumping noise as one vehicle limps to the side of the road with a flat tire. Two medics hop out and ready themselves to make the necessary repair without surveillance or weapons.

Live bulls' eyes.

I head in their direction, surveying … searching … studying … trying to find anything—no matter how small and seemingly insignificant—that could be out of place. *Ok, Reardon, keep your guard up and trust your instinct to know what's wrong when you see it.* I'm no "Ivy Leaguer" yet, but damn if a bullet or bomb is going to keep me from getting out of here.

I blink once, twice, swiping sweat from my forehead and watching with a vigilance that snaps every nuance, object, and person into place. When the memory hits, I do a double take in all directions. Where the hell is she? She's always here at this time, covered in a burqa, like a blue-shrouded ghost as she walks to the market. Could she have gotten a tip that there's an impending ambush? Wouldn't be the first time something like this has happened. Insurgents want to protect their own, often tipping off locals before an impending attack.

I finally spot her, feet kicking up dust as she walks along the far wall of the school. She's taking her usual path, walking on the same side of the road, head straight, body erect, nothing to indicate she's nervous. Exhaling a deep breath, my body uncoils from a posture so stiff it felt as if my spine was chiseled stone.

I reach the truck with the flat tire just as one of the doctors, a dark-bearded, weary-eyed man, lifts the spare tire and rolls it towards the front of the truck. Throwing me a glance, he calls out, "Do you have a jack. Ours is broken." That's no surprise. Everything is broken here. My eyes pivot back to the woman.

Fuck! Two large sandaled feet jut out from beneath billowing robes. A beefy hand reaches inside just as the figure charges ahead.

Breathe, Reardon. Breathe.

I shoot once then twice. The target drops sending sand and stones rocketing in all directions as his suicide vest explodes. Ten seconds more and we would have been diced meat lying alongside his body parts.

Adrenaline pumps through me as I swivel my weapon right then up before aiming straight ahead. Sammy, doing the same, begins treading carefully towards what remains of the body. The medics freeze and a quiet descends, suspending us in the breath of a moment that stretches forever.

And then it happens.

"IED!" Sammy hollers, hurling himself off the side of the road. I jump onto the medic and we topple over the side of a gulley just as the force of the explosion rips waves of dirt and pieces of metal in all directions. Its deafening, fire-breathing roar courses through my body, rings in my ears and singes my skin. We roll down a ravine, my body over his, stones and coarse earth scratching and piercing our skin until the bark of a tree slams us to a halt.

Crack. Crack. Crack. A fire of bullets splinter holly branches that ricochet as we dive for cover. Remnants of a bombed-out Humvee scatter like pieces of a plastic toy waiting to be assembled. Two of its rear tires are strewn on opposite sides of a scorched road stained with leaking oil and blood.

"Incoming fire from the southeast corner!" Sammy shouts.

"This is Eagle 367. Do you copy? TIC," Hank bellows into the radio. "I repeat, troops in combat. Sniper fire coming from one hundred meters outside the marketplace, approximately 180 degrees southwest." The response is curt and sure.

"Roger that. Clear to engage contact."

The relentless snap of bullets leaves no time to think or speak. I drag the medic beneath me in a slow crawl. Machine gun fire ricochets on all sides. Keeping low, we inch forward taking cover behind a stack of abandoned timber.

"You alright?" My voice is lost in the deafening roar of gunfire. Head bent and gasping for breath, he nods. With our backs pushed against the protection of a mound of cedar, I calculate that our chances are not good. We're surrounded. Any movement will get us killed and leaves me no option but to wait for a reloading pause so I can take out the rooftop sniper doing the most damage. In this contest, there is no second-place prize.

The medic's breathing hard and an ugly gash on his head bleeds into his swollen right eye. "What're you thinking we can do to get out of this mess?" he shouts above the blistering gunfire.

The bulk of shots appear to be coming from approximately 150 meters to the west. Counting intervals between blasts, I wait for their reloading pause. In that sliced moment of time, I pivot, stand, aim, and fire in rapid succession before dropping down again. Muzzle flashes hit all around us and then … fucking blessed silence.

Heart racing, I glance at the medic. "I'm thinking I'm being fucking underpaid for this shit."

There's cheering from those under direct fire from that particular area, but it's not over and the next deafening round of firepower is relentless.

Thwack, thwack, thwack.

The sound becomes louder until enemy outposts are exploding with fire. Apaches swoop in to attack the insurgents holding us down and damn if it's not like the cavalry arriving in the nick of time. Hank's radio crackles in the distance. "RTG continuing to engage. Taking a hard left." And the area explodes. We stay low waiting for them to finish. "Targets down, Eagle 367, Eagle 1 RTB."

Job completed, the Apaches return back to base. There's a rousing cheer from the men. It's unbelievable. A 150-pound explosive device packing enough power to blow apart 32,000 pounds of steel detonates, followed by a full-throttle, surprise enemy ambush, and the number of casualties in our platoon: zero. This is one for the record books. Pumped with relief, we jump up laughing and swatting each other. Looks like I'll live to see the end of another day.

The medic stands and when our eyes meet, his gaze speaks volumes about life and death and witnessing hell on earth.

He stares at a form lying facedown, and my eyes travel to the gaping hole that's oozing blood and brains from the prone body. Doc Sanders, our platoon physician who's joining the convoy, checks for a pulse then shakes his head. An unscathed package with a pink tip stands within reach of his outstretched fingers. Mingled rage and despair course through me as I approach the corpse. Picking up the contents of the packet, I hold the plant protectively to my chest and look up only when I hear the Pakistani medic. Each of his words hug the formality of a British accent, calling out, "I owe you my life. It is a debt of honor I will forever attempt to repay."

I'm tired. Confused. Devastated. I don't understand this dance of life and death. Can't grasp why, with what seems like the mindless toss of a coin, some survive and others don't. Nothing I can do about it now. Only thing left is to grab life by the balls and hold tight, moving forward until I'm so far ahead there's no looking back.

I point my chin towards the medic. "Consider your debt absolved. I've already been rewarded. You're alive and…" I hug the package tighter "…after a stop in Kabul, my tour is over." As an afterthought I add, "What's your name?"

"My name is Sunny."

"Sunny, I'm Chase. Chase Reardon." I shake his hand for the first and last time because inside there's one fact I know as definitively as I know my name.

This pigeon is flying the coop.

CHAPTER ONE

The Present

"That's him." The metal chair in the sparsely furnished area of the seventeenth precinct house presses cold and hard against my back. I check the image on the computer screen, tracing the hollowed cheekbones and cold-as-stone eyes that stare from beneath sharply arched brows.

"Are you sure, Ms. Cesare?" Detective Wilson questions, studying the screen. I first met Detective James Wilson at the hospital shortly after my attack. A lead detective from the Special Victim's Unit, his calm and reassuring demeanor put me at ease. But now, the day after, the reality of the attack settles like a festering wound. It's as if the culprit staring from the computer screen still holds me at knifepoint, the sharp tip of his blade pricking my lip and pressing against my neck. I try to shake the compulsive hatred mirrored in his steely gray eyes, but I know, as clearly as I understand the sun will rise tomorrow, that Dimitri Ostopenko is never going to forget. Revenge seals his soul and hatred rules his actions.

"Yes, absolutely." I manage to croak. Disgust tightens my stomach and inches up to my throat as I relive the coppery stench of the ruthless mobster's blood spurting over my body. Covering my nose with the back of my hand, I squelch the queasiness.

Detective Wilson thumbs through a lined legal pad, glancing through hand-written notes. He's old school but thorough. "You said the contents of the envelope left for you at the front desk of your apartment building…" he pauses trying to find the right way to continue but comes up blank and just plows ahead "…contained a severed finger. Is that right?"

"Yes."

He's determined to confirm the accuracy of all the information he collected from me last night. "And you thought it belonged to your boyfriend Chase's sister, Fiona, because you recognized the same ring on her finger several times before?"

I nod. The ring couldn't be mistaken for anyone but Fiona's. The turquoise stone sported veins so thin they disappeared into its sheened perfection. I had admired it several times as it graced the index finger of Fiona's left hand.

Alert eyes shift to Chase. "We're going to need to question Fiona and your father. I assume they are … available." The implication hangs in the silence.

C. J. Pastore

Chase's response is cold and clipped. "My father's been sober for over eight years now, Detective, and Fiona has been drug free. They have nothing to add or to do with my problems with Dimitri."

Sourness collects in my mouth as the past morphs into the present, spinning recall into reality. My body starts to shake. Vivid visions of Dimitri's attack spring to life. My stitched hand throbs, my swollen eye aches, and an icy dread settles inside my bones. The metallic smell of his blood continues to assault making it seem as if a battery of hemorrhaging victims is splayed across the room.

"Are you alright?" Detective Wilson's concern is buffered by the image from the screen that pins me to my seat. I try tearing my eyes from it, shaking myself back to the present, but frozen with anxiety I can only gape at the face that now appears more monster than human. His knife-wielding hands forcing me from the lobby of my apartment building and into the basement, where he groped my breasts and tore at my clothes; the dankness that clung to the walls; the ominous silence when his member was too flaccid to penetrate, and the rage trapped in his tight, raised fist that he readied to crash into my face. Heart hammering, I remember the shard of glass clutched in my hand slicing into the underside of his arm and his blood spurting like spray from a waterfall. A flicker of disbelief emanated from eyes that would appear deadened if not for the sparks of driven hatred that flared in their depths.

All these images merge to hold me hostage. I can't process what I should be doing or saying. Until … I hear that familiar voice and feel the warm caressing of my arm. It's only then that I'm able to reconnect to the reality of the faded walls and marred, dull floor of the precinct room.

Chase bends and tenderly strokes my forehead. "It's ok. You're going to be alright." He cups my face in his palms. "Alicia, deep breaths. In … out."

The warmth of his hands soothe the chill coursing through me, and I do as he says. When I can finally look up, the first thing I notice is the mounted clock, a large and lumbering appendage jutting from the wall, its second hand jerking forward, a reminder of the previous minutes that felt like hours. The second is the man I've fallen in love with, the man who has changed my life, who has swept me from a simple, coddled existence into a world of passion, love, and fear.

I lean into Chase's arm and try to catch the sob lodged in my throat. I fail and quietly weep, keeping my face pressed against his body. He says nothing, just pulls me towards him and cradles me in a comforting embrace. I relish the contact, marveling at how one person can illicit the change from crippling trauma to soothing relief. There is no time or space for shame. My fear is too raw, too overwhelming to allow for the triviality of embarrassment from my loss of control.

"Mr. Reardon," Detective Wilson interrupts, eager to get on with the investigation. "If you could tell us if you recognize this man, we could wrap this up."

Chase lets go of my arm and it only takes one brief glance before he nods tersely. "That's Dimitri Ostopenko."

"Are you certain?" Detective Wilson is merely doing his job, but Chase is annoyed.

"Don't undermine my history or insult my intelligence, Detective. The man has relentlessly stalked me, my family, my friends, and anyone close to me for well over a decade."

The detective clears his throat. "I know. I've combed through the file. You were a brave kid. What were you, fourteen at the time?"

His gaze a lifetime away, Chase doesn't answer.

"I want you to know we will apprehend this thug."

Thug is an understatement. More like a beast bent on using violence to amass power and wealth. Dimitri Ostopenko, aka The Finger for his propensity to cut off the digits of those who cross him, is a ceaseless demon hell-bent on avenging Chase for his losses. Time, age, and jail have not and will never reform Dimitri's need to destroy all that Chase holds dear. In Dimitri's psychopathic mind, Chase was instrumental in his conviction and incarceration and responsible for all the havoc that wreaked: the murder of his eldest son by rival crime gangs in Moscow, the disappearance of his wife and younger children into the witness protection program, and the financial hit to his underworld business dealings. For Dimitri, it's a personal vendetta—the nastiest type of grudge to carry because it leaves no room for negotiation. Dimitri feels no remorse or culpability, only rage and retribution.

"We're done here." Chase's tone is blunt, leaving no room for further questioning as he wraps his arm around me and guides me out of my chair. I feel a pressing inside my chest and a cold sweat trickles down the back of my neck.

"We may have further questions. After Ms. Cesare rests perhaps we can come by and illicit her coopera—"

"You ever been in a situation where you didn't know if your next breath would be your last, Detective?" Chase gives the detective a penetrating stare. "Maybe it was during a gang war or a drug bust where it was you and your partner against a battery of armed and desperate killers defending their turf and merchandise." The detective looks down and shuffles with discomfort. I swallow my unease because I'm guessing Chase has some inside information about a chilling incident Detective Wilson was forced to confront. "You watched your partner get gunned down. You survived and got the bastards. Now you get to celebrate by reliving the moment of hell over and over again without warning. They're called flashbacks, and Alicia just had the last one she's going to have triggered by you or anyone else from your department. You have any more questions, you consult me." He pauses for a moment. "As far as I'm concerned, I did my part. I helped you arrest and convict one of the worst organized crime leaders in a decade. How long were you looking to nab this Russian kingpin on drug and weapon trafficking, even murder? Three, four years and you couldn't get the bastard. Then I come along, a gullible fourteen-year-old with photos ..." Chase pauses, his voice cracks, and he shoots me a quick glance then in a hard tone, finishes. "I got clear pics of him viciously raping my friend. Devie Raykhelson was only thirteen years old, in case you don't remember. I secretly snapped them while hearing the screams of what she suffered at the hands of that madman. Detective Wilson looks as if he's about to say something, but Chase is not finished. "You finally got your man. So what if it was on charges of the rape of a minor instead of racketeering and murder. It was enough to keep him from seeing the light of day for a long time. We'll protect you and your family, the police told me. Yeah, right. He even stalked us from jail having his clan of thugs harass us wherever we went. And now he's let go because he participated in a chemical sexual suppressant program. You released a ruthless racketeer. I have no more use for you or your assurances of justice and security."

He takes my hand and guides me towards the door. Even in my state, I can see that blaming the detective for all that's happened in the past is unwarranted. It's not Detective Wilson's fault that Dimitri was released then slipped through the system's fingers. He wasn't even involved in the previous investigations and eventual conviction. Still, I can't fault Chase's ire. He's suffered at the hands of this maniac for a long time.

Detective Wilson doesn't answer, just leans forward, arms outstretched, hands pressed into the top of his desk as he chews on his lower lip. When he looks up, his sharp brown eyes bore into us. "Once again, I can assure you that we are doing everything in our power to capture and arrest this felon. The FBI is involved as well as the prosecutor's office. We will find Ostopenko."

Before we walk through the door, Chase stops in his tracks, still as statue, and asks in a stern, flat tone, "Tell me something, Detective. Dimitri's expertise is knowing how to minimize risk. He eluded you guys all those years, so it's not like him to take such a flagrant chance of getting caught by openly revealing himself in a lobby of a high-rise residential building on the Upper East Side. I want to know how he got past the doorman in Alicia's building when I can't even get through without being stopped although they've seen me multiple times and know me well. How the hell did he get in and out so seamlessly?"

Detective Wilson's answer cuts through the ensuing silence like a blade slicing flesh. "He had help. We believe it was someone you know well." He searches through countless folders that clutter his desk, chooses one held together by a rubber band so stretched the folder oozes papers, index cards, and sticky notes. Rifling through it, he finds what he's looking for and places it on his desk. Staring straight at us, from the lobby of my building, is a photo of Devie Raykhelson.

CHAPTER TWO

"I just don't understand why Devie would want to help Dimitri. Does she hate me that much?"

I'm sitting on Chase's living room sofa, ensconced in his white terry robe after taking yet another shower to try and remove the stench of that monster from my memory. The fact that his essence lingers like some trapped viper is sickening and infuriating. I sink into the plush comfort of Chase's robe and take a deep breath inhaling soap, sun, and sandalwood—all him, all reminders of our recent trip to Italy and the South of France. More at ease, my mind drifts back to today's sordid details.

I knew Devie never warmed to me. In fact, the few times we met she was downright hostile, but there was no easy way to shake her off. She and Chase shared a childhood bond that encompassed more than walking to school together, having lunch in the cafeteria, and hanging out on the football field. At the time, Chase's mother was dying from cancer and his father had taken to binge drinking. I don't remember all the details because even though we grew up in the same town, by the time I was old enough to understand, Chase's mother had died and his father stopped drinking and turned his life around. But for Chase and his sister Fiona, the damage was done. Chase said for years he believed he didn't fit in, said he felt *like a commoner outside* and Fiona, although mostly clean now, struggles with bouts of drug abuse.

Devie had no easy time of it either. Her mother was a chronic drug abuser. Heroin was her drug of choice. When not incoherent, Elena was sleeping with just about anyone who kept her well stocked with drugs—and that included Dimitri Ostopenko. It was a match made in hell. She received a steady supply, and he was able to whore out a beautiful woman for profit. Dimitri also figured he could seize the opportunity to force himself on her young daughter. Never thought for a second that a mere teenager would be smart and brave enough to bring him down.

So ... there's all that *and* the not so small fact that Chase and Devie were once lovers. Yes, I admit I'm envious. Who wouldn't be? Devie radiates sulky elegance: tall, angular body, dark hair fashioned in a sleek bob, porcelain white skin, and dark eyes with just the right modicum of slant to imply exotic mystery. Attractiveness personified, she wears her clothing with the expertise of a model and the grace of a dancer.

Works as a model, too, for top design houses and magazines. It's impressive how she lifted herself from a blighted past to become successful and productive. She and Chase have that in common as well.

My thoughts are interrupted by a clipped voice and a no-nonsense tone I've come to know well.

"I have no idea what hold Dimitri has on Devie. I don't even know if Elena still sees him." He clasps his mouth shut. I think my swollen eye, stitched hand, and precinct meltdown keep him from angrily adding, "*And I don't give a fuck.*" Not spoken but implied. He takes a deep breath, reining in his temper, and shoots me a sympathetic glance before the litany of orders I also have come to know, to follow.

"I don't want you anywhere near Devie. Do not take her calls or accept her visits and if you spot her in your vicinity, call me immediately." His phone jingles, but he's so worked up, he doesn't even check to see who it is and just lets it ring until it shifts to voicemail.

His decrees might prove difficult since Devie occasionally models for the same design house I work for. As if reading my mind, he interjects, "If she happens to be modeling at Estelle Designs, leave immediately."

Even though that seems unlikely given that she's wanted by the police for questioning in my abduction, I shoot him my incredulous "*how the hell do I just leave work?*" expression.

He emphatically responds, "Just tell them you feel sick." His hair is spiked from his rifling hands, and he nervously rubs the side of his chin with his palm, but it's the expression in his eyes that pierce my heart. They shout hurt and betrayal. He's grappling with the idea that someone he befriended and defended since adolescence has aligned with the enemy. I take his hand, lift it to my lips, and kiss his palm. I simply cannot give this man any more worry.

"Ok. I'll do as you ask."

He relaxes immediately, his body loosening from a stance as rigid as rock. His cell bleats again and he ignores it, not even bothering to see who's calling. It's early afternoon on Monday, a usually serious work day, and he has not checked his schedule once or taken a single call. Nor have I for that matter.

"Good. No worries about bumping into Devie at work this week. You need to rest that hand and eye." I don't bother answering because an argument is the last thing I want now. My plan is to try to ease my way back into the office later in the week. I have some sketches to update for a new line I'm being encouraged to develop and other designs that are being sewn that will require my input. Besides, last thing I want is to be reduced to invalid status because of the attack. No one at the office or in my immediate family know what happened, and I want to keep it that way for as long as possible.

Playing with a strand of my hair, Chase pulls me closer. He's unusually quiet and—I'm sure—still upset about what happened. He even had Sunny, Sammy, and another Marine buddy Mac move my belongings into his place last night while I slept in a Nurse Jackie-drugged coma. Yep, three former

Marines and a Pakistani army medic sorted, organized, and closeted every stitch of clothing I own, adeptly moving them from my apartment to Chase's bedroom suite without my permission or knowledge.

Sunny, dressed as usual in his loose-fitting white button up jacket and black trousers, brings me a cup of tea sweetened with honey and brandy. Sunny is the former Pakistani military medic who shares a comradery with Chase that belies a mere employer-employee relationship. It's a connection that began in Afghanistan and has strengthened ever since Sunny turned up in New York and Chase gave him a place to live and a job. Each would give his life to protect the other, and they form only one part of a tight band of combat comrades in Chase's life. I take a sip of tea allowing its warmth to seep into my fear-chilled bones.

"Humph!" Sunny looks at Chase and grunts, shaking his head. I watch as he retreats to the kitchen, hoping he isn't still giving Chase a hard time about moving me in without my consent or a marriage proposal. Sunny's a conservative thinker in that regard.

"How are you feeling, Alicia?" Sammy steps into the room, shoots a nervous glance at Chase before turning his eyes back to me and smiling. A tad too cheerfully for my liking. I'm thinking he must have been here at the apartment for a while waiting for me to settle in after my precinct visit. I know he holds himself accountable for my predicament. Sammy's responsibility is to see I remain safe from Dimitri and his underworld gang of criminals. It's a job he takes seriously. He and Chase met as part of the same special-op team in Afghanistan. That was several years ago and to this day they remain tight. They are Marine battle brothers, part of a link of comrades who would risk their lives for each other and their loved ones. It's a bond that's hard to grasp by those who have not seen war.

"I'm fine, just a bit tired." I want to take another one of those pain killers prescribed by the hospital to help deaden the throbbing in my hand, but the thought of closing my eyes and inviting back the terror of my ordeal compels me to stay awake. "I just think I'm going to relax today, lounge around in this robe." I take in its scent again, immediately relaxing when all I smell is Chase. Sammy fires another jittery glance at Chase before nodding and leaving the room. I have no idea why he's still at the apartment. Something's up, but damn if I know what it is.

The persistent ringing from Chase's cell interrupts my dark thoughts. Sighing, I take another sip of tea allowing the brandy to loosen my tension while I bask in the relief that I've turned off my phone. Chase unlocks his arm from around my shoulder and leaves to take the call. I'm glad because the ignored chiming only serves as a painful reminder that it's not a normal workday with accepted calls, emails, and meetings. It brings attention to all the thorny issues that remain in our relationship. Besides, I'm well aware that he is in the middle of a competitive bid for another development project in Brooklyn.

An empty silence settles when Chase leaves. It's difficult to identify or describe the aloneness. It's like knowing, in the far reaches of your consciousness, that someone was once with you and you can't put your finger on who it was or where it's disappeared to, but an indent remains that had once been filled.

No one in my family realizes that I know I had a twin brother. He was stillborn, weighing less than two pounds at birth, while I was born a healthy, robust six pounds six ounces. It's like I absorbed all the necessary nourishment leaving him none to survive. My mother didn't cope well after my birth. I was the change-of-life baby, the happy little surprise that I get the feeling she wasn't really happy about. Since I was born, she's grappled with bouts of depression that knock her into bed for weeks at a time like some lifeless apparition of her real self, and I get to blame myself each and every time she succumbs to its dark depths. The problem is she never told me I had a twin. When I was twelve, I accidentally overheard the details from a family member during a conversation she was having with my sobbing mother. Now, my father and three older brothers tiptoe around the truth so as not to slip and upset my mother. It's like circling a blaze that never withers.

"A penny for your thoughts." He massages the area on my forehead that rests between my brows. "I can always tell when you're concerned about something because this area furrows." He continues to rub his thumb softly across its surface. My loins stir. His touch is tantalizing when he bends and places a feathery kiss on my lips. I don't know if Sammy is still in the room or where Sunny is, and still I lean into his touch, ready to bare all. When my lips tighten on his, he pulls back and even though desire cloaks his eyes, he shakes his head no. My hope of becoming lost in lust evaporates and before I can protest, he speaks four simple words.

"We have to talk."

I groan inwardly because talking is the last thing I want now. I want … No, I *need* to escape in his embrace, feel the warmth of his lips on mine, and spin with him into an oblivion of pleasure.

No such luck. With Chase, no means no. I blow out a frustrated gust of air.

"What is it that can't wait until we've spent some time together?" I discreetly reach in and massage his crotch in the hope of getting him to change his mind. He leans into my touch and just when I think he's all mine, he pulls away.

"We're getting company."

What.

"W-who?" I sputter, unable to finish because I don't want to see people.

"I tried, really I did." He's shaking his head, looking all serious and … well … frankly bewildered. "They wouldn't take no for an answer." He rolls his eyes and throws his hands in the air. I recognize that frustration and realize immediately that my family's the cause. They know.

Closing my eyes, my brow furrowing into what's probably permanent lines, I utter, "How did they find out?"

He doesn't speak, barely moves, just looks at me nervously and hands me a copy of the Daily Post folded back to page six. The headline grabs me first: **Summer of Safe Slammed**. Yeah, well, we all know who the person slammed was, but I read on anyway.

A twenty-one-year-old woman was attacked at knifepoint and dragged to the basement of her building on First Avenue and 76th Street where she was sexually assaulted before managing to escape her assailant. The incident took place on Sunday at about 7:00 p.m. The police have not identified any suspects or persons of interest at this time.

The article doesn't mention my name but gives away enough information for the people who know me to reach out and ask if I'm alright.

"They're like a herd of charging rhinos. You said so yourself. I couldn't lie and pretend nothing happened." Chase is beyond exasperated when he sees me holding my head in my hands.

"I know. I know." I exhale in some vain attempt to relax. "When will they be here?"

"In about an hour or so. Your father was making other arrangements for the restaurant, and then they're driving to the city."

"What do you mean he had to make other arrangements? What about Antonio?" Even though my father had other professional visions in mind for Antonio, my brother only wanted to train to be a chef and work in the restaurant. He finished his study at the Culinary Institute and proceeded to update the menu and operate the restaurant to rave reviews.

Chase looks down dejectedly then back up. "He insisted on coming as did Francisco, who's arriving at Grand Central..." he studies his watch then looks up "...in about an hour and Massimo, after he finishes rounds at the hospital, about the same time."

Terrific, just terrific. Groaning out loud, I wonder how I'm going to cope with the onslaught of concerned family. I hold onto one last ray of hope that it might not be as bad as I think.

"Do they know the particulars of the attack?" I'm holding my breath, praying that they don't know all the gruesome details—especially that I had been nearly drowned in Italy, then chased by some masked madman, and now attacked by Dimitri in New York. To make matters worse, I left the apartment that night after promising Chase I wouldn't because he considered it unsafe.

Chase's grimace does not convey optimism. "Massimo knows all about my past problems with Dimitri. He was there one afternoon when I was attacked after school by one of Dimitri's henchmen, and I'm fairly certain Fiona explained the situation to Antonio. They have been seeing each other for over a year now, and Antonio did help us search for Fiona when she disappeared a few weeks ago."

This is not good.

"Um … and…" He pauses.

Oh no, there's more.

"Virgil phoned from your office. He said they figured out it was you when I called in sick for you this morning. He's coming by later as well." I shake my head in disbelief. Family is one thing, but my boss and work associates are quite another.

"You couldn't put him off? I really don't want to combine office with family." My mind conjures an onslaught of cloying concern and baffled questioning.

Do you know how just about everyone has that one meddlesome relative with opinions on what you should and shouldn't be doing? Well, compound that one by five and you have my family—and that's only immediate family. Thank heavens extended family lives in Tuscany or this would spearhead into a *Matrix* sci-fi replication gone bad.

Chase takes my hand and lightly kisses its bandaged surface.

"They care about you and want to see that you're alright." He takes my other hand in his. "But if you really feel you can't handle the company, I'll meet with them at your apartment and assure them you're ok."

He's pale, his lips are taut with worry, and tiny lines trouble the sides of his eyes. Blame. Remorse. Shame. They're pelting him like a hailstorm.

I take his face in my hands, pull his lips to mine, and whisper, "Don't."

Mouth inches from mine, he asks, "Don't what?"

"Blame yourself."

He swallows and when he answers, his reply is barely audible. "How can I not?"

"That's easy to answer." The words tumble out, one after the other, a string of earnest beliefs that capture the essence of who he truly is. "Because you're passionate, because you navigate through life with a pressing need to take care of others and see that they're safe, because you're generous." I pause, waiting for my comments to sink in, then plunge ahead. "The list goes on, but I need you to understand that I am going to be alright, that together we will defeat this monster who has tormented you for so many years."

"That's just it," he continues, his tone taking on an edge. "I don't want you involved in my mess."

"Well, it's a bit late for that, don't you think?"

He's shaking his head with that stubborn, determined look I've seen on many occasions. I know he's about to say, "*It's never too late because I'll do whatever it takes to protect you,*" in that no-nonsense tone he acquires when he's agitated and wants to make a point.

Before he can open his mouth and speak the words I already hear in my head, I interject, "But I understand now, and I'll be on my guard. I won't be fooled as easily." My mind invokes my encounter with Dimitri, but there's a hiccup in my troubled thoughts. What was it he said? Then, clear as water, it materializes. *Maskirovka.* That's what he called it, even taking time to explain as if he was a teacher speaking to a wayward student. "I tell you," he intoned, his Russian accent thickening with his sarcasm. "It is Russian term for shrewd skill, a pretend action that masks your real intent." Knife held to my throat, I was so close I could see spittle forming on the corners of his mouth. "Like playing game of make believe."

I shift uneasily, thinking of that sardonic voice and for the first time since my attack, fear morphs into anger. That sadistic bastard! He deliberately incited a carbon monoxide scare in one of Chase's buildings to call Chase away so he could have easy access to me, and I stupidly stepped into his trap. I ignored my promise to stay put and left the apartment to pick up a package from the lobby that I believed was from Sammy. The ruse continued when Dimitri placed a severed finger sporting a turquoise stone ring inside the envelope. I shiver. There was no mistaking that jewel. It wasn't Fiona's finger, but it was Fiona's ring. I don't care what anyone says about it being a figment of my imagination. I know craft and design, and there was no mistaking the flawlessness of that stone. Chase's worried eyes chisel into mine, and I force a smile. Why rehash details and worry him more?

"I better get ready to face the maddening crowd. Probably best if I see everyone, show them I'm ok. No need to have their imaginations running haywire thinking it's even worse than it actually is."

He nods and follows me into the bedroom to help me dress, throwing a quick glance at the bathroom—no doubt worried that I'll wet and infect my stitches with yet another shower. There's no need for that, though. I've erased the toxic smell from my memory, but his aura lurks like a smothering blanket woven from ubiquitous threads of retaliations.

CHAPTER THREE

They come en masse, one immediately following the other like a crowd before a parade—only more somber especially after they get a good look at my eye and hand. Chase insists I sit on the sofa where feet up, hand resting on a pillow, I plaster a smile on my face that I hope conveys *"I'm fine, no need to worry"* assurances.

My parents freeze when they first spot me. Not wanting to show their shock, they quickly come over to offer hugs. My mother pulls me to her in a fierce hold. Massimo peers at my face, kisses me gingerly on the cheek, asks how I'm feeling, then heads to the liquor cart where Chase has already poured him a scotch on the rocks. He downs it then turns his attention to Chase where, from the looks of it, they fall into a charged conversation. My other two brothers follow suit, the only difference being their drink of choice. Friends with Chase since high school, I'm sure they have no qualms discussing what happened and why. To their credit, they don't stare or fret.

Yet.

Surprisingly, Beth arrives too and after perfunctory hellos to everyone, heads immediately in my direction, carrying two glasses of wine. I've known Beth since grade school so no surprise she is the first to break from the stoic discretion and false smiles of the others to get right to what's on her mind. She sits next to me, hands me my glass, and gives me a quick kiss, followed by a deadpan stare.

"I woke up yesterday morning with Astroglide, a finger condom, beef jerky, and a package of Mentos in my purse. Should I be concerned?" Snorting a laugh, I nearly spit out the wine I'm sipping. "It's good to see you laugh, but ..." Beth hesitates then leans towards me to whisper, "This relationship with hard-to-get lover boy..." she discreetly nods her head in Chase's direction "...seems to be on the fast track. Have you thought it through?" She looks up, casually brushes her hair from her forehead, wincing when she pointedly meets my one eye-opened one eye-shut gaze.

"I'm..." Mouth open, my voice trails off when she interrupts.

"You've wanted this guy for a long time, but do you really know him? I mean, is this just an infatuation that hasn't had time to morph into anything more?" She tosses another look towards Chase making sure he's not listening before returning her attention to me.

I try to jump into what now appears to be a monologue, but she's obviously not finished.

"I'm saying that for you, he may be nothing more than a fascination that you see in ways that defies reality."

Hmm, a relationship built on seeing and believing what's not really there? I take another large sip of wine to free my thoughts. Could this be the whole love is blind concept springing to life on my feelings' white board. I shake my head because this is simply not the case. True, it's been a rapid-fire union of yearning and dynamite sex, but I know that what I'm experiencing, the desire, the need, the want, the fulfillment are very real. Beth reads my skepticism and wants none of it.

"You're not going to like it, but I have to say this. Since you connected with Chase in Europe, you've experienced unheard of heartache and uncertainty. He's there and then he's not; he wants you and then he doesn't, and all the while your emotions speed on a roller coaster ride." She raises her hand to stop me when I attempt to explain. "I know he helped bail you out after your arrest in Monte Carlo, but he has a shaded past, and you ..." Beth pauses closing her eyes to collect her thoughts, wanting to be sure she's not going to offend. When she opens them, she swallows biding her time, and I can tell she's going to say what she's said countless times before. She doesn't let me wait long. "You haven't had much experience with men and well, you may just need to date others, give yourself some time to make comparisons." Lowering her head, her voice caught in her throat, she whispers, "He's hot, I'll grant you that, but his combination of bastard tendencies and emotional baggage are a lot to deal with." Just when I think her soliloquy is over, she sighs and resumes. "There's one reason and one reason only that explains our dating the bastard tendencies type."

I take another sip and quirk a brow in anticipation.

"Availability." That's why you need to know how to avoid the nastiest of the lot and that requires practice. Besides, he left you stranded in Milan. There. I said what I felt I needed to say because I care about you, so don't hate me. I just need to know that you're alright, that you're not making a mistake."

Beth's right. Before Chase my life was staid and predictable. I worked hard at Parsons, even won a contest for a jacket I created that is now selling well in stores around the country. And yes, in many ways Chase and I conflict like splashes of hues from a Pollack canvas. Since we met, my life has been a series of ups and downs with little time between to carve my own path, be my own person. And now he's moved me into his apartment when I've barely had time to adjust to living in mine. How can I be with him if I haven't first learned how to be alone with myself? At the moment, he's frightened and blames himself for my attack but afterwards, when his fear passes, is this what he'll still want? What I'll want?

The balance between need and want can be shaky. To be perceived as a defenseless dependent like a weak link in a chain of life events is demeaning. No, there isn't any way this attack should seal our relationship. There has to be some parity of successes and economies. Otherwise, I'm nothing more than a damsel in distress, someone in chronic need of care and watching.

"Oh no, I've thrown you into your typical tailspin of worry. Not my intent. I just want to make sure you're moving at your own pace." Beth throws a glance at Chase then back at me, her impish grin a sure sign she's changed gears. "Is he still giving you mega orgasms?" She doesn't even pause before throwing out another observation. "Forget I asked. You've now added pink to your black and blue face. Any more colors and you'll pass for an artist's palette." She's brought me back from my funk and now she's all serious again. "How are you? Really?" This time she pauses, giving me time to respond.

"I'm fine, just a bit shaken." I involuntarily shudder causing Beth to take hold of my good hand and give a gentle squeeze.

"This maniac who attacked you … does he have something to do with you nearly getting hit by that boat in Santa Margharita?" When I don't answer, she puffs out a breath and staring straight ahead asks, "It's someone from Chase's past, right?"

"Possibly." I hope my vague response is enough to satisfy her initial curiosity. Last thing I need is a flashback.

Beth takes the hint but doesn't let me off the hook. "I heard the Countess was involved."

Devie's raven hair and predilection for red lipstick and black silk outfits, garnered her the nickname Countess

Dracula. The pull of a slight Russian accent on certain words just adds to the Transylvanian mystique.

"The lead detective seems to think Devie helped my attacker enter the building by distracting the doorman." Offering no other particulars, I let my response hang in the ensuing silence.

Beth navigates through my sparse answers and rather than pry further changes tack. "Marcel was asking about you. Said that after you kissed at the club, you flat-out disappeared."

"I owe him a phone call or at the very least a text. Everything happened so fast afterwards. I drove to Summit to meet Chase and then ..." My voice fades.

"I bet Chase was furious when he saw those posts of you and Marcel dancing and kissing. I'm sorry it got you into trouble, but he deserved it the way he treated you after his sister disappeared."

"We were both at fault. I agreed to hold down the fort and fell asleep, and he shouldn't have hurled insults. Anyway, it's done and over with." A few more sips of wine and my muscles start to relax, allowing our run-ins with his past to slide into the distance. "Have you spoken to Andre recently?" Beth met Andre in Paris and a torrid love affair ensued that extended to the South of France and then Italy, all traveled to by way of Andre's motorcycle. Marcel is Andre's friend who Beth introduced me to in Paris. He's the sexy, French speaking, romance kissing, touchy-feely kind of guy who sweeps you off your feet with courteous smiles and warm compliments. Chase is not a fan.

"We talk regularly. We met for dinner on my last trip to Paris, and he's coming into town in early December. We should plan to all get together."

I happen to look up and notice my father staring in my direction. I know he wants to speak to me, which means we're bound to have one of his ball and chain, guilt and shame chats. Too late to escape now. "Sounds great. Keep me posted." Beth gives me a quick hug before getting up to offer my father a seat on the sofa. I move into a sitting position because I don't want to worry him further by appearing to be an invalid. He's already been monitored for his heart.

"Hi, Papa." He reaches over, wraps his arm around me, and kisses me, his mustache tickling my cheek, then sits back and says nothing. I know he's thinking how best to approach the subject without upsetting me further, so I jump in before he begins. "The doctor says my hand is going to heal nicely. There's no nerve damage and my eye just looks worse than it really is. I'm able to open it a bit now and my vision is fine."

Ignoring my prattling, he reaches into an insulated bag and hands me a package of frozen peas. I peek over and see there are three more inside. I place it against my eye like I've been doing on and off for the past twenty-four hours. I think Chase gave me frozen green beans. Maybe, I can cook them as side dishes. Seems a waste to just toss out good food. My father clears his throat, not allowing me time to drift for long.

"Chase tells us you've been stalked by someone for a while now. Is that true?"

Staring ahead, I answer, "Yes."

"Yet you never told your family about the problem." Earnest eyes meet mine, and I dread the lecture that's sure to follow. Both my parents left their families in Romagna, a town in the Tuscan region of Italy, shortly after they married to open a restaurant on the south shore of Long Island. For them the unity of family held the key to life. My not going to them in a time of need was like driving a wedge into that bond.

"I didn't want to worry everyone, especially since I … um … figured the situation was under control."

Small white lie.

Well, maybe not so small, but I never did imagine an attack of this sort. Guilt is already pushing me into a defensive argument with myself.

"I hear you promised to remain inside because the threat was very real, and then you left to accept a package. Both do not sound like solutions to a problem under control."

Et tu, Brute, and I stare pointedly at Chase, but he doesn't come to my rescue. No one does. I'm in this conversation for the long haul.

"It pains me that you did not think you could ask for my help, or your brothers' help. We would have stayed with you, saw you through the danger while Chase was called away.

"I know." My guilt ratchets up another notch.

"Do you not trust our help?"

Two more notches.

"Of course I do. It's just that I didn't want to get everyone worked up. You're all so busy, and Mamma has just started to feel better." I'm swallowing back tears because, for me, my mother's depression triggers a mixed bag of feelings ranging from guilt and blame to loss and worry. Watching her slide into a depression is like seeing a garden flower wilt into the earth. She disappears into her thoughts and lets the covers bury her unhappiness.

I would do anything to avoid plunging her into another episode.

"And if something worse had happened to you? How do you think she would have felt? As it is, she is beside herself with worry. We all are."

My fingers hastily brush away my tears. "I'm sorry."

He hands me a handkerchief. "I don't want to give you any more grief. I only want to help. But I can't, none of us can, if you do not share your problem." He pauses and I breathe a sigh of relief thinking he's done. No such luck.

"You are more than we could have wished for in a daughter. You create beauty not only with your designs, but with what you carry inside: your empathy, your love, your willingness to help, often putting others before yourself. Your mother and I..." he pauses "...how could we live with ourselves if we did nothing to protect you when you were in danger? His tearing eyes are my undoing and nodding assent, I cry into his hankie. This must arouse Chase's pity because when I look up from blowing my nose, he's standing next to us. My father kisses my forehead and shaking his head tosses Chase a pitying look. "Just like her mamma. On the outside all soft and pliable and inside…" he makes a tight fist "…a will of iron." Then patting Chase in commiseration, he leaves to join my brothers by the liquor cabinet, no doubt to continue the discussion on how best to handle the Alicia situation.

"Your father's chats pack a potent punch."

I sniff back a sob. "They're the worst. It didn't help that he knew I left the apartment alone." I give him an accusatory glance.

Pretending he hasn't heard, he quips, "Someone should find a way to harness that guilt to sell to parents with noncompliant kids. They'd make a fortune." He sits and wraps his arm around me, pulling me closer. "How are you holding up?"

"I'm ok." I reach over and gently kiss his lips. He's responsive but just barely. It's funny how he still holds back in front of my family.

"And for the record," he whispers, running his finger slowly across my lower lip, "I did not tell your father about you leaving the apartment." My breath catches with the trace of his lingering finger on my mouth; feelings are stirred that have no business coming alive in a crowded room of family and friends. They don't linger for long.

"You look like you went a round with Ronda Rousey." Virgil, my boss, stands stock-still peering at me from the doorway. Impeccably clad in a tailored blue suit with matching shirt and silk tie, Virgil has the eyes of a mischievous poet. "I refuse to lie. This is terrible." He bends to kiss both cheeks before taking the seat Chase vacated for him. "We just knew it was you when *The Chaser* called in sick for you this morning." Virgil has been referring to Chase as The Chaser ever since they first met and he couldn't keep his eyes off Chase's tight torso and ass. "You were the star of our gossip session. Everyone spouted such horrible scenarios: vicious knife attack, forced entry, kidnapping … that I had to see for myself how you were doing." The consummate gossip Virgil craves info but doesn't misuse what he learns. Pure and simple, he's not vicious.

"I'm fine. Just a bit sore. It looks worse than it is."

"Have the police identified your attacker?' Virgil did not reach an executive position at a leading fashion house without knowing how to get right to the point of a problem.

"They're working on it. I had to … um give a description and look at some photos today." I'm deliberately vague, preferring to leave it that everyone is unsure of the attacker.

"Sounds like a lunatic with a grudge."

You don't know the half of it, buddy. "Yes, that's what the police believe also."

"Listen …" Empathetic eyes peer into mine. "Take all the time you need to recover, but I will admit you're needed. Your jacket is selling well in several of the luxury department stores and the Chronicle had someone nosing around looking for you to interview for a spread in their fashion page, something about *The Craft of a Fledgling Genius*."

Good heavens, am I even worthy of that moniker? Virgil looks at me with wicked glee. "Charlotte needed a rabies shot when she realized it was your label they were writing about and not one of Estelle Designs. She wants you to create more for our brand." That's a switch—not the foaming fury, the positive recognition part. Charlotte generally uses her title as president of Estelle Designs, to devalue or dismiss just about everything I do. She acts like my ideas are nothing more than innocuous attempts at originality. *It's homogenized, nothing more than a simplistic replica of every other jacket flooding the market today.* Her scathing remark remains lodged in my mind like an armed sniper taking aim at my ideas.

"And look. The fox has decided to see for herself what's happened to you." Virgil flashes a smile in Charlotte's direction and gives a wave. My head swivels, and I catch sight of icy blue eyes surveying the room. She gives a slight head nod in recognition of me, then turns towards Chase, and the frost thaws. She always did have a thing for Chase. "However did *you* manage to snare him?" she had the audacity to ask me when she first met him in the office. And when Chase helped me arrange for a jazz band to highlight Estelle Designs' runway show during fashion week, which was my idea I might add, she badgered me for his private cell number so she could "personally offer her thanks on behalf of Estelle Designs."

Chase turns when she taps his arm, a look of surprise widening his eyes. Charlotte smiles and kisses both his cheeks in that *I'm so sophisticated I dish out European kisses* maneuver.

Ugh. My eyes follow the line of Chase's jaw and the curve of his lips as he gives her his drop-dead gorgeous grin. Leaning towards him, she speaks into his ear like they're in a crowded bar and not his living room. Nodding, he goes about pouring her a glass of chardonnay. When she reaches out and picks a piece of lint off his sweater, I have to contain myself from jumping off the sofa and slapping away her hand. They continue their conversation, Chase standing straight with Charlotte leaning in, her earnest eyes boring into his as she makes some kind of point. Chase responds nodding his head, and she reaches into her purse and takes out her phone to record something he's just offered. Virgil must notice my scowl because tipping his head towards me, he adds, "I better get over there before Charlotte sinks her fangs into The Chaser's neck." He clears his throat and stands. "So when can we expect you back?"

I don't acknowledge his comment about Charlotte's behavior towards Chase. Both he and Charlotte are my bosses so only a fool would bad mouth one to the other. "I think I'll be back on Wednesday." My plan was to rest tomorrow, continue to ice my eye, then don a pair of exotic-looking sunglasses and go to the office the following day. Terse words from the far corner of the room drift in my direction.

"Not happening. The doctor said at least five days." Chase looks at me before continuing to pour a Sapphire and tonic for Virgil.

Honestly, he has radar for ears.

"Take all the time you need. "You don't want to rush back before you're ready." Virgil's gaze darkens when he scans my bandaged hand; he's probably thinking what Chase remarked after it happened. *What if it had been your right hand*? As soon as he leaves, Charlotte glides towards me like a snake eying its target.

"Aren't you a sight! How are you feeling?" She takes a sip of wine, scans the room making sure to smile at Chase and wave at Virgil, then looks back at me and continues talking, never giving me the chance to answer. "I'm sure Virgil mentioned that your jackets are selling well." She raises her shoulder as if to say *how the hell is that happening*. "Perhaps when you return, you can originate a line for Estelle. Nothing too bourgeois, though."

What? Possible meanings rifle through my brain like a scanner on fast forward. She must notice my confusion because in a monotone, she clarifies, "You were inexperienced when you created your initial design and now, well … you can add more verve to them."

Ah, she means don't be as boring with your new work as you were with the first. A person needs an interpreter to decipher what she says. Besides, it couldn't be further from the truth. The jacket is chic with a svelte silhouette. But there's still the whole boss-worker dynamic going on so I don't tell her what's really on my mind like why doesn't she just fuck off and take her criticism with her.

"Thank you for your faith in my ability, Charlotte. I'll take it under consideration."

"We look forward to seeing you back in the office soon. Do check in with HR to determine how many sick days you're entitled to as a relatively new employee." Her job as bitch personified complete, she slithers away.

I look up and see Mac and Sammy chatting with Chase. Their heads are bent in contemplative conversation that to the casual onlooker would appear to be no more than friendly chatter. I know better. Three veteran Marines, bound by an oath of brotherhood sealed on a battlefield, are not going to just sit back and leave my attack in the hands of the local authorities—especially since it was spearheaded by a ruthless adversary who has stalked and terrorized Chase for years. Chase may be a successful business man, with Sammy and Mac as partners in various ventures, but what really links them is the indelible imprint of their past that remains as intact as fossils fixed in rock.

Chase must notice me rubbing the temples of my forehead because their mini meeting ends. He pours a glass of white wine for me and saunters over, taking Charlotte's vacated seat and casually throwing his arm around my shoulder and pulling me close. It's like musical chairs only with one person left seated instead of standing.

"Figured you could use a bit of wine." I take a sip, then another, and another. He sweeps the glass away from reaching my mouth a fourth time and places it on the table.

"Not a good idea to chug alcohol when you're taking pain killers." He's right, but his monitoring of my behavior is irksome and a reminder of all the times I've been in trouble with him since we first hooked up in Monte Carlo.

"I'm sure a glass of wine won't turn me into a druggie."

"I believe this is your second glass."

It's my third but why clarify. I haven't taken anything for the pain today. When I happen to glance ahead, I spot Charlotte staring our way, her gaze pinpointing Chase, her eyes crinkling with her smile. Humph, that White Witch better hope that broad grin doesn't crack her face. Chase is unaware of her flirting or at least he's pretending not to notice. He's a player that's for sure. When we met in Europe, I imagined he had a Costco-sized bag of condoms packed in his suitcase. How else could he have been able to pull out just the right one at just the right time with the dexterity of a magician sliding ropes of scarves from his sleeve? And me? No experience, no handy birth control, no naughty moves. I was the perfect make-over project for someone with his know-how. Show the beginner how to make love, how to behave and lose her childish impetuousness, and let's not forget how to obey orders. Chase is very big on following the rule book. Another *humph* from me and he lifts his glass of club soda and drinks, obviously hydrating before having to deal with my grumpiness. I watch his Adam's apple ripple beneath his chiseled chin and heave a sigh. To say I'm conflicted is an understatement. It's easy to understand what the White Witch sees in Chase. He's the whole package, an Adonis who's generous, caring, and sexy as all hell. I wouldn't be getting through this mess without him, but then again, I'm in it because of him and his past.

Charlotte's a player too, or so I hear. She's got to be at least thirty, plenty of time to shore up a battery of conquests. Virgil hinted that she's scored with several fashion account executives and brand coordinators. Having sex with her must be like getting into the sack with a block of dry ice that smokes every now and then.

"If you keep scowling like that, your face could stay that way. At least that's what my mother used to say." Chase takes my hand and lightly strokes my knuckles with the pad of his thumb. "Did Charlotte give you a hard time?"

I blow out a gust of air, shoot him an *I dare you to try and stop me* face and grab my glass of wine, making sure to sip slowly.

"I'll deal."

"She had only good things to say about you. How bad can it be?"

Oh my god. She's pretending to be nice to me in the hopes of wooing him. Judging from the wary look in Chase's eyes, I must be wearing the same glare I used to level and scatter my brothers when they did something annoying. "How bad can it be? Let's see. Do we want to focus on how she believes my work is tedious or how she wants to milk me for my designs? Oh, and let's not forget about her hint that Estelle Designs will only pay me for a limited amount of sick days because garment I brought. I had not planned for a drug bust when I dressed this morning.

With brusque, swift efficiency, he opens and studies my passport. I hear nothing but my hammering heart and in the heavy, hanging silence, he looks up and curtly announces, "Alicia Cesare, you are under arrest for possession of an illegal substance. Please come with us." And he waits while I scoop up my bag and hat to follow him and his partner off the beach and to their waiting vehicle. The last words I hear are Beth's hushed whisper, "I'm not leaving you," and she grabs her bag and follows.

CHAPTER SIX

y legs shake, my cover-up sticks to my body with perspiration, and I crave a glass of water for my parched throat. I've been sitting in this small, cramped room at the local police headquarters for several hours and still questions continue to be fired my way with no offer of a break. I knew it was going to be bad after they took a mug shot and led me to this back closeted area. The worst part is that I have no idea how long I am going to be detained, or if I'm even allowed a phone call, and with my guilt so evident I'm too scared to ask.

The officer standing in front of me strokes his lip and surveys me from quick eyes that indicate he's no amateur in the art of lying, before tossing out another series of questions, some repetitive, some new.

What is my reason for being in Monaco? Where did I arrive from? Where am I staying? Where do I come from?

How am I traveling? Where did I buy the drugs? Have I ever been arrested before for selling drugs?

I answer honestly but stop short of giving him Thomas's name. Instead, I say I got the hash in Nice from a friend of a friend, who I really didn't know, and that it was given to me not bought. He seems satisfied with the vague answer, and I'm lulled into believing that like Nice, recreational use of small amounts of hash in Monaco is if not legal then tolerated. I am wrong. Just when I think I'm done, another round of questions start, some variations of the original cluster, others different. The question *have I ever smuggled drugs*? really shakes me up, and choking on tears, I'm only able to shake my head because the thought that I might be considered a drug trafficker is so frightening, it renders me speechless.

Eventually he shuffles some papers on his desk and gets up and leaves, firmly shutting the door behind him. I don't know if I'm locked in or free to go, but fear roots me to my seat, forcing me to remain in the stifling office where the only movement I make is to put my hair into a ponytail with an elastic I have around my wrist. Alone, my mind runs rampant and I imagine myself languishing in some dank French prison, my life and career ruined. How could I have been so foolish and reckless? I steady my breathing and continue to stare at the faded white wall ahead.

Another officer, one I've never seen before, enters and curtly returns my belongings to the table, speaking rapid fire French and gesturing toward the door. Still afraid to say anything or get up and leave, because who needs attempted escape added to a drug arrest, I remain in my chair until he once again taps my passport and slides my tote closer to me, pointing again at the door. I take them, slowly stand, and walk out of a room that could double as a sauna.

"So, she's free to go?"

I'm in some sort of vestibule, scanning the area where Beth was waiting for me, when I hear a familiar voice. It's now dark and knowing Beth would never just leave me, I start to panic when I don't see her. I search the room again and find her cell phone under a chair in the far corner of the room. When I bend to retrieve it, I hear the voice again, clipped, serious, no nonsense. This is not happening.

Slowly standing, I remain fixed to my spot, sure my imagination is playing tricks on me after a long and tense day. When I glance over my shoulder, I notice the back of a tall, broad shouldered man with the rigid stance of a soldier. He's dressed in khaki shorts and a checkered collared long sleeve shirt with the sleeves rolled up.

Oh god, what is Chase Reardon doing in Monaco, and how the hell did he know I was arrested? I don't hear the clerk's response but see some paper work being stamped and handed to him. He turns around and his eyes pinion me with a glare that has me quaking more than the arrest and police inquisitor combined. So much for relief at being released. He's furious. Gathering my courage, I'm finally able to speak.

"Hi," I whisper and give him a little wave."

"Hi." He pauses for a moment before walking toward me in purposeful strides, his eyes giving me a rigorous check to ensure that I'm OK. "You've been released. Do you have everything, including your passport?" When I nod, he issues an abrupt, "Let's go."

I open my mouth to try and tell him I need to find Beth, but before I can say anything, he places his hand around my arm in an iron-clad grasp and close to my ear says, "If you don't move NOW, I will throw you over my shoulder and haul you out of here."

No use arguing. I know from past experience that he means business. I follow him out of the station and to what I assume is his car. He opens the door, and as I sit and buckle my seat belt, he slams it shut so hard I wince. Once behind the wheel, he asks me what hotel I'm staying at and proceeds to drive me there in silence, a silence that stretches until it becomes deafening.

Feeling I owe him some explanation, I tentatively remark, "Thanks. I really appreciate you helping me. I plan on paying you back for any fines you had to pay to get me released."

He doesn't respond at first, but when he does, I regret saying anything at all. "You think this is a situation that can be rectified by paying back money. Ok, tell me. How much does it cost to correct poor judgment or recklessness or stupidity for that matter? How much does jeopardizing your life go for today? How much, Alicia?"

I figure they're rhetorical questions so I remain silent.

Looking down, I twist my hands in my lap and prepare for more of his verbal onslaught.

"You crossed the line today, and believe me there will be retribution but it won't be meted out in dollars and cents." He looks at me with eyes that radiate anger then squints at my neck before turning to look back at the road. "Are those tattoos on your neck?"

I rub the side of my neck, remembering how I had them done after his kisses in the coffee shop. No smooches or hugs tonight, and I swallow to moisten my dry mouth and steady my nerves.

"Um, yeah, but today they're more like fashion statements than unsightly markings." My too-high voice and too-quick words sound like someone giving a bad sales pitch. I clamp my mouth shut, not wanting to give him any more ammunition, but can't stop myself from thinking why is it any of his business if I have a dozen tattoos? He's not my father—although, he was none too pleased either when he saw them.

Chase stares at me hard. "You are edging toward a behavioral precipice."

What? Has to be some weird expression that indicates I'm not making good choices, and I wonder how many other *Chaseisms* I'm going to have to endure before this night is over. Either way, it does not sound like where I want to be right now, especially with that grimace plastered on his face. Good god, I hope these tattoos are not going to be what throws former Marine Chase Reardon over his edge. Besides, don't Marines usually have tattoos running up and down their huge, muscled arms? This is ridiculous. Instead of discussing tattoos, I should be asking him what I need to do as a result of my arrest, like should I get a lawyer or am I going to have to appear before a judge, but all I seem to be concerned about is what my actions say about me. Last thing I want is for him to think I'm some flake who wanders from mishap to mishap without considering consequences. The truth is I never imagined recreational marijuana use would illicit such an over the top response here, especially since all I had in my possession was enough for one or two joints at best. Maybe if I explained, clarified the situation, he'd be less inclined to think so little of me.

"I just want you to know ..." My voice is hesitant. I'm nervous, unsure of how to continue, but I plow ahead anyway. "I didn't think I would be arrested. I thought marijuana use was widely accepted today. It's legal in Colorado and ..."

There's a beat of silence before he cuts me off with a sweeping gesture of his hand that first points to the sea to our left and then to the palm trees silhouetted against the darkening sky on both sides of the road.

"Does this look like Colorado to you?"

There's something about the impatient delivery of the question that demands an answer, and I'm tempted to shout "sir, no, sir!" like I once saw a private bellow to his commanding officer in a movie.

I hide my smile and offer a simple "no," wondering if

someone needs to show him his discharge papers to remind him he's no longer on active duty.

There's so much tension swirling that when I finally see my hotel, I have to restrain myself from jumping out of the car and calling out, "thanks for the ride," before running into the lobby and up to my room. Instead, he comes around, opens my door, and helps me carry my things inside, making no attempt to leave once we get inside my room. I start rummaging in my suitcase for a pair of shorts and T-shirt, determined to call a cab and start looking for Beth once I'm dressed and he's gone.

"Leave them," he orders and pats the side of the bed, telling me to sit.

Not wanting to agitate him further, I do as I'm told and nervously wait for what he's going to say. He starts pacing while he appears to be thinking. Stopping, he looks directly at me before continuing.

"We have a situation here where choices are required."

I have no idea what he's referring to. It's obvious I've already made bad choices or I wouldn't have been arrested. He offers nothing more, so I am forced to look up and ask,

"What do you mean?"

"What do you think should happen as a result of this debacle where you put your safety and Beth's in jeopardy?" He's speaking in a quiet, even tone, but I can gauge his angry mood by the darkening and narrowing of his eyes. Besides, answering a question with a question is never good in these situations.

"I'm waiting for an answer, Alicia. Don't try my patience."

"I … I don't know," I stammer. I'm afraid to make the offer to pay him back again because it made him so mad the first time I said it. Still beside myself with worry about Beth's whereabouts, I ask the inevitable because I know that's what he is waiting for.

"What are these decisions you mentioned that I need to make?" I stare him straight in the eye before looking back down again when the full weight of my predicament hits again.

"Here's how it's going to go down. The way I see it, you have two choices: you can either submit to my punishment …"

My head shoots up, but it's impossible to read his expression. The palms of my hands start to sweat and my mind races to figure out what he plans to do.

"Or," he continues, pausing for effect most likely to heighten my concern. He's being a bastard, but I'm the one in the hot seat and in no position to argue until I finish hearing what he has to say.

"Or what?" I finally murmur.

"Or I call your father, explain what happened, and ask him what he would like me to do."

I blanch. That can never happen. My father would insist I clean up my own mess and then return home immediately. I would have no choice because all funds would be cut off and not having secured a job yet, I would be forced to give up my new apartment and continue working in the restaurant while living at home or a friend's house until I found a job.

All totally unacceptable. But as bad as that would be, it wasn't what I dreaded most. I couldn't bear to give my father any more worry than he already has. With my mother sick and the pressing demands of his restaurant and the vineyard, he is overworked and overwrought. Just last month he had to wear some sort of heart monitor because the doctor heard an arrhythmia during a routine exam. He was still waiting for the results. I just couldn't disappoint and hurt him with this news.

"Well," he interrupts my thoughts, "What will it be?"

Resigned to what I have to do, I shrug and say, "I choose your punishment."

"Without even knowing what it will be?" he admonishes. "Have you learned nothing about exercising caution from this recent situation?" His voice raises for the first time since I saw him earlier.

There is no satisfying this man right now. Anything and everything I say just makes him angrier. His tone holds an edge that indicates he's not going to go easy on me. Best to opt for honesty.

"I could never hurt my family by letting them find out about my arrest and for the most part, I trust you. You helped with my release and saw me safely back. So what's my punishment going to be?" I sound much braver than I feel.

He doesn't even pause, just looks me straight in the eye and says, "An over-the-knee spanking with twenty-five hits."

I remain still, trying to digest this information, and in a brief moment of panic eye the door.

"Don't even think it." In one fluid motion, he sits down on the bed next to me, reaches for my hand, and pulls me over his lap.

"The sooner we start, the sooner it's over." My head hangs down and he grips my hands behind my back with his left hand while his right leg pinions my legs. Could this be any more humiliating?

At first I feel his hand resting on my bottom and then it's raised, landing the first resounding slap that stuns, and forces my eyes open before I close them again to wait for the next. *Slap!* Ow! Five more follow in rapid succession. This hurts like hell. Another five and my backside stings so badly, I try to wriggle free, but it's like I'm trapped in a vise. More follow, each in a different spot, each with the same relentless intensity. He doesn't stop until the promised twenty-five are administered. I know because I silently kept count.

When he finishes, he lifts me off him and helps me stand. My legs are shaky and I can't bring myself to look at him. I turn away and cover my face with my hands. The tension and fear caused by my arrest and Beth's disappearance surface with a vengeance. If anything happens to her, I would never forgive myself. Guilt, remorse, and let's not forget a very sore ass, prevent me from getting a grip on my emotions, and I sob into my hands.

Chase wisely keeps his distance, remaining silent while I try to pull myself together. After a bit, he walks over to me, removes my hands from my face, and pulls me into a hug, gently stroking my hair and telling me everything is going to be ok. Conflicting emotions bounce around my mind, but I let him hold me because even though there is a part of me that hates him for what he just did, the comfort of his arms and soft words offer a reassurance I crave after the events of the day.

"Please, I need to go find Beth," I finally manage to say. "This is all my fault."

He frees one of his arms from around me and I wonder what he's doing, but I still can't bring myself to look at him.

"Shh, don't worry," he says, lifting my chin so I meet his gaze. There's regret tinged with concern in his eyes. "We'll find Beth. I just texted a buddy of mine and he's going to start searching. It's a small area. She can't have gone far."

I step back and wipe my tears with the back of my hands.

"I'm coming. Just give me a minute to change."

He pauses, then adds, "I don't think that's a good idea. You've been through enough today. Besides, you need to be here in case Beth shows up before we find her."

It's sound advice and agreeing, I make sure to add his phone number to my contacts and give him mine so he can keep me updated. As soon as he leaves, I start pacing the room, wondering about where she could possibly be. Maybe they took her to another location for questioning, and I wrap my hand across my mouth and try to stifle my tears. Poor Beth. Good god, what if she was attacked or kidnapped? She doesn't even have a phone to reach out if she needs help. My thoughts run riot until, unable to bear them any longer, I decide to take a warm shower to try to relax. The water feels good and I let it spill over me, soaping away the sand, salt water, and grime from a long and tiring day. I lather and rinse my hair. Refreshed and a bit more settled, I towel and gingerly rub my backside. I slip on my short silk robe, loosely tying the front, comb out my hair, and again start my pacing, too nervous to do anything else. My phone pings a text and I immediately lift it from the night table.

Getting close to finding Beth. Keep u posted.

Well it's some news, and I have renewed hope that she's safe. I resume my pacing, but my legs ache and my head is spinning. I lie in bed on my stomach, vowing to only rest for a bit. The next thing I know I hear a light tapping on my door. I get up quickly and let in a tired but smiling Chase.

"We found Beth. She's fine."

I exhale a long and welcomed sigh of relief. "Where was she?"

"Seems like she was riding around on a motorbike with some Frenchman looking for the U.S. embassy to get help for you. They never would have found it because there isn't one in Monaco. Anyway, I told her you were fine and she said she'll speak to you in the morning."

Andre must be staying with her, and I'm happy she has someone to be with after all the trouble and worry I caused.

"Thank You." I stand there in front of him, at a loss of anything else to say for fear I'll start crying again.

He reaches in with his thumb and pushes back a strand of

my hair, and I lean into his touch and close my eyes when he lets it travel across my lips.

His "you're welcome," comes out in a husky whisper, and I'm tempted to take his lingering finger in my mouth and suck, but he drops his hand. My eyes sweep back to his, and blue to green our gazes lock. He leans in and brushes my lips with a kiss, tender and warm, and I lean into his body, melding my mouth to his. And then ... he pulls away, shaking his head almost as if he's reminding himself of something.

"I should go. You must be exhausted." He steps away and turns toward the door, and it's as if the lost moment is already carving a small hole inside me.

"Wait." My heart ricochets into my throat and I have to swallow hard to catch my breath and maintain my nerve. I walk towards him and he slowly turns to meet my gaze.

"I brought a bottle of Rosé from Nice. Join me for a drink, just one nightcap before you leave."

The slight widening of his eyes tells me he understands the implications of the invitation. There seems to be some internal battle of indecision being fought, and I think I hear him mumble *what the fuck* before he pulls me toward him and plants a hard, deep kiss on my lips. My legs nearly cave, and I melt into his body, wrapping my hands in his hair and kissing him with an unleashed passion that lay buried until this moment.

He backs me against the bed, and we keep our embrace while he uses one hand to untie my robe. It opens, and I hear him gasp soft words of praise as his smoldering hot eyes rake over my body.

Slowly, he glides his hands down my shoulders, lifting the robe and letting it slide down my back and fold onto the floor.

"Are you sure you're up for this?"

I look into the eyes of the man I have desired for so long and whisper, "I have been hoping for this for a long time."

There's a slight intake of breath before he lowers me onto the bed. Straddling my prone body, he holds my face in his hand and kisses me again, a deep passionate kiss that parts my lips and encourages me to slip my tongue into his mouth. Gradually, he moves his mouth to nibble my ear, gently tugging the lobe with his teeth before lowering it to my neck and planting soft kisses beginning with the first star tattoo, then gradually descending to the next and the next. When he reaches the last, he gently sucks and moves his hand down toward my breast, using his forefinger and thumb to gently pucker my nipple. Sensations riot across my skin and deep inside my belly thrums. I close my eyes and moan.

He pauses and I use the opportunity to lock my hands in his hair and pull his mouth toward mine, thrusting my tongue inside and holding his lips to mine. He groans then disengages from my kiss, lowers his mouth to my breast, and strokes my nipple with his tongue before gently tugging it with his mouth. Lightning shoots through my body, and I arch my back in a reflex motion that is new to me.

Through a haze of pleasure, I place my hands on either

side of his face and lift his head. Looking into his hooded eyes, I reach up with shaking fingers and unbutton his shirt. Then, stroking his muscled chest, I lean in and plant small kisses down his navel before falling back onto the bed when his mouth locks on my breast again. Arching up from the bed to meet the tension of his mouth on my breast, I feel him slowly insert one finger inside my warm, wet folds. My swollen nub vibrates with need as his finger teases then presses further inside, and I mindlessly grip the sheet, inviting a multitude of new sensations to undulate over me.

"You are so wet." He inserts a second finger, moving both in repetitive and pressing motions that have me submitting to a need that escalates when his mouth and tongue stroke and suck my nipple. The sensations are so intense I don't know if I want to pull him closer or push him away. Overwhelmed, I attempt to remove his mouth from my breast but with facile dexterity, he takes my hands in a firm grasp and holds them above my head before moving his diabolical mouth back to my breast, where he again sucks and tugs the nipple.

"Uh, uh, uh," I whimper, barely recognizing my voice as he moves to plant feathery kisses across my chest and down to my navel, sending electrical sparks of excitement through my body when his lips reach my apex.

"God, but you taste sweet." And his mouth plants wet, open-mouthed kisses that begin traveling up until once again he latches his mouth around my breast, causing my nipple to bud.

A mounting pleasure I can't control washes over me until I feel I am going to burst from within. Removing one hand from my wrists, he once again places one, then two fingers inside me, and as their movements quicken, he lifts his mouth from one breast and begins tugging and licking the nipple of the other. This time, my body tenses, my legs stiffen and arching upward, I'm gripped by ripples of mind-bending, continuous undulations. When I finally descend, I slowly become aware of Chase straddling me, shirtless but still in his shorts. Trying to catch my breath, I hear him chuckle.

"How was that?"

I can't speak. I can't move. And there's this white rush of noise in my ears. Before I can gather my wits to answer, he removes his shorts and underwear, and I watch him spring loose. I swallow and move my gaze toward his face as he reaches for a condom. He tears it open and slides it on in one fluid motion. Shifting his body on top of mine, I close my eyes when he slowly slips inside.

"You're very tight." Holding himself up, he studies my face.

I turn away from his penetrating gaze, and he stops and gently grasps my chin so our eyes meet. It's in that heartbeat of a moment that I know he realizes I have never done this before. He doesn't move, just continues staring into my eyes.

I close my eyes, not knowing what to say or do, then opening them implore, "Please, don't stop. I want this."

"Why?" he asks, his hushed voice catching, and I don't know if he's asking why didn't I tell him I've never done this before or why do I want it, so I answer with the only truth I can summon.

"Because anyone else would have just been a substitute for you."

He lets out a groan, and I know he's exercising every ounce of restraint he can muster to remain inside without moving. And still he waits, his biceps straining with the effort to support himself above me, his eyes searching as he whispers close to my ear.

"Are you certain this is what you want?"

I open my eyes and stare into his. "I've never been surer of anything in my life."

He responds with a slow, deliberate motion that allows any burning to ease as my body adjusts to his fullness. Gradually, I moisten in slippery need with each measured movement.

I begin to feel that same mounting pleasure from before, and when I'm wet with desire he gives one quick thrust, stifling my cry of surprise with his mouth in a searing kiss. He stills, burying his face in my neck, but I want more and I raise my hips to continue the momentum. Once again, he moves with that same patient rhythm. I reignite with a pulsating escalation of pleasure as his methodical thrusts intensify, carrying me to just that certain point before he slows, leaving me to drift just short of release. It's like being on a balanced seesaw that hovers with small rivets of movement but never moves completely up or down, and all I want is to feel that upward swing to the top.

"I want you to savor this moment," he rasps. "To remember

it always."

He bends and kisses my parting my lips, moving his tongue to match each measured motion below. The sensation is sublime and my pulse escalates. I hear him groan deeply from the back of his throat as bit by bit, he continues the momentum while keeping our lips locked. Every thrust takes me to heights I never imagined and tearing my lips from his, my body arches with each sweet penetrating plunge until I soar on ripples of mounting pleasure. I hear him groaning with each thrust before he too reaches his release, allowing me to continue to glide in undulating ecstasy. When he slows and eventually stops, his body resting on mine, I feel the full brunt of his weight and move my head to the side in an attempt to still my rapid breathing. He gently pulls out and I wince more from loss than pain. Rolling onto his back, he takes me with him, continuing to hold me until our breathing returns to normal.

I lie limp on top of him and taking my face in his hands, he lifts it and kisses my forehead then softly, tenderly my lips. "How do you feel?" His voice is hesitant, unsure, and I can't understand why.

"I've never felt better," I answer, smiling.

He continues stroking my hair back from my face until I can no longer keep my eyes open. I want to say so much, to share how wonderful it all felt, to ask if he will be spending the night, but the events of the day and this wild end has me struggling to stay awake. The only movement he makes is to reach down and remove his condom before tossing it into the waste basket in a clean, neat shot.

"Score," I tiredly murmur, giggling. And he moves to his side, pulling me closer, leaving one arm possessively wrapped around my hip.

"Best one yet."

Nestling into his arms until we comfortably fit together, I drift off into one of the most peaceful slumbers I can recall.

CHAPTER SEVEN

"Hey, beautiful, rise and shine. It's time to get moving."

Chase stands before me, fresh from a recent shower, towel wrapped around ripped abs, his dark, silky hair dripping water as he vigorously dries it with a second towel. I could wake up to this sight forever. Stretching, I get up and scoot to the bathroom to relieve myself. I brush my teeth and shower, taking my time to try and lessen the morning after shyness I'm feeling. The cool water is invigorating, easing the soreness of my tense muscles. I reach for the liquid soap and begin rubbing and washing until I reach below. It's tender, but I continue to stroke with my fingers until the feelings from last night awaken. *Mmm, so this is how it's done.* I allow the sensation to wash over me with the water. I hear a knock, look up, and see Chase. He eyes my body then pulls off his towel and steps inside the shower.

"Are you sore?" When I don't answer, he presses me against the wall and hands on either side holding me captive, adds, "There are other ways."

I stare into his eyes and he places his lips on mine, first gently then deepening the kiss. I feel his swollen member brush against my groin. I know there are other ways. I may be inexperienced, but I don't live in a bubble, so when I reach down and begin stroking his already swollen member with my hand, I hear a hiss of pleasure. Empowered, I lower my body and take it into my mouth, continuing to suck and pull until he throws his head back and moans.

"Are you sure you want to do this?" he queries through gritted teeth.

I am. I also want him to stop asking if I'm certain about what I want to do. I'm not some teenager who doesn't know her own mind, but how do I explain and put him at ease without offending? The rock-hard answer is staring straight at me so, not stopping to reply, I continue my hard and steady sucking, firmly gripping his backside to pull him closer. Occasionally, I pause and lick the tip of his penis and marvel at the power I have to initiate such pleasure.

"My god, Alicia," he pants, head thrown back, then stops talking when I keep the momentum. "I'm going to come."

I don't stop and I hear him groan as he spills inside my mouth. It takes me by surprise, and I'm not sure I like the feel, but eliciting that kind of reaction is satisfying. I stand, rinse out my mouth under the shower, and as soon as I turn back, I'm lifted by a pair of hard, muscled arms. I wrap my legs around his waist and my arms around his neck, and he kisses me deeply. With me in his arms, Chase reaches back, turns off the faucets, and carries me out of the shower to lay me face up on the bed. Taking me by my ankles, he pulls me toward the end of the bed where he's standing, bends my knees, and spreads them. I'm open, vulnerable to his ministrations. He lowers himself and places kisses first up my inner calf then my thigh and then *there*. Writhing with desire, I pant out a plea, and slowly he replaces his kisses with his tongue circulating it slowly and then rapidly, with firm thrusts. I'm awash in sensation and shamelessly lift my hips towards him for more.

"Please," I murmur between deep, heavy breaths and try to raise my hands to reach for him.

He keeps going, probing and swirling his tongue until I tremble with desire. Stopping, he inserts one, then two fingers, pulsating them up and down inside me until I succumb to wild, shuttering ripples of ecstasy and cry out his name as each electrify me. When I return to Earth I notice him smiling like a Cheshire cat who just had his cream. He slides me further back onto the bed so I can extend my legs and settle my rapidly beating heart. Heavens alive, a girl could easily get used to this. Chase lies down next to me and gently kisses the stars on my neck. Oh no! I couldn't go another round without serious consequences. Was there such a thing as death from orgasm? But he stops and begins stroking my hair. Eventually, my breathing returns to normal, and I feel thoroughly sated and relaxed.

"For a novice you're good. Have you ever done this before?"

"No." I pause then raise a questioning brow. "Have you?"

He throws his head back and laughs. "Yes."

Of course he has. What a ridiculous question to ask. And just like when you first develop a rash that flares every time you scratch, I start to wonder how many women he's slept with. A dozen? Tens of dozens? My imagination runs amuck with the math because even as a beginner, I can tell he's adept at lovemaking. He knows when and where to touch, and he's gorgeous and successful. I sigh and he reaches over and kisses me.

"You're sexy as all hell," he says, and I think he means it but I have nothing to compare.

"Well now I understand all the fuss about sex." I rest my head on his shoulder and he turns and strokes my hair. Every part of me relaxes, allowing my mind to drift, and I start to wonder again what he was doing in Monte Carlo and how he knew I was arrested.

"Chase?"

"Hmm?"

"Do you know when we first met here in Monte Carlo?" I purposely leave out the word arrest.

"You mean after you were arrested?"

So much for avoidance. But he doesn't seem mad and continues to smooth back my hair.

"Mmm hmm. How were you able to get to me so quickly?"

He slowly exhales. Our trysts are affecting him too.

"After you were arrested, Beth texted Thomas the information and location of the police station with a photograph so he knew where you were being held. Concerned, Thomas phoned his sister Julie, asking what he should do. Julie knew from my sister Fiona that I was at the Grand Prix in Monte Carlo, gave him my number, and suggested he call and ask for my help. Thomas phoned then emailed me the photo and address of the police station where you were being held so I could find you and see what was happening. And here I am."

Terrific. Just Terrific. My arrest has rocketed through the local media grapevine. Well, it's too late now to change things and useless to keep worrying.

"You left the Grand Prix for me. That must have been hard. Do you love cars?"

"I enjoy studying how they're built and how fast their engines run, especially the F1 cars in the Grand Prix circuit."

I have no idea what he's talking about, but it sounds like a big deal to him. I kiss his nose then his lips, but he stops any further progression and tilts his head back to look at me.

"We have to finish packing and get ready to leave."

This surprises me because I'm not scheduled to leave until tomorrow.

"I'm supposed to meet Beth and Andre tonight at the casino. You're welcome to join us."

"No, you can't."

"No?" I'm having a hard time wrapping my head around his emphatic answer. "What do you mean, *no*?"

"You have to leave Monaco today. Police orders."

My eyes widen and my mouth drops open.

"What? I'm being thrown out of the country!" I immediately sit up and pulling the sheet with me, stand and start pacing, muttering all manner of irrelevancies to express my disbelief. "Unbelievable. Just unbelievable. I've never even been thrown out of a bar. Never even got sent to the principal's office. Well, once when I gave Benny Shuster a black eye, but he deserved it." I stop and look at Chase, who continues to let me ramble before finally interrupting my walk-a-thon of worry.

"Technically, Monaco is not a country."

"What?"

"It's a principality. You've been kicked out of a principality and …"

Oh god there's more. I close my eyes, bracing myself for what he has to say.

"You can't return for five years."

I stop pacing and shake my head. There are no words. I throw up my hands in frustration then grab the sheet before it slips to the floor. "I've smoked pot maybe twice in my life, and the third time I attempt to smoke an iota of hash, I get arrested, thrown out of a coun—principality and banned from returning. What would happen if I attempt to smoke again? Twenty years to life?"

Without hesitating, he stands, moves closer and looking

me square in the eye, says, "I assure you there will be no next time." The simple statement has me trembling and noticing my fear he steps back and tempers the warning by adding, "It's good you got caught. Drug abuse is destructive."

Abuse? I want to say three times does not constitute misuse, but I'm in no position to argue, so I wait in silence for what I am sure is going to be a lecture.

"Substance abuse, alcoholism, all of them destroy ambition. They rob you of large chunks of productive time, prevent success … interfere with healthy choices and relationships, the list is endless. You said only three times. But how do you know three won't become thirteen or thirty or more? And it was foolhardy to whip out a joint in a public place in a country you know little about."

He's right, and worried that some international criminal record will make it impossible to get a job or live a normal life, my mind conjures all sorts of awful scenarios. What if they don't let me leave the country? Confiscate my passport and turn me into the authorities? This time I could be thrown in jail. I've heard about French prisons. Dirty, cramped, prisoners snacking on cockroaches, and I have no one to blame but myself. This is not something I would have done on a public beach at home. What made me think it would be alright in another country? Locked in my internal prison of worry, I don't notice Chase standing inches away. When I look up, he strokes my cheek with the back of his hand.

"Hey, it's over and done with. Time to move on." He gives

me a quick hug and smiling, tosses his head toward the door. "C'mon, you foxy felon, go get dressed and grab that sexy straw hat. I'll drive you to your hotel in Camogli. A buddy of mine will drive my car to your car rental lot."

My worries scatter, because all I process now is that he's staying. I freshen up and put on a sundress that I designed and sewed especially for this trip. It matches the hue of the sea here, and its tapered form hugs in all the right places. I happened to have found a pair of sandals in the same color, which is next to impossible with blues. Chase is patiently waiting and has the suitcases ready by the door.

In all the haste to leave, I realize I haven't spoken to Beth about the get-out-of-town order. "Chase, wait. I have to return Beth's phone."

"I took care of it. It's already been delivered to her room."

The man is incredibly organized and efficient. With all our sexual carrying on, I have no idea when he found the time to do this.

"Thanks, just give me a sec. I want to make sure she knows I have to leave and that she has a way to get to Camogli."

A groggy Beth answers her phone, mutters a sleepy "are you Ok?" followed by a thick tongued, "I have a ride there with Andre," before signing off with a slurred, "see you then." Beth is incapable of coherent thinking before noon.

Lifting our suitcases into the trunk, I notice he's favoring his right hand, and I know precisely the reason why, because I still can't comfortably sit. Good for the bastard. More sweet revenge follows when, Mr. Rules Are To Be Followed realizes that I'm the only one who can drive to the car rental garage as per the contract agreement.

"Do you know how to drive a standard?" he asks, doubt creasing his beautiful face.

"Yes." He's skeptical, and I do an internal cartwheel of joy.

"Who taught you? Massimo?"

I contemplate answering yes just to put him at ease, but since I'd recently been teetering on some behavioral precipice, lying doesn't seem to be an option. "Not exactly. I taught myself when I drove here from Nice."

I think I hear him groan, but he says nothing more and gets into the passenger seat. I slowly lower myself into the driver's seat.

"By tomorrow you'll feel a lot better," he offers, looking a tad guilty.

Well thank you Doctor Spanks, and suddenly it dawns on me that he must have done this before or how else would he be able to spout healing time. Ugh, I bet he even enjoyed it, but before I can ask if that's the case, he's belting himself in, adjusting the passenger's side rearview mirror, checking my rear view mirror, reminding me to buckle up, asking if my seat is properly positioned for me to comfortably reach the pedals, studying the shoes I'm wearing to make sure they'll allow me to work the pedals properly. He finally grips the hanging door handle and stares ahead, waiting. You'd think we were blasting off into outer space. I stifle a smile. This is going to be so much fun.

Lowering the roof, I turn on the radio and put the car in first. After only two stalls and one jerky start, we exit the lot. Traffic is light and I accelerate, shift gears, and speed away, relishing the motion of my neck pulling back against the head rest. One glance at Chase shows me he's gripping the dashboard and moving his feet as if he's controlling the pedals and driving.

"Keep your eyes on the road, Alicia," he admonishes then quickly adds, "Can you concentrate with this music blaring?"

I ignore his ridiculous question and shift, burning some rubber and jerking us forward as we speed ahead. With the wind rustling my hair and Michael Bublé crooning "Feeling Good," I am freer and more alive than I have ever felt. My happiness must be contagious because I see a slight tug of a grin, and I reach out and caress his hand. His smile evaporates.

"Two hands on the wheel and don't take your eyes off the road."

I answer by slamming on the accelerator and shifting gears, throwing us once again forward then back as we speed ahead. Blissful silence, and I have to stop myself from laughing out loud.

The car rental office is easily located, and I drive into its adjacent garage and park in the first available spot without any mishap. Chase is rubbing his neck as he gets out of his seat, and I think he looks a little paler than usual, but he waves good-naturedly to his friend: a muscular guy, clean shaven from the top of his head to the bottom of his broad neck. Across the breadth of his forearm is a tattoo of a fire-breathing dragon expelling some kind of huge weapon. He glances my way through eyes that are alert, wary, and warm all at the same time, and with the same erect military stance as Chase, he shakes Chase's hand with a hint of a smile.

"Glad you made it, bro."

You'd think I careened into poles and pedestrians on my way here.

Chase introduces him simply as Mac. Mac shakes my hand, nods and offers a short but friendly, "nice to meet you," before quickly turning to help Chase transfer our bags to the other car. Like Chase, he's not a talker.

Chase opens the passenger door for me but instead of getting in, I nonchalantly remark, "I thought I would try driving your car."

"Maybe in your next life."

Laughing, I playfully tug at his ears. "So, now you're Buddhist?" Then I slip into the passenger seat and quickly buckle up before he hits his checklist.

Chase takes the wheel, looking far more confident and excited than before. He gives a warm thank you to Mac and as we drive off, I call out, "It was nice meeting you, Mac."

"A pleasure, Alicia." He casually salutes in my direction.

It's a beautiful day and with the top down and the wind blowing, I feel a newfound pleasure in just being. It's as if the missing pieces of my life have been fit into place.

"You look radiant," he comments, glancing in my direction.

"That's because you're here." I reach over and softly kiss his cheek before pointing my finger and mockingly commanding, "Eyes on the road, Reardon!" He smiles, bites my finger, and yelping, I yank it away.

Chase handles the car well, and it's easy to see he enjoys driving. His shifting is seamless and the ride smooth. We lapse into a comfortable silence, and my mind ruminates on what lies ahead. Having Chase drive with me is an unexpected bonus. I relish this chance to learn more about him. He's obviously accomplished a lot in a short span of time, and it's a little bit intimidating. I need to recalculate, determine what I have to offer. It can't be all that one sided, and I let my mind walk through my accomplishments/experiences: recent graduate with 4.0 cum, about to receive a prestigious award, one almost sexual encounter with Thomas (he groped, I fiddled, until we were caught by his sister who promptly kicked us out of her car—that one gets A for effort), and last but not least one drug bust with subsequent arrest and detainment. Not an impressive relationship resume.

It's obvious he's had considerable sexual experiences. He knows just where to touch to arouse, and his speed and facility producing condoms rival a magician pulling rabbits from a hat. What if he's clumping me into the virgin pity category and that's why he's staying? Like maybe he's thinking, *"Oh shit, there's no way I can just leave, it being her first time and all.*" And didn't I hear him say "what the fuck," right before he kissed and touched me like I've never been kissed and touched before. What if I was just a, *what the fuck*, fuck. Like he was thinking, I'm here, she's here, why not? Even worse, he could be mistaking my lack of experience for naiveté. The abyss of negativity deepens.

"A penny for your thoughts? You're awfully quiet. Everything OK?" He reaches out and gently kisses my hand.

"Sure." I'm not ready to confide, so I just say, "I was thinking how sweet this car drives. It really is gorgeous."

"It's a Mercedes Benz SL 65 AMG Roadster. But you don't really want to talk about cars." He pauses and quickly glances at me before asking, "Was I too hard on you the other night?"

I think for a bit and even though I was mortified at the time, it wasn't intolerable.

"I don't plan on letting you repeat it any time soon." I catch a hint of a smile and my former suspicion surfaces again. I look at him and narrow my eyes, but he stares straight ahead with his best poker face.

I decide on levity. "Not really. I have three older brothers. I've been pinched, poked, prodded, punched, pigtails yanked and tied in knots, pulled up by the straps of my overalls, and held upside down by my ankles so my backside could be used as a rubber dart target ..."

"That beautiful ass," he laughs. "Was it Antonio?"

"No, Francesco. Antonio was the diligent scout who practiced different kinds of knots by tying me up to earn merit badges. Then he'd conveniently forget to untie me." He's really laughing at this point.

"I got my revenge, though, by hiding anything and everything that was important to them. Homework, house keys, car keys, textbooks, laptops, cell phones, and then myself when they came looking for me to get their belongings back."

"What about Massimo?"

"No, he never participated in any of their pranks. He was my protector."

Chase pauses for a moment and then taking my hand says, "Like me. I want to be your protector, but what I wouldn't give to have access to your ass to help make you scream with pleasure."

Excitement and fear course through me, but I murmur, "OK ... maybe I'd try that."

I hear a sharp intake of breath, and he reaches over and quickly kisses the tattooed star closest to my ear, making my insides quiver with anticipation.

"There is a rash side to you but I admire your bravery. Soon," he croons and puts me at ease by adding, "we'll build up to it so you're ready and wanting."

I think that if this conversation goes on any longer, I'm going to jump him in the car.

"What about your family?" I ask to tame my mind and body from reacting to thoughts of mind-blowing sex.

"What do you want to know?" his tone is tense, his stare at the road ahead unblinking, and I'm caught off guard at his rapid change in mood.

It's obvious he doesn't want to talk about his life, so to narrow the question I ask, "What was it like growing up with a younger sister?"

He pauses, and for the briefest moment his lips purse and his forehead furrows, and I think I have stumbled onto another uncomfortable topic of conversation. But he catches himself and his features relax.

"Fiona was a tomboy. She did everything she could to keep up with me and my friends. Climbed trees, played softball, basketball, and any other sport we were engaged in. Whatever Fiona lacked in size and strength, she made up with in speed. Fastest short and long distance runner."

His expression softens and a faint trace of a smile graces his lovely lips.

"Like Massimo with you, I was her protector."

"What does Fiona do now?"

His smile fades and he squints one eye in a nervous reflex motion. I have inadvertently hit another nerve and regret asking the question, but it's too late to take it back. His past seems to be a riddled with taboo subjects, and I wonder what unhappy secrets it holds. I know I nurse mine, but I can still talk about happy times.

Finally he answers, "She's an amateur photographer and really quite good. I think she may have just sold one of her portraits. She has a son, Liam, and they live in Long Beach with my Dad. He converted the downstairs into an apartment for them shortly after he moved there."

"You have a nephew. That must be fun. Do you spend time together?"

"Liam is a great kid, a three-year-old whirlwind of motion. I'm teaching him how to play soccer."

And just like that, Chase's mood shifts and he's smiling again. I have no idea why he's uncomfortable talking about Fiona. I know that since his mom died my mother has kept in touch with Fiona, but she never indicated there were any problems. Then, she never would intrude upon or reveal another family's issues. She believes in the privacy and sanctity of family. I decide to follow the same credo. No need to stoke Chase Reardon's somber side, especially since something tells me it's deeper and wider than I imagined.

CHAPTER EIGHT

y the time we stop in San Remo for lunch, my stomach is grumbling. I didn't eat yesterday and this morning only had a croissant and coffee that Chase brought to the room while I was dressing, so when we stop at a restaurant called Victory Morgana Bay, taking a table overlooking the harbor, just about everything on the menu makes me salivate. I decide on the trenette al pesto, a dish made with homemade flat spaghetti tossed with a pesto sauce. It's delicious with the basil and scattered haricot verts blending into a savory burst on my tongue. The local Pigato wine Chase orders easily washes everything down.

Afterward, sipping an espresso, I sit back relaxed, enjoying our time together. The quiet interlude makes me realize that there's so much more I want to know about this man, but except for his lack of inhibitions in bed, he remains a puzzle. I grapple with how to approach this delicate give and take exchange of information without having him think I'm prying into things he doesn't want to share, but the truth of the matter is that I know very little about him.

"I can tell when you want to ask me something but don't know how to say it," he says, interrupting my thoughts. The man is positively clairvoyant when it comes to knowing what I'm thinking. It doesn't help that my face mirrors my thoughts.

"You know me well." Pausing to gather my thoughts, I try to figure out a way to tactfully approach the subject. Coming up at a loss, I simply ask, "How do you know when I have something I want to talk about?"

Leaning toward me, he quietly says, "You become extremely still and your brow furrows so that I want to smooth it." He reaches over and touches the spot above my nose and delicately rubs it with his forefinger. My breath catches and I literally have to shake my head to stay focused on my intentions to have him share.

Smiling, he sits back and says, "So … what is it?"

Oh, he knows the hold he has over me and relishes the fact that his touch can unnerve and muddle my thinking.

"I … I …" I'm stammering, and realizing it shouldn't be this difficult blurt out, "How many other women have you slept with?" The question just pops out of my mouth, and I can only blame some filtering defect that malfunctions when I'm in his company. He seems taken aback and doesn't immediately reply, making me feel I should break the awkward silence with an explanation.

"It's just that my sexual history is obvious, and I can tell that you've … um, had lots of experience in that department so I'm curious as to how many women you've slept with." I lean forward, locking my eyes with his and wait.

"You mean at one time or all together?"

Not the response I anticipated, and my brain fast forwards into picturing how such a setup works. I mean who does what to whom and when? It's a lot to think about. All thoughts halt when his raised eyebrows and wicked grin tell me he's joking, and I poke him in his side. He pulls back and snorts a laugh.

"No, I'm an exclusive type of guy. One woman at a time." Then he looks at me and in a low melodious voice begins talking. "My first time was with Lauren Martinson. I was fourteen and she was a senior, so she was probably seventeen or eighteen. We were under the bleachers at school smoking, and before I knew what's happening, she unzips my pants and begins doing well, you can imagine what. We met under those bleachers until school ended for summer break. Next was Maxine Caudwell, but we all called her Maxi. She was the nurse who came to help my mom after her surgery. One night Maxi suddenly showed up in my bedroom. I was lying on my bed listening to music with my headphones on and didn't hear her at first. Without saying a word, she lied down next to me and started kissing and touching me in all the right places. She taught me how to pleasure a woman. I thought I was in love and was devastated when she was reassigned and never returned my calls. Then there was a series of four or five classmates who more or less amounted to fast flings. I was lonely and angry, especially after my mother died, and looked for any pleasurable fix I could find to ease the pain." He pauses and takes my hand, turning it to kiss my palm and holds it in his hand before continuing. "One of those was Devin Raykhelson." I notice a fleeting shadow of pain dart across his eyes, but he doesn't stop talking. "She's an old friend who was forced to deal with many challenges growing up. We often hung out together, talking, listening to music, drinking beer, smoking weed. One night we kissed and the friendship turned into a torrid sexual fling that petered out as quickly as it began once we realized it wasn't what either of us wanted. Soon afterward I enlisted in the marines, had several more sexual liaisons when I was on leave—each lasting no more than a few weeks. After completing my tour of duty, I attended Yale where I met Addie Walker. She was smart and attractive and gave me my first taste of heartbreak when she left me for some wealthy hedge fund guy from Connecticut. Since then, there's been casual sexual flings, but nothing serious. And just in case you're curious…" he stops and takes my hand "…I'm not seeing anyone now."

Well, that explains his speed and facility with a condom. Still holding his hand, I quietly take the time to study his face. He never breaks eye contact. In his earnest expression I see the young and vulnerable boy who sought love in sex and I reach over and brush his lips with a kiss. He lets out a deep breath, and I realize that this conversation is making him nervous.

He smiles and continues, "Not long afterward, I bump into a green-eyed vixen who's sketching in a coffee shop, and when she suddenly kisses me with a passion and longing I never experienced before, I feel confused so I act like an asshole and walk away. Besides, I knew her brothers would kick my ass if they found out I was sleeping with their younger sister."

Laughing, I ask, "So what about now? What changed that?"

"You were too irresistible to ignore and worth taking the chance." And he holds me by the chin and raises my lips to his for a warm and delicate kiss.

We linger a bit longer opting for more current topics to discuss, and Chase tells me he has to leave for business in a few days but can drive me to Milan before flying back to New York. I mentally calculate that we have four days to enjoy the Italian coast together. I'm glad I didn't burden him with an invite to the awards ceremony in Lake Como when he has unavoidable business commitments. I still wonder where this relationship is headed. An attraction from afar has been transformed into a multitude of new feelings inside so that when we're together, desire, affection, and an aliveness that sees a future radiant with potential spring to life. I am falling fast and hard for this guy, and I can't help but think I could be a heartbeat away from heartbreak. Self-doubt and inexperience can be monikers for relationship failure, especially when one partner has accomplished a great deal while the other has yet to make a noticeable mark. Intellectual compatibility and shared experiences, like oxygen breathed in to fill the lungs, keep a relationship fulfilled and alive. What if my professional and experience lag causes him to become bored? Will I constantly be trying to catch up, striving with every life event to prove my worth? I have three older brothers and the idea of that is sobering.

Chase interrupts my reverie when he picks up the check and automatically pays it in full. I make a mental note to be sure to pay the next time around. I want him to know that I am on my way to becoming an independent wage earner, that is as soon as I find a job. I wince because this is yet another hole to breach.

If Chase notices my troubled silence, he chooses to say nothing. We continue driving, and with an ease that I recognize he has for conversing about sports or music or art, he starts talking about his favorite bands and books and entices me to do the same. It seems we both enjoy an eclectic mix of different sounds, but he favors jazz, while I like rock. He laughs when I tell him that although I love reading the classics, especially the Bronte sisters and Virginia Wolf, I am a romance novel junkie. He tells me he prefers non-fiction, especially books about World War II and the Viet Nam War. It is a pleasant drive along the coast with a cloudless sky overhead and a gentle breeze tempering the heat. Too quickly, we reach my hotel, a small structure nestled on a hilltop overlooking the harbor town of Camogli. A sudden wave of melancholy grips at the thought of him leaving but I don't feel comfortable asking if he'd like to stay. There's not much worse than a clingy first-timer. A psychologist would have a field day with my confidence issues.

He walks me into the lobby and before I can object, slips the hotel clerk his charge card to keep on file. Then, after checking in, he suggests we have a glass of wine in a nearby café while the room is being readied. My spirits lift immediately. We walk along the harbor and find a small trattoria that's serving beverages at this time. In Italy as in much of Europe there are distinct times that restaurants remain open. If you're not out and about between 12:00 and 2:00 PM or 7:30 and 10:30 PM, you're not eating, unless you count gelato and espresso a meal.

Chase orders a bottle of Vermintino, and tanned, with his tousled hair falling smooth and silky over his collar, he looks young and carefree, making me realize how guarded and taciturn he normally behaves. It's as if he's attached to some monitoring device that consistently reminds him to remain focused and in control. I'm beginning to understand that in Chase's world there is little to no room for making mistakes. I reach over and stroke his cheek, and he leans into my hand.

Then in a rare, unguarded moment, he says, "I enjoy being with you. You make me feel like I matter." He pauses for a moment and with an impish grin adds, "And I think I may have turned you into a sex fiend."

"Fiendish only for you," I whisper, reaching in and kissing him again.

"That's good because I don't share."

Hmm, I muse, *maybe it's a good thing I've had no former*

lovers. Something tells me that not only doesn't he like to share during a relationship, any "befores" would illicit unpleasant scrutiny. Still, I would have liked to compete with at least one juicy sexual tryst. Seems my self-doubt is sprinkled with some competitiveness.

We finish off the Vermentino and hand in hand take a walk along the harbor. I love the feel of his hand: strong but not too rough with long fingers that wrap around mine in a hold that's firm, but not cloying. We stop to watch the boats scattered in the harbor and taking me in an embrace, he bends toward my lips and plants a leisurely kiss that on contact escalates into a reaching and touching melding of bodies. Holding the back of my head with one hand and cupping my backside with the other, the intensity of his kisses make my knees weak. I immediately melt into him, wrapping my hands in his hair and pressing myself into his body.

"Hotel now," he says out of breath. "Or I will have to raise your dress and take you here."

He grabs me by the hand and we walk quickly toward the hotel, stopping at intervals to kiss again. Thank heavens my room is ready, and once inside it's a race to see who can remove whose clothes first. I tear open his shirt, marveling again at the rippled muscles of his chest. He pulls off my dress, then reaches down and tugs at my panties, tearing them off my body. We're wild with need, and as I unbutton and lower his pants, he kicks them off, and we fall onto the bed. He takes me in his arms and fondles my breast, rubbing the nipple between his thumb and forefinger before bending and taking it in his mouth and gently tugging it with his teeth until my body arches toward him in need.

I futilely grasp for his swollen penis, but he's faster and in one swift motion, he grabs my two hands in a firm grasp, holding them firmly above my head, and swiftly turns me onto my stomach. He tells me to push my knees forward, and I shimmy them until my backside hangs in the air. Open, waiting and vulnerable, I quiver with anticipation. Kneeling behind me, he releases my hands and slowly massages my backside, allowing his pinkie finger to barely tickle my anus. My body jumpstarts then stills at the new sensation. He pauses. I hear his deep breaths, and the waiting for what will happen next excites and unnerves me all at the same time.

"God, how I want you." He takes the forefinger of his other hand and inserts it into my front while his pinky finger continues to do a little dance from behind, and awash in sensation, my body presses downward and he inserts another finger, pressing both inside. I moan, then gyrate, pushing myself toward him to increase the momentum of his fingers. Biting the inside of my mouth and whimpering from their slow thrusts, I listen for the tear of the condom package. Again and again he pushes his fingers inside me, coaxing my legs further and further apart, and just when I think I can't bear another moment he pulls out his fingers, pushes my legs further apart, and tears open a condom with an adept skill that still catches me by surprise. He thrusts his swollen member inside, and

I gasp from the deep penetration. He rapidly continues to thrust until he hits that sweet point, and I explode in ripples of ecstasy. He groans as he reaches his climax, and when he finishes, we both fall onto our backs, exhausted and sated, our heavy breathing mingling as we wait in silence for it to slow. He's the first to move and I hear him flushing his condom and washing his hands in the bathroom before coming back to lie down next to me.

"Hi," he whispers, taking me in his arms. "How are you feeling?"

I decide that it's endearing that he continues to ask. It shows his concern, not only because much of it is new to me, but because it is his way of asking if I enjoyed the experience.

I caress his face and kiss first one eyelid, then the other, before answering, "That was …" I pause because I'm not sure there are words to describe what I felt. "Incredible. It was incredible."

He holds me tightly, and I know he's pleased because he nuzzles his lips into my neck, and between kisses answers, "Good. I'm glad." I'm flattered that he feels the need to satisfy me, and it's empowering to know that I can illicit this response from him.

"Rest, get some sleep, love," he says, still holding me to him. The endearment lifts me to new heights, and I close my eyes and fall into a peaceful slumber. It would be one of my last for a long while.

CHAPTER NINE

wake with a start. Chase is lying on his side, his body spooned around mine, his arm holding me to him. It's early, the sun just beginning to give form and shape to the unfamiliar objects in the room. There's a light tapping on the door, and I slowly disengage from Chase's arm, slip on my robe, and go to see who could possibly be at the door at this early hour.

"Who is it?" I whisper warily, looking through the peephole.

I see a tousle of hair and a large brown eye staring ahead. It's Beth, fist raised, getting ready to knock again. I quickly open the door. One look at me and she breaks into a toothy smile, grabbing me in a hug before holding me at arm's length and giving me a good once-over.

"Thank god you're alright." Pulling away, she studies me again. I haven't uttered a word, but her eyes narrow as they take in my appearance. "What have you been up to, girl?" Standing on tiptoes, she attempts to peek past me into the room. Dressed in a clingy black sundress, her hair hugging her shoulders in soft waves, she looks as if she's been out partying all night.

"Shh." I hold my finger to my lips. "And I should be asking you the same question. What time is it anyway?"

"It's about five. Andre and I have been out dancing and walking on the beach." She hesitates and I easily fill in the blanks. "Why are you blocking the door? Is there someone in your bed?"

"Possibly."

"What does that mean?"

"I'll give you all the details later."

"Ok," she reluctantly agrees, "but it seems a lot has happened since your arrest, and I want the full scoop."

"Ok, but not now. I'll call you later."

And walking away, she suddenly stops and hovers in place as if her feet are stuck. Then without warning she jumps and lets out a whoop. Turning to face me, she flashes a grin.

"It's Chase Reardon inside, right? He showed up to bail you out, and you hooked up."

"Shh." I hush her again, but her enthusiasm is infectious. She throws her arms around me, locking me in a bear hug before pulling away and shamelessly asking, "So was it good?"

Then pointing her finger in a random circle around me, quickly adds, "Forget what I just asked. Your mussed hair and pink cheeks tell me all I need to know for the moment. Let's meet for lunch at the hotel café, just the two of us, that is if you can separate yourself from lover boy long enough to grab a meal." I don't have time to answer because she quickly adds, "And speaking of long enough, how—"

I cut her off midsentence. "You're impossible. I'll see you and Andre at the beach for an early afternoon swim. We'll decide on a time for lunch then."

We hug again and as she's walking away, she does another jumping yelp without looking back then continues on her way. Gently clicking the door shut, I tiptoe back to bed, noticing Chase is still asleep. Lying on his back, with one arm resting above his head and the other at his side, he looks young, carefree, and I resist the urge to gently brush his hair off his forehead. Sensing my presence, he stirs and squints open one eye.

"Good morning, beautiful." It comes out as a deep hum, and before I can respond, he reaches out and grabs me by the tie of my robe and pulls me toward him and onto the bed. My robe falls open and wrapping his arms around me, he nuzzles my ear with his nose. "Snuggle with me?" he asks, a lopsided sleepy grin plastered on his face.

I turn on my side and bury my head in the crook of his arm. A perfect fit and very comfy. I must fall back into a deep sleep because the next thing I know, there's slivers of bright light sifting through the blinds and my body feels leaden with hungover sluggishness. Slowly sliding into a sitting position and propping pillows behind by head, I see Chase is already showered, dressed, and busy working on his laptop. When he hears me stirring, he looks up and smiles.

"I would say good morning, but it's almost noon."

Oh no, I must have slept in. "Why didn't you wake me?" I groggily answer. I didn't want to sleep away valuable time we could be enjoying together.

"You were sleeping so peacefully and these past couple of days were rough going for you. You needed the rest."

This is true, and I feel the difference immediately. Energized, I hop out of bed, run to Chase, and throw my arms around him. "Give me fifteen minutes and we'll go for a swim at the beach."

"More like an hour and fifteen minutes," he grumbles, but he's grinning. I am ready in fifteen minutes—record time for me. Clad in my bikini, I reach into my suitcase for a sundress and slip on a coral cami sundress then give my packed beach tote a final check. It's stuffed to the brim with clothes and assorted sundries sans any pot. I took time to carefully pack because I realize you never know what you might need during a day at the beach. I still shudder when I think of my arrest. I want to ask what was required to secure my release, but I hesitate to bring up the subject. No need to rile him and upset myself when things are going so well.

While I putter around, Chase patiently waits, returning his attention to some charts on his laptop. When I'm finally ready, I look at him and grouse with mock annoyance, "C'mon, stop dawdling. Jeesh, you're slow."

He's up in record time and on the way out swats my backside, making me jump and yelp. That has become one busy area of my anatomy lately.

The Ligurian Sea is a shimmering expanse of turquoise tranquility. My mind configures different designs of beachwear in the same color with a backdrop of accessories that match the color of sand and rock that spread across the landscape. I resolve to take my sketchpad to the sitting area after lunch with Beth and begin drawing.

"How about something to drink?" Chase asks and thoughts of work slide away.

"I'd love a glass of Rosé."

"Then, Rosé it is."

I motion for the waiter from the beach café. "Mi scusi, una bottiglia di rosa e due bicchieri d'acqua. Grazie."

"You speak Italian," Chase remarks casually, but I can tell he is surprised.

"A bit. My mother and father occasionally spoke Italian at home and would encourage us to speak it whenever possible, correcting our enunciation and grammar. I also studied it in high school."

"What about you. Did you study any language?"

"Yeah," he snorts, an ironic twist to his mouth, "the language of hard knocks. I'm fluent." He laughs, but his expression holds regret and a tinge of what looks like shame.

He's suddenly quiet and once again I regret asking a question about his past. I want to try to understand this complex man, but each time the subject of his past is broached, he withdraws behind a wall of silence. It's sobering and bewildering. And what's with this school of hard knocks comment? He's a Yale graduate who's on his way to becoming a successful real estate developer. How bad can it be? What he needs is some fun to get his mind off his dreary thoughts.

Playfully kicking sand at his feet, I jump up and run towards the water shouting, "Let's go for a swim."

"What about the bottle of wine we ordered?" he shouts after me. Thorough and precise, Chase rarely does anything spur of the moment.

"They'll leave it chilling on the table." I turn and wave him in my direction before running and diving into the serene surf.

He's at my side as soon as I surface, and in one fluid motion disappears beneath the water and lifts me onto his shoulders. Trying to adjust my balance, I attempt to fold my arms around his neck, but he grabs me by my ankles and tosses me backward before I can establish a solid grip. I surface, sputtering water and laughing. Happy that his good humor's back, I immediately dive under, grab ahold of his ankle and tug. It's like trying to lift bricks, but finally a soft swell in the water works in my favor, and he slides to his side and under. He surfaces from behind and wraps his arms around me, nibbling my neck with gentle bites that send ripples of pleasure through my body. I turn and kiss him deeply, immediately feeling his response below. Lowering my hand, I reach under his bathing suit and began rubbing, but he removes my hand and shakes his head. I pout and try to convince him.

"It's all being done under water. No one can see."

But he's adamantly opposed. "Save yourself for later when we get back to the privacy of our room."

Sometimes he can be such a prude, and at other times he doesn't have any inhibitions. We swim a bit further out, but not being a strong swimmer I turn back toward shore. Chase hollers and points to show he plans to continue, making sure I reach shore before swimming further and further until he's nothing more than a dark dot on the horizon. I relax when I see how competent he is and return to the lounge chair. Beth and Andre still haven't arrived, and I imagine they must be keeping very "busy" in the bedroom. The wine has been opened and left chilling in a bucket of ice on a table next to our chairs, and I pour myself a glass. It's delicious, dry and crisp.

Relaxing and sipping the wine, I notice Chase swimming back toward shore and while I'm pouring a glass of wine for him, I hear my phone's ringtone. It's from home and I immediately answer. The voice sounds sluggish and the connection is poor.

"Mamma, is that you?"

"Yes." Then silence

"How are you feeling?"

Her voice cracks, like she's about to cry but is holding back. "I'm fine. How are you?"

Tears prickle and I fight past the lump in my throat. She sounds sad, her words stretched and flat. "I'm good. Are you home alone?"

"No, Nelda is here, making up the bed." Nelda is a part-time housekeeper who usually comes once a week to help, but recently has been at the house several times a week. "I wanted to see how you were doing." Silence follows and if it wasn't for the background hum of the vacuum cleaner, I would have thought she hung up.

"The weather's been great. I'm at the beach waiting for Beth," I offer, hoping to engage her in conversation.

"Ah, the cote d' Azur … breathtaking. Take time to notice when the sea turns an amethyst color. Duplicating that hue would make a one-of-a-kind design." And it's like she used every ounce of her strength to articulate those words, because she adds in a soft, slow voice, "I'm going to go now. Take care of yourself. I love you." Before I can say good-bye, she's gone.

I swipe away my tears, think about calling the restaurant to make sure everything is ok but dismiss the idea. Nelda is with her and very responsible. Why worry my father when everything appears to be under control. I look at Chase, who's back and taking a business call.

"Was the contract signed? We need that sale before the upcoming purchase can be finalized."

I tune out the work-related conversation, reach for a tissue to wipe my eyes and blow my nose, then take a few more sips of wine forcing myself to stare at the sea and relax. I'm relieved to hear his continued conversation because I don't want him to see me like this, mostly because I don't want to explain. Lying back, I let my mind drift until Beth's throaty laughter brings me back to the here and now.

"There you are and drinking already. I think I'm going to have to join you. Can't let you get day drunk alone."

Laughing, I look up and notice a large love bite on her neck. "Naughty, naughty," I tsk, pointing to my neck as a reference point.

She just chuckles some more and says, "If you think this is bad, wait until you see Andre's." Beth's humor is like salve for my worrying wound, and I crane my neck for a peek at Andre's neck, but he's bending over in some snug strip of blue the Europeans call a bathing suit, lathering his legs with sun screen. The view is interesting, but when he straightens and turns, I do a double take. Ay dios mio! That is some serious bulging. Unaware, Andre remains rooted in his spot, gazing ahead and smiling at a cluster of children running toward the water.

Beth brushes back her hair with her fingertips and drolly remarks, "Enjoying the view?"

"Mmm, it's … expansive, could make an interesting picture to hang in the bedroom."

"Yes, indeed," Beth quips. "It could even hang beautifully above a kitchen table or a desk in a study, or … well, it's versatilities are endless."

It's becoming harder not to laugh out loud, so looking down I pretend to rummage through my bag. Finished with his call, Chase glances in my direction, squinting his left eye ever so slightly before getting up to shake Andre's hand and kiss Beth hello. I was surprised by Chase's recognition of Andre then realized they must have met when he was out looking for Beth the night of my arrest.

We fall into light conversation until eventually, giving into the sun and heat, Beth and Andre decide to go for a swim. I take the opportunity to mention to Chase that Beth and I plan to have lunch together, and he indicates that he has some business to attend to.

Then pausing, he quietly mentions, "I rented a villa in Santa Margharita with plenty of room for all of us." He takes my hand and looking earnestly into my eyes says, "Stay with me there. It's larger than your hotel room and has ample space for your friends. Afterward, I'll drive you to Milan." He seems hesitant, unsure, and I'm taken aback by the seriousness of his request. It's as if he doubts my desire to be with him.

"I'd like that," I respond, squeezing his hand, and he visibly relaxes. "I'll be sure to mention it to Beth over lunch."

We spend the rest of the time swimming, dozing, and making idle vacation chatter about things of little consequence. I pin my hair up into a bun and sit back, contemplating home. It's always like this. Just when I think I've forgotten, memories surge back and I'm caught in twists of sadness. Just to see her smile again would be a gift. I decide to rest my concerns until I can phone later when I'm alone. I must have sighed because Chase takes my hand, holds it to his lips, and brushes it with a kiss.

"Why so sad?"

I didn't think I was that transparent, but I never was any good at masking my feelings, and he reads me well. I shake my head and smile, not wanting to burden him with the truth.

"I'm just thinking about what needs to be done for my job search."

He kisses my hand again before looking me in the eye and says, "I don't think that's quite the truth, but I'll let it slide for the moment. Later however, quid pro quo."

I have no idea what tit for tat he's referring to. "What do you mean?"

"I freely shared my sexual history at your request and now you owe me a personal truth."

I pause, scrambling to determine what he could possibly want to know. I draw a blank. "You already know my sexual history. There's not much else to say about it."

Without missing a beat, he answers, "I'd like you to tell me about your mother."

Caught off guard, I look away so he can't see the tears welling. I'm embarrassed, crying in front of him about my mother like I'm not grown up enough to enjoy a trip without thinking about home. How do I explain that every one of her relapses shadows me, like lightening before a storm, that they prickle at the onset then burst into an uneasiness that only abates when I see them subsiding. Where do I even start?

I wipe my tears, take a deep breath, and turn toward him. "OK. But not now. I can't talk about it here"

"Whenever you're ready, I'll be here to listen." He smiles and takes the back of my hand and gently brushes it with another kiss. And several bricks of the wall I've built begin to crumble, with more and more following until I decide that if I'm going to talk about it with anyone, it will be with him.

CHAPTER TEN

I'm seated facing the path Beth has to follow to reach the café where we are meeting for lunch. There's a lovely garden gracing both sides of the walkway to the restaurant, and I revel in its verdant vibrancy. Beth arrives a few minutes later, flushed and slightly breathless, her soft dark curls haloed around her face and cascading to her shoulders. She immediately initiates conversation as she sits and scoops up her menu.

"How scary was the whole Monte Carlo scenario? I thought for sure they were going to keep you incarcerated. That's why I reached out to Thomas and ran off to try and get help. I never imagined Chase would be here. Convenient, right? I bet you were ecstatic to see him."

"Mmm, very surprised indeed. But he was furious with me so it wasn't exactly a happy reunion." I left out the part about my punishment because it's too embarrassing to mention.

"OK, so what aren't you telling me? How did you manage to, you know, hook up. I want all the tantalizing details."

I shake my head, laughing. "I don't know exactly. I was upset because you couldn't be found. He was consoling me, and well … one thing led to another." I don't want to go into detail about a relationship that's so new, and with nothing to compare it to, so I ask her about Andre.

There's playful mischief in her eyes and her lips quirk up. "Can you believe he drove all the way from Paris, then spent half the night with me looking for you? And…" she leans in and whispers "…he's unbelievable in bed. Those speedos don't lie." Raising her head and sweeping her hair off her face, she nonchalantly asks, "So did Mr. Hard to Get Lover Boy give you an orgasm?"

Some young student type with his head buried a tad too deeply inside his menu lowers it and peeks over at me, a droll smirk plastered on his face. I shoot him a scowl and he dives back behind it.

When I don't immediately answer, Beth plows on. "You're very particular, and I know you were waiting for the right person and the right time, so I hope it … well, that he …"

Beth at a loss of words is such a rarity, and I know she's concerned and doesn't want to offend, so to spare her any more discomfort I smoothly interject, "They were fantastic."

"Your first has a *they*?" I nod and shrug and she lets out a soft whistle. "Impressive. First time for me was a bust. Lying on the cold backseat of Sammy Preston mother's SUV, he came ten seconds after he penetrated. Next time, he made it to twelve seconds. I don't think I had an orgasm until I was sexually active for many months, but when it hit … Wow! Fuckers just kept getting better and better."

Mr. Student nearly topples out of his chair, trying to catch a better glimpse of Beth. Needing time to digest where my relationship with Chase is headed, I don't offer anything more. Beth has experience and an uncanny ability to drift from lover to lover without concerns about long-term issues. I have never felt this way about anyone before and to be falling for someone who's intelligent, gorgeous as all hell, and accomplished in an array of different areas continues to intimidate. I mean, I'm flattered he's still here, but what if I remain stuck in the younger sister category of Chase Reardon's list of conquests? I can hear him now, ruminating to another girlfriend about his former lovers. "… *and then there was Alicia, the younger sister of a good friend from High School*." I reach for my soda wishing it was wine.

"I can tell you're trapped in your usual web of worry. I should slip you some Valerian root so you stop dwelling and enjoy the moment."

I nearly spit out my soda. "Let me get this straight. You're suggesting herbal supplements as a relaxant to someone recently arrested for smoking hash."

"A blip of a mistake on an otherwise stellar record. Although, you do have this devil-may-care side of your personality that will give him a run for his money." She smirks.

"Not that he doesn't need to be kept on his toes and reminded he can't always be boss."

Me keep him on his toes? Interesting premise but something I never considered, and I file this information in the "must give more thought" category of my brain. Then to deflect, I explain that Chase is here for only three more days before having to fly back to New York for business.

"He rented a villa in Santa Margharita and invited you and Andre to join us there. He says it's large enough for both of you to have your own space and privacy. What do you think?"

Beth ponders for a bit, shrugs, and offers, "That's fine with me, but what about you? Will we be crowding you?"

"No. Not at all."

"I'm not sure how long Andre is going to be traveling with me. He has several weeks off for vacation, and I'll probably drive with him to Milan, unless you were planning to have us travel together."

"No, that works for me. Chase offered to drive me to Milan before leaving and I have lots to do there."

The urge to augment my portfolio is increasing as the Lake Como event approaches. I had invited Beth to attend as my guest but now reassure her she's under no obligation to come if she wants to spend the evening with Andre. I don't know what to expect but assume the event will include several speeches and announcements that could be tedious if you weren't in the design field.

Logistics resolved, we ask for the check but are assured it's been paid. I have a feeling Chase is picking up all the expenses, and instead of being relieved, I'm unsettled. The thought that I have no idea where I'm going to find a job or how I am going to support myself continues to cause me angst. I do believe I'll find employment and be on my way to financial independence, but it doesn't seem to be happening fast enough. I'm not afraid of hard work, and except for a few minor lapses in judgment I'm focused and responsible. The problem is Chase has mostly seen me at my worst moments, where he's had to pick up the pieces of my mistakes and chastise me along the way, like I'm some errant child in need of direction. What if all he saw after he sprung me from jail was a recent graduate in need of a pity bang? The term appears like an unwanted guest hauling an oversized suitcase.

This tailspin of negativity is tiring and quite frankly a bit depressing, so pushing work from my mind for the time being, I return to my room. Chase must still be working at the beach or maybe in the lobby's library, because the room is empty. The bed looks inviting and exhausted from wine, sun, and food, I remove my clothes and crawl under the light coverlet for a nap. It's warm outside but a sea breeze wafts through the open window and the room feels refreshingly cool. I close my eyes and succumbing to sleep, feel myself weightlessly drifting higher and higher until all I can see is an iridescent sea below and a blanket of blue sky above. When I descend, I'm cocooned in a comforter, so smooth and silky, it cushions my body and cools my feverish skin. My eyes flutter open and I see him emerging from shadow into sun, giving him dimension and substance. He's wearing jeans and a black T-shirt that stretches across his broad shoulders and hugs his biceps. My eyes wander toward his lips and the curved, knowing grin that spreads them as he silently watches and waits. Automatically, I reach down and touch myself, circling and pressing my fingers, lightly then firmer, until I moisten. I use my other hand to fondle my breast while he walks toward me and sits on the edge of the bed. He's so close I feel his breath tickle my navel. I insert my finger and raise my body to deepen my touch. He does nothing but watch—a silent observer who wants only to see my arousal. My eyes plead for more and eventually he joins me in bed, lowering his mouth to mine, pressing and possessing, thrusting his tongue inside as his swollen member presses against me. When we part, his eyes study me, and he casually removes my hand from my pleasuring and places it above my head. He takes my nipple in his mouth and tugs with his teeth then gently sucks. I moan and slowly he inserts himself inside. Gyrating, he increases then slows, keeping me wanting. I feel something smaller enter me from behind, perhaps a small finger, and impaled I am wanton with need and press my body into one and then the other. Rocking back and forth, unknown sensations take me to new levels of arousal, until reality pierces my dreamy haze and I feel a warm strong hand covering mine, moving two of my fingers in circles around my vagina.

"That's it, baby."

And sleepily I moan, the haziness of my dream now tapered by real touch, real sound, real movement. Floating between slumber and waking, it takes me a while to realize Chase has joined me in bed, transforming my sensual dream into reality. I am lying on my side and facing me he uses his hand to slip two of my fingers inside me then takes my thumb and maneuvers it along my clitoris. I am so wet that I wrap my legs around his so both our hands can exert more pressure. Chase gently turns me onto my back, never stopping the motion of our hands, and reaches to caress my breast, tugging my nipple between the thumb and forefinger of his other hand. My legs stiffen and I arch my back and moan again. I attempt to pull my hand and his away from me and reach for his penis, but he takes both hands and holds them above my head. His grip is strong and all I can do is lift my hips toward him in an effort to get him to respond to my need.

"Shh," he says "Soon. Let's not rush this." He climbs on top of me and gently tugs at my nipple with his mouth, sucking until it stands firm and supple, as ripples of pleasure cause my hips to once again gyrate and lift off the bed in an attempt to increase the pressure of his fingers. Arousal triggered by my dream and compounded by Chase's touch is more than any foreplay I need and keeps me just on the cusp of orgasm. The feeling is agonizingly sweet.

"Please," I whimper. "I … mmm … I can't …" And squirming, I helplessly succumb to him, revealing each vulnerability so he knows exactly where to touch to illicit the greatest response.

"Oh yes you can. Hang in there," he whispers in my ear.

I moan in frustration. Now it's as if he has points to score and a battle to win. Inexperienced, I can't compete, and I feel him insert one, then two fingers inside me, and again my hips raise upward, as if catapulted by some mechanism I can't control. Slowly and methodically, he continues making no attempt to penetrate. My god, where did he learn this restraint? I am both lost and consumed as he incessantly increases the pressure of his hand, inserting his fingers deeper and moving them in a slow back and forth rhythm while his tongue circles my nipple, taking turns with his mouth to tug at it. Damned if I am going to give in, but my slender frame doesn't afford me the strength to move with the weight of his body pressing me into the bed, or allow me to free my hands that are being held in a viselike grip above my head. It doesn't help that I am wild with need. I have no choice but to submit to the myriad sensations vibrating through my body as his fingers continue to twirl and press inside and his mouth pulls and tugs first on one and then the other nipple.

It isn't until my eyes beg with silent need and he—arms, body, and swollen member strained from sexual want—craves more that he slips on a condom and pushes himself inside, rapidly thrusting until I spiral toward a shuddering and seemingly never-ending climax. Several more hard thrusts follow and groaning loudly, he reaches his. I lie motionless on my back, my body weighted with sated tiredness, and wait for my breathing to slow as he lifts himself off me and falls onto his back. I turn toward him and he puts his arms around me, kissing me gently on my lips then my eyelids and the tip of my nose.

"That must have been some dream. Were you dreaming of me?"

I pull myself closer, wrap my arms around him, and bury my face in his neck, giving it little kisses. I identify the insecurity imbedded in the question, god knows I've felt it often enough, and I'm moved by his need for my recognition.

"It's always about you. Only you." I continue kissing his neck and nibbling on his earlobe.

"He lifts my chin and brushes the hair out of my eyes. "Keep that up, and I'm going to have to go another round." He lies back and quiets, eventually drifting off to sleep.

I wake groggy and achy, only to notice that Chase is showered, dressed, and working on his laptop at the desk in the corner of the room. He looks amazing in dress jeans and black linen shirt, his hair still wet and swept back. Rubbing the sleep from my eyes, I sit up and fight to win the battle to keep them open.

"What time is it?" I ask, standing and stretching.

"It's almost seven. He gets up and wrapping his arms around me, plants small kisses up and down my neck. Like magic, everything south of my waist awakens. At this rate, I am never going to leave this room. To my disappointment, he says, "Go get dressed. We'll grab some dinner before we go meet Beth and her Frenchman."

I hop out of bed, rejuvenated by the thought of having more alone time with him. "OK. I'll be ready in fifteen minutes."

"Maybe when pigs fly," he mutters, more to himself than aloud.

I'm tempted to go over and tickle him silly, but that would warrant body contact—a sure stop sign for any immediate leaving.

It's another lovely evening, clear, dry with a light breeze. I'm wearing a tangerine silk twill dress, its dipping neckline revealing a hint of cleavage that is more teasing than gauche. Hair parted to the side and styled with a soft wave, I opt for a bit of mascara, some blush, and tinted lip gloss. Chase does a double take when he sees me. Suddenly shy, I smile and to taper my embarrassment pipe, "Let's go Mr. Slowpoke. Do you think we have all night?"

"After you, mademoiselle." He holds the door open then tweaks my nose and makes a honking noise when I pass through.

We drive to a small restaurant that overlooks the harbor. Bobbing sail boats and fishing vessels provide a live mural for the restaurant's outdoor area. Seated at a table that looks out onto the sea, we order a bottle of Grechetto Bianco—a light white wine from the Umbrian region—and fall into light conversation. Chase looks magnificent in the soft glow of candlelight, and the wine and prior lovemaking mix together like a tonic that relaxes my body and loosens my tongue.

My phone sounds and I'm tempted to ignore the call, but it's from home so I hold up my finger to Chase, asking for a minute and answer.

"Hello." The smooth timbre of my father's voice reaches out like a warm hug.

"Hi, Papa, yes, I'm fine. How are you? Have you just finished at the restaurant?"

"Oh, it sounds like you had a busy night. Did Mamma stop by?"

I hear my voice taper to a disappointed whisper when he answers.

"Has she gotten out of bed at all today?" I close my eyes and whisper a small prayer of hope.

"No, I'm just a little concerned and …"

"Sure, I know it takes time. I'll try and reach her in the next day or two."

"Yes, I'm having a wonderful time. I'm in Santa Margharita."

"Of course. I promise not to worry."

"I love you too. Say hello to everyone. Bye."

Looking at the harbor my eyes travel to the water, and its gentle rippling calms my frayed nerves. I look up and see Chase watching me closely. He says nothing, just reaches out and strokes the top of my hand. I meet his gaze, start to open my mouth, shut it, and turn again to watch the boats and soak up the sounds of the sea. I don't know how to begin, but I realize it's now or never. It's not going to be easy to talk about my mother, but I have held on to this for too long. Chase has asked, and I need to talk. He looks expectantly at me but wisely keeps silent to give me time to gather my thoughts. When I finally start to speak, the words spill out like water in a moving brook.

"Earlier, at the beach, you asked about my mother. Well, you were right to notice that this is a topic that preys on my mind." I push past the tightness in my throat and force myself to continue. "My mother has been intermittently ill for some time now. She suffers from bouts of depression that force her to take to her bed for weeks at a time. It's like she slips into some deep, dark place where no amount of cajoling is enough to coax her out of its depth. They're especially hard to see because she usually has this innate ebullience … this joie de vivre that allows her to easily connect to others. She loves to cook and create and sew and taught me so much of what I know today about quality craftsmanship and design." I pause here and take a large gulp of wine, swallowing the lump in my throat along with it to help me express what I want to say next. I don't want to cry. I need to share this burden that I have shouldered alone for so long.

"What no one knows is that I know why she really suffers from this depression." I take another sip and think what the heck and finish the entire glass before softly uttering, "It's because of me."

Chase opens his mouth to say something, stops himself, and reaching for my hand continues to listen. It's good he remains quiet because now I can't stop. It's like I've reached a summit that I struggled to climb for years, and I can finally unload the baggage it required to get there. I take in a deep breath and slowly exhale before going on.

"My mother had me later in life. The story goes that when she missed her period, she put off taking a pregnancy test or visiting the doctor because she thought she was experiencing perimenopause symptoms. It was only after she began feeling tired and nauseous that she went to the doctor and pregnancy was confirmed." I sip some more wine Chase has poured, stare into the distance, and continue.

"So I was born and I've heard they were thrilled to have a daughter. My brothers say I was the princess who had my own nursery, and then eventually my own room when they had to share. But even with all that attention, I often had this feeling that something was missing, that there was this gap, this emptiness and I could never understand why. My family was there for me. My father showered me with love and attention, and my earliest recollection of my mother is that of a vivacious woman who sang and danced with me in her arms. But then there were those times when she would look at me, letting her eyes linger as if it was not just me she was seeing and a faraway, lost look would take hold of her, and I also ached with the loss expressed in her eyes."

I start to cry and Chase gently dabs my face with his handkerchief then hands it to me to use when the tears don't stop. I take another deep breath to get my emotions in check.

"During one of Mamma's depressive bouts, my aunt Maria

came to help, and I overheard her telling my mother that it was all in the past and best forgotten. I had no idea what she meant, so I walked closer and listened from outside the door. I heard my mother in a small but firm voice say,

'A mother can never forget a child who has died. He was perfect, ten fingers, ten toes, but so tiny and so blue and cold, and I kept thinking what I could have done differently. Maybe I could have eaten healthier meals, taken more vitamins and then …then he too would have been born as strong as Alicia.'

I heard my mother sobbing and my aunt softly consoling, murmuring, 'That is the way it sometimes works with twins, in the womb the stronger takes from the weaker in order to thrive.'

Those words were spoken more than ten years ago, but I remember them as if it was yesterday. Even when I do manage to forget, every time my mother becomes depressed, I'm reminded all over again. I had a twin brother who was too weak and malnourished, was stillborn while I was born alive and healthy. And I ask myself why? Why did I live and he die?"

At this point I am crying so hard into the handkerchief I can't continue. I have held this inside me for such a long time that the pain of its release is gut wrenching. Chase stands, takes me by the hand, and sits back on his chair with me on his lap. He says nothing for a long time, just holds me, stroking my hair, and letting me cry. I finally collect myself enough to pick my head up and wipe my tears.

"I'm sorry." I stare at the harbor, using its serenity to

calm. "It's just that I know the feeling that grips my mother. I understand it because the same emptiness, the same void lies inside me."

He studies me for a long time, remaining real quiet before softly answering, "Then let me fill it."

My eyes shift to his and it's as if his words—those five little words—are enough to move mountains to fill a gap that has continued to widen until this moment. I don't reply immediately. Frankly, I'm a bit embarrassed, unravelling like this when we've only just become intimate. But his words take me by surprise and a feeling overtakes that makes me think I would do anything to protect this strong, kind-hearted, beautiful man, this man who has no idea of all he has to offer in a relationship. But right now, all I want him to understand is how much I appreciate the time and patience he is taking to listen.

"I'm sorry for burdening you with my sadness."

"How can you possibly be a burden? You're a beautiful, spirited woman who has brought happiness into my life these past several days. You make me forget my pain, and I want to do the same for you."

I kiss him softly on the mouth, and he gently traces my upper lip with his finger. "I love the way your upper lip gently lifts and is all pouty and full. It begs to be kissed." But he doesn't kiss me. Instead he stares straight ahead, a faraway look in his eyes, and real quiet says, "I never could figure out how this dance of life and death works. Why one is allowed to continue, while another is eliminated. When I was in Afghanistan I was torn by thoughts about why some died, sometimes right in front of my eyes, while others, including myself, were spared." His eyes seem faraway, and he becomes very still. "One time, shortly before my discharge, this truck traveling in front of ours hit an explosive device and was wiped out, completely blown off the road. It was not more than a few feet in front of us. Over and over, my mind replayed that scene, searching for a logical explanation, thinking that maybe there was something I should have seen or could have done to prevent it. I don't know how long it took before I finally realized that harboring this obsessive guilt was not going to help me survive, and I wanted more than anything to return home alive and in one piece. So I accepted it as fate and moved on. I'm not saying this is what you should do. I'm just telling you this so you understand that I can relate to what you're saying." And he gently kisses me again.

I'm stunned. I knew he was in combat, but never realized until now what he must have endured. It doesn't lessen my pain, but it certainly puts it in perspective.

He pulls me from my thoughts saying, "Let's go back to the hotel. I have something I'd like to talk to you about."

I'm physically tired and emotionally spent and want nothing more than to leave with him, but I remind him of the plans I made for us to meet Beth and Andre later for drinks.

"Not going to happen tonight. Text Beth and cancel. You're upset and it's just a matter of time before exhaustion sets in.

Besides you already drank too much wine."

In spite of my sadness, I smile at how quickly he shifts from empathetic listener to bossy decision maker, and this time I welcome the change. I'm not in the right frame of mind to go out drinking and socializing. He must have already paid the check, because he lifts me off his lap and extends his hand for me to take, and as we reach the exit he wraps his arm around me and asks, "Want to take a walk along the harbor?"

"Sure." I put my arm around his waist and rest my head on his shoulder, feeling more free and comfortable than ever before.

"Is your mom being treated for her depression?" He breaks through my reverie, and I let out a deep breath of frustration that's been festering every time I wonder why her medication is not working.

"Yes, of course. But she hasn't been responsive to her usual medication so new medication was prescribed. We're all hoping that once it takes affect she'll feel better. The last recourse is electric shock therapy and …" I can't finish because we all understood the repercussions of this treatment, and although it would be administered safely and humanely, both my mother and father were attempting to avoid it because of the potential memory loss and other negative side effects.

Chase pulls me closer. "If you want I can place a call to a buddy of mine, a medic who works with veterans dealing with post-traumatic stress disorder."

"Can he treat my mother for her depression?

"No, I don't think so, but his brother is the renowned Dr. Michael Leonard, who has had tremendous success treating patients who suffer from depression."

"I recognize the name. Massimo recommended him, but when he called, there was a six-week waiting period for an appointment. Massimo made the appointment, but by the time it came my mother was too tired and upset to make it. I think they may have another appointment, but I don't know when that is."

"If it's ok, I'd like to make some calls. See what I can do."

I nod and he reaches down and gives me a light, lingering kiss. We stop and stare at the harbor, and in the moonlit distance I notice a boat drifting apart from the others. Untethered, it seems to be moving away from the safety of the harbor. Slowly and rhythmically, it glides deeper into the shadow of the sea. My eyes lock on its drifting until Chase takes my hand and we walk back to our hotel.

CHAPTER
ELEVEN

Spinning in a funnel-shaped tunnel, something continues to pull me from a deep slumber. Then I hear it, a controlled and urgent whisper coming from inside the bathroom that becomes louder the longer it continues. I look at the clock and see that it's 3:00 AM. Chase must be talking to someone in New York.

I quietly go to the door to listen.

"Dammit, Devin, Does she need to get back into rehab?" *Brief silence.*

"Well, she's no good to him if she's high all the time, and we're approaching that time when she has the tendency to relapse." *Long pause.*

"What the fuck! When?" *Silence.*

"I thought he was supposed to be behind bars for at least another seven years. Now you tell me he was released over a month ago." *Longer silence.*

"Chemical castration! Does that even work? What that bastard needs is to be castrated. Period. " *Silence.*

"I know. I know. I'll be in New York on Friday. In the meantime, Mac will fly back to keep an eye on things." *Silence.*

"Did you see any of his henchmen?" *Silence.*

"Shit!"

This is spoken so loudly, I jump even though I'm on the other side of the door. "I'll kill him if he touches you." *Silence.*

"I am calm. Just keep your eyes and ears open and stay close to Mac." *Silence. Pause.* "Yeah, you too. Be careful."

He's anything but calm and my nerves kick into high gear. Jesus, what was that all about?

There's a long silence and not wanting to be caught eavesdropping, I run back to bed, stubbing my toe on a chair so hard I have to bite my lip to keep from crying out. My heart is pounding and an unfamiliar churning twists my stomach into a knot of fear. When he opens the door, light from the bathroom spills into the dark room, spotlighting him like an actor caught on stage. Rubbing his face with his hands, he takes in a deep breath and looks nervously in my direction. Lying on my side, I feign sleep. Then no longer able to bear seeing the worry ravage his face, I get up and go to him, wrapping my arms around him and letting him rest his head on my shoulder.

"What's wrong?"

He says nothing.

"Please, tell me why you're so upset."

He looks at me and strokes my cheek with the back of his

hand. "I just want to go back to bed. Come back to bed with me."

His lips crush down onto mine, demanding, taking, thrusting his tongue inside and kissing me like someone who's visited death and is now welcoming back life. I return the kiss, putting my arms around his neck and holding him tightly. We walk back to bed and once there his hands and mouth are on me, kissing and stroking, stopping only to pull my nightgown up over my head.

His eyes rove up and down my body. "You are so beautiful," he whispers. And he kisses me fervently, then suckles behind my ear, stretching the length of his body on top of mine. This is going to be fast and furious. He is rock hard, and I know he won't be able to wait much longer.

"Hand me a condom," I demand, palm out, and he reaches over to the end table and grabs one from the drawer. I tear it open and smooth it over him. He's instantly on top, using his arms to support him and slips inside. It surprises me how wet I am and my body, honed to his touch, reacts instinctively. I raise my legs and wrap them around his upper torso to deepen the penetration. Drive after deepening drive follow until I feel that delicious mounting of pleasure that escalates with each thrust, and soon I am lost in a sea of pleasure. Just when I think I cannot go further, he pumps harder and faster with a strength that makes me lower my hands and hold them weakly at my sides. My breath catches, and I whimper with each pounding momentum until lost in an explosion of sensation,

I'm plummeting off a cliff with Chase following, groaning and shuddering with his release.

Breathing heavily, we remain entwined and feeling caught and lost in only him, I want to hold onto this moment. Exhausted, he falls onto his back. I lie motionless, waiting for my breathing to slow, then roll to my side and gently kiss his lips. He returns my kiss before deftly removing and knotting his condom, tossing it in the waste basket near the bed. The minute he hits his pillow, his eyes blink slowly, and I see he's starting to fade. I cover him with the light coverlet, and he throws his arm over me, holding me to him. His breathing deepens, but his hold remains tight. I'm too overwrought to sleep, but I don't want to untangle from his grasp, afraid I'll wake him if I move. He has told me nothing, and the shreds of information that play over in my mind are not enough to form a complete picture.

He called the person he was speaking to "Devin." Who was he? I rack my brain to figure out where I heard the name before. Devin. Devin. My mind repeats the name, trying to pinpoint the where and when of its familiarity. Reckoning finally dawns when I recall the context. It was when he was running through his list of former lovers that he mentioned a Devin Raykson—something or other. I remember thinking at the time what a unique name Devin was for a girl.

In my mind I hear him saying, "She was a childhood friend ... had many challenges growing up. The friendship turned into a torrid sexual fling ..." That's who he must have been speaking to. That churning in my stomach begins again as uncertainty and jealousy vie for position. He spoke to her with such tenderness, such concern. I don't want to pry if he doesn't want to share, but it's upsetting that a former lover holds his confidence when he refuses to share with me. Then, in creeps concern, making it impossible to harbor jealousy when words like henchmen and chemical castration are being tossed around.

Do I even want to know what this is about? And if I did, how do I approach the subject? Um, excuse me, who exactly is this person who's been chemically castrated and why might you want to kill him?

We haven't been together long enough for this level of shared confidences, and he doesn't need any more of a headache than he already has. But he was such a solicitous and empathetic listener when I explained about my mother. I just have to think of ways to encourage him to confide, to make him see that he can trust me to help. We'll be spending the next several days together, which should give us the opportunity to share and get to know each other better. Beth and Andre have their own relationship brewing and will most likely want to spend chunks of time together, allowing us to have the house to ourselves. With time and patience, we'll sort through this mess because that's what people do in relationships, and I want this to be more than a mere vacation fling. Feeling settled and more assured, my eyes flutter and pressing into the warmth of Chase's body, I'm lulled to sleep. But it's a fool's optimism

C. J. Pastore

that relaxes me, because like all the best laid plans of mice and men, malevolent obstacles lurk.

A more somber Chase is working on his laptop when I wake. As usual he is showered, shaved, and dressed in jeans and a neatly ironed checkered shirt with the sleeves rolled up. The tight pull on the edges of his mouth and fine wrinkles along the sides of his eyes are the only indications of his troubled night. His profile, as he bends toward his work, looks as if it's been chiseled by an artist. Even fraught with worry, he's beautiful. I brush my teeth and go sit on his lap, snuggling and breathing in his soapy scent. He takes a deep breath and exhales, and I know he's relieved that I am here with him. I say nothing more about the overheard conversation, hoping he'll explain when he's ready.

Wrapping his arms around me, he kisses the top of my head. "Did you sleep well?"

"Yes," I lie. "And you?"

He doesn't answer but continues to hold me tightly. His phone rings and he glances to see who the caller is but doesn't answer.

"Why don't we get an early start to Santa Margharita? The house is ready and we can use the time to settle in before Beth and her Frenchman arrive."

He has met Andre several times and yet still refers to him

as the Frenchman. Actually, Andre is quite good looking. I know he doesn't deign him with a name because he overheard my comments on the beach. It's so adolescent, but I don't comment because it's trivial compared to his current problems.

"Sounds great." I shower and dress in record time, slipping into a short sundress. We complete our final packing, and Chase does a brief walk-through to make sure nothing has been forgotten. I don my hat and sunglasses, and when we walk towards the car, I notice a broad-shouldered, muscled guy with a pale neatly trimmed Van Dyke leaning against the driver's side. He's dressed in jeans and a black T-shirt, and I'm taken by surprise when he greets us and takes the suitcases.

"Hey, bro. How's it going?" Chase says, shaking his hand and grabbing him in a one-armed embrace.

Bro?

"You know, keeping out of trouble." He laughs and somehow I think he's doing anything but.

"Good morning," he says.

I don't immediately answer because I'm trying to figure out why he's here. Then remembering my manners, I answer, "Good morning."

They're both so busy packing up the car that I can't seem to ask who the fellow is without appearing rude. When I go to get in the passenger side, Chase comes and takes me by the hand and opens the back door for me to get in. Now I'm really confused. I know they seem like good friends, but am I supposed to sit in the back while the two of them chat together in the front? Very bizarre. But then Chase goes around and gets in the backseat and sits beside me.

"Who is he? I finally ask.

Once the fellow gets in the driver's seat, Chase makes the introductions.

"Alicia, this is Sammy. Sammy, this is my girlfriend, Alicia. Sammy's going to be staying with us for a bit." Sammy waves to me from the front seat.

I wave back and then quietly ask, "How do you know Sammy?

"Sammy McPhee and I go way back. Right, Sammy?

"You bet, Casey me boy."

What? I asked a question. Got two supposed answers and still don't know how "Casey me boy" knows Sammy McPhee. And Chase has the nickname Casey? Sensing my annoyance, Chase takes my hand and kisses it.

"I'll explain later, when we're alone. OK?"

"Ok," I murmur and even though my mind races with unanswered questions, Chase introducing me as his girlfriend gets top billing.

CHAPTER TWELVE

t's a quick fifteen minute drive to the villa in Santa Margharita. On both sides of the winding road, narrow homes press into the mountain like large sherbet colored popsicles. We continue our ascent until we reach a house that overlooks Mare Ligure, a striking stretch of the Mediterranean Sea between the Italian Riviera and the island of Corsica. The villa is a gated structure bounded by orange, lemon, and olive trees. Pulling up to a short driveway, Sammy stops to press a code into the security system, and the iron gates open. Once inside, there is a cleared pebbled area with ample room to park the car. Sammy and Chase grab the suitcases, and I notice Sammy is carrying an overnight bag. Is he staying with us?

The main entrance is on the left side of the structure and opens easily with the key. We enter into a large hallway that leads into a huge eat-in kitchen complete with black marble countertops and stainless steel appliances. Blond wood cabinets line both sides of the kitchen, and there's a wall of windows that look out to the sea. Breathtaking.

A nondescript door opens from the kitchen onto a quaint terrace that also offers vistas of the sea. Brightly-colored potted plants, a wrought-iron glass table, and chairs for eating and lounging are spread about. It is a lovely place to enjoy a home-cooked meal.

The master suite is located at the end of a long corridor. It also opens onto an attached balcony that looks out to the sea. A cherry wood canopied king-sized bed dressed in white Egyptian cotton sheets and matching coverlet graces the far wall, and a stone fireplace is built into the opposite side. The master bathroom has a giant sunk in bathtub with Jacuzzi, and I have all sorts of thoughts about what we could do inside its inviting depth. Five guest bedrooms are at the other end of the house, each with their own full bath. Sammy heads toward one of them with his overnight bag in tow.

"What do you think?" Chase queries, hesitating a moment before placing my suitcase down.

I am spellbound. "It's beautiful, simply beautiful." I run and jump into his arms, kissing his face again and again.

He laughs, lifts me up, and swings me around. It's so good to see him happy and carefree.

Wrapping me in his arms, he asks, "How long do we have until your friends arrive?"

"Oh no! I forgot to text Beth the address."

"It can wait. I want to show you the beach. Put on your bathing suit and be ready in five minutes, or I will come in and drag you out to the beach with whatever you happen to be wearing. I plan on removing your clothes anyway."

I have no intention of being carried to a beach—even a private one—without wearing any clothes, so I hustle into the bedroom and rifle through my bag for a bathing suit and cover-up. Anticipation is a good motivator to move quickly.

"Well done. A personal best for getting ready." The wiseass applauds before taking my hand and walking with me through the front door and around to the side of a steep, rocky hill. I notice getting to the beach requires a vertical descent on makeshift steps carved into the rocky incline. There's not even the hint of something to hold onto, and wearing flip flops is not helping. Chase insists on first stepping down a few steps and then reaching back to hold onto my hand to guide me.

"Next time you need to wear sneakers." He turns again and offers his hand.

My vertigo has kicked into high gear, and I try to only look at one step at a time while taking deep breaths to control my fear. I don't say anything because who needs to deal with a phobic diva when henchmen and convicts are wreaking havoc with your life.

We are halfway there when I happen look up and see how high we are and how far we still have to go. I freeze, attempting in vain to reach onto something to control the dizziness. My stomach jumps into my throat as both sides of the steep incline dance the rumba. Chase turns to extend his hand, takes one look at me, and walks up a step so he is directly beneath me. He wraps his arm around my back and guides me to a sitting position. I have a hard time catching my breath as I clutch both his arms. After a bit, he reaches out and smooths the hair away from my perspiring forehead.

"I … I'm sorry. Heights make me dizzy and …" I can't even finish the sentence I'm trembling so badly.

"Shh, it's OK. We're going to sit here awhile until you catch your breath." He holds onto my hand and picks up my chin, making sure I look at him while he quietly continues to talk. "The water on the beach is very calm. You're going to enjoy swimming there." Words freeze on my tongue, and I sit clutching his arms. He calmly continues, "Tomorrow we can go sailing to Portafino, a small island right off the coast. There's an excellent restaurant there called Bar Georgio that serves grilled Baraonda, caught fresh that day. Doesn't your father do the same for his customers?"

And we start talking about different foods and my father's restaurant and other random topics until gradually my shaking stops.

"I'm going to stand now then lift and carry you the rest of the way down. He gently takes my held hand and kisses it. "Are you ready?"

I nod, and in one quick motion, he sweeps me up and carefully carries me the rest of the way down. He never once wavers, shifts, or stops, just continues our descent in a fluid balanced gait until we reached the beach. I was never so happy to have my feet hit flat ground. One quick glance around shows me that the beach is a mixed strip of sandy and pebbly surface bordered by steep inclines on two sides and the sea on the other. It is completely private.

"Thank you," I murmur, a bit embarrassed. "I should have mentioned that I don't deal well with heights, but I didn't think it was going to be this steep."

Chase takes me in his arms. "You don't ever have to hesitate telling me your fears." He gives me the sweetest, most gentle kiss that deepens once I wrap my arms around his neck and press into his body. When we break contact, he throws me a mischievous grin and dashing towards the sea shouts, "Last one in has to give the other a body massage." He kicks off his bathing suit and running to the water, dives effortlessly into the surf.

Hmm, a win-win wager. Stripping, I run toward him, leaving a wake of clothes behind. The water is glorious, calm and cool, and I float on my back relaxing and enjoying the ever constant cloudless sky and gentle breeze that keeps the sun from feeling too hot.

Chase swims to my side but lets me stand before taking me in his arms and asking, "Better now."

"Much." I love this man and how he makes me feel, as if together we could conquer anything, and looking into those blue eyes and sweep of dark lashes, I murmur, "You make me unafraid to just be me."

He hesitates for a moment then bends and kisses me, lifting me so I can wrap my legs around him. I run my hands through his hair and pull him toward me to deepen our kiss.

He pulls away and between deep breaths manages to get out, "Can't here. No condom."

"It should be ok," I answer, breathing just as heavily. "I've started my period." And I quickly resume our kiss, my arms wrapped around him.

Chase lifts me, flexes his thighs, and thrusts toward me, penetrating with a suddenness that makes me gasp. Even in the water, I'm slippery with need for him. Staying inside, he holds me by my backside and slowly lowers me. The salt buoys and gently ripples against my breasts. I open my eyes and see Chase looking at me through hooded eyes. I bob and weave with him inside as the movement of the water lifts and lowers my buttocks held firmly in his hands. With one arm wrapped around me, he slowly presses the pinky finger of his other hand against the opening in my behind, and I involuntarily clench those muscles. Gently he inserts the tip. Impaled from both ends and weightless in the water, I'm starting to feel that delicious building. He begins thrusting slowly at first then harder and faster. I meet his thrusts using my legs to both hold onto him and push him deeper inside. He stops momentarily, and I feel the press of the tip of his pinky finger move further inside. With both teasing and tantalizing insertions, my head rests on his shoulder and I whimper. I don't know if I want him to pull his finger out or insert it deeper. In an instant he pushes it in deeper while plunging his penis in rapid insertions. It is my undoing and I spiral into an orgasm that seems to continue forever. Calling out my name, he follows, and clinging to each other we finish in panting flurries of sensation. Hearts racing like we ran a sprint, we remain locked together. When he lowers me, I feel wobbly and he steadies me as I regain my footing.

We stand there looking into each other's eyes, and he traces his finger across my lips then lightly kisses them. "I have never felt this way about anyone before. I would give my life for you."

I kiss him back as I begin to understand that this is his way of telling me he loves me. He takes my hand and we slowly wade back to the shore and onto the beach. I am thoroughly sated and exhausted. I feel some cramping beginning and realize I should insert protection. I reach for the beach bag and take one out.

Chase is studying me carefully. "Is everything alright."

"Fine," I say. I want some privacy so I can put it in. "Just turn around, ok?"

"Why? Do you have to pee?"

Is he serious? "No."

"Then what? I'm getting concerned."

Gee, he needs to know everything. "I just need to put in, you know, some protection for my period.

"Want some help?" He raises his eyebrows and grins mischievously, moving in my direction.

I swat his hand away. "Just look the other way."

He turns around shaking his head, and I insert the damn absorber. We put our bathing suits back on and spread out on large towels. It feels good to be lying in a dry bathing suit, soaking up the warmth of the sun.

"Will Sammy be joining us for a swim?" There still hasn't been any explanation as to why Sammy just happened to show up.

"No, he's got work to do."

Starting to doze, he drops the subject. I decide now is the time to get some answers before he conveniently uses sleep as an excuse to postpone any discussion. I turn on my side and using my elbow to support my head gently stroke the side if his face with my finger.

"How do you know Sammy?" He doesn't immediately answer, just slowly opens his eyes, and I get the feeling that he knows I'm not going to let the subject rest. I think I hear him sigh.

"Sammy and I met in Afghanistan. We … worked together on many of the same assignments, and now we're partners on several real estate development projects, the last being a commercial building that includes a club."

This is news. Mr. Military owns a club. There must be some measure of fun buried inside … deep inside.

"That's cool. What kind of a club is it?"

"Music, dance, lots of jazz, some rock."

"Mmm, sounds like fun."

No answer.

"Is Sammy here for pleasure or business?" This seems to have turned into a one-sided game of Twenty Questions.

Chase sits up, lets out a deep breath, and stares moodily ahead at the sea. I join him, resting my head on his shoulder. He kisses it and eyes staring ahead, body straight, head erect, he starts talking.

"There's a problem back home that's been brewing for some time. Sammy's here to help me deal with it." He hesitates, moodily staring at the sea.

"Does this problem involve anyone close to you?" He's really making me work to get answers, but that phone conversation has jangled my nerves and I'm curious.

"I think I mentioned someone by the name of Devin when we were having breakfast in San Remo."

I notice he leaves out that it was when he was telling me about his former lovers, but I don't comment. I want him to continue.

"Devie and I grew up together. She was this tall, gawky kid who hung around wanting to play basketball and softball with the boys. We became friends. She was easy to talk to. Her mother had a substance abuse problem. My dad had fallen into a spiral of binging after my mother became ill. We could relate. We would hang out at her house. More freedom there to smoke weed and drink beer."

I raise my brow at the mention of pot, and he tugs my hair. "I was young. I know better now as should you."

I look down, appearing more contrite than I actually feel.

It was one joint that I never even got the chance to smoke for heaven's sake.

"What about Devie?" I want to stick to the essentials.

"I must have been fourteen, Devie a year or so younger. We always met at her house to walk to school together, but this one day, when I got there no one answered my repeated knocks."

Chase's eyes are haunted, and my heart races as I steel myself for what comes next.

"Standing on a crate, I peeked into her bedroom window and saw some guy, her mother's boyfriend at the time, sexually abusing her. It took every ounce of strength for me not to go in and try to kill the bastard, but he was a good foot taller than I was with muscles the size of cannon balls. It just so happened I had a camera with me that day. Took a slew of photos of the bastard right in the act then ran and pounded on the door until I was let in. I convinced Devie to go to the hospital and report the abuse, and with the incriminating photos he didn't stand a chance. He was tried and convicted. Was supposed to be in jail for a very long time. Problem is he's just been released. Good behavior and participation in some program that uses drugs to suppress sexual drive earned him a get out of jail early card."

His sardonic laugh is sobering and taking in a deep breath, I ask in a soft voice, "Doesn't he have to be monitored for that type of sex offense?"

"He should be, but he's ruthless and relentless, even made threats after he was convicted. He found out about The

Freedom of Information Act from some lawyer friends and used it to contact the Board of Elections to get home addresses of anyone he wanted. Always knew where to find me and Devin no matter where we were living."

I shiver in spite of the heat. "So Sammy flew here to help you deal with this problem?"

"Not exactly. We were at the Grand Prix together and now…" Chase stops, his eyes raised as if he's unsure of the right words to use "…and now," he repeats, "we're, um, attempting to keep track of the bastard." Again, he hesitates before smoothly continuing, "Sammy's a whiz with computers. Understands how to use them to monitor movements and pinpoint locations of people."

"He could even be here, in Europe?" It sounds ludicrous to me that a convicted felon out on parole could travel to a foreign country.

"No, but let's just say he has friends."

Suddenly, I'm glad he's taking precautions. "Please be careful when you go home. Will Mac and Sammy be there to help?"

"Mac's back now, looking after things." He turns and holds my face in both hands, staring me in the eyes with an expression of firm resolve. "I want you to know that I will do anything to keep you safe … anything." He drops his hands like he's surrendering to some cemented truth and continues in an even, slow tone that's laced with sadness. "You and I may have grown up in the same town, but we came from different worlds. Every day I watched people trapped in a ceaseless marathon, always running, forever racing … making hopeless attempts to outrun problems like drug abuse, alcoholism, pesky bill collectors …" He pauses for a moment, garnering the courage to continue, and swallows before adding, "Shame." He stares ahead. "When I was younger, I would think of ways to cover up the embarrassment of having a father who, on any given day, could be found passed out drunk on the front lawn. I wanted to make it seem as if my life was just like everyone else's. But no matter how hard I worked at it, I couldn't make the problem go away. Now, I say to hell with it, but then I felt like some kind of outsider forced to peer in at those who never had to deal with my problems."

When on the school bus in the morning, I vaguely recollect stretches of time when I would see a man passed out, flat out drunk by the curb or on a front lawn. Kids would point and laugh. Not me. I knew he was the father of the handsome hunk of a boy with electric blue eyes who had a very sick mother and who would often be seen hauling the drunk man over his shoulder and carrying him home. A burden that held more than its weight in pounds. I swallow past the lump in my throat. Sadness now could easily be perceived as pity, and he doesn't need to feel more shame as a result of my misconstrued reaction.

"Well, it's obvious you've moved on. Your attempts at success have not been fruitless." I'm trying to remain upbeat, but he remains lost in a past that's woven a web of despair around his mind, body, and soul.

"Yeah. I managed to bury it in the marines, but once I got to Yale, it surfaced like some dormant, fire-breathing dragon sprung to life."

"I'm confused. Are you saying you had an easier time fighting the enemy in Afghanistan than dealing with your fellow students at Yale?"

"No, of course not. I'm just saying it was easier to forget the past and do your job as a marine than it was as a college student."

"How can that possibly be?"

Shaking his head, he responds with a sardonic, humorless chuckle that whispers through his nose and throat before surfacing as a disgruntled, "humph," and when he suddenly pauses, I know it's to try to find the right words.

I wait.

"Perfect example was when I was dating this girl from my economics class. Her family had this framed family tree proudly displayed in the den of their country house that showed they could be traced back to John Hancock. Addison Hancock Walker was her name. Once, when I was invited for the weekend to their summer home, I overheard her folks talking. They used words like 'commoner' and 'seems to hover on the sidelines like he's locked out.' Her grandmother even jumped in, asking if anyone had met '*the boy's* family.' That's when I figured out they were discussing me. It was like being at a job interview where you thought you were in contention for management but turns out you were only being considered for pool boy. Yet, despite their snobbery, the truth is, they understood the reality of the barrier between us, and they didn't try to pretend it didn't exist. I was just like all those other poor bastards, who fought through life, hauling the shitload of baggage that comes from dealing with an alcoholic parent."

He pauses here, then turns to look at me. "Just know, I will do whatever it takes to shield you from that world."

Yet another sworn oath to protect me that sounds more like a barrier constructed to separate us. I remain quiet. Ahead, the expanse of serene sea and cloudless sky defies my tumultuous emotions, encouraging rational thought to prevail over raw emotion.

I understand his longing for normalcy. What child doesn't want to fit in, especially when trying to figure out who they are and what their place is in society? He and his friend Devie were robbed of a childhood when they were forced to deal with adult problems because one or the other parent was too drugged or drunk to take notice. The substance and alcohol abuse surrounding them made them easy targets. I get it. I may not be from *his world* as he puts it, but I'm not some pampered princess too blinded by affluence to recognize hardship.

I'm sensitive to the predetermined strata of distinctions Chase refers to. I know how judgmental people can be, believing that where you live and the type of car you drive determine your value and status in society.

I recognized the type when they came into the restaurant,

tanned from rounds of golf at "the club," insisting on a table without a reservation on a crowded Saturday night, their manicured, pedicured, and coiffured wives with six-figure designer handbags slung over their shoulders, looking glum faced and acting rude to waiters and bartenders when they didn't get their way. Causally mentioning their Upper East Side pied'a terres on Madison or Fifth and their summer homes "out east," meaning somewhere in the high-priced stretch of beach know to locals as *The Hamptons*. All golden real estate with their "humble" family homes in Rockville Center the go-to for maintaining family roots. Power driven by wealth, and from its summit people attempting to control, categorize, and separate others deemed beneath their pinnacle. It was all about domination, making it no wonder that Chase chose real estate as his strategic move toward wealth. But that he should think I fit into that category rather than into his former life of problems and hardships is unsettling. Once again, he leaves no room for gray area, choosing to believe social and economic layers are either black or white. Yet contrary to his prejudices, I understood it all too well and when I finally begin talking, it's with a tenacity that contradicts predetermined notions of where people belong.

"Those separate worlds you speak about, well I don't believe they can't be bridged. You are the perfect example." I point my hand toward him before emphatically continuing. "You have an honorable military stay, a Yale degree, and a successful real estate business. You're caring and giving, interrupted your trip to the Grand Prix to help me. "You're …" I hesitate for a fraction of a second because I'm not sure if I want to say what's next on my mind but plow ahead anyway thinking, *What the hell, I'm trying to make a point.* "Leaving to be with your friend back home. You take care of your sister and nephew. You're not that lonely, defenseless child anymore. My mind zigzags back to that haughty family's discussion about Chase, and I can feel myself frothing at their presumptuous attitude. "Besides, Addison's family sounds like assholes." It's humor I fall back on, the go-to for those periods of time when emotional intensity seems to smother and darken the way forward.

"I mean …" I pause and roll my eyes, shaking my head in mock wonder. "Who in their right mind gives their daughter the middle name Hancock? That's why you can't listen to assholes, because if you do, you know what happens?"

Now I'm bristling with righteous indignation at how they spoke about him, but he's smiling so I relax. He was so solemn before, I didn't particularly like the divisive tone of the conversation.

"I'll bite," he says. "What happens?" He starts nuzzling my ear, which is never good for my conversing abilities.

"It's simple," I murmur, leaning my neck toward his kisses. "You. Mmm. Become…" my breath catches and I murmur between hitches "…an asshole. Might even name your child Dick Harding or Susan Pierce Bush or Thomas Paine Ash …" I'm on a roll but don't get the chance to finish because his kisses are roving down my shoulder and toward my breast, dangerous territory for meaningful thinking.

"I happen to know for a fact that not all assholes are bad. Take yours for instance." And he changes his kisses to soft nibbles.

Caught in a sensual web of touching, I'm no longer listening. Maybe it's because we both need a release from our heavy conversation, or maybe this is just how we connect, but we forget about economic differences and social ills and make the sweetest, most tender love to each other.

CHAPTER THIRTEEN

I wake to Chase gently rubbing sunblock onto my back and legs.

"You're burning. Turn over so I can get the other side." I do as he says.

"Mmm," I purr. His touch tingles and my nerve endings jump to attention. He is thorough, smoothing lotion over my body with strong, agile fingers, knowing exactly how to stroke and circle.

"You're turn now. Let me rub you. I was the one who lost the race before." Any more of a sunblock rubdown and I'd ignite.

"Gladly." He turns and lies on his back.

Even groggy from my nap I look forward to touching him, marveling at his muscular chest and broad shoulders and the way his waist angles, giving him a V-shape physique. Very sexy.

He lifts his head and opens one eye. "Enjoying the view?"

My cheeks color at being caught staring, but I nonchalantly answer, "What's not to enjoy? I'm sunbathing with an Adonis."

He smirks, lowers his head, and gives in to my slow, methodic rubbing across his shoulders. His breathing deepens and his features smooth, revealing a youthful candor that's rarely shown when he's awake. I can only imagine the toll those revelations took on him. I still don't know the name of that criminal who's at large. I make a mental note to ask Chase for a description and his name. Sighing, I let it go and text Beth the address of the Villa.

Her response is immediate: *Great! cu at 2. Bringing DDG.*

This light exchange is the balm I need, and I smile knowing that she's still going hot and heavy with Andre, her most recent drop dead gorgeous fling.

I thumb: *k, then decide it would be wonderful to prepare a home-cooked meal.* The kitchen is well equipped. Chase and I could drive to the market in town for supplies, and we could all eat on the terrace overlooking the sea. There's a superb Umbrian pasta recipe for strangozzi al tartufo nero. The homemade pasta is easy to make, only requiring flour, eggs, and a little salt. Finding black truffles might be challenging, but there's a gourmet market in town that's worth a try. Black truffles are mainly found in the Apennines near the borders of Umbria and Marche, not terribly far from where we are. Mentally completing the menu, I also include grilled Orata and a tri colore salad with extra virgin olive oil and fresh lemon juice dressing.

I hesitate waking Chase, but when I notice him stirring I turn to my side and gently stroke his cheek. "Hey, sleepy head." I kiss him softly.

Two blue sharply focused orbs pin me, and I am amazed at how quickly he transforms from relaxed slumber to wakeful alertness. With the speed of a panther, he reaches out and pulls me on top of him then just as quickly turns again, and I find myself lying on the towel with him on top.

I yelp, giggling, and he says, "I love waking up to you." He plants soft kisses on my lips, my face, down my neck. "But I think we've had enough sun for today." He continues kissing me then gently nibbles my lower lip, making me forget what I was about to suggest. It isn't until he stops that my wits return.

"Beth and Andre are coming later, so I thought we'd shower then drive into town for supplies and I'd cook us dinner."

"You can cook?" he asks skeptically.

"Yes, I happen to be a good cook."

"Like chef good?"

"Amateur chef. You can be my sous chef.

"Does suos mean I have to shush and follow orders?"

"Yes…" I give him a mock serious look "…and be on wash detail."

"Can I wash you?"

"We're planning a meal. Get your mind off sex." Grabbing on to his lower lip with my mouth, I gently suck before planting delicate kisses above both of his eyelids. I shake my head to ground myself so I adhere to my own advice. I remember Sammy is staying with us and ask, "Do you think Sammy would like to have dinner with us?"

"Sure, he loves a good home cooked meal. I'll mention it to him."

Gathering towels, lotion, and other beach paraphernalia and sticking them all in the beach bag that Chase slings over his shoulder, we walk toward the steep steps that have not crossed my mind since Chase carried me down. Looking straight up to the top, my head spins and my heart races. Surely going up is going to be easier than walking down.

When I make an attempt to climb the first few steps, Chase comes up from behind, grabs me under my knees, and scoops me into his arms, saying, "Oh no you don't. Can't have you toppling over because you're too dizzy to keep your balance."

"There is no way you can carry me up all these steps." Shaking my head, I squirm to get down.

He just pulls me closer and tightens his grip. "I can and I will."

He immediately begins the ascent as if climbing seventy steps carrying a 107-pound live load is an everyday occurrence. Halfway up, I take a tentative peek down the steep incline from over his shoulder and start to feel as if the rocky sides are shaking. I quickly avert my eyes. Chase's face offers a far better view anyway.

When we reach the top, he is barely winded, and for the first time I begin to wonder about the type of military training he received and his current workouts. I figured he belonged to some type of gym because of his ripped abs, muscular biceps, and tight narrow waist. God, even the image has me breathless, but this strength and endurance is beyond anything I ever imagined. I actually have to run to catch up to him, and with so much to do there's little time for further conversation about the past.

The Italian market in town is well stocked and does sell black truffles. The price is exorbitant at about two hundred dollars for the equivalent of two ounces, but I haven't been spending much of my own money thanks to Chase, and I revel in this opportunity to buy everything needed to prepare an excellent meal. It will be my way of showing my appreciation for all he's done. At the checkout I step up to the cashier as Chase places the last of the items on the counter and take out the correct amount of Euros to pay.

"I got this," he adds, pushing my hand gently to the side while removing cash from his wallet.

One good look at Chase has the cashier spellbound, and I use it as an opportunity to tell her in Italian that I am paying and do not under any circumstances accept any money from the gentleman. She immediately reaches out her hand to me, ignoring his outstretched hand, and just as I'm about to hand it over, Chase takes my hand and pushes it aside, saying, "I have this."

I repeat again in Italian that the senor is not to be allowed to pay since his mamma is ill and his money is needed for her care. Now the cashier is adamantly refusing Chase's money, shaking her head in sweeping motions. Without changing his expression and with agile speed, Chase moves his hand behind my head to cover my mouth while simultaneously shifting and pinning me under the crook of his arm. I can't move, I can't speak and rip roaring mad, I try kicking his legs while squirming and pulling at his arm, but he doesn't budge. I hear the cashier and other employees and shoppers within sight laughing. Chase ignores them and simply hands over the cash, as if there isn't a hellcat of a woman squirming and squealing at his side. He even takes the time to study the receipt.

"Excusa, those two black balls cost how much?"

Oh no! Did he just call the tartufo nero two black balls, and I fervently hope he's not going to return them. But he listens to the cashier's explanation in choppy English and satisfied, loosens his grip, grabs the shopping bags in one hand, and whisks me away with his other, walking out of the market, pulling me along as if nothing is wrong.

I am furious and like a petulant child I refuse to budge.

He turns around looks at me as if I'm being unnecessarily difficult. "Let's go, I thought you were in a hurry to prepare this meal before your friends arrive."

"What! Are you serious? How dare you just manhandle me that way."

"What way? I told you I had it covered."

"And it was important for me to pay this time. Tell me, did you or did you not attend kindergarten?"

"What?" Now he really looks confused. "Of course I did. We had problems, but we weren't illiterate." The man is clueless.

"I just thought you missed that year... maybe because of some brain MISHAP, because isn't that where you're supposed to learn how to USE YOUR WORDS to express yourself?"

He pauses then shrugs and says, "I did. I told you I was going to pay, but you didn't listen, so I did what was necessary to finish up so we could get going. So let's move it or we'll never prepare this meal in time. I'm starving and you must be hungry as well. You don't want to get a headache from not eating."

This argument is going nowhere fast. I let out a frustrated groan and proceed to the car with him. Once inside I continue to sulk. Arms crossed, I stare ahead in stony silence. Chase is uncomfortable. I sense it. He clears his throat and nervously taps on the steering wheel as he drives. I don't care how long it takes to break the silence, I'm not saying a word. It's a while before he finally speaks.

"I like being able to pay. For too long that wasn't the case." A shadow passes across his eyes, his face reflecting quiet sadness.

I realize that for all his outer strength, there is a vulnerability that I need to be mindful of. I hate that I may have contributed to his sadness, especially the lie about his deceased mother.

Reaching over, I take his hand and brush a soft kiss in his palm. "I'm sorry for getting angry. I appreciate everything you've done and keep on doing. Thank you for paying."

"You're welcome." Relieved, he gives me a slow smile that graduates to an ear-to-ear heart-stopping smile.

Then he reaches out and raises the forefinger of my hand and gently sucks on it. My breathing becomes shallow, and I clench my legs together in need. The shift from anger to arousal astonishes me, and I don't seem to know how to harness it. Removing my finger from his mouth, he uses it to tease my leg at the hem of my sundress then placing it to my side uses his hand to slowly lift my dress past my thigh. He knows my body so well that without taking his eyes off the road, he moves it to the inside of my leg and caresses my inner thigh. Slowly, he slips it beneath my panties with the light liner I have in place. Palming me, he gently massages my clitoris with his thumb. I lean into it and clutch his arm. The worrisome thought of succumbing while driving on the open road in broad daylight is fleeting as ardor conquers discretion. I realize this is his attempt to apologize, and I can't seem to accept fast enough. The ever present swirling movement of his thumb makes me want to grab the dashboard and push myself further toward it, and I bite the inside of my mouth to avoid the temptation. It's like trying to refuse water when you're dying of thirst.

"Are you having cramps?"

"No," I breathlessly murmur.

I feel his finger slowly entering me as his thumb continues to tease my clit and giving into the pleasure, my head leans onto his shoulder and my eyes flutter closed. When he pulls his hand away, I'm bereft but see the reason why when a pickup truck passes on our right, offering a clear view of the interior of our car from its higher vantage point.

The opportunity is lost because the villa is immediately ahead and with guests arriving soon there is no time to play.

"Later," Chase leans over and whispers in my ear before gently raking his teeth along my earlobe, sucking. God, he's hot and my body tightens in anticipation.

Once in the kitchen we wash up and immediately get to work. The kitchen is well-equipped with spacious marble countertops and two stainless steel ovens.

Chase begins unpacking, randomly placing groceries in a spread across the counter, then proceeds to rummage through all the cabinets, placing every pot and pan he can find on the counter as well. Dear Lord, what a mess.

"Um, I don't think we need all those pots and pans. Why don't you put back the crock pot and the electric fryer? Also, we won't be needing all those colanders. One will do." I try not to look up to the heavens for help. "You can also put back the Dutch oven, the stock pot, and the double boiler."

Measuring flour, I place it in a mound on a large work board in preparation for making the pasta. I carve a crater in its center, add eggs and a pinch of salt, then mix and knead until the dough can be rolled into a circle that's similar to one made when making pizza. When I demonstrate how to cut the dough into narrow strips, I'm amazed how efficient and precise he is. Each pasta strip is a replica of the other, looking like he used a pasta machine instead of cutting them by hand.

The sauce is easy, only requiring olive oil, sautéed garlic, grated truffles, and parmigiano reggiano and pecorino cheese. I dress the fish with fresh lemon, parsley, capers, white wine, and a bit of olive oil and heat the oven grill so it's ready. Chase sets the table and adds a centerpiece of sunflowers we purchased at the market and a chilled pitcher of Compari, gin, and fresh sliced oranges. By the time we hear the doorbell, the kitchen is cleaned, the food prepared, and the wine chilling.

Beth enters a whirlwind of energy and long legs in her cutoff shorts and loose fitting floral blouse. She throws her arms around me then steps back and studies me with one brow raised.

"Look at you, girl. You look amazing."

I scoff. "Must be the bit of sun I caught today."

"Or …" Beth pauses, eyes wide, and whispers close to my ear, "All the fucking you *caught* with good-looking lover boy over there." She gives a discreet nod in Chase's direction.

"Maybe that too," I answer, glad no one is paying attention.

Arms spread and weighted down by two heavy backpacks, Andre strides toward me in jeans that appear painted onto his body. My eyes ricochet to his face, ready to defeat any contact with what my mind refers to as the *Battle of the Bulge*. Andre lowers the bags and grabbing both my arms pulls me toward him in a hug.

"Ah, zair is the beautiful Alicia. I remembehr your love for the Provence Rosé." Disengaging, he reaches into one of the bags and pulls out a chilled bottle of wine, handing it to me then kissing both cheeks. Very French … and that accent … all z's and melted vowels, like savoring a warm chocolate croissant.

He ambles through calling out, "ahlow," to no one in particular, banging bags into walls until Sammy appears to help.

Shutting the door, I walk on to the terrace and notice Chase pensively watching. I toss him an innocent smirk, knowing he's seen what no one with working eyes could miss.

My suspicions are confirmed when he whispers in my ear, "Doesn't that Frenchman have clothes that fit."

"Oh…" I shrug, placing the bottle of wine on the table "…I didn't notice."

"Like hell you didn't."

He pours me a Negroni from the pitcher and taking it, I can't help but look down and sheepishly smile. He lifts my chin and wrapping my hair around his hand, pulls my head back and plants a deep, penetrating kiss on my lips. I nearly melt on the spot.

"Just reminding you where your eyes belong." Then he disappears to greet our guests. I nearly down my drink in an attempt to quench my parched throat.

The meal is a huge success and with Chase's arm leisurely draped around my shoulders, I lean contentedly against his side, sipping Limoncello and watching Sammy perform a card trick. I know Chase sees how Sammy keeps guessing the right card no matter where it is in the pile, but for the life of me

I can't decipher how he's doing it. It isn't helping that I have a serious buzz from the Negronis I drank before dinner, the glasses of Rosé I had with dinner, and the Limoncello I'm enjoying now.

Beth is explaining how she had her suitcase sent ahead to our hotel and that she would be traveling by motorbike with Andre when my alcohol high takes a nose dive.

"Ah, Alicia," Andre casually tosses out, "Marcel made me promise to tell you that he wishes you well at your awards ceremony in Lake Como. It is next week? No?"

My heart does a somersault and I force a smile but have not looked down once. I may be winning the Battle of the Bulge, but the brewing war with Chase has yet to start. I glance nervously at him. His eyes are frosty, his body still, but he says nothing. Maybe he doesn't mind, but as soon as I think it, I realize that he is not the type to let something like this slide. I inwardly sigh because I know I'm going to have some explaining to do, and I don't relish dealing with him when he's angry.

Remembering my manners, I inconspicuously murmur to Andre, "Thank Marcel for his warm wishes." Andre nods and unaware of the cold war developing, sits and amicably begins chatting with Beth. Sammy looks at me and I swear I see pity in his eyes.

I get up and begin clearing the dishes. I need time away to think about how I'm going to broach the subject of an innocent Parisian encounter that is being interpreted as a deceitful slight. I get as far as the kitchen waste basket when Chase suddenly appears behind me. I jump.

"You startled me." Reaching behind me with my free hand, I pull his head down and kiss his cheek, hoping to thaw his icy mood.

I go back to scraping the plates, thinking of how to begin explaining when he wraps my hair in his hand and gently tugs my head to the side, exposing my neck. My libido kicks into high gear and placing the dishes on the counter, I close my eyes and surrender to the slow-moving kisses that travel the length of my neck, one for each tattooed star. A warmth moves toward my navel before resting in a heaviness between my legs. It's like my body is a violin playing to the strum of his bow.

"Who the hell is Marcel?" Chase whispers close to my ear between these endless litanies of kisses that are now sweeping toward my collarbone.

I don't answer, because even though I hear the menace in his words, desire renders me speechless. He pulls my hair tighter and begins nibbling and sucking behind my ear in just that right spot. I take in a deep breath.

"Mmm." I softly exhale as my body continues to absorb the warmth of his kisses. "Just someone I met in Paris."

He tugs a bit harder, exposing more of my neck as he nuzzles his nose behind my ear and uses his tongue and mouth to gently suck and tantalize my earlobe. The warmth of his breath scented with sweet orange and Compari tantalize, and head bent back, I surrender to his caresses.

In that same soft and deceptively measured tone, he asks, "And what is this awards ceremony that *Marcel* knows about, but I don't?"

The far reaches of my consciousness register that this is not going in the right direction, but I'm so fucking turned on, my libido has my ears plugged and my tongue anesthetized. It's only when the tugging registers discomfort that I'm stirred from my sexual stupor and can elaborate.

"I submitted a sketch of one of my designs to a crowd-funding site." He lets go of my hair and stops nuzzling. "The design was chosen as a winner. It's being made in my choice of fabric and print and offered for sale in a beginner designers' showcase." I can't keep the excitement from my voice. "I'm to be the recipient of an award for the submission and the ceremony and cocktail reception is in Lake Como next week."

He steps away, widening the space between us, and all I want to do is reach out and pull him to me and kiss his lips and feel his arms around me. But the tense pull of his lips and his stiff carriage keep me at a distance. From the terrace muted sounds of conversation and Beth's throaty laughter carry, and I relax knowing our guests are preoccupied, giving us privacy to talk. Thank heavens he breaks the awkward silence first, because I feel anything I have to say about Marcel is only going to exacerbate the situation.

"I don't understand why you didn't let me know. Have you invited Marcel to attend?"

And in an instant his anger turns to hurt, and my heart

sinks because the last thing I want is to cause this man any more angst.

"No! Of course not. He only knows because Beth mentioned it when we met. I originally invited Beth, but I think Andre is going with her to Milan so she'll probably want to spend the last part of her vacation with him."

"Doesn't that guy have a job?"

"What?" The change of topic is baffling, but then I realize he's referring to Andre and add, "Yes, but he's on vacation."

"Oh, you mean like in high school when we had summers off."

I get the impression he's using his anger to shoot the messenger. He must realize his behavior is unreasonable because he switches tactics and asks, "So you'll be attending alone?"

I take a deep breath and finally say what I have wanted to say since we met in Monte Carlo. "Not if you'll come as my guest." And before he answers, insecurity and self-doubt become kicks-ass bad, pummeling self-esteem, downgrading sureness and declaring all-out war on confidence, making me spill out a torrent of contradictory explanations.

"But I understand if you can't. I didn't ask because I knew you had to leave for work, and then there were those personal problems that came up and I didn't want to burden you with another request. You've already done so much." I'm nervously babbling, but can't seem to stop. "These events can be dreadfully boring if you're not in the business and ..."

He bridges our gap in two large strides, takes me in his arms, and kisses me deeply, thankfully ending my tedious soliloquy. Releasing me, he stares into my eyes and says, "I want more than anything to be with you when you receive your award. This sounds like a big deal."

I let out a deep breath and smile. Keeping me in his arms, he adds, "Why would you think that your life wouldn't interest me enough to take the time to be with you during such an important event?"

I shrug my shoulders and remain silent, because how do I put into words that I don't want to be perceived as a taker—as someone who usurps other people's needs and replaces them with her wants. For as long as I can remember I kept my yearnings quiet, my ambitions buried, only letting them surface in the bursts of color and design when I sketched. It was a big deal for me to submit an entry, and when I won I told no one except Antonio. Somehow, he understands. Closest to me in age, he saw how I would blend into the shadows when my mother was ill or my father too busy at the restaurant to attend school performances. I often went to great lengths to hide invitations or simply chose to "forget" to bring them home. As the youngest, everyone seemed busy with more important issues like medical school, running a restaurant … depression, and I learned early on how to skirt around the sadness and deal with my guilt by melting into the background.

My throat tightens and I look away from Chase, hoping for more time so I can shift my thoughts in a different direction.

"It's not that I don't want the recognition. It's just that everyone is busy with their own jobs and problems and my issues are…" I pause, searching for the right words "… comparatively less important."

Lifting my chin, he looks earnestly into my eyes, pausing a bit before answering, "If you continue to sell yourself short like that, others will also. Success is something you pursue with skill, imagination, and tenacity, and when you earn it you don't stop there. You grab it and use it to achieve more. You don't want to demean your success or the empowerment it affords because it seems less significant than someone else's or too burdensome to others."

I try to fit these words into the way I see myself. For me, success has always been about working hard and persevering. But Chase is right. It doesn't end there. They're just stepping stones to greater accomplishments.

The realization is startling and for the first time it's clear that ambition and success are attributes I aspire for. I merely kept them under wraps, believing their exposure revealed greed and selfishness.

I look at Chase. He remains quiet, pensively staring at me while tracing his forefinger over my upper lip.

"What are you two up to in here?" Beth interrupts, walking into the kitchen all smiles, flushed from wine and laughter. "Thank heavens you're both still dressed. I had no idea what to expect you were gone so long."

Without having to think twice, I answer, "Just enjoying

dessert."

Before Chase can pull away, I wrap my arms around his head and pulling him to me, give him a slow, deep kiss as a thank you for his wise words. When I pull away, he's wide eyed and quite frankly a bit breathless. I hear Beth chuckling as I walk back to join our guests on the terrace. This whole self-realization empowerment concept, well, I think I could get the hang of it.

CHAPTER FOURTEEN

wake up with what feels like an ice pick jabbing the left side of my head. My eyes refuse to open and my mouth feels like cotton. I should have never mixed drinks. Forcing myself out of bed, I head into the shower. The sudden spray of water hits and closing my eyes, I groan and rub my temples. Gradually, the warm water rejuvenates, and I gently massage shampoo into my scalp, rinse, then wash with a rose and honey scented soap, wrapping myself in a plush white towel when I'm done.

I comb out my hair and leave it hanging. I can't bear to pull it back or tug at with a dryer. I plan to spend the early part of the day sketching, but desperately need a cup of coffee first. Slipping on a pair of denim cutoffs and a loose fitting white camisole, I head for the kitchen and rummage for an espresso pot, spotting one in the far cabinet. I hear the faint sound of conversation coming from the home-office room at the end of the hall where, I assume, Chase and Sammy must be working. Espresso brewing, I see that there's also an electric coffee pot for American coffee and decide to make a pot to bring to Chase and Sammy. I have no idea what time Chase woke and imagine he and Sammy have been working for quite a while.

The espresso finishes first and I pour it over ice, waiting for the ice to crackle before I begin sipping. Then I open a bottle of chilled mineral water, pour it into a glass and squeeze lemon into the contents before drinking. The liquids refresh and my headache gradually recedes. I place the coffee with two cups and cream and sugar on a tray and head to where Chase and Sammy are working. The door is closed and their voices are muffled. Curiosity makes me pause and listen before knocking.

"They're at record highs through Central Asia into Europe, each worth about twenty-three million." Sammy's voice is clipped, urgent.

"And his involvement?"

"Full force with global tentacles."

"You know it's personal as well as business, so I'm not taking any chances. I want discreet surveillance and protection of the principal starting now."

Sammy mumbles a reply I can't make out and in the silence that follows, I tentatively knock then enter.

Fired tension crackles around the room. I see it in Chase's stiff demeanor and in Sammy's too bland expression, like he's erased all emotion so as not to reveal a horrid truth. I hesitate, unsure of what to say, but Chase gives me a warm smile and comes over to help with the coffee. There are two laptops open on the desk displaying maps with grids that he discreetly closes before making room for the tray.

"I hope I'm not intruding. I thought you both might like some coffee." I'm all thumbs and fumble with the cups, but Sammy graciously removes one and pours himself a cup.

"Thanks, Alicia. Just what I needed." He takes a sip and turns to look out the window.

For miles, nothing stretches but foliage, sand, and sea. I pour some coffee for Chase, adding a bit of cream, and he takes it, closes his eyes, and sips then rests the cup back on the tray. He tugs me by my hand and taking a seat, pulls me onto his lap.

"You look fetching as ever this morning..." he pauses, contemplating my face "...except maybe for these shadows." He gently traces his thumbs under each of my eyes, and I close them and lean into his touch. "Do I detect the remnants of a hangover, young lady?" He softly nuzzles his nose in my neck.

He looks as glorious as ever in jeans and a black linen shirt, sleeves rolled up and his hair hanging boyishly in his face.

"Yes, but you seem none the worse for wear," I grouse.

"That's because I know to drink plenty of water, pace myself, and not mix different types of alcohol. If memory serves, you failed at all three."

Why doesn't he just write a book about me and title it "Misdeeds of a Miscreant." His nibbling and kisses feel too good to comment, so I quietly nuzzle closer and bask in the warmth of his touch. It's not until he pulls me closer by the back of my head and kisses me deeply, his tongue doing a slow dance in my mouth, that Sammy clears his throat and begins gathering up the laptops and strewn papers littering the desk. I'm a bit embarrassed, but Chase is nonplussed and as Sammy prepares to go, he emphatically repeats, "It begins NOW with the principal," to which Sammy curtly nods and leaves.

"Now, where were we?" He gently rakes my earlobe with his teeth while his hand slides under my cami until he reaches and lifts one side of my bra. My pert breast pops out and reaching in, he gently twirls my nipple before lowering his head to tease and taunt it with his tongue. I am lost and barely realize that I'm being lifted and placed horizontally onto the desk where a minute ago there were laptops and papers spread. Chase unzips and lowers my shorts. I am wearing white lace panties that barely cover my backside with a matching uplift bra, and his eyes mirror revered expectation.

"You are so sexy." He bends my knees and places my feet on top of the desk then slowly lowers my panties, rubbing his hands down my thighs before lifting one foot and then the other to remove them.

My back initially protests the hard surface but as Chase's mouth moves south, my hips reach up to meet his lips and any discomfort evaporates. Bending my bent leg outward, he places soft kisses on my inner thigh, slowly moving his mouth upward until it reaches that special place that makes my breath quicken. His tongue is relentless and gasping, I fist my hands in his hair and pull him even closer. Stopping, he gently pulls me nearer the end of the table and inserts first one then two fingers, moving and twirling them until my back arches and I groan. I pull his mouth to mine and sweep my tongue over his lips and into his mouth, my body writhing in pleasure as he moves his way down, nibbling my neck until he reaches my breast. With a quick tug, he pulls up the other cup of my bra, using it to buoy my exposed breast. Immediately my nipple points in anticipation.

"I love how responsive your breasts are to my touch." He takes hold of my nipple and alternates sucking and tugging at it until it almost hurts.

The intensity rocks my body, and I try to pull his mouth from me in some vain attempt to control and lessen the impact, but he ignores my efforts and switches to my other breast. Heat flashes down my spine, reaching the heaviness between my legs.

Craving release, I arch my back and haltingly murmur between rapid escaping breaths, "Please, I … I … Mmm," and I reach with my hands to clutch onto the back of the desk, using it to help me thrust up. Fuck He's diabolical. I don't know how much more I can take.

Pausing, he looks up and says, "What, Alicia? What do you want?"

I can barely hear let alone speak as he goes back to teasing and sucking one nipple then the other while moving his fingers in and out slowly then faster and faster until I'm so wet I crave more. But he doesn't stop, only repeats, "Say it Alicia. Let me hear it."

And between escaping breaths I pant, "You, I want you."

I hear him groan deep in his throat before unzipping his jeans and springing loose. There's the quick tear of a condom wrapper, and he is inside me within the breadth of seconds. His thrusts are hard and the surface unforgiving, but my body pulsates with each movement until I feel myself building. He raises one of my legs over his shoulder, and I grab onto the sides of the desk as he sinks in even deeper, teasing, slowing his gyrations, and then increasing them faster and faster and bringing me almost to the top.

"Give it to me baby. C'mon."

Hearing his voice, I scream out as I spiral into ripples of ecstasy that continue to peak as his thrusts lengthen and strengthen with his release. Dazed, there's a rushing in my ears, and it's taking me a while to regain focus and catch my breath. It's like I'm hovering in another dimension, somewhere between rapid excitement and balmy satiation. When I finally do reach the here and now, I feel Chase's arms under my shoulders, gently raising me from the desk.

"Are you ok?" He queries, hooded eyes scanning my face.

"Never better." I wrap my legs around his waist, helping him lift me off the desk, then slowly lower them as he keeps his arms around me to help steady my wobbly legs.

"How's your back?

I stretch to work out the kinks then massage my lower back before answering, "Good. I think it's realigned so I'll never slouch again."

He laughs then quickly takes off his condom, knotting it and tossing it in the wastepaper basket.

Sweeping his eyes from the top of my mussed hair down to my wobbly toes, an ever so slight grin tugs at the corner of his mouth. "Well, I'm proud to claim responsibility for your state of dishabille."

So true. I can actually feel my hair expanding in long wild waves with heaven knows how many knots running through it. I quickly slip on my clothes and pull its unruliness into a high ponytail. I've regained my senses. My legs and arms are working in tandem and my brain function, complete with sight and hearing, has begun to process information.

"Give me a couple of hours to finish here then we'll take a boat over to Portofino for lunch. There's a great restaurant there called Bar Georgios that I think you'll enjoy."

My eyes appraise his just fucked state and in no way does it match mine. His hair falls neatly and smoothly over his collar, and his broad shoulders are held erect as he buttons his unwrinkled black shirt, allowing me to graze my eyes down to his happy trail and lower, where his pants hang commando style. Oh my. I have to shake my head and scold myself to buck up and get moving, but it would be nice to take the initiative as a preview for the next round while showing him that my sexual stamina can rival his. Well, almost.

"Sure," I answer when I find my voice. "I could use some time to work first also."

Before I lose my courage, I walk briskly toward him and in one swift movement, reach up and pull him to me. With both hands locked in his hair, I plant a long, hard good-bye-for-now kiss smack on his lips, making sure to break away before he has the chance to assume control. Then without saying a word or looking back, I turn and walk away, thinking there's got to be a Heisman equivalent for this kind of restraint.

Setting up shop at the large kitchen table that faces the sea, I'm awash in color and light, a perfect combination for producing ideas and precise lines. My mother was right. There's an amethyst hue to the sea that I want to capture in a design, but my mind keeps shifting back to my mother. Best to call home before starting. The connection goes through quickly, and I hear Francesco's deep hello.

"Alicia, you live. We've been wondering about you. How are you?" It's Francisco and his upbeat tone helps me breathe a sigh of relief.

"I'm good. How is everyone there?"

Francesco knows that Mamma is a major concern so he gets right to the point. "Everyone's fine, and get this ... Papa was able to schedule a last minute appointment for Mamma with some well-known specialist. She agreed and whatever went down in that office, she's up and about a bit more. This morning she got out of bed, showered, and had some breakfast."

"That's great." I feel tears of relief prickle. "Is she there?

Can I talk to her?

She started some new meds so she's resting. Do you want me to check to see if she can come to the phone?

"No, let her sleep. I'll call again when it's earlier in the day for you. Would you tell Papa I called and let him know I'm well and having a great time."

"Yeah, sure. And, hey, don't forget to bring me home a souvenir. Preferably some sexy Italian woman who wants to start new with a suave American."

"I'll get right on it." It feels refreshingly ordinary to have this conversation, like a cool dip in the sea on a hot day.

"You do that."

I know Chase's phone call is what helped my mother get that appointment, and a warmth I've never felt before permeates, making my heart swell with gratitude and delight. The depth of these feelings are both uplifting and frightening, like two separate roads that intersect before diverging in opposite directions.

A looming question glares in large neon letters, flashing: *what if he doesn't feel the same way about you*? My breath catches and my throat tightens. I can't bear the thought. Even thinking of him leaving for home and my stomach knots. *Shake off these negative feelings. Embrace the moment and head down,* I am pulled into my sketches.

CHAPTER FIFTEEN

hase maneuvers the motor yacht as well as he handles a car, and we glide out of the harbor and into open water where he allows her to hit a nice speed. Standing erect at the helm, he squints to see ahead, adjusting the angle of the rudder to change our direction toward Portofino. He's relaxed and the contrast between his acquired tan and blue eyes is stunning.

"Want to steer?"

Did I hear right?

"Sure."

He steps behind and wraps his arms around me as I take the ship's wheel then lowers his head and nuzzles my neck. Even with me at the wheel, he's relaxed and I'm guessing it's the miles of empty, open sea that's helping. We are moving at a fair pace and the sea, sun, and cloudless sky, with Chase holding me, makes me think that if there's a heaven this must be what it's like.

After we've traveled a safe distance from the harbor, he suggests we stop to go for a swim before arriving in Portofino.

"Sounds perfect. I turn and give him a quick kiss.

"We're out in the open, so it should be fine, but we need to be careful. There's lots of boaters and sometimes it can get congested. Let's be sure to swim together."

I shrug. "Ok."

I hear his concern but the water is calm, and there aren't any boats in our immediate vicinity. The spot seems perfect for swimming. Chase takes control of the helm, makes a wide loop, leaving a spray of water in the wake of the boat and slows it to a stop. It bobs gently in the current, and I spot a swimming ladder along the port side. I can see several boats in the distance, some of them stopped and others traveling to and from the surrounding harbors.

"Just give me a few minutes before you go in. I have something to attend to first." He gives me a peck on my nose then walks over to Sammy where they huddle in conversation. Chase points to something in the distance, and Sammy grabs a pair of binoculars from on board and peers in that direction. Chase, intent on what Sammy sees, keeps his eyes fixed on that area then quickly turns toward me and raises his finger asking for a bit more time. Nodding, I resume my stare into a blanket of blue sea and sky that never becomes tiresome. Closing my eyes, a breeze tickles my face and rustles my hair, though the sun continues to warm as its strengthening rays are absorbed by the salt water. I feel sweat trickle along my forehead and neck and when I open my eyes, the sea looks too inviting to wait any longer. Raising my sundress over my head, I strip to my bikini and head toward the ladder. I toss a glance in Chase and Sammy's direction, but they're immersed in conversation and not wanting to disturb them, I gingerly climb down the ladder and lower myself into the water. It's cool and still, and diving below the surface, I swim underwater until I'm a reasonable distance from the boat. When I surface, I glance toward the boat, sure that Chase is swimming toward me by now. He's not. Instead, he's at the stern, gesturing wildly at me with both hands waving in the air.

"Come on in. The water's great," I shout, waving back and dive below, opening my eyes this time to try and see some of the undersea life while I wait for him to join me. Breaking the surface, I lie back and float, arms and legs spread, my weightlessness drifting with the light current.

I hear it before I see it. A revved humming from behind that becomes louder and louder. I rub my eyes and push back my hair, but before I can turn to see what's there, my ankles are gripped in a viselike hold, and I'm pulled under. The sudden plunge takes away my breath and flailing my arms, I try to escape, but I'm tugged deeper. It's like I have two bricks tied to my feet, and no matter how hard I try to kick them off, they remain secured. Swallowed by sea, I open my eyes hoping to glimpse what has such a fierce hold of me, but all I see is unending water, smothering and trapping me as I'm yanked further and further under. Fear succumbs to panic, giving me the strength to bend forward and grab onto whatever or whoever holds me prisoner. I yank fiercely at what feels like hair, twisting and turning until my arms ache. Nothing works and the strong hold and tugging continue. Something buzzes overhead, but I'm too deep and too panicked to see what it is.

My breath and strength feel as if they're being torn from me, and all I can think is *please, God, don't let me suffocate in this coffin of sea and sand.* Just as my body goes limp, I'm held fast under my arms and tugged upward. I break through the surface of water, coughing and gasping and kicking so hard it takes me a while to see that it's Sammy who has me in a firm grasp.

He's looking me square in the eyes and from somewhere far away I hear him shout, "It's alright Alicia. You're going to be Ok. I need you to stop fighting me and relax. Do you understand?"

Adrenalin courses through me, and I flail and sputter, curling my fists and punching wildly until the furor in my head finally clears and I quiet in his grasp. When we reach our craft, he agilely hoists me up the ladder and onto the deck where I collapse in an exhausted heap. I'm having a problem catching my breath and my body seems locked in place. Sammy climbs on board, picks me up, and carries me below deck. He sets me on the canvas-covered dining bench and the boat takes off at a speed rivaling a Pensacola boat race.

Shivering uncontrollably, I can't move or speak. Sammy

returns with a towel and wraps it around my shoulders. I still can't stop shaking, so he grabs a blanket and wraps that around me too. My chest hurts, my ears are popping, and a cold has seeped into my bones that racks my body with chills. I hear Sammy rummaging around the galley, and he hands me a steaming cup of tea. I wrap my hands around its warmth, but I'm shaking so badly I have to work at getting the hot liquid into my mouth.

Taking a seat next to me, Sammy's worried expression is shaded with compassion, and I realize that his quiet presence is helping me calm.

"Wh-what happened?" My voice is so shaky and raspy, I don't recognize it as mine.

Sammy looks down at his hands. "There was a boat headed straight toward you. We saw it but you couldn't. Luckily, I was able to reach you first and pull you under before you were hit. Sorry you got so frightened. There was no time for a warning."

"I don't understand." The reality of my plight makes my voice steadier and stronger. "Didn't the boater see me in the water? I shouted and waved to you guys. How could I be missed?"

Sammy's usually assured composure skips a beat. I see it in the tightening of his mouth and the slight flexing of his upper arms before his usual bland expression slips back into place.

"I think whoever was at the helm had been drinking. Sorry, but I couldn't make out much of him. I'll leave it to Chase to fill you in on the details. He'll be down shortly. Just hang tight."

I have no desire to move. I don't think my legs could support me and my hands are still shaking. I rub my face, massaging my temples with my fingertips in a vain attempt to try to piece together a chain of events so surreal they swirl in a convoluted muddle. I hear Chase descending below deck, and I try to stand but my head spins and my legs wobble. He takes me by the arms and gently sets me back down.

"Are you alright? You seem to have trouble standing."

"I'm fine, just a bit shaky."

He's uncharacteristically quiet, and I sense a hotwired tension that can spring loose at any time.

My apprehension is confirmed when he asks in a controlled, measured tone that indicates he is anything but, "Why didn't you do as you were told and wait for me? You could have been killed, dammit." He stops talking and glares at me with a mixed expression of worry and fright, a combination I've come to realize as a potent trigger for his anger. Before I can answer, he hauls back and punches the far wall causing me to flinch and jump.

How unfair of him to think it was recklessness on my part that nearly got me killed, and with the snap of a finger, my fear and fatigue turn to anger. I have had enough of being reprimanded like an errant child and standing to face him, I snap, "You act as if I deliberately made myself a target for a speeding boat then decided on a deep sea dive without the benefit of oxygen."

My chest is heaving, and I have to keep my shaking hands behind my back. He is not an easy adversary to take on in an argument. A slight grin replaces his former grimace, and he reaches out and lightly brushes my cheek with his hand then places it behind his neck. Stretching back, he closes his eyes. When he opens them they mirror the desolation of a much older man. My heart wrenches and forgetting my anger, I wrap my arms around him. He holds onto me tightly and kisses the top of my head.

"I'm so sorry," I whisper.

"No, I'm the one who's sorry. If I had let anything happen to you, I couldn't live with myself," and he tightens his hold on me.

I don't understand why he's taking responsibility for something that clearly would have been an accident, but he's so forlorn I say nothing. Besides, in his arms I feel at home and safe with mad boaters and underwater rescues melting into the distance. He holds me for a long time, and I rest my head on his shoulder. My chills have subsided and suddenly warm, I let the blanket drop. He looks at me, desire glazing his eyes, but this time he won't make the first move. After my ordeal, he's leaving that up to me, and I want him. I need him.

Pulling him to me, we kiss with an unleashed passion that takes his breath away and makes my heart skip a beat. I lean into his embrace as he unhooks the top of my bathing suit and he grazes my back with his fingertips. He is moving slowly, but I crave more. I deepen my kiss, shrugging first one shoulder then the other, letting my top fall to the deck while never breaking my hold on his lips. He groans into my mouth before moving his lips to plant gentle kisses down my neck around my collarbone and toward my chest. Fear has transitioned to lust, and I move my hand inside his bathing suit and palm his cock while I use my other to cup his balls. It springs to life with just the lightest touch of my hand, and I massage it slowly, letting my hand slide up and down its length.

"No, not this way." His voice is low and gravelly. "I want to be inside you."

And with deft hands, he produces, tears open, and slips on a condom. Holding my hands, he sits on the seat of the nook and lifts me onto his lap, cupping my ass with his hands. I guide him inside with my hand as he bends and suckles on my breast. Twisting my hands in his hair to pull him closer, I use my raised feet as an anchor and move up and down, relishing the power I have to manage momentum.

"That's it, baby. Nice and easy." He moves his head back and closes his eyes.

I'm so wet I glide up and down easily, and the mounting pleasure makes us crave more. He uses his hands as a boost, allowing me to increase the speed of insertion in time to my quickening. Once again he pulls on my nipple, grazing it with his teeth then gently sucking.

It is my undoing, and I push down and pull up until I feel tightening spasms from my gyrations. Beads of sweat pepper his forehead and droplets from my wet hair trickle down my back. The intense building feels like heat from a lightning bolt searing through my torso and up my spine. Throwing my head back, I pant with need until I unravel in an upward rippling of sensation that seems to plateau forever. I hear a loud groan from Chase as he thrusts and climaxes, lengthening my orgasm further. My heart beats rapidly in tune with Chase's as we remain entwined until we catch our breath. Pulling my legs from around him, I curl on his lap, nestling my head in the crook of his arm. My eyes flutter closed as sleep overtakes, and I barely feel him reach down to remove, knot, and toss the condom in a nearby waste basket. He wraps his arms around me and holds me close. I try to stay awake but depleted energy from my near-death dive and sizzling lovemaking make it impossible for me to win the battle to keep my eyes open, and I drift off feeling safer and more at home than ever before.

When I wake Chase is still holding me.

"Hi," he whispers tenderly.

I look up and take a deep breath. Groggy, my arms and legs feel leaden, and it takes me a while to acclimate to where I am. Memories of the boat, the swim, and the rescue seep into consciousness, but Chase does not give me any time to dwell. He lifts me onto my feet and waits until I appear steady. I look at the small nook where we have both been sitting and can't believe he remained in such a cramped space with me on his lap while I slept.

"How about some lunch?"

Groggy, I nod.

"C'mon, I'll help you shower."

I don't think he trusts my steadiness, and the boat, although now docked, continues to rock. He takes me by the hand and guides me to the shower. The cool spray of fresh water runs off my body, rinsing away the residue of sea salt and sweat, and slowly I feel my achy limbs wake. Chase hands me body wash and shampoo from my carry bag, and I rinse away the salty residue of sea water.

He waits outside the shower, giving me privacy yet not leaving me alone. He even has a towel ready when I step out and wraps it around me. I reach up and plant a kiss on his cheek before quickly drying and reaching for my clothes. Luckily I packed clean underwear and dry clothes because I have no desire to put on my wet bathing suit. I quickly slip into a pair of shorts and a T-shirt and comb out my hair, twisting it into a braid to tame its unruliness.

I'm just about to gather my belongings to leave when Chase looks at me for a breath longer than usual, like he needs to tell me something but he doesn't know how to start.

"What is it?" I immediately ask.

"What do you mean?"

Ugh, he's being deliberately evasive. This time I'm not deterred.

"Is there something I should know that you're not telling me?"

"No ... well, yes." He rubs the side of his face with his hands probably to buy some extra time before saying, "I decided we should return to Santa Margharita. You're not up to lunch in Portofino after your … uh … mishap." He reaches out his hand for me to take and just like that the subject is closed. Except I don't want the conversation ended without any input, so I take his hand but hesitate.

"It seems like a waste to have spent good money to rent such a beautiful boat and not at least have a meal at our intended destination."

"Don't worry about the money. In fact, I was thinking we could go back to the villa and prepare another one of your great lunches. We can stop at the local market for supplies, and hey, you can even pay." He raises his hands in mock surrender. He's won because I can't resist when he turns on his charm.

The car ride to the market should give me the opportunity to mull over the past events and discuss them with Chase, but it's as if my mind is shuttered from remembering what actually happened. Any attempt to retrieve the memory, and the covering darkens until what remains is nothing more than a hazy mirage of blue water and bobbing boats.

At the market we agree on a menu of grilled lamb chops, a mixed green salad, and pasta with a light pomodoro sauce. We select a bottle of Pinot Nero because it's impossible to find a bad bottle of red wine in Italy even in a supermarket. The cashier obviously remembers us because she's grinning from ear to ear and when I start to pay, she snickers and pointedly stares at Chase. He smiles, turning the pockets of his shorts inside out to show they're empty.

"Tartufo nero, no denaro."

At this point the clerk's scoffing has turned to raucous laughter. She can't tear her eyes off Chase, and I have to wave my money in front of her face before she acknowledges I'm trying to pay. Without so much as a glance at me, she takes it, hands over my change, and still staring at Chase, slowly licks her lips.

Ugh, really! I take Chase's extended hand while he grabs the groceries with his other, and we leave before she hurdles into his arms. So this is what it's going to be like. Maybe I should carry some kind of bludgeon to wave around whenever we leave the house. The thought makes me laugh, and Chase looks down and smiles too, but the shared moment slowly evaporates, like wisps of lifting fog, with each passing kilometer to the villa.

CHAPTER SIXTEEN

*L*unch is quiet. Very quiet. Beth and Andre are out, and Sammy seems to have disappeared. The meal is delicious, the lamb grilled to perfection and so tender it melts in my mouth. The pomodoro sauce is light and the added fresh basil sweetens any lingering acidity. It complements the fresh spaghetti cooked al dente but not too firm. The only way to accomplish this is to stand by the pot and periodically taste, stir, wait, then taste again. You can't be too rushed or the consistency is compromised.

We should be enjoying the meal, laughing, talking, and sharing stories like lovers do in books and movies. Instead, Chase is withdrawn. It's as if some switch in his brain turned off after we arrived at the villa. I try for levity, referring to the oncoming boat as a test to see if I'm as hardheaded as my family says, but he barely smiles. If anything, he retreats more. Tomorrow we leave for Milan, and the following day he flies home. I want to ask how things are there, but he's slipped into such a sullen silence I don't think he'll answer honestly—or even worse: he might consider it prying.

After we clean up, he gives me a peck on my cheek, says he has work to finish, then disappears into the back room and shuts the door, and it's like the door of a vault closing in my face.

Sighing, I reach for my sketchpad and begin imagining the colors of a vibrant seascape to incorporate into my designs. I only surface when the natural light has become so dim I realize I can no longer comfortably draw. When I study my finished product I see that, despite the bright color of sun and sea, I have created a tight fitted dark ensemble that looks funereal. I push aside my pad and get up to make myself a cup of tea. I decide to check if Chase would like something because I keep thinking some contact, any contact, will allow us to reconnect, but as I reach the closed door, I hear him speaking on his phone. His voice is edgy, tight, like a whisper trapped in a black hole.

"He's hell bent on it, and he's not getting to me that way. I won't allow it."

Silence.

"Who the fuck knows? He moves underground like some fucking mole with an army."

Silence.

"Stay low and close to Mac, Devie. He's not going to stop. I'll see you tomorrow night. Thanks for looking after Fiona."

Silence.

I stand frozen like a statue carved to depict hurt and surprise. A tiny voice inside my mind keeps repeating, *he's leaving tomorrow and never said a word.* I want to cover my ears to shut out the din. I swallow to fend off the tightening in my throat and like a marionette moving by the hand of another, I walk back to the kitchen. The tea kettle hisses angrily and turning the burner off, I sit at the counter in stunned stillness. He wasn't scheduled to leave for another two days. What could have happened to make him push it up a day? But that's not the worst of it. It was the way he said her name, the way it slipped off his tongue, like a silk scarf that wafts with a breeze that makes my stomach knot and my heart race. *Devie.*

I raise my head and decide to pour myself that cup of tea. My mind is racing in so many circles I don't realize someone is standing next to me, so when I look up I'm surprised to see Chase. My first reaction is to go to him, to wrap my arms around him, and hold him close, and then I notice the change in physicality. His face does not emote. It's as if someone has taken an eraser and removed smiles, frowns, joy, and even fear from its contour. I study his eyes, but he seems to be staring right through me. Even so, I want to nuzzle my nose in his neck and tell him everything is going to be ok, but I'm stilled by his blank gaze. It's like he's been transformed into an apparition.

He speaks first. "There's been a change in plans and I have to fly home tomorrow."

"Oh." My voice is barely audible, and I pause to give

him time to explain, listening so carefully that I think I stop breathing for fear I'll miss something.

"There are some problems I have to deal with." He pauses as if he wants to say more, but his lips clamp shut and he remains silent.

I finally exhale. "Ok, I understand." But really I don't, because he hasn't offered an honest explanation and his body language indicates he's not going to.

What hurts the most is that he's making no attempt to touch or hold me and more than anything that's what I crave. I glance toward him and what I see touches the depth of my core, making my heart pound and my stomach tighten. He stands rigid, his face blank, his gaze far away. It's as if he's already left. A tiny voice inside mocks, *He's breaking up with you. He's breaking up with you.* Over and over again until it's no longer a whisper but a long, loud lament. I continue staring straight ahead because I know if I look at him again, I'll cry, and I won't give him that satisfaction.

I don't have to fight this urge for long because I hear him say, "I have work to do that's going to take some time so don't bother to wait up. We'll need to get an early start."

I can only nod and after he leaves, there's a bottomless desolation so deep, I become lost in its emptiness. It isn't until later, when dusk has given way to darkness, that I recognize the expression of concern and warm comforting arms of Beth.

"Ali, please tell me what's wrong? Are you ok?"

I turn in her hug and surrender myself to the tears that I

have been holding at bay for what seems like an eternity. Beth sets me down and takes a seat across from me, but doesn't let go of my hand. Her silent touch is reassuring, and I wipe my tears and laugh nervously, shaking my head and apologizing for phases one, two, and three of a major meltdown.

"Ali, apologies are not necessary. Please tell me what happened?" She hands me a glass of water, which I gratefully sip.

"I don't know …" And I stop speaking because I really don't know where to begin. She nods but remains quiet, giving me the time to gather my thoughts and continue. "Everything was going well until today, and I'm just so confused. I don't know where it went wrong, but, Beth, I think Chase is breaking it off with me."

"What do you mean you think? Have you asked?"

"Well, not exactly. He just suddenly turned weird … all distant and aloof, like we were strangers."

"Did you argue about something?"

"No, it all started after I was almost hit by that boat."

Beth's eyes pop. "What!"

"I'm fine. Some drunk boater nearly crashed into me while I was out swimming off our craft." I don't feel the need to explain about my rescue because I just want to put the whole episode behind me and focus on where my relationship with Chase is headed.

"That's strange. He was pretty into you at lunch the other day. He couldn't take his eyes or hands off you. Nobody changes that fast, even a mercurial bastard like Chase Reardon."

That may be true, but there's a clear distinction between a good fuck and an emotional connection. Yet he was so solicitous when we discussed my mother's depression and when I needed help because of my vertigo. My mind slips into rewind, and I recall our conversation on the beach yesterday when he talked about our different worlds and how he would do anything to protect me from the problems of his past. Did he think I was some coddled child who couldn't deal with adult issues?

"Ali, you're doing your usual obsessing. Let's cut to the chase." And she winks and gives me a nudge. "Is the sex still good?"

"What?"

"You know, multi-orgasms? Types? Where?"

This catches me off guard. I look up and feel my cheeks heat. She's like a sex census taker. It's so like Beth to get directly to the point she deems significant.

"I can tell by your blush that it's been good. Out with the details." She stands back, stares me straight in the eye, and waits.

"Um, it's been good so far …" I swipe away my tears with my fingertips and lean in whispering, "Often more than one," and looking away add, "not necessarily in a bed."

I don't know how to answer to different types. Memories of being sprawled on a desk with my legs wrapped around his waist while he plunges into me and feeling his fullness inside while his pinky circles that area behind as we swim in the Ligurian Sea spring to mind.

"I'm going to have to douse your face with water if it becomes any more heated. Listen, good sex is half the battle, but so is good communication. Talk to him. Hold his feet to the fire and demand answers. Tomorrow, when you're driving to Milan, is the perfect opportunity. For now stop all this mental masturbation and let's drink wine, do same dancing, have some fun." And she shimmies and takes me in another hug.

When I nod, smiling, she swings into motion, grabbing her IPad for music and shouting to Andre to come open some wine. With the snap of a finger, Andre appears, making me realize that he must have been hovering just outside the kitchen, afraid to interrupt my meltdown. Laughing, he takes Beth in a tight embrace and plants a deep kiss on her lips.

"Anything for you, ma cherie." Beth jumps up and wrapping her legs around him, grasps the back of his head and gives him a lingering kiss.

Their arduous openness, as they seamlessly drift from one experience to the next without drama or upheaval, is refreshing. Beth has the uncanny ability to seize opportunities for enjoyment while dismissing moments of sadness with the clear notion that given time, they will pass. It's not that she's never felt sorrow. Beth's younger brother died from Leukemia when he was only three years old, and her mother, who is a graphic artist, grapples with Lupus. It's more that she doesn't succumb to its grip, doesn't worry about future ramifications or what ifs.

I decide to give them privacy and search for some wine. They may need a room, but I wanted a drink. I rummage through the cabinets and the fridge before realizing we are out. When Beth surfaces for air, she suggests I take a ride with Andre to the market to buy wine while she showers. It's fine by me and grabbing the villa's keys and my purse, I follow Andre to his motorbike. He puts on his helmet and I hop on, realizing too late that I forgot to take along Beth's helmet. No matter. I crave this getaway, and with the wind whooshing in my face and my hair whipping behind me, exhilaration replaces tension. Spotting the market, I holler in Andre's ear, pointing behind me, but he shouts back asking if I want a longer ride.

"Yes," I yell and speeding up, he serpentines through traffic. Andre's a proficient driver, fast but not reckless. Laughing, my arms wrapped around his waist, our jackets ballooning with gushing air fragrant with pine and bougainvillea, I embrace the freedom of the moment—a time where nothing is real except for the motion of this bike.

Andre eventually turns toward the market and effortlessly maneuvers into a small space in front. I attempt to slide off the seat, but my foot catches and I fall sideways, scraping my thigh and wrenching my ankle.

Andre rushes to me. "Are you hurt?"

I quickly get up, wincing a bit when I put weight on my ankle.

"I'm fine. Just blame my klutziness." I brush myself off, embarrassed by my clumsiness.

"Klutzeenes? What is dees?" Andre asks, taking me by my arm and guiding me toward the entrance. I feign another trip, widening my eyes and exaggerating the motion as a definition.

Glint in his eyes, he remarks, "I, too, have dees klutzinees when I try to dance, but it ees my partner who limps away." I chuckle and it feels good to be talking and laughing about small nothings.

After purchasing several bottles of local Vermentino and a loaf of thick crusty Italian bread, and a large slab of pecorino cheese and dried sausage, I pay and we head back. It is probably the first time I have paid for anything since I met Chase in France and it feels refreshing, liberating as if I am not too young, not too inexperienced, not without job and resources so as to be unable to pay my way. Yet a part of me feels it's unfair to blame Chase for these insecurities. He is just trying to make his way in a world where his past doesn't haunt, doesn't reach out and lock him in its hold of alcoholism, sickness, and insufficiency. His successful escape is what I appreciate most. That, and his ability, his unrequited need to reach out and care for those he loves while expecting little to nothing in return. It is this selflessness that makes me yearn for his touch and his love and makes me want to return them in equal measure.

When we get back, Beth has finished her shower and has Adele's "Rumour Has It" blasting. With her typical bouncing energy, she grabs my arms and swirls me into a dance. My ankle gives one sharp throb before quieting to a dull ache, allowing me to move without pain. Andre uncorks a bottle and pours us each a glass of wine then starts dancing, grabbing one of us in his arms and then the other, his jerky movements and heavy steps giving clear warning to keep a safe distance. Clapping and singing we swing to "You made a fool out of me … rumor has it … rumor has it." When the music slows we sing louder, putting our heads together before starting to dance again when it picks up. Arms raised we shake and shimmy to the beat. After the song ends, we clank our wine glasses toasting, "salute" in unison.

A bit heated, I begin pouring us glasses of chilled sparkling water, when I think I hear my name being called. I look up and see Chase standing in the distance.

"Could I have a word with you, please?" He stands rigid and his formal tone seems out of place.

I leave Beth and Andre sipping their wine and dancing close to some slow blues song and follow Chase to the room he's been using as an office. When he doesn't once turn, I begin to feel as if I'm being summoned to the principal's office. He's all tense and quiet, and I know there is a serious argument waiting for me. I steel myself for what's to follow as we enter the room and he closes the door. I don't have long to wait.

"Where did you go?" His words are clipped and his gaze penetrates.

Taken off guard, I extend my hand toward the window in

the direction of the road and answer simply, "To the market to pick up more wine."

"How?"

"What?"

"How did you get there?"

I swallow because now I know where this is going. "With Andre on his motorbike."

"Your hair is very windblown and you're limping. Were you wearing a helmet?"

I didn't think I was favoring my sore ankle, but I should have known he would notice. "Um, I … I …" Stammering, I try to keep my answer light, but I just know it's going to make him angry. "I forgot it and the market is so close that—"

He doesn't let me finish. "I don't care how close the distance is. It's reckless to drive on a motorbike without a helmet." He stops, concern lacing his voice. "And you left without saying a word. Did you fall?" He bends to look at my ankle then satisfied it's not serious, impatiently demands an answer. "Well?"

Am I ever going to *not* be in trouble with this man? Feebly, I answer, "I slipped getting off the motorbike." I look down and wipe my sweaty palms on the sides of my shorts. "I didn't tell you I was leaving because I didn't think you wanted to be disturbed."

"So you hop on a motorbike without a helmet with some French guy you hardly know rather than bother me. Where's the logic in that!"

You'd think I disappeared for a week the way he's carrying

on, but I can see he's been worried. His hair spikes where he's been tugging at it, and his forehead furrows in a deep crease when he looks at me. The man is a walking puzzle. One minute he acts as if I don't exist, and the next he's angry because I didn't tell him where I was going.

Bemused, I answer honestly, "I didn't think you'd notice or worry."

"Of course I realized you were gone. Next time, tell me when you're leaving and no motorbike without a helmet."

I don't want to argue with Beth and Andre here so I swallow the ugly retort on the tip of my tongue, shrug, and answer with a simple "Ok."

When he looks down at his phone, I realize I've been dismissed, but as I turn to leave, he abruptly looks up. "What's your plan for the rest of the evening?"

"Just some wine and cheese and dancing. Want to join us?"

"Here?" And I think I hear a hint of alarm in his voice.

"Yes," and with deliberate nonchalance, I add, "maybe even a game or two of strip poker."

His head jerks up. "You would do that?" His eyes meet mine, lips forming a tight line of disapproval while he waits for a reply.

"No…" I roll my eyes and blow out air in exasperation "…I'm joking." Whatever's eating him must have started with his sense of humor.

He's all bristling business once again, studying his damn phone as if it holds the secret to world peace then adds without looking up, "I can't join you. I have too much work to catch up on. Sammy might though. Is that ok?" he asks tersely.

I don't immediately answer because I realize he's deliberately not looking at me. Instead, I wait until the split seconds of silence hang so heavy in the air, I almost need to cover my mouth to keep from answering. Finally he looks up and god damn it, it's the look that never ceases to tug at my heart. Eyes so blue I can get lost in their depths even as they squint to study me beneath a worried, furrowed brow. It takes every ounce of effort not to take him in my arms and bury my face in his neck, to breathe in his clean musky scent and plant kisses up and down behind his ear. We're so close I hear his breath hitch, and I know he's feeling something too, but he stands stiff and unmoving. I swiftly shake my head and envision giving myself a kick in the pants as a reminder that this is how he is choosing to behave so he has to be the one who decides to come back from whatever godforsaken hole his head has decided to burrow inside. Maybe it's his ass.

"Sure," I answer, feigning nonchalance.

When I begin to leave, he remains silent, staring through the open window at a stretch of sea that even under these unhappy circumstances preens beautifully. When nothing more is offered, I realize that this time I have been dismissed.

He gives me one final fleeting glance and with a tinge of regret pauses. "Um … ah …" Motionless, I wait for some glimmer of his old self, but he only mumbles, "Don't forget to ice that ankle."

I swallow the fuck you sitting on the tip of my tongue and walk out without once looking back, making sure to give the door a fierce tug behind me.

"So you hop on a motorbike with some Frenchman … Next time tell me when you're going somewhere," I parrot then mockingly salute at attention outside the closed door. *Asshole.*

CHAPTER SEVENTEEN

'm alone. Sitting in the Foyer Bar of the Four Season Hotel in Milan, I moodily sip a glass of champagne and stare above the bartender's head while he shakes a martini. Beth and Andre may join me later, but our plans were never finalized. Chase left for home yesterday and the subsequent void is now a widening chasm. I envision his chiseled profile and can still feel the chill that permeated the car with each passing kilometer to Milan. I close my eyes and swallow over the lump that seems wedged in my throat, but I refuse to shed one more tear thinking about that icy wall of impenetrable silence. Any attempt to connect with a question, thought, or shared feeling was met with a one word response or non-committal shrug until all emotion was filtered and left behind was a shadow of his former self. I want to forget. I need to push any thoughts of Chase Reardon from my mind and move on, but it's proving impossible. Like a jingle that repeats over and over in my mind, I cannot rid myself of his smile, his scent, his face with its hint of a sexy, dark stubble and how it feels when I run my fingers along the side of his cheek. I shake my head and try to focus on reality.

When we arrived at the hotel, which was his selection and at his insistence, he helped me check in, took one look around the lobby, then brushed my lips with a kiss and said, "Take care." And just like that he was gone.

I raise my champagne flute to my lips, a silent tribute to myself, finish it and order another. I resolve to make it my last. I leave for Lake Como in two days, and I need a clear head to work on the latest addition to my portfolio, which I plan to start first thing in the morning. There's a sun-drenched study adjoining my suite that is perfect. Sipping champagne, with myriad thoughts of elegant designs offsetting lost love, I don't initially notice the gentleman seated to my left.

It's not until I hear him say, "If you hold the stem of that glass any tighter, I'm afraid it might snap and cut your lovely hand," that I realize he's speaking to me.

When I turn I'm met with a pair of deep set hazel eyes and a smirk expanding the width of his face that brings an automatic smile to mine.

"That's better. You have a beautiful smile. How long have you been in Milan?"

I note the hint of a British accent. His t's are emphasized and "been" sounds like "bean."

"Since yesterday. Before that we were in Santa Margharita."

The "we" slips out before I can catch myself, and I nervously take a sip of champagne, followed by another.

"Santa Margharita, eh? A beautiful harbor town with lovely beaches."

"Yes, I had a wonderful time."

He studies me for a moment, saying nothing, then casually but not presumptuously remarks, "Somehow I doubt that."

It takes me a moment to process his reply because I can't fathom how someone I've never met before can read me so well. He sits quietly, staring ahead, sipping his martini. When he speaks again, it's with an assuredness that holds a lifetime of experience.

"Your expression when you said 'we were in Santa Margharita' was marked by sadness. Your mouth turned down and you blinked several times before taking rather large sips of your champagne. I certainly am glad you changed the course of the conversation to 'I' because the alcohol consumption the 'we' triggered was bound to have you tottering off your seat in no time."

I look at him in stunned silence, and for the second time that day I smile.

He continues staring ahead, but a smirk tugs at the corners of his mouth.

He eventually looks in my direction and extends his hand. "I'm Donald Meet and yes, the same as in I'm happy to *meet* you."

"Well, Donald Meet, it's a pleasure to *meet* you." I turn to shake his hand.

"Everyone calls me Donnie. And you're?"

I pause before answering. "Alicia." I deliberately withhold my last name because I can hear the other part of my "we" chastising me for sharing my full name with a complete stranger while sitting alone at a bar in a foreign country. I take a deep breath and lift my glass, conscious to sip and not gulp in some vain attempt to numb my pain.

"It's easy to drown sorrows in alcohol," Mr. Meet continues, again reading my mind, and I think that maybe he's some kind of soothsayer like the ones in ancient Greek myths who act as precursors to unpreventable doom and destruction. God, I am depressed. Tearing me away from my thoughts, he quickly adds, "But the ensuing numbness is never long lasting, and the next morning there's a nasty hammering inside the noggin." He looks appraisingly at me with a frank, non-judgmental gaze.

I put my drink down and suddenly curious, ask, "So, Mr. Meet, what brings you to Milan?"

"I'm here to address a Mental Health Conference."

"You're a Psychologist?"

"Yes, that's right." He takes a large sip of his martini before raising his eyebrows and adding, "I specialize in alcohol and substance abuse."

This time I laugh out loud, and he laughs right along with me. I like him. He's straightforward and unpretentious. He tells me he's from Bath, a city in South West England about ninety minutes outside of London and that he became interested in the study of alcoholism after his mother, a recovering alcoholic, died from cirrhosis. His honesty and earnestness are intriguing and endearing, and I feel myself pulled into his confidence. Unwittingly, I glean information about alcoholism that I never knew or understood before and eventually feel confident enough to take the conversation in a slightly different direction. I don't want to make him talk about work related matters when he's relaxing during some down time, but curiosity prevails, so nervously clearing my throat, I pluck up the courage and ask, "In the course of your work, do you ever deal with the children of alcoholics?"

He doesn't have to think twice before answering. "Yes, although I mostly refer them to other specialists for help."

"Oh." My breath nervously catches before continuing, "Do they often need help?"

"Yes, of course."

I slowly exhale and resist taking another sip of my drink. Instead, I meet his gaze head on and ask, "And why is that, Mr. Meet?"

"Well ..." he leans his head to the side before answering "...for a variety of different reasons. Children growing up with an alcoholic parent or parents live with constant uncertainty, never quite knowing what havoc the addicted family member will wreak next. They have little to no sense of normal family life and lots of their time is spent either caring for the alcoholic parent or covering up for him ... or her." He pauses as if lost in thought then continues, "These children can grow up feeling isolated and unworthy, with a need to control everything and everyone in their life to feel safe."

"I see."

I swallow and briefly look away to rein in my emotions. I don't want to embarrass myself by crying in front of this kind stranger. Mr. Meet spares me any concern because when I look at him again he's staring straight ahead, sipping his drink. I take another sip of my champagne, but its bitterness bites at my tongue. Thoughts of my time with Chase skirt through my mind as I try to sort them with this newly acquired information. I realize I need a clear head to think it all through and drinking at a bar is not the way to do it.

I ask the bartender for my check and extend my hand. "It's a pleasure, Mr. Meet, or is it Dr. Meet?"

"It's Donnie and the pleasure is all mine." He reaches out and shakes my hand.

"Thank you, Donnie." I sign for my drinks and leave.

Walking to my room, I'm intrigued by how a chance meeting with a complete stranger can help transform a jumble of disconnected puzzle pieces into a discernible image. I recollect our conversation at the beach when Chase described the repercussions of growing up with an alcoholic father. He described it as feeling like a commoner ... an outsider looking in. I dismissed it at the time, making a joke that if he was a commoner, then I was his captive. But I saw his pain. I just assumed success erased its impact and made it easier for him to move on. Now I see that it might not be that simple. And that impenetrable barrier he's erected is like a mind fuck structure. I can't even begin to fathom why he put it up in the first place. Was it because that drunken boater resurrected unpleasant reminders? When I think back, this all started after that mishap. My nearly getting slammed by a boat, and let's face it almost killed, must have made him feel completely out of control. Head bent in thought, my mind circles round and round these course of events until they lose their defined boundaries and collide in chaotic confusion. I do remember that there was something Chase said on the beach that caused me particular angst. What was it? Aargh! I'm exhausted and my brain just wants to shut down, not go round and round in futile circles like some jammed carousel ride. When I finally do look up, I notice that I must have taken a wrong turn to my room. I'm in an unfamiliar corridor where a peculiar silence hangs, broken only by the echo of my footsteps resonating off the walls and down the stretch of empty hallway. Strange. It's dimly lit, and leaning against the wall on top of a spread of drop cloths is a ladder. A vacuum-packed quiet continues to swathe its length, and I realize I must have wandered into an area of the hotel closed for renovations. I turn to retrace my steps back toward the elevators when I think I hear something from behind. It's faint at first but then becomes louder. I slow my pace and listen. Nothing. When I continue, I hear it again—the sound of footsteps echoing mine. I shrug off any disquiet, thinking it must be workers, but this end of the corridor is empty and eerily quiet. I quicken my pace, heading toward the exit signs, and this time it sounds even closer. I'm tempted to stop and wait for what the rational part of my brain indicates must surely just be another hotel guest. I don't know what sixth sense exists to warn of approaching harm when none seems warranted, but something inside me screams danger, and I increase my stride in a frantic search for the correct hallway. Footsteps now slam down the hallway in short, fast slides behind me, becoming so close I think I can hear labored breathing echoing off the walls. I propel myself forward, racing to lengthen the distance between us, and when I take one quick glance behind, I see a tall figure, face covered in a black ski mask, gaining momentum. I stifle a scream and in a blind panic trip when my toe catches on a drop cloth. Staggering forward in several gawky steps, I manage to thrust my hands out and regain balance without falling, but slowed by this stumble, I feel his heavy breaths on my neck as his hand grazes my back in an attempt to grab me. I pull it in and continue running, screaming and racing past closed doors, quickly turning left when I see the corridor leading to the elevators. The pounding pace of footsteps is quicker and louder, a clear indication that whoever this madman is, he hasn't given up. Dashing toward the exit sign, I hear a grunt and repeated thumps as if someone is banging into the walls on either side. More thrashing sounds resonate, but I continue running, panting and panicked, until I nearly fall headlong into a cluster of revelers spilling out from the elevator. Laughing and joking, they don't even notice me, and I use it as an opportunity to lose myself in their group until I reach my room. Oblivious, they linger in front of a room three doors down where they continue their boisterous chatter. Hands shaking, I clumsily slide my room card, relief washing over me when I see the green light, and then quickly lock and bolt myself inside. My palms are sweating and my heart's pounding. One by one, I hit switches until the room is bathed in light. Adrenalin courses through me and unable to remain still, I begin pacing, trying to figure out what I should do next. I need to report the incident to the front desk, but just as my hand reaches for the phone, I imagine the Italians at the front desk snickering as they report that some hysterical American woman claims she was chased by a masked man in one of the hotel corridors. I can hear it now.

"So, Signorina Cesare, you say you were returning from the Il Foyer Bar this evening when a man in a ski mask started chasing you?"

"Yes."

"Did anyone else…" snicker … snicker "…see this masked man?"

"No, but he chased me until I reached my room and …"

"So you were alone when you left the bar?"

"Yes."

"What did you enjoy drinking at the bar this evening?"

"Champagne."

"Our champagne is the best. How many glasses did you have?"

There wouldn't be any need to continue. The implications would be obvious. No, this was best left unreported. I wish Beth and Andre were here, but they continued on to the Park Royale Hotel and weren't sure they could join me tonight. My fear turns to anger when I think that I willingly complied with Chase's request to stay at The Four Seasons instead of The Park Royale where I could be enjoying the company of friends instead of running from some maniac. And where was the damn control freak anyway? Probably off protecting Devin whatever-her-name-is. I undress, wash up, and make vain attempts to calm down, but as soon as my tension ebbs, it's replaced by empty sadness. Exhausted, I slip under the covers naked and bringing my knees up, curl into a ball. The tears start as soon as my head hits the pillow so I turn into it and sob. Eventually, drained and empty, I drift off into an unsettled somnolence.

The last thing I remember are his words. "I will do anything to keep you safe … anything."

CHAPTER EIGHTEEN

*g*roggy from a restless night where nightmares of speeding space ships manned by faceless forms had me running from one deadly confrontation to another, I drag myself out of bed. Keep me safe, my ass. Since I took up with that man I've had nothing except headache and heartache, but a morning kissed by sunshine has a way of clearing the mind. The warmth of the sun when I step onto the balcony sooths my ire and dissipates last night's memory until it's nothing more than some misconceived notion of danger. Still, I find myself checking my door is bolted and peering through the peephole to confirm that it's room service delivering my ordered triple espresso on ice and not some masked maniac.

I crave the relaxation of a bath and fill the large tub with warm water, adding lavender bath crystals and lighting my scented candle. I sink into the soothing suds and lie back to unwind. Sipping my coffee, I relax. The urge to sketch is paramount, and my imagination conjures up the finishing touches on my current design: a soft suede wrap coat that falls just above the knee. I imagine it worn over sleek silk pants and matching top.

Toweled and dressed, I pin my hair in a loose wrap and get to work, using the natural sunlight to ease into the gentle curves and sharp angles of different designs. Sketching is mind cleansing, and soon everything is swept away except the contour, drape, and color of my rendering. The trick is imagining how it should drape. Should it dance or fall sleek and straight, or perhaps be a combination of the two. With each line and curve, it develops its own personality until it pops off the page in a swirl of movement and grace. This is a gentle catharsis for me, one that simultaneously empties and fills as it carries me to sated contentment.

It's a grumbling stomach that makes me realize I haven't eaten, so I stop to order a quick lunch from room service. When it arrives, the minestrone soup is hot, allowing the grated parmigiano reggiano cheese to melt on top. There are two slices of freshly baked bread that are still warm from the oven, and I dig in with gusto. Within twenty minutes I'm back at work, not wanting to waste the natural light on a long lunch break. Exhausted, I stop around five and check for messages. Beth texts a good luck wish for tomorrow night and writes that she's extending her trip to travel to London and visit her aunt. I plan to stick to my original plan and return home the day after the awards ceremony to prepare for job interviews and my move into my new apartment. I close my eyes and will myself not to shed another tear for Chase. But they come anyway, so I cover my eyes with my hand and quietly sob. Taking in deep breaths, I wipe my eyes and blow my nose, suddenly realizing that someone is going to have to reach out first to break this ridiculous silence. Keeping it simple, I text him, "miss u," but before I can hit send, my phone pings and a message appears. My breath catches when I see it's from him.

It reads simply, "There's no sun without you."

And once again I start to cry but these tears don't hurt, and soon I'm laughing and crying from the relief that those words unleash. The ring of my phone catches me by surprise and when I answer I hear that familiar deep voice and think there is no greater joy than this moment.

"Hi, it's me." He pauses, the lilt of concern catching in his voice when he asks, "How are you?"

Let's see, I inwardly muse. *Nearly killed by a drunk boater, dumped unceremoniously by a first lover, chased by a masked madman …*

"I'm good," I lie, taking a deep breath and wiping tears from my eyes. "How is everything back home?"

"No worse than before I left Italy."

His voice is sad. I want to take him in my arms and sooth away his troubles, but obviously I can't, so I opt for the next best thing and say, "I wish you were here."

"Yeah, me too. Do you have time to talk? I mean what are

your plans for the evening?"

"Just lying low. I sketched most of the day. So I'll pack and turn in early. I leave first thing in the morning."

I hear him sigh, and I'm not sure if it's relief or regret I sense before he says, "That sounds smart. Give yourself the opportunity to prepare for your big night, tomorrow."

"You remembered."

"Of course I remember. Listen I …"

I don't let him finish. "It's ok. I understand. There are problems you need to address at home." I close my eyes before asking, "How is your um … friend doing?"

He pauses as if trying to think who I mean. "Devin?"

"Yes." And I hold my breath because I don't know if I'm ready for what might follow.

It's obvious they have a shared history and a close bond, so when he answers, "She's holding up," in an aloof and noncommittal tone, I exhale in relief.

"That's good. And you? Please tell me you are keeping safe."

"I'm fine. What about you?" I pause for too long because he adds tersely, "Is there something you're not telling me?"

"No, I … it's nothing really. It's just that I thought there was someone following me last night when I left the hotel bar and was heading back to my room."

I'm deliberately vague so as not to give him added worry but realize this is not going to be easy when he asks, "You were alone? Where's Beth and her Frenchman?"

Will he ever call him by his name? "Beth and Andre had other plans."

"Did you see who it was?"

"Well …" I hesitate again, then finish saying, "Not exactly."

His strained, raised voice brusquely responds, "I can always tell when you are holding something back. Did you or did you not see this person?"

Well, that didn't take long. Two minutes into a long-distance conversation and he's full of reproof and demands.

Tentatively, I add, "I couldn't tell. I believe a man judging by his height and build, but he was wearing a mask, a ski mask I think, so I couldn't make out his features."

"What the fuck?" A ski mask! Are you sure?"

"Yes. But he disappeared after I ran into a group of people returning from a party."

"Did you report the incident?"

"No."

He's mad. There's a string of mumbled swearing and I'm pretty sure I hear him punch a wall, making me jump even though I'm four thousand miles away. I hate when he does that, but I don't say anything and the long pause on his end tells me he's trying to rein in his temper.

I finally hear a long exhale of breath and in a husky murmur, he asks, "Are you ok?"

"Yes. I must be a walking target these days." I laugh nervously and when he doesn't respond, I take advantage of the silence to lighten the mood. "It's lonely here without you, very quiet. No one to criticize my driving … let me know I've drunk too much, tell me I'm reckless." I smile because I hear a snort of laughter, before I softly add, "No one to kiss. Or hold …" I swallow and pause before whispering, "Or love." I want to feel the warmth of his arms around me. God, I miss him.

"Yeah, I miss you too." He sounds distant as if he's drifting away from me.

A sorrowful aloofness clings to the flatness of his tone and with this unexpected shift of mood, I feel tears welling again. His quick return to business snaps me back to reality.

"Listen, I have to make a quick call and then I'm going to phone you right back. Do not leave your room until you hear from me."

Now I hear alarm in his brusqueness and I desperately want to put him at ease. "I'm fine, really. There's no need to be concerned."

"For God's sake, don't give me a hard time about this." Panic clings to his words making me tremble, and I don't realize I've been holding my breath until I start to answer.

"Alright, I promise to stay put."

He's quickly gone, and I barely have time to pace the length of the suite before my phone tone jingles, startling me even though I'm expecting the call.

"Hey, it's me." His voice is still clipped but softer, and I know he's attempting to stay calm for my benefit.

"Hi …" He doesn't give me the chance to add anything more.

"Listen, Sammy is coming. He would have been there sooner, but he had an accident. He's at the hospital."

I don't understand why Sammy is still in Milan. I assumed he was helping Chase back home, but concern trumps curiosity. "My god, is he going to be alright?"

"He's fine. He's under observation for a concussion and he got some stitches in his head, but he figures he'll be released within the hour and then he's going to spend the night in your suite. Do not open your door for anyone but Sammy. And no room service. If you're hungry, eat something from the mini bar. Don't leave your room until you have to check out tomorrow and then only with Sammy."

My mind is slow to register his words and maneuvering through them, it checks off each command, but the meaning behind them remains elusive, like peering through a window during a heavy rainstorm. I notice the contour of the room still looks the same. The bed, flanked by the night table and lamp, is where it has been since I arrived. Just beyond is a table with a vase of flowers and a bowl of fresh fruit on top. I can always eat the fruit if I get hungry later. No need to overpay for lousy food from the mini bar. My drifting is interrupted by a loud command that makes me jump.

"Alicia, are you there? I need you to focus. Did you hear what I just said?"

I shake my head to clear it and tracing the fingers of my left hand across my mouth, I let them linger before removing them to answer. "I'm here." And those two words thrust me back to a reality riddled with unanswered questions I can't seem to ask. Instead, I say, "Do you want me to call you when Sammy gets here?"

"Yes, do that."

It seems premature to end the conversation here. When I realize what I need to ask, an awareness ignites, revealing that once answered there would no turning back to the false security not knowing offered. Staring straight ahead, I close my eyes and plunge ahead anyway.

"Chase, is someone deliberately trying to hurt me?"

The pause of no more than seconds seems interminable, and in that silence I have my answer.

That's why I'm not surprised when he answers, "Maybe. I think at the very least someone is trying to frighten you."

"But why? What could I have done to warrant these attacks?" I sputter in disbelief.

His answer is slow and heavy, each word cloaked in shrouds of regret that I have to strain to hear.

"You date me. It's because he wants to hurt me."

I can't believe what I'm hearing. I know Chase had a shady past, but this is beyond anything I ever imagined. "Who? Is it that rapist?"

I'm still trying to make sense of something my mind deems delusional. I hear a deep sigh and know that it pains him to have to continue, and for the first time since we met, I'm not sure I want to hear what he has to say. I drag over the desk chair and force myself to sit in anticipation of what's to follow.

"I didn't want to have to tell you this over the phone. I thought if I left things would stop, but they haven't, and given what's been happening, you have a right to know the truth. He pauses, and I imagine him pacing, staring straight ahead while massaging the back of his neck with the palm of his hand.

"His name is Dimitri Ostopenko. He's a high-ranking member of a Russian gang that runs an international drug and arms cartel. He's ruthless and stops at nothing to get what he wants."

"My god." Rubbing my right temple, I attempt to loosen the band of tension that makes my head feel like it's trapped in a vise. Disbelief leaks through my filter of fear and I sputter, "But … but I don't understand. Why does someone like that want to hurt you? How do you even know him?"

Chase's quiet magnifies any surrounding sounds. Somewhere in the far end of the room, a clock ticks. A door shuts in the hallway and the rattle of room service dishes clank on a service cart with the cushioned *tap, tap, tap* of rubber soled work shoes following. I relax only when the footsteps disappear down the hallway. The light in the room continues to fade as night approaches and still Chase remains on the line. It's as if he's afraid to let go of the only connection that bridges the miles that separate us. I hear him breathing in and out, undertones of air swollen with pent up anger and frustration. He is struggling to find the right words and when they finally come, they reverberate in my mind like some old malfunctioning CD that repeats one stanza of a song over and over again.

"Dimitri Ostopenko is the man I photographed raping Devin."

CHAPTER NINETEEN

The light taping on my door startles. I look up and stare in its direction, waiting until I hear it again. Following Chase's instructions, I ease my way toward the door and peek through the peephole. Sammy's broad frame fills the aperture, and I quickly unlock the door and let him in. There is a bloodied bandage above his left eye and a bump the size of a golf ball protrudes from his temple. He immediately steps in and turns to lock and bolt the door. I throw my arms around him, relieved to see he's ok and here to help, then involuntarily wince when I get a close up look of his injuries.

Mouth twisted in a sardonic grin, he snorts, "You should see the other guy." I grab some ice from the bucket, wrap it in a linen napkin, and hold it to his forehead.

"Now how does this look? You doctoring me when I'm supposed to be looking after you."

"It's the least I can do." The words tumble from my mouth before I can stop them. "You were attacked trying to help me last night, weren't you?"

"More like jumped from behind. I lost you after getting caught in a group of partiers, and then when I figured you had taken a wrong turn, I followed but someone was smart enough to catch me by surprise. Don't worry. He won't be coming back any time soon."

Sammy flexes his fist and squints his eye, before taking the napkin of ice from me and holding it to his bump. There's something simultaneously ferocious yet discreet about Sammy. He walks with the lithe, quick movement of a cheetah that packs the strength of a lion. I notice how powerfully wide and strong his hands and biceps are and imagine that he could easily kill with those bare hands.

"Why don't you go and try to get some rest. I'll bunk here on the sofa and get you up in the morning to check out. Be sure to lock your bedroom door."

I nod but first head toward the minibar, bending to take out two small bottles of gin and a tonic water. Tonight white wine won't cut it.

"Care to join me?"

Sammy shakes his head. He is on duty and, like Chase, he takes his job seriously. I'm relieved because I really don't need someone who's been drinking on the lookout for a thug who may want me dead. I give him another quick hug, go into my room, and shut and lock the door. I pour myself a gin and tonic, take a few sips and when I begin to relax, decide to call home. There is something about the familiarity of family that I crave. My mother picks up after the second ring and her throaty voice is tinged with pleasant surprise when she hears my voice.

"Alicia, honey, how are you?"

She sounds strong, vibrant, and I'm thrilled that she's up and about.

"I'm good."

My voice catches and I immediately clear it but obviously not in time because she asks, "What's wrong? Are you alright?"

What is it about mothers that enable them to detect distress in their children even from a distance of 4,000 miles? I take another large gulp before forcing myself to calmly answer, "I'm fine. How are you feeling?"

"Much better thanks to this new doctor I'm seeing and different medication I've started. The combination of medication and therapy is helpful, and he's easy to talk to. But enough about me. What have you been doing? How is Milan?"

"Milan is wonderful." I take another sip. "I sketched most of today, and I'm leaving for Lake Como in the morning."

"I know. For your awards ceremony. We wish we could be there." Her tone tapers in regret before she is interrupted by my father, who I hear in the background asking who's on the phone.

She buoyantly calls out, "It's Alicia," and then quickly tells me, "Alicia, your father wants to speak to you."

I breathe a sigh of relief because I wasn't sure how long I could maintain the serenity facade. Our conversation is brief. He asks how I am, where I'm staying, and if I need anything and then satisfied with my answers, tells me to be careful, says he loves me, and hangs up. I'm sure my mother wasn't finished talking, but as soon as my father has all his questions answered, he's onto whatever's next.

Despite my predicament, I feel lighter, spirited, and more hopeful. It's possible that, with Sammy and Mac's help, we can tackle this problem. I don't want Chase to think I can't be counted on, that I'm like some porcelain doll that cracks if not protected and coddled. It's infuriating how he suddenly left, thinking that would keep me from danger. Ironically, it found me anyway and we were both miserable in the process. That man needs serious reminders on how to maintain a relationship. I finish my drink, undress, and climb under the cool sheets, leaving my nightgown draped over the end of the bed. Fear and fatigue war in my mind, but weariness wins and I drift into a dreamless sleep that even nightmares refuse to visit.

Check out goes well. No attempted assaults, viscous pursuits, or vengeful threats. Just me, a solicitous clerk, Chase's credit card—in absentia—and one bodyguard.

Even though it's morning, the rocking of the car sooths

me into an easy doze. When I wake, I see we are driving down an avenue lined with cypresses and magnolias that leads to the opulent grounds of what looks like some sort of villa. I have no idea why we are here and uneasy, I start to check off all the things I need to do to get ready for tonight: washing and styling my hair, deciding what I am going to wear, plucking, tweezing, shaving and completing all other sorts of unpleasant necessities, as well as applying a decent amount of makeup before deeming myself ready. And I have to prepare some words to say when I'm announced. Butterflies flutter in my stomach.

"Sammy, do we need to stop here? I don't want to rush you, but I have to get to my hotel."

"We are at your hotel." He gets out, opens my door, and greets a bellman dressed in charcoal gray and starched eagerness.

I shake my head to clear the lethargy from my nap and follow Sammy through a magnificent entrance. Once inside, I whisper tersely, "There's been a mistake. There is no way I can afford to stay here." Then realization clicks and scowling, I squint pointedly at him. "Did Chase make these arrangements?"

"Yep."

"But why?" My voice is strident, strained in frustration.

"Don't know."

Ugh, his uncommunicativeness is as annoying as Chase's, but I'm not deterred.

"Well, you're going to just have to turn around and take me to the hotel I originally booked."

It's perfectly suitable and I abruptly trek back to the car that is exactly where we left it, although our suitcases have been removed. I slam the door to the passenger seat and sit with arms crossed, staring at a blanket of green that stretches for miles. No matter. Thug or no thug, there is no way I'm letting Chase dictate where I stay without the common courtesy of a discussion. Besides, I can't continue to accept extravagant gifts from someone who slept with me and then left, even if I understand the reasons. Fact is, he's not here and I have no idea when I will see him next. I push down the lump beginning to form in my throat as tears threaten. Better to hang onto the anger, much less painful than rejection. Sammy gets into the driver's seat and says nothing for the longest time.

Then, leaning his head toward me and raising his eyebrows, he casually asks, "Are you going to be the one to tell him or are you going to make me do it?"

I pinch the top of my nose with my two fingers and close my eyes, because the truth is I don't want to have to deal with Chase and I can't, in good conscience, push Sammy into an argument with him after all Sammy has done to help. The two of them have each other's backs, and it would seem as if Sammy didn't do his job if I didn't cooperate.

"Fine. I'll check in, but be sure to communicate to the control tower that I don't plan on eating anything here. Probably costs fifty Euros for a damn sandwich," I mutter, slamming the car door.

It's infuriating how even from another continent the man remains in charge. And why does he continue to spend money on me? Can't the damn fool see that it's him I care about and not all this opulence? It's like he has some potted money bush growing on the terrace of his swank Park Avenue penthouse and all he has to do is pluck some hundreds to toss my way to make everything alright.

One long look at the splendor the Hotel Villa d'Este is enough to give me second thoughts. Nestled on the banks of Lake Como, it is surrounded by a spread of grass and garden. Chestnut, cypress, and palm trees cluster along footpaths dotted with azaleas and hydrangeas. Such a glorious path to stroll with a lover … Wrong focus to visit now, and I safely shift to logistics. Villa Passalacqua, the site of the awards ceremony, is only about a mile away and easily accessible by car. That will help add to preparation time and clutching my cosmetic case and purse, I walk ahead with Sammy to check in. The hotel clerk is all efficiency when I give him my name.

"Your room is ready Signorina Cesare. This is Elio. He will show you the way." An elegantly dressed gentleman in a dark jacket and bowtie elaborately holds out his arm as if ushering in the queen of England. Even though I have no idea where I'm going, I lead the way because it seems to be protocol. When we reach the room, Elio steps forward, opens the door, and waves out his arm for me to enter. It's like I've been selected to appear in some Pomp and Circumstance Reality Show.

The suite is fashioned in cherry-colored Como silk with a draped king-sized bed that looks like it sleeps six, yet another depressing reminder that I'm flying solo. Sammy ignores my repetitive sighs and silently watches Elio place my suitcases on a wooden table laced with canvas straps. Sammy does a quick walk-through then mutters something about having to leave for a bit. The realization that he's probably going to case the place is sobering. I have stepped into a world that I had previously only read and heard about in the media. The click of the room door shutting and the ensuing silence shifts my eyes toward the small balcony that looks out onto the lake. Stepping out, I look across the breadth of green-blue water and snow-capped mountains, and I have to commend Chase's choice over the smaller, cramped quarters where I would have been staying. Still, I would trade locations in a heartbeat for just one glimpse of him. The empty feeling makes my body ache to its core.

I don't know how long I remain rooted there but thoughts of the evening ahead eventually pull me inside and once there, my eyes are riveted to an item I hadn't noticed earlier. Resting on top of the far corner of the bed is a beautifully wrapped box. I walk over and pick it up. Tucked into the ribbon is a card printed with my name.

I open the small envelop and read:

For the woman who paints my world beautiful.

I scan the room but there's no one, except I do spot another wrapped package on top of the armoire. It also has a card labeled with my name and when I open it, I read:

My world changed when you stepped into my life. xo.

Behind this is yet another wrapped box, from Tiffany's I think, with a card that reads: *To the gem of my life, with love.*

I have no time to decipher the spin of these words because in the dimly lit corridor of the bathroom a shadow casts a familiar shape. I don't speak. I don't think. I just run and jump into his arms, and he lifts and spins me laughing. I kiss every inch of his face from his eyes to his cheeks, until finally my lips move to capture his. Lowering me, he deepens the kiss, slowly raising my dress and cupping my buttocks in a tight hard grasp. Fear and anger dissolve along with any need for explanations, and I fold into Chase's arms, relishing his soft breath on my neck.

"Ah, baby, I've missed you." And I melt further into the timbre of his voice.

It isn't until he gently wipes tears from my cheeks with his thumbs that I realize I'm crying.

"I'm so sorry. I never meant to hurt you." It's a painstaking and sorrowful admission, but I don't let him continue.

Instead, I take his hands in mine and kiss each before wrapping them around my waist. There will be plenty of time later to talk about why he left.

Cupping his face in my hands, and looking into his eyes, I shake my head in disbelief and stutter, "When … how …" before gathering my thoughts and continuing, "Were you able to get here so quickly?"

"I told one of my buddies I had an important event I promised to attend, that there was no way it could be missed, and that it involved the most beautiful woman I had ever met. So, he agreed to loan me his private jet complete with pilot and crew."

Poof. Just like that, another indispensable "brother" appears, who will do anything to help. It doesn't take me long to realize that he must have planned this all along because there is no way he could have pulled all of this together so quickly. He bends his lips again to mine and kisses me, grazing and gently tugging my lower lip with his teeth before thrusting his tongue inside, and I feel I have reached an oasis after combing a desert floor. Here. Now. At this very moment in time is when I know that I've fallen in love with this man. And it's not the gifts or endearments that have transformed a young girl's crush into heartfelt feelings of love and appreciation. It's having him here. It's understanding the sacrifices he made to be here, that he left a hornet's nest back home to participate in my professional celebration, that despite having to address potential serious harm to his family and friend, he still behaves like I matter, that my achievements are important. And it's here and now that I realize he will continue to encourage, participate in, and make sacrifices to foster my success. It's who he is and how he thinks. It's the part of him that's selfless, the part that can facilely shift words spoken and promises made into actions that, even at the young age of twenty-one, I understand are indispensable. The realization renders me speechless.

"You. Taste. So. Sweet." He buries his head in my neck, softly nibbling and kissing until my belly quickens and my legs weaken. In a heavy whisper, he adds, "I want to devour you." I groan and reach up to pull him closer, but he resists. And just as quickly as he began, he pulls away. "But I can't. You have a big evening ahead with presents to open and services to enjoy." Holding me at arm's length, he walks to the largest package and offers it to me.

"A present? Why? It's not my birthday."

"No," he says, hooded blue eyes gazing into mine as he gently strokes my cheek with the back of his hand, "But it is your moment."

I unwrap the box, gently lifting the tissue paper to find the most elegant dress I have ever seen. I stroke the sapphire-colored fabric, holding it up to admire its sleek, simple lines. The design is magnificent, draping low in the back with a side slit that continues from the ankle to the knee. Also tucked in the box, is a sheer matching shawl to drape over my shoulders.

"It's beautiful. Thank you and thank you for thinking I make your world beautiful."

I attempt to take him in my arms, but he holds me away. "Open this next." He hands me the smaller narrower box. Excitedly, I tear off the wrapping paper and inside are a pair of black T-strap high-heeled shoes with tiny sapphire crystal clasps. Holding them gingerly in my hands, I stroke the soft leather and look up at a loss of words.

He steps closer, folding my hair behind my ear, before

lowering his head and whispering in my ear, "Later, I am going to fuck you long and hard in nothing but those shoes."

I lean into the soft wisp of his words and my lower belly strums in anticipation. Reaching down, I attempt to wrap my hand around his member, knowing that it would be impossible for him to ignore the enticement, but he grabs it midway and slowly takes my pointer finger in his mouth and sucks before gently pulling it out and taking me to package number three. I'm panting with need and can wait for the gift, but he hands me the package and insists I open it now. Exhaling, I blow strands of hair off my forehead in an attempt to cool down. I'd forgotten how long and far he can extend his self-control. I turn to my gift and open the soft white ribbon and remove a dark velvet blue box. Inside there are a pair of pearl earrings that extend from an elegant white gold base with two small diamonds on each side. I step forward and placing my lips on his, I reach lower with my hand to once again palm his penis, which I notice with a smug smile is lengthening. This time he groans, pressing into my hand and allows me one kiss before disengaging and holding me at arm's length.

"Tonight is your night and now is your time to prepare. I've arranged for a series of beauty treatments for you at the spa."

We have so much to discuss, to attempt to resolve, but for this moment all I want is to revel in his touch. I look up and pout, reminding him that there's nothing like steamy sex to clear the mind and beautify the face. His response is an appointment printout showing me where and when I am to go for facial, massage, and hairstyling.

"Do I look that bad that I need a complete makeover," I say, trying to bait him to come closer. It works.

He reaches out lifting my sundress and tickles my thigh with the soft up and down motion of his fingertips. "Everything about you is beautiful. I missed you so much it hurt to breathe." And grabbing me in an embrace, he nibbles my earlobe, grazing it with his teeth before he lifts his head and gravelly whispers, "If I had my way, I'd tear these clothes off you and ride you until you scream out my name."

Heavens alive. *How does he know to say these things?* I pull him closer, clutching his shirt collar, pushing his mouth toward mine, until I can thrust my tongue to meet his. He slowly slides his fingers up my arms before disengaging with a frustrated groan. He grasps my chin, gently lifting it, allowing me to meet his gaze. He's smoking hot, eyes shuttered, body tense, and yes, lower extremity raised. Leaning his head back, he gently strokes my cheek. "Not now. We have the whole evening after you receive your award."

Frustrated, I grab the info from his hand and turn away mumbling, "Promises, promises. Just don't decide to disappear."

As soon as the words are out of my mouth I regret them. He looks dejected, head bent, mouth pulled taut with one eye squinting, lost in regretful recall.

"I didn't mean that." Taking him at arm's length, I give

him a peck on the check. Any closer contact and I'd ignite. He smiles pointing to the door as my cue to get moving.

"Be sure to wear those tight sexy boxer shorts later. They'll provide a good show when I tear off your clothes and jump your body at the awards ceremony." I tug the door closed before he can respond and head to some kind of cucumber, vitamin C, oxygen blast, exfoliating facial.

Later, waxed, clipped, plucked, polished, and primped, I return to finish dressing. My hair is swept behind in a loose, low twist that compliments the plunging back of my dress and the graceful dangle of the pearl earrings. I slip on sheer thigh-high stockings, noticing that their lacy tops blend with the garter belt and skin-colored lace and satin panties and … I'm not the only one noticing. Chase sits at the leather-topped writing table and glances in my direction as I dress. When I finish, I walk toward him. He stands and when we lock eyes, it's hard to determine who's staring at who more. He looks ravishing: tall, lean torso, flat stomach, broad shoulders, all tucked neatly inside his suit. I run my tongue across my lower lip and continue to stare. God only knows how I'm going to get through the long evening without undressing and tackling him to the ground. He takes me at arm's length, eyes worshipping, and I don't think I've ever felt more cherished. No need for words, he takes my hand and leads me to the car for our drive to Villa Passalacqua.

CHAPTER TWENTY

lanked by stretches of manicured gardens, Villa Passalacqua is at the top of the list for refinement and elegance. And the parade of luxury cars, it's like a motor show. Maserati, Mercedes, Rolls Royce and Lamborghinis breeze up the roadway to the villa. With the excitement of a little boy looking at his model car collection, Chase points them all out, stopping to remark on a Lamborghini Hurácan.

"Look at that uniqueness," he gushes. "Remarkable rear end, small yet edgy with unbelievable looks and performance. She's a real beauty." Eyes dancing with mischievous mirth, he glances at me sideways. "Riding in that baby is pure bliss."

"Yeah, well the driver better perform as well as he does innuendo, or she may just rev up on her own." Without waiting, I get out only to stop and stare slack-jawed at the opulence ahead.

Wrapping his arm around me, he whispers in my ear, "I can assure you his clutch precision and shaft control are impeccable."

Before I can say another word, he takes my hand and leads me up stone steps toward a pair of Venetian bronze doors. They open into a vestibule where someone waits to tag off our names and complete the registration process. Inside, a spiral white marble staircase covered with plush red carpeting is lined with waiters holding silver trays with crystal glasses of champagne on top. Large urns of hydrangeas occupy both sides of the entry hall and stylishly attired guests fill the room. To say I'm overwhelmed is an understatement, and it isn't until Chase gently raises my hand and kisses it that I realize I have been clutching his in a viselike grip.

He leans down and whispers in my ear, "You are the most beautiful woman in this room."

I take a deep breath and relax, more from the proximity of his lingering breath on my neck than his compliment. Scanning the room, I spot Toni Townshend, fashion editor of Belle magazine, exuding kick-ass attitude in a bold, tapered tuxedo with a low cut ecru silk tank. At the far side of the room, to my left, Francois Georges, world renowned fashion and portrait photographer, chats with fashion designer Ralph Soren.

Panic and excitement collide, and I scoop a filled champagne flute from a statuesque waiter costumed in some formal garb from eons ago and take a swallow to attempt to relax. It doesn't work. My heart pounds up to my throat and back down again, my palms are sweating, and my stomach flutters with butterflies. At this rate I'll need a tranquilizer gun to calm down.

Chase looks at me, eyebrows knitted together and remarks quietly, "Breathe, Alicia. You can do this." Then staring straight ahead, tersely adds, "But I might have to poke the eyes out of some of these old men who are eye banging you."

I look at him as if he's sprung a second head. I'm that sure I'm the last person anyone is noticing in this room. But then just ahead, I see a well-dressed gentleman sporting impeccably groomed white hair, with matching trimmed goatee and deep blue eyes that burrow into me. He nods and raises his glass in a silent salute. I revert my eyes back to Chase and pull my best poker face that has never been convincing but is still better than admitting he's right and giving him cause to knock the guy out along with any prospective job opportunities.

"Not going to work, sweetheart." Eyes fixed on me, he nods. "Santa Claus, three o'clock, just begging to have that leering grin knocked off his face."

It's as if we're on a military expedition instead of a fashion soiree, and I roll my eyes in disbelief.

"Mock all you want. You may think these assholes are interested in the artistic merit of your portfolio, not that you're not gifted or that it isn't creative..." he quickly pauses, raising his hands palms up to accentuate the comment "...but most are perusing with their dicks for the quickest way into the panties of the fresh new kid on the block."

"As if I would ever let that happen."

Before I can say anything more, the lights dim and a spotlight is shone on the staircase, hushing the crowd. The music from the pianist in the adjoining music room mellows and attendants dressed in tuxedos with pink silk bowties and matching cummerbunds herd us to either side of the staircase in preparation for the fashion show that's about to start. Eyes travel toward the uppermost balcony where a parade of models descend the wide spiraling staircase. One at a time, they pause on each level to turn and display clothing that ranges from long dresses with bold geometric shapes to athletic wear that doesn't resemble anything I would ever wear on a sweaty jog. I notice the third to descend is wearing a cropped smoky gray jacket. My eyes follow in stunned wonder while my mind thrums with a disbelief that peers through a window of recognition. It's mine.

"Congratulations, baby," Chase whispers in my ear, and I can't help but match his ear-splitting grin.

The remainder of the show is a blur. My feet seem to hover and although I try to focus on the other winners, each seem to vanish inside a whirl of excitement. I never imagined what it could feel like to see my design worn with such professional elegance. It's thrilling.

There is a final round of applause as all the models complete the catwalk and disappear into one of the rooms. The lights brighten and we are quickly escorted into the music room where a podium stands. Vanilla-colored walls with antique Venetian chandeliers grace the walls and an ornate domed ceiling adds a palatial feel. Again, my heart pounds and my palms sweat. Breathing deeply, I slip into a surreal, out-of-body mode. The music stops and a slightly-built gentleman takes to the podium, silencing the standing audience with two outstretched hands that slowly wave in a downward motion. Speaking Italian first, then switching to English, he welcomes us, reiterates the purpose of the occasion, then introduces the chairwoman and creative director of the fashion event and contest. She is groomed in a floral dress that softly cascades to her calves with beautifully crafted Carlo Pazolini shoes peeking out. In Italian, she discusses the entries and with a fluid motion of her hand, invites all the chosen candidates to the podium. When I reach that part of the room, I look into the audience and immediately spot Chase. Our eyes lock and it's with newfound lucidity that I decide what I'm going to say. It's a good thing too because it isn't long before I hear my name announced.

Moving toward, the microphone with a grace and fluidity I hadn't known I possessed, I pause momentarily and begin. "Tonight I am reminded of Robert Browning who wrote, 'Ah, but a man's reach should exceed his grasp, or what's a heaven for?' Thank you for making my envisioned design a reality and for allowing me to lengthen my reach with this honor. A heartfelt thank you, also, to that special someone in my life who helps me believe I should always reach for the stars."

Rocked by the applause and riding on a cloud of euphoria, I float back to my spot next to Chase. Brushing his fingertips down my arms, he takes me in a hug and chastely kisses me on the lips. The consummate gentleman with the business acumen of a professional, he knows where to draw the line at a public forum. It's a good thing too, because just that light brush of his lips makes me ache for his touch.

The other winning contestants find their way to the microphone and instead of listening, I find myself craving the feel of his arms around me, imagining his tongue thrusting in my mouth and his hands caressing, fingers moving, oh those magic fingers, circling and touching those hidden places. I don't actually moan, but I am startled by the mellow voice of a man who interrupts my foreplay fantasy with an extended hand.

"Miss Cesare?"

"Yes." I glance up, a tad too quickly.

Standing in front of me is a gentleman with cognac-colored skin and a set of lucid hazel eyes that meet mine with such an encompassing sweep of knowing that I begin to feel guilty for my former naughty thoughts.

"I'm Robin Virgil May, artistic director at Estelle Designs. I hope I'm not interrupting anything." He smiles patiently waiting for me to respond.

My cheeks heat, but I shake his extended hand. "It's nice to meet you, Mr. May."

He looks left to right then back again, and I'm thinking

that maybe he's lost something, but before I can offer my help, he clutches his chest and quips, "Oh god, for a moment I thought my grandfather was here, risen from the dead, most likely straight from the depths of Hell if memory serves. He was Mr. May. Everyone calls me Virgil."

My mouth curves into a grin, both from his comment and his sweeping gaze up and down the length of Chase's taut torso.

"You must be the someone special." He pauses then continues, eyes wide, voice a low, slow crescendo. "Mmm hmm. You'd make me grasp for the stars also." As if he hadn't just said anything out of the ordinary, Virgil extends his hand to Chase and introduces himself.

Chase takes it, clears his throat, and replies, "Chase. Chase Reardon."

He pointedly keeps eye contact, and although his face reveals nothing, I can see by the slight narrowing of his left eye and the upward tilt of his head the wheels in his mind turning. Then obviously satisfied that there's no way in hell Virgil is ever going to attempt to get into my panties, he offers to get us some champagne.

Virgil follows his departing with a shamelessly decadent stare and nodding his head, murmurs, "Your Mr. Chase is a chaser," before giving me his full attention and continuing. "Well, Miss Cesare, I was hoping I could have a few words with you."

I stop worrying my bottom lip with my teeth to fight back a grin. "Of course, and please, call me Alicia."

"Alicia, congratulations on your winning design. There's no doubt that my team at Estelle is impressed with its elegance and timeless simplicity." He's all business now, his compliment measured, tone formal, and I get the impression that despite his former playfulness, Robin Virgil May is a perfectionist with a keen eye for aesthetics and an astute business mind. "There's a small group of us here who are interested in meeting with you. Is that a possibility?" he continues.

I'm stunned. I wrap my mind around his question as it processes his credentials and the prestigious brand he represents.

"My flight leaves tomorrow evening. When were you interested in meeting, Virgil?"

"In the morning. Does nine o'clock work?

"Yes, sure."

"Do you know the Villa d'Este?"

"I do, I'm actually staying there."

He appraises me for a moment, probably wondering how a young upstart can afford such elegant accommodations, then hiding any initial surprise smoothly continues, "We're all set. See you at the Villa D'Este restaurant. Oh, and bring any up to date work you may have. We understand you are traveling, but even a few sketches of your designs will work."

"Yes, thank you, Virgil. I look forward to seeing you tomorrow at nine." We shake hands and he vanishes into a cluster of mingling guests.

By the time Chase returns, carrying two champagne

glasses, I'm wired with excitement.

"Guess, what?" I don't wait for a response before rambling on. "I have an interview tomorrow morning. Well, I think it's an interview or it may be a preliminary meeting." I barely pause before breathlessly continuing, "With Virgil and his associates ... from Estelle Designs."

He places the untouched glasses on the nearest tray and wraps me in a hug, discreetly taking my earlobe in his mouth and scraping it with his teeth. "Very impressive, Miss Cesare," he whispers so close I can almost taste the champagne on his lips. "I'd say it's mission accomplished here. How about we leave and take some time to get ... reacquainted."

My breath quickens and an electrified shiver wraps around areas that have no business being aroused now. I mutely nod and he presses his hand to the small of my back and guides me through the exit where other guests have also started to leave.

Inside the darkened car, Chase doesn't wait long before pressing three kisses on my lips, the last one long and lingering. Reaching for the back of his head, I pull him closer and wanting more, my tongue easily slides in to meet his. Not breaking our kiss, I turn toward him and shift to my knees, leaning into his body and running my fingers through his hair. He slowly nibbles and tugs on my lower lip, sending shivers down my spine.

"I missed those lips, the way their soft and pliant at first, then turn insistent and needy."

We're both breathing heavily, and I have to restrain myself

from tearing open his shirt and running my fingers down the length of his chest. The beaming lights of another car spotlights us and Chase maneuvers me out of its glare. Hand on my breast, he teases my nipple with his thumb and forefinger. I let out a quiet pleading sigh as I feel it tense against the fabric of my dress and I instinctively reach between his legs to palm his lengthening member. He groans and presses into my hand. It's becoming more and more difficult to ignore the ever present lights of the other car, and I'm beginning to think its occupants are purposely stalling to watch. Oddly, I'm not bothered, but Chase pulls back his hand and sits up, taking me with him.

"I think it's time we take this to a more private place."

It seems my brain filter has not caught up to my libido that's now sprinting, because I blurt, "But not in a bed." Swallowing, I quickly murmur, "Are you ok with that?"

I catch the glimpse of a grin as his eyes darken with need. "Is that a trick question? Hell yeah, and I know the perfect spot." We draw apart and I sink into my seat as Chase calls out, "Show's over, buddy."

Once in motion, he takes my hand and gently strokes my knuckles with the pad of his thumb. "We've got a lot of catching up to do. I couldn't stop thinking about you when we were apart, what I wanted to do to you *here* …" He removes his thumb and strokes it across my bottom lip before lowering it to the side of my chin and slowly down my neck and across my collar bone. I lean into his touch feeling goose bumps spread up my arms. He lowers his hand down my chest. "And *here* …"

He gently tugs on my nipple, which is hotwired to points below, and even though he hasn't removed his eyes from the road ahead, he knows my body so well it's as if he's looking at me to reach all the right places to touch. My thighs squeeze together in a vain attempt to relieve the building heaviness and pushing them apart, he presses on my clit through my underpants with that same pad of his thumb, circling it in pressing arcs until I can't remain still anymore. My back arches from my seat as I press his thumb with my hand to increase the pressure. He pulls his hand back using it to shift gears and increase speed, and I bite back a frustrated groan.

Get it together, Alicia. I've become so addicted to this man's touch, I don't even want it in a bed *and* didn't even mind that someone was watching. What was with that? And as if that's not bad enough, my mind replays the past, reminding me that he suddenly leaves and just as suddenly returns dragging a shitload of baggage with him and no explanations. Now at the first sign of his attention, I throw myself at him. It doesn't get more pathetic.

"You're suddenly awfully quiet." He reaches over and smooths my furrowed brow with the same dangerous pad of his thumb that seems to be getting a lot of action during this short car ride.

The high from before kicks back into place when I realize that, ever since I took up with this man, my life has become a series of mood-altering adventures. Besides, who am I kidding? The minute he touches me, I smolder like a West Coast brush fire. I want him. And I know firsthand that the hurt caused by his absence is heavier than any emotional baggage he carries. We're just going to have to talk and work through our issues, but that can wait until after our "perfect spot" liaison. I stomp on the "you're so pathetic" mantra inside my head and wave a big hello to libido.

CHAPTER TWENTY-ONE

The spot is an awe inspiring plane tree on the Villa D'este grounds that stretches to the heavens, with a white trunk that spans the length of a meeting hall wall.

"You like?" he asks, eager for my approval. Overwhelmed, I can only nod.

He takes my arm and helps me across the tree's blanket of flattened roots and pushing me against the trunk, locks his lips onto mine. I let my shawl drop, and swept by the neediness of the press of his lips on mine, as if he's drowning and I'm what buoys him, I lean into the perfect fit of his body. Without breaking his kiss, he grips my hip and pulls my leg until it's wrapped around his waist. His hands fist in my hair, loosening the pins until it falls down my back. I moan as he pulls tighter, exposing my neck and moving his mouth to nip and suck behind my ear then down to my collarbone while his other hand slides to squeeze the curve of my ass. The heat of his kisses burn through my body, and I lean into the pressing firmness of his cock, pulling him closer by his collar, impatient to feel its thrust inside. The ache between my legs becomes heavier and acknowledging my need, he lowers his hand and slowly raises the hem of my dress, caressing my inner thigh before gradually slipping his forefinger under the silk of my panties and sliding it in. My breath hitches and he slips in another finger. I bury my head in his neck to keep from moaning.

"Please." My plea is so needy and breathless, I barely recognize it as mine.

He pushes in a third finger and my hips thrust forward in an attempt to deepen the insertion and satisfy my craving. He pulls his hand away, and I want to scream in frustration, but instead I pull him toward me by his jacket lapels and bite his lower lip before taking it in my mouth and sucking. Then I lower my shaking hands to unzip his pants and watch him spring loose. God, this man is well endowed. I take it and slide my hand up from the base to the head, pulling and tugging and relishing his groan of pleasure. Lowering myself, I take it in my mouth and suck long and hard while he grasps the back of my head and brings me closer. I look up to watch his teeth clench as he peers at me through hooded eyes.

But two can play this game and when he tells me, "Just about there, baby," I give one more wet, teasing slide of my mouth before releasing him and raining little kisses up its length. I should have known better.

Before I fully stand, he has me turned with my palms pressed against the surface of the bark and very close to my ear whispers, "Baby, that's not how it works here."

I shudder from the feel of his warm breath on my neck and the threatening delicious promise that clings to his words. Slowly lifting the hem of my dress, he guides the palm of his hand up my thigh before wrapping it around my waist and pulling up. My bottom thrusts out and with his other hand, he lowers my head. Then with one sharp, swift tug, he tears my panties, exposing my ass and gives it two hard slaps. I bite back a moan, not wanting to give him the satisfaction of knowing how hot this is.

"You like that little touch of roughness, don't you?"

So much for keeping it quiet. He circles my clit with that ever ready thumb, and shamelessly I push harder against the tree, wanting to feel more of him inside. "You are so fucking beautiful."

My body is on fire and I don't know how long I can hold on. He again inserts one, then two fingers, and I bite my lip and whimper. I refuse to beg, mostly because the devilish fiend will only use it to prolong my misery, but I'm panting with need, and it only takes one quick glance behind to see that he's aimed and ready.

Between clenched teeth I whisper, "I can't hold on much longer."

He finally tears open a condom I never even saw him take out, wraps his arm around my waist, holding me against him and thrusts inside. Hard. I nearly scream with pleasure from the intensity of the hit. He eases back and wraps his hands around mine before placing them back against the tree, and I know it is to cushion them from the harshness of the bark, but I don't care about that. All I want is him moving inside, thrusting and hitting that sweet spot, until I burst into rushing splinters of whiteness.

I don't have to wait long. Sliding in and out, he lowers our hands and thrusts harder, and I bend even further to give him more access. It must be exactly what I need, because I cry out his name and dissolve into waves of little deaths that continue to rise before subsiding into ripples that go on and on and on. He lets go of my hands and wraps his arm around my waist, holding me in position but eliminating the strain.

"Are you ok?" he whispers close to my ear and when I nod, he doesn't wait long to continue his thrusts like before. Legs quivering, arm muscles straining, he throws back his head and groans out his release.

I am boneless. If it wasn't for Chase still inside and holding me up by my waist, I may have sunk to the ground in exhaustion. My loose hair sticks to my back and beads of perspiration dot my forehead and neck.

"Christ, Alicia," he lets out between pants as our breathing gradually begins to slow.

He pulls out and straightens slowly, taking me with him, then adeptly removes and knots his condom and places it in his pocket. I turn to face him and stand on my toes to give him a soft kiss, because even in heels that rival stilts, I'm shorter. He deepens it and when we separate, he bends and retrieves my torn panties.

"Can't have some pervert walking by later and stealing them." I look at the torn shreds and frown. My favorite pair, but definitely worth every tear.

"Oh, you'd rather the pervert be you."

"Damn straight." With raised eyebrows and a wicked grin, he holds them up and sniffs before slipping them into his pocket.

Wobbling, I hold onto his side so I can remove my shoes. Walking in spikes, on knobby roots and soft grass, after an orgasm with a sex god can be challenging. Also, broken necks do not mix well with pending job interviews. Lifting my foot, I notice the gaping runs in my thigh highs and slip them off as well.

"C'mon, let's get you back to the room for some well-needed rest so you can wow them with your talent in the morning."

"Well, Reardon, you may think it's my talent they're interested in..." I look up, grimacing, and shaking my head "...but I happen to know for a fact that all they really want is a piece of your pretty ass," I taunt and then slap his backside—*hard*—before sprinting ahead like some Olympic runner who's just heard the gun go off.

He's on me in no time and taking me in his arms, begins tickling under my ribs until I'm twisting and turning and laughing so hard I'm ready to collapse.

"No, stop," I sputter between bouts of laughing that take my breath away and make me bend at the waist to try and escape.

"This is what wise asses get when they think they're funny." His tickling is relentless and ready to drop from his wiggling fingers, I futilely try to pry his hands away, but I'm laughing and gasping so hard it's impossible.

"Wait, I … no more, please …"

Finally, he takes pity and stops, wrapping and tightening his arms around me, and I snuggle into his embrace. He rests his chin on my head and breaths deeply.

"I want you running toward me, never away." He pulls my head back and gives me a long, tender kiss.

I'm breathless with neurons singing as they carry the meaning of his words to my consciousness and then back again. "That works two ways, Reardon."

Our eyes meet, and in that heartbeat of a moment, I see a lifetime of need and yearning before he shutters the gaze and nods, grasping my hand for our walk back to the room.

Inside, Elio eyes us with a knowing smile. "I see you have been enjoying our beautiful garden and its timeless tree." My face turns the color of the Communist flag sans sickle and star, but his eyes are kind. There's a slight tug of a grin before he relaxes his features and wishes us a pleasant evening.

I must look a mess. Wild hair, no stockings, shoes, *or* underwear. I attempt to smooth my hair in case we run into others, but the mirror ahead shows me I'm a walking just-fucked billboard so I give up. When we climb the magnificent staircase to reach our room, I spot Sammy in the distance and, although it's a balmy evening, an icy chill works its way up my spine. I nestle closer to Chase, wrap my arm around his waist, and rest my head in the crook of his arm, willing away masked mobsters and hoodlums.

CHAPTER TWENTY-TWO

y cell phone alarm pings for the third round. No matter. I am up and awake and trying on outfit number four. Do I wear the charcoal gray pencil skirt with matching jacket or the black linen dress and white blazer? I eliminate the gray suit because its jacket makes me seem like a live advertisement for my winning design. Maybe the black dress? No, too funereal. I pull out and try on a navy skirt and white silk blouse. Definitely not. Looks like a school uniform. Instead of preparing for a high-powered "woo 'em" interview, I'm spinning in a fashion freakout. Blowing hair from my eyes, I look up and catch Chase staring, propped up against pillows all sleepy eyed with rumpled, sexy as hell hair and a wide smile. He reaches for my wrist and pulls me on top of him.

"You look beautiful in all of them." He kisses the tip of

my nose, then my eyes, until he works his mouth down to my collarbone and … Not helping. I pull my head back.

"Thank you. But it's not that simple." I sit up, push my hair back with both hands, and take a deep breath before explaining. "I need to present as professional … but not boring or flat. Confident ... but not cocky or too bold. Intelligent … but not geeky or nerdy." Now I really don't know what to wear because instead of clarifying the situation, I've managed to push brain overdrive into full-fledged meltdown. I leap off the bed ready to mix and match yet another outfit when two simple sentences stop me in my tracks.

"Definitely the gray skirt and white silk blouse. Offset them with the black T-strapped shoes … nothing boring about them."

He's right. Put together it's a perfect ensemble. I smother his face with kisses and rush off to dress. The outfit feels like a hit. I present confidence and intellect, and when I pull my hair into a tight knot and offset it with the slight dangle of the pearl earrings, sophistication and elegance. Nothing depicts prudish austerity, which would be the kiss of death at this company.

I grab my portfolio, and Chase whispers close to my ear, "It's a good thing you're off to an important meeting, because looking as you do now, I would make sure to keep you *busy* for the rest of the day." He nuzzles his mouth near the back of my ear.

Leaning into his embrace, I inhale his musky scent before disengaging and shakily offering, "Wish me luck."

"No need for luck. Your talent speaks for itself. Go show 'em what you got."

Sunlight streams into La Veranda, the expansive windowed extension of Villa D'este that overlooks the lake on one side and a stretch of green garden splashed with beds of violet and yellow pansies on the other. Straight ahead "The Tree" looms, its tall, wide branches reaching like arms ready to embrace me for a repeat performance of last night. I shake my head to regain focus and drag my eyes, inside noticing planters of large dome-shaped hydrangeas along the perimeter of the room. Tables dressed in crisp white linen display plump strawberries, pink grapefruits, bunches of purple and green grapes, assorted rolls and breads and different cheeses and cured meats. Waiters in white jackets and black bow ties pour coffee from silver pots and fresh-squeezed orange juice from tapered crystal pitchers. I have no appetite right now, but the surrounding color and quiet elegance wake my senses and boost my confidence. Looking ahead, I once again see Elio, who nods in my direction as he pours orange juice to a portly guest seated at the far table. Does the man ever sleep?

Gripping the handles of the leather case of my portfolio, I turn to my right and spot Virgil seated at a round corner table that faces both lake and garden. There are two women with him that I don't remember seeing last night, but who obviously will be a part of the interview process. I take a deep breath to steady my hammering heart and move toward the empty seat waiting for me.

"Hello, Alicia." Virgil waves, summoning me over and standing to shake my hand. Dressed in an ecru linen suit, salmon-colored shirt, and matching silk tie with a similar colored handkerchief peeking from a front pocket, he presents impeccable style and elegance. All that's missing is a straw fedora with matching trim to complete the look.

"It's a pleasure to see you again, Virgil." I shake his outstretched hand, noting the warmth and strength of his clasp.

"Alicia, this is Mimi Hardwick, one of our fashion sales representatives, and Charlotte Henry, a designer with our international branch."

"A pleasure to meet you, Ms. Hardwick." I extend my hand to her first and then to Ms. Henry, who appraises me from the palest blue eyes I think I have ever seen. The sides of her mouth pull back in a smile, but the rest of her face remains still, no crinkling or widening her eyes or raising her eyebrows. Just a wooden smile with eyes so frosted my inclination is to pull back my hand. I don't. I can't fathom whether it's bitch or Botox causing the bad vibe, but since this is a job interview, I maintain a warm smile and shake her hand.

"Nice to meet you, Ms. Henry." I meet her gaze head on before shifting it to the others. Lowering my portfolio, I place it next to my chair just as Virgil begins.

"Alicia, there's no doubt that we are quite taken with your winning design. The clean tapered lines and fitted flair of the jacket is in line with the style and form we look for at Estelle

Designs. And that you were able to create some of it from the use of recycled fiber is admirable. Could you share with us what you believe your strengths are and how they would enhance Estelle Designs?"

I am not baffled by this question. In fact, I had prepared for it. Chase explained that this question is often used in preliminary interviews. My response is direct and confident.

"I believe my greatest strengths are motivation and perseverance. I want a rhythm and grace in my designs, and I don't give up until I feel I have accomplished them. It's important to craft designs that satisfy my creative and ecological standards, as well as meet customer demands. I persist until I feel I have satisfied them all."

"Sounds obsessive. Have you ever designed for customers before?" Ms. Henry asks in a hollow monotone, her bland expression and opaque eyes offsetting the pale perfection of her face. *Definitely a bitch*, but I remain unruffled. I want this job. The company is growing with international exposure on the upswing making the experience invaluable.

"No, Ms. Henry, but I believe that what I lack in experience I make up for with skill and hard work. I embrace challenges and learn quickly." She pauses, shuttering any intake of emotion then looks away without comment.

Pulling a strand of her unruly blond hair behind her ear, Ms. Hardwick glances at my portfolio.

"I see you've brought samples of your work. May we see some of your sketches?"

"Certainly." Grateful for the break in tension, I open my case and hand over my sketch pad.

Virgil leans in and they scuttle together to peer through my work, stopping to study the lilac suede coat. To ease my nerves I look first at the water and next at the garden, but staring me straight in the face *again* is "The Tree." I shift my eyes to the lake and wipe my mind clean of any of last night's tryst. Virgil hands me back my pad, then conducts the remainder of the interview. His positive demeanor and quick wit help me gather my thoughts and respond with intelligence and skill. The waiter brings us coffee and juice, and I take a moment to sip some water.

As he continues to serve, Ms. Henry stares at Virgil and in perfect Italian remarks, "She seems young."

I put down my glass and stare ahead, pretending not to have understood, but my heart pounds. The thought crosses my mind that maybe I should address the comment, but decide against it. She doesn't need further reason to dislike me. Virgil says nothing and as breakfast is being served asks if I have any questions.

I actually do and don't hesitate to ask, "What does Estelle Designs value most in its employees?" I often thought beforehand that the answer to this question would reveal so much about the culture of the particular company.

"All the attributes you mentioned: motivation, hard work, creativity … Also, the ability to integrate color, style, and texture in fashions that dance with the wearer's movements."

His eyes drift and I imagine him conjuring his latest design. He pulls himself back to the table and asks, "Where do you get inspiration for your creations?"

I don't even have to think about the answer to that question. "Anywhere and everywhere. I just left the south of France where I was mesmerized by the different shades of the sea. In Nice, as the sun starts setting, the ocean appears lavender with a tinge of heather. That helped me select the color of the suede jacket."

Virgil's eyes shift in contemplation. "Yes, it's no surprise Matisse settled in the Provence region to create."

I take a nibble of bread and a bite of cheese as the others dig into their omelets. Definitely better to be on the other side of the interview process.

"I notice you often glance at that magnificent plane tree that graces the garden," Ms. Hardwick interjects, her mouth curving into a warm smile, her guileless eyes reflecting curiosity. "It's majestic with such an inviting trunk. Do you plan to use that as motivation for one of your designs?"

I nearly spit out my water and lift my napkin to my mouth to stifle my choking.

Virgil reaches over and pats my back. "Are you alright?"

"I'm fine, thank you," and regaining composure, muster some shred of professionalism to answer, "Um … I haven't considered that possibility but perhaps. I hear it's over five hundred years old." I quickly take a sip of water, hoping my face isn't the color of the bowl of strawberries sitting at the center of the table.

After a beat, Virgil notes, "I believe Cesare is an Italian name. Is your family from this region?"

"My parents were born in Romagna, a town in the Tuscan area. In fact, my father and his family still own a vineyard there. I've spent many summer holidays with them."

Ms. Henry's façade finally takes a hit. Her hand moves to her throat and a rosy hue forms across her collarbone. *Touché, Virgil.*

There's an awkward silence punctuated by the clank of forks and knives as they eat while I pretend to. Once we finish, plates are cleared and it isn't long before both women excuse themselves and leave. Virgil remains, and for a moment I don't know whether I should leave as well. I have my answer when he begins talking.

"There's no doubt you are a good fit for this company. I'm going to arrange for Human Resources to contact you when you arrive back to New York so we can arrange to have you meet other members of our staff."

"Thank you, Virgil. I believe I would be the right team player for Estelle Designs. I look forward to hearing from you."

We stand and as I'm about to leave, Elio scurries over, "Excusa me signorina …" He looks at me, eyes twinkling and arms eagerly extended. "I believe you left this when you and your gentleman friend were under our magnificent tree last night." He hands me my shawl.

As I struggle to remain matter of fact, Virgil throws back

his head and laughs. "That would make one helluva a design."

What can I say except thank you to Elio, who beams then hands Virgil a cream-colored fedora. I knew it! I take my portfolio under my arm and buoyantly wave, "Buongiorno, Grazie," then walk out, all the while thinking, Robin Virgil May is quite the discerning character. I like him.

CHAPTER TWENTY-THREE

ntering the room, I hear Chase speaking on the phone and freeze, every muscle and nerve on alert in anticipation of the nature of the conversation.

"Is it owned by an NGO?"

Pause.

"If the property is still for sale, I need to know the status of zoning."

Pause.

"It's an SRO?"

Pause.

"Then contact the RSA for that information."

Pause.

"Yes, it makes a difference." His voice is abrupt, impatient. "I need this info ASAP."

It's like he's speaking in code, but it's work related so I relax.

"Alicia?"

I love hearing that man say my name. "Yes, it's me."

He comes out, fresh from a shower, hair still wet, pants hanging just below his waist, no shirt. My eyes rake over his torso, coming to rest again on his chest. Heavens alive, even spent from a job interview, he's delectable.

In several quick strides he's at my side and sweeps me into a hug.

"How did it go?"

"I think it went well." Virgil made it clear he liked what I had to offer. I believe I also made an impression on one of the other two interviewers."

"And the other?" Shrewd eyes wait for my answer.

"Not so much. I think she thought I was too inexperienced."

"She said that?"

"More or less, but in Italian."

"So she obviously didn't know that one of your many talents includes speaking Italian."

"No."

"Screw her." My eyes widen and I can't help but laugh. "I mean it. Some people just take an instant dislike. It's irrational, not steeped in any logic. Probably thought you looked too good."

I laugh again. "And you're not biased?"

"Maybe, but my opinions are steeped in experience with the interviewee's talent. Intimate knowledge of what creativity these fingers offer."

He reaches in, taking the index finger of my right hand, and places it slowly in his mouth, sucking gently before reaching for my thumb and doing the same. My knees nearly buckle, and I lean into his body. There's a loud, angry rumbling from my stomach that I ignore because any skin to skin, never mind skin to mouth, has me panting for more. A loud tapping at the door penetrates my preoccupation.

"That's probably room service. I figured you'd have no appetite during the interview so I ordered you some breakfast."

In pops the ubiquitous Elio, sporting a huge grin and pushing a wheeled cart holding several domed silver platters. Ceremoniously, he uncovers plates of vegetable omelets, fresh fruit and cheese, warm rolls, mini muffins, and ... well, what appears to be a condensed assortment of the entire dining hall buffet. There's even a hot double espresso and a large glass of ice. I smile because once again Chase has spared nothing. When not being overbearing and over-controlling, he really is sweet and considerate.

"Come sit. You need to eat."

Thanking Elio, he hands over a generous tip. I dig in. The omelet is still hot and oozes melted cheese peppered with diced tomatoes and mushrooms. I hadn't realized how hungry I was and once I start eating, I don't stop until my plate is clean. Hunger sated and sipping an iced espresso, I lean back and stare out at the sea and rise of snow-capped mountains in the distance. Captured in a single gaze, the two are hypnotic to an eye used to the flat coastal terrain of the south shore of

Long Island. My mind shifts to home where job interviews, family, and a new apartment wait, along with who knows what from this new relationship. And like a sudden awakening from a leisurely slumber, I ready myself for the face-to-face conversation that's been begging to be had since Chase's arrival.

As if hearing my mind speak, he looks up over his cup of coffee and utters, "We need to talk."

I turn my gaze toward his, taking in blue eyes, the sweep of dark lashes and stubble along the sides of his face and across the cleft in his chin, all in sharp contrast to the crisp white linen collar of his shirt. I hesitate because I want this moment to linger in the space between the words that must be said until it obliterates any reason for their existence.

When I don't answer, he lowers his cup and strokes the side of his chin before adding, "There are things that are being put in place for when we get home that I think you should know about."

I understand there is a lot to discuss, but first and foremost I need to hear from him why he just upped and left. I think that if I can grasp that, I will be able to deal with what follows. I just don't know how to phrase the question, let alone brace myself for his answer because the monster hovering has less to do with mobsters and childhood differences and everything to do with the importance of maintaining a relationship. How can there be a "we" if he thinks I can't grasp the breadth of his problems? I'm not some guileless innocent who's danced through life wearing rosy-colored shades. Not wanting to be motivated by anger or defensiveness, I lead up to his leaving by asking first about his sister and friend.

"How is Fiona?"

"She's doing well."

I nod, relieved, and swallow before asking, "And your um … friend, Devin?"

He seems to do a double take as if surprised I'm asking. "She's fine too." His voice is clipped, impatient, most likely because I'm avoiding the topic he wants to address. "Listen, Alicia, I appreciate your concern for these other people in my life, but what I want to talk about is you and your safety."

He looks up, mouth taut with concern, riveted eyes staring into mine. His sadness tugs at my heart, and I get up and sit in his lap, burying my head in his neck and breathing in his scent of sun and sandalwood. I need this closeness before continuing, and he must feel the same because he wraps his arms around me and holds me close.

"I'm sorry for leav—"

I put my finger to his lips. "Shh." I lift my head and stare ahead, lost in thought, trying to find the right words. They're hesitant at first. This is new territory for me, but eventually I let them unfurl into a forthright, honest explanation.

"I won't lie. You hurt my feelings terribly. You left without any explanation or display of emotion. That tore me up more than any fear from these threats." I clear my throat to keep from crying. "More than anything I want us to be able to get through this together and that can't happen if you're running off at the first sign of a problem."

He looks long and hard at me, and I wait, recognizing his need for time to gather his thoughts. "My past is so … so sullied. It's like some fucking boulder on my back that threatens to topple and destroy everyone I care about the moment I let my guard down. But you … you're different. You're all sunshine and innocence, like a breath of fresh air. I couldn't bear to see you marred by my ghosts."

"What am I twelve?" Leaning back from his embrace, my eyes flash anger and frustration. "I'm not some kid who can't handle adversity. We either have a partnership or not. And if we do, it means we stand by each other even when— No, especially when there are problems. I admit, this hoodlum …" I refuse to call him a gangster because that would make it seem like he has more power than I care to acknowledge at the moment. "Well, he poses a threat, but you have eluded him so far and done quite well with your life. What makes you think we can't achieve even more together?"

As soon as these words are spoken, his reasons for leaving melt into the distance along with my need to delineate them. It's as if I've shaken off an albatross and floating lighter and higher, a gathering strength enables me to lift Chase with me until the phantoms from his past diminish in relevance.

Not answering my question, he stands, taking me with him, and savagely whispers, "I could never live with myself if I let anything happen to you." The words seem torn from him, leaving a hollowness where they had been festering. And just like that, we reach the crux of the problem. I may be ready to understand that I have to deal with that possibility, but he obviously is not. How do I make him see the distortions of his logic? You can't erase someone from your life with no explanation because there are problems.

"I know. But running away was never the answer. I haven't experienced your past, and I won't pretend that I know what it feels like for you, but that doesn't mean I can't cope with its ramifications. Besides, you left Sammy here to protect me. Which I might add you failed to mention. We have to keep our lines of communication open. If I had known Sammy was here, I could have called to let him know I lost my way or that I thought I was being followed. Maybe he wouldn't have gotten ambushed. Your leaving was never a solution. And, I don't believe your demented nemesis gives up that easily."

He whistles out a frustrated rush of air. "He doesn't, but I thought my leaving would keep him in a chase after me. I should have known better. With him it's personal. Always personal."

I'm confused. I can't fathom why this maniac continues to blame Chase when he was only a child protecting his friend. "Is it because you disrupted his illicit trafficking business when you turned in the photographs?"

"No, not just that."

"Then what? I don't understand."

He takes in another deep breath and grasps me tighter,

before slowly exhaling. "You smell good."

He lifts my chin and kisses me tenderly on my lips. I think he needs this pause, this rooting to the here and now, before navigating the path the conversation is leading us down. When he continues, his tone is measured and flat, as if he's stepped into another time and place.

"After The Finger was convicted, he was placed in solitary. Officials said it was to protect him from other inmates who don't take kindly to sex offenders, especially those who abuse children. Truth is, they were trying to nab him on other charges: drugs, arms trafficking, racketeering, just to name a few. But they couldn't build a case. He was good at covering his tracks and keeping away from all the dirty work involved in running and stashing the heavy drugs and arms he smuggled. When I presented the photographs, the authorities knew they could put him away for a long time for rape, so they took what they could get. Keeping him in solitary was their clever way of preventing him from running the business from the inside. When he dropped off the radar, his enemies realized his vulnerability and went after his assets." Chase stops, closes his eyes and for a moment I think he's going to reveal something, but then his expression becomes shuttered, and I know he has decided to take a different course.

"The Finger? I thought his name is Dimitri." I want to be sure to process each word, name, and place correctly.

"That's what his clan calls him. I learned that when I was jumped and knocked to the ground one day after school.

Rubbing my face in the dirt some bastard whispers in my ear, 'The Finger sends his regards.' Didn't take a rocket scientist to figure out he was referring to Dimitri."

It's mind boggling how a vendetta that started with two adolescents could continue well into their adulthood. I start to feel sorry for Devin, a helpless victim in this debacle. And where in heavens name were the adults who should have been protecting these kids? The answer brings me back to what Chase tried to convey on the beach in Santa Margharita, and I imagine Chase's father and Devin's mother lying in drunken or drugged stupors, unaware of what was happening. The realization that one problem served as a road map to worsening problems locks into place new and unsettling thoughts that leave a lingering sour taste in my mouth.

"Anyway," Chase continues, interrupting my new found insights, "his oldest son, Yuri, must have taken over the business while he was incarcerated, because the next thing I hear is that Yuri has been gunned down in Moscow. Part of some mob massacre. To make matters worse, Dimitri's wife and his other kids disappeared. She most likely cut a deal, gave up info and names the authorities were looking for and then was placed, with their children, in the witness protection program. In either case, he hasn't seen or heard from her or his children since. "

"And he holds you accountable?"

"No question about it. An eye for an eye is his creed, and now that he's out of jail he wants his pound of flesh. The Finger plots revenge like normal people take pleasure in hobbies. He's constantly looking for the perfect stratagem or ploy to get even. And he has loyal troops who extend his organization's global force. I can't imagine why he hasn't been tried for additional crimes, but whatever info his wife revealed didn't include him. I'm thinking it involved some marital confidence privilege she chose and the feds were satisfied with who they were getting."

There's so much nervous energy coursing through my body that I stand and start to pace. Taking my hand, Chase stops me and rubs my arms.

"No need to worry. We have protection."

"Is this why you enlisted in the marines?" This must have been on my mind because I'm really not surprised when I blurt it out.

"Partly, but mostly I signed up because the road had converged for me after graduation and I chose the wrong path. I started drinking, *a lot*, even bought a gun in the hopes of protecting myself and Devin. I was angry, frustrated. Spent many late nights carousing with friends, and before I knew it I was drinking every day, staggering home at all hours. One morning I woke up on the front lawn after having been passed out from a drunken binge. Didn't even realize I was brandishing a loaded gun until I staggered inside the house and saw it stuck into the waist of my pants. I had no recollection of where I had been or what had happened the night before. I was just grateful I hadn't killed anyone. I enlisted the next day. Best thing I could have done. Not so good for Fiona, though, but that's another story for another time. For me, there was benefit in the regimentation and discipline, and I had a free college ride."

"So you met Sammy and Mac during your enlistment?"

"Yeah, I met Mac in training camp and Sammy in Afghanistan. Others too. We've got each other's backs. Don't worry. But I need you to understand some things."

Oh god, there's more. I don't know how much of this open communication I can handle. But I asked for it and at this point there's no turning back.

"Ok." I wait and don't realize I'm holding my breath until he continues and I let it out in a long, slow exhale.

"I believe there is less of a threat now. Dimitri broke his probation and given his history, there's an international all-points bulletin out for him. He's gone underground and that means he has other things on his mind besides me ... or you. But I don't like to take chances. So, Sammy is ... well he's going to keep an eye on ... things." He pauses and looks at me and then into the distance.

I know that look. He can't meet my eye. He's holding something back. Then realization hits. Sammy's job is to watch me and suddenly, the idea of a personal bodyguard becomes so preposterous given my innocuous life that I laugh. Chase's eyes spark blue then mute, his previous contrite persona replaced by a hard and determined expression that catches me off guard.

"I can't imagine what you find amusing about this, but I

assure you I will have you on board with Sammy on the watch."

I immediately stop laughing. "Oh, so now I need to be watched. I've been mostly on my own this entire trip and doing just fine thank you very much."

"That depends on how you define just fine," he retorts, extending a finger to begin a count. "Let's see. Arrested for possession of drugs, almost hit and killed by a rushing boat because you're unable to follow simple instructions, jumped on the back of a Ducati without a helmet for a wild ride with some Frenchman, fell off said motorcycle, chased by a masked maniac after having one too many drinks."

It's amazing he has any fingers left after counting transgressions. "You can't just issue orders for me to obey like you're my commanding officer. And ... and all of those things are not true," I finally manage to stutter, waving my hand to accentuate my point.

"Oh yeah, which part?"

"I ... I did not have too much to drink before being chased by the masked maniac." This gross understatement sounds ludicrous even to my ears and another giggle bubbles out until before I know it I'm bent over, laughing so hard I have tears in my eyes. I'm afraid to look up at staunch marine Chase Reardon, so I just hug my sides to keep from dropping and then spent from laughing so hard, wipe the tears from my eyes. When I finally do muster the courage to look up, I'm surprised to see him grinning.

"You know, there's a recklessness lurking in your normally

sedate manner that could be fun if it wasn't so damn scary. Listen …" He pauses, pushing back his hair with both hands then trails one behind to rub the back of his neck, both motions I've come to realize signal mounting stress. "I'm sorry if I came on too strong, but I need you to cooperate. It won't be for long. There's so many people looking for the bastard, it's just a matter of time before he's either caught or killed."

I really can't see that I have any alternative and under the current circumstances it does make perfect sense, but with Chase's overcautious behavior and overactive need to be in control, I want clarification. "What does this watching over involve?"

His relief is immediate. His shoulders relax and his hands unclench. "It will be discreet. For the most part you won't see Sammy, but he'll always be near. You'll be able to reach him at any time, day or night."

Being in life threatening situations because of mobster vendettas are not obstacles I imagined having to deal with, and I'm having a hard time wrapping my head around the idea of an around-the-clock protector.

Incredulity collides with confusion, and I blurt out, "Always be in reach? When does he sleep?" *Or for that matter have any kind of life.*

Chase doesn't even pause before answering. "Not your concern. We have that worked out."

And the 'you only need to know what I think you should know' commandeer is back, but I'm too tired to argue. Last night's shenanigans followed by the early morning interview have taken their toll and thinking about all the packing I have to do for tonight's flight doesn't help.

Closing my eyes, I sigh and nod. "Ok, I understand."

He's at my side immediately, folding his arms around me and holding me tight. I lean into his embrace and ironically feel safer than I ever have before. This should be disconcerting, but instead I've never felt more alive. It's like my inner core has been energized with so much hope and elation, I can feel the turn of the earth on its axis.

"You know…" he looks down at me and gently places a loose strand of hair behind my ear "…when I'm with you, I feel like I'm home."

That does it. Packing, schmacking. It can wait, and slowly I start unbuttoning my blouse.

CHAPTER TWENTY-FOUR

There are many redeeming perks of flying first-class but none better than the wider seats and additional leg room. Now we sit bolt upright waiting for takeoff. Chase holds my hand and squeezes gently as all 800,000 pounds of plane and cargo hurl down the runway and, God only knows how, into the air. Once airborne there is the ok-to-unfasten-seatbelt ping, and a flight attendant appears with a toothy smile and a work-mode gaze trained to affect interest where none exists.

"Can I get you something to drink?"

"I'll take a glass of cabernet and she'll have a chardonnay."

I can use that glass of wine. It's hard to fathom my return home because home is usually reminiscent of the familiar and so much has changed since I left. New apartment, potential new job, new boyfriend, and let's not forget one bodyguard. I recline trying to quiet the thoughts that bombard my mind like colliding molecules under a microscope.

This relationship was complicated enough when it was removed from the stress and strain of everyday living. Thrust back into our different lives with the added pressure of lurking danger, it seems as if it could disintegrate into fragments of fear and uncertainty, and yet … I've never felt more energized. The world is in such sharp focus, I can still smell the flowers and dewy grass of Lake Como and feel the spray of water when a wave hit the shore on the beach at Santa Margharita.

I love this man and life without him would seem empty and dark. As if reading my mind, he raises my hand to his lips and brushes it with a kiss. Smiling, I use it to stroke the side of his face and gently tug on his ear lobe.

"I've been thinking," he states matter-of-factly before earnestly continuing, eyes brightening and so full of yearning that the shift makes me turn to meet their gaze. "Come stay with me for a bit. I have a suite at the Carlyle we can enjoy. It'd be like extending your vacation, but you'd be close enough to prepare for your interviews without having to navigate through the clutter of packed boxes." He stares ahead as if trying to find the right words before turning to face me again and adding, "I'm not ready to let you go yet."

I'm moved beyond words because underneath the practicality of logistics is the pure and simple fact that I want to be with him. Leaning closer, I take in his clean, soapy scent before kissing him on the neck, and when I lean back, I see he's waiting expectantly for a reply. This I find surprising. I thought my answer obvious and my intentions clear.

"Ok. I'd like to have more time together too." On the outside I'm all cool and calm, but inside I'm somersaulting with elation. I have to be at my new apartment next week to wait for furniture deliveries and begin unpacking, and I know the Carlyle is on 76th and Madison so we're close enough to travel to and from if necessary. Smiling and resting his two hands on the sides of my face, he pulls me closer, locking his lips on mine for a kiss. When I finally come back to the here and now, there's an expectant presence loitering to my left and looking up, I notice our flight attendant sporting the same toothy smile and bland gaze, standing on the sidelines, holding a tray with two glasses of wine.

Leaning back, I look away, feeling my cheeks warm. Nonplussed, Chase gives her a killer smile and takes first my glass, handing it to me to place on my tray, then his and with a quick dismissive thank you, returns his gaze to mine.

"Now, where were we?" he continues, eying my breasts with raised eyebrows and a grin that rivals Dennis Quaid's.

I slap away his hand just as he's about to reach toward my chest. "Don't you dare. We're on a crowded plane for heaven's sake."

"You don't think worse has been done while ten thousand feet in the air? Once, on a flight to LA, I noticed this guy in front of me disappear into the rest room. Normally I wouldn't think twice about it, but there was something about the way he furtively swept his eyes, as if trying to determine if anyone was watching. A minute or two later, the woman seated next to him follows. When she reaches the lavatory, the door swings open, and she's pulled inside. They're in there together for only a few minutes when some burly guy heads down the aisle toward that same bathroom and now I know there's going to be trouble. Sure enough he flings the door open because, as I suspected, he's a federal marshal, and there they are, the guy hanging loose with his pants around his ankles, bare ass exposed, the woman with her skirt tossed above her head, pressed against the sink, both going at it like two rabbits in heat with the whole section of our plane as an audience."

"No! How could they possibly manage? I can barely maneuver to pee." I'm laughing because the image is hilarious, but something tells me that this was no "I just happened to look up and see that something was not right" reaction. I see how Chase effortlessly flicks his eyes across a room, gleaning information about who's doing what, like a digital camera snapping, storing and retrieving images. When Sammy can't recall someone they're discussing, I'd hear Chase clarify, "he was the little guy, always drinking on the far left side of the bar, whiskey straight up, never any clinking of ice," or "she was the tall pianist, face like a giraffe, small eyes, always looked slightly stoned," and Sammy's face would light with recognition. No doubt Chase's ability to record and remember, coupled with his military training, came into play on that plane.

"Who knows. Libido is a creative motivator." Bending his head toward me, he brushes his lips on the turquoise star directly below my ear, working gradually down to the others until, leaning into his touch, my breath quickens and there's that delicious ache between my legs. A rather husky throat clearing interrupts, and I see from the corner of my eye that Ms. Toothy is yet again waiting, ready to offer us anything but privacy. She must have been on the same flight as the two rutting passengers and doesn't want a repeat performance in passenger seats.

"What would you like to order tonight?" she asks, raking her eyes in a brisk, sweep over me then shifting them all sparkly to Chase.

I haven't checked the menu and disengaging from Chase, I make a feeble attempt to reach and scan it. Chase looks up flashes another one of his winning smiles, which I'm sure has her knees wobbling, and orders fruit and cheese platters for us, nodding in my direction to make sure I'm in agreement.

"Sounds good." Taking a sip of chardonnay, I lean back and relax.

The wine is dry, crisp, not too fruity. Our banter and nuzzling lulls me into a sense of normalcy that reminds me I'm a soon-to-be employed fashion designer returning from a holiday with a lover, who has invited me to stay with him for a bit. Other uncertainties melt into a hazy mix of improbabilities, too fathomless to be real. I must doze because when I look up, my tray is down and on it is a platter with a sprig of red grapes, some strawberries, and a cluster of four assorted cheeses surrounded by water biscuits. Chase is busy on his laptop, his half-eaten plate resting to the side. I rub the sleep from my eyes and focus on my food. It looks fresh, colorful, not like the processed cheese and cellophane wrapped crackers served in coach. I take a few nibbles and then some sips of wine. Glancing at Chase, I notice his brow is furrowed and his eyebrows are drawn together in a combination of perplexity and annoyance. I don't want to know why, preferring to hold onto my drowsy serenity. I finish the fruit and spread a soft bit of brie onto a cracker, munching and sipping, feeling the wine wrap around my limbs and lengthen my sleepiness. Then, leaning back to take advantage of the recline and added leg room, I glance at Chase, who is still busy tapping keys and studying his computer screen. It never ceases to amaze me how little sleep he requires and how focused he remains without any. Reaching into my pocket, I pull out an eye mask to block out the light from his computer, and slipping it on drift into a dark, weightless sleep, the hum of the plane's engines fading into the distance.

There's a slight shift in the sound of the plane. Light floods the cabin as window shades are opened and fresh croissants and muffins are served with orange juice and coffee and tea. Some have ordered omelets and toast, but I softly ask for the bread and muffin basket for myself and Chase. Chase is asleep, head bent to the side, lips parted. He looks young and untroubled, his often furrowed brow now smooth and his hands resting open at his sides. I gently rub his arm and give him a soft kiss on his cheek. His eyes open, not quickly with his usual sudden, I sense danger surprise, but slowly, easily, with a languidness that exposes youthful vulnerability. He turns, looks at me and smiles, his expression such a mix of unabashed joy and openness that I'm jolted into a sudden awareness that I will do anything to protect this man. Challenges and differences may temporarily block our path, but they will be just that— temporary because some imaginary line connects us so that even when we're apart there's a yearning that draws us together, a bond that enables us to transition memories of shared moments into realities of now. It's our wanting to be together that will drive us to conquer adversity. I know it. I feel it, and the clarity strengthens my resolve to withstand any waiting turbulence. Simple truth: I want to be with him and he wants to spend time together too.

He leans over and holds a warm croissant to my lips. "Taste. It's good."

I take a bite savoring the buttery flavor. "Mmm, this is good." I chew and take several sips of orange juice, the sugar coursing through me, jolting any residual sleepiness.

There's that last minute hurriedness when passengers get up to use the bathroom and rustle around in their bags, reaching for combs, phones, lipstick and any other assortment of products and gadgets that prepare them for what waits after landing. Ms. Toothy appears looking a bit worn after the long flight but still sporting the same faux expression of interest that stares through me as if I really don't exist. That all changes when she reaches Chase.

"May I take that from you, sir?" She looks at him, all warmth and smiles, reaching for his empty plate and glass when he nods. She says nothing to me, merely leans in and removes my plate and utensils.

"Thank you," I pointedly say.

Without looking back, she throws out a hasty, "You're welcome."

I'm thinking I better get used to it, because no doubt this will happen again.

"Alicia." His voice is low but clipped, tinged with an, 'I need to have your attention now' inflection. His tight shoulders and clenched hands radiate tension, and I'm sure I'm about to get lecture 128 about all the precautions we need to take, but instead he says, "Would you consider staying with me at my place? There's plenty of room and privacy and well, it might be more comfortable than staying in yet another hotel."

I see no reason I should refuse this offer. I had already made up my mind that I want to be with him and his apartment on 72nd and Park is close to my new apartment.

"Sure."

Relieved, he sits back before abruptly turning toward me again and adding, "Could we wait before letting your family know we've been seeing each other." He blows out a deep breath. "Uh … your brothers and I swore this oath about not dating siblings, and I think I should speak personally to Massimo first."

I almost laugh at how worried this is making him because the last thing I want is to be harried by my family demanding details about this relationship and badgering me to bring Chase by for dinner. That he's an old friend of Massimo just adds another layer of issues.

"Ok, best to wait for the right time." But I wonder when that will be given the current circumstances. There's no way I want my family to learn anything about Chase's problems and with my mother just starting to feel better, she doesn't need to go into a tailspin because her daughter has a bodyguard protecting her from a roving Russian mobster. Suddenly the full weight of the situation crashes in on me and worrying the inside of mouth, I imagine myself running through dark city streets in some vain attempt to get help while fleeing from attacking hitmen as Chase lies huddled and hurt in some alleyway.

"Are you ok? You're as white as a ghost."

There's no time for explanations because the aircraft hits the runway with a jolting bounce that propels us forward before shifting to a manageable speed and hollering to a halt.

Lugging our carry-ons, we straggle down long corridors with other passengers dragging overstuffed suitcases on wobbly wheels. Chase has his laptop and business papers in a bag slung over his shoulder, along with my portfolio under his arm, and still he has not let go of my hand. I know it's his way of saying I have nothing to worry about and even though the events of the past several days tell a different story, I believe it. I feel the movement of life overtake me. Everything is sharper, from the colorful scarves that dangle in the airport shops to the aroma of roasted coffee beans from the Starbucks kiosk. Even the people we pass look more alive as they scurry down corridors or slip into restrooms to freshen up before meeting family and friends in arrivals. This happiness must be infectious, because people look at me and smile or are quick to say excuse me and thank you when passing. In comparison, my former world seems nothing more than a dress rehearsal.

"Happy to be home?" Chase asks, slowing his runner's pace to Customs to pull me closer.

"Happy to be home with you." He gives me a big-hearted, ear-to-ear, goofy grin so unlike his usual guarded expression that I laugh out loud.

"C'mon, let's move so we can get out of here. Sammy is waiting to pick us up at the arrivals gate once we clear Customs." I lengthen my strides to a steady jog to keep up.

Labeled *Priority*, our suitcases come quickly. Sammy seems to appear from nowhere. He and Chase greet with a silent nod as only good friends can and immediately fall into a rhythm of grabbing and loading suitcases. Wrapping Sammy in a hug, I give him a warm hello. It's the least I can do. The man saved my life—twice—and the nasty cut above his eye, while looking better, still hasn't completely healed. He looks pleased, his eyes widening slightly before he hugs me back and straightens with a "Hey, Alicia. You look good."

"Thanks, Sammy." Overloaded with bags, we head toward the parking lot.

"Alicia's coming home with me," Chase informs Sammy and Sammy nods, staring ahead and driving, no questions asked or explanations necessary. I text my parents that I landed safely and heading to my old apartment (small white lie) then move on to reading a text from Beth, who's in London visiting family. '*New shape of legs* ( )' she texts from all her motorcycle riding. I miss her and even though I would enjoy having someone to talk to about this new relationship, she'd freak out if she knew about the mobster madness, and there's a very real possibility she'd blab to my brother. Disastrous.

Traffic is light on both the Van Wyck and Grand Central, and we make record time. Chase's apartment is in a high rise on 72nd and Park. The wide avenue is planted with colorful flowers along its midsection without the usual hustle and bustle of trucks and buses and jaywalking pedestrians clogging intersections. Sammy pulls to the curb and a doorman appears, pushing a cart to help with the bags.

"Good afdanoon, Mr. Reardon. Welcome home. Did you enjoy your trip?" He lifts the bags from the trunk and places them onto the cart while Chase types and sends a final email.

"It was good, Boris."

Chase takes my hand and escorts me through the doors and into a small, elegant lobby flanked by a cozy sitting area. The floor is a snappy black and white marble and two polished-brass elevator doors wait against the far wall. Chase hits the button and one immediately opens. Stepping inside, I'm suddenly nervous and a bit unsure. I'm so new at this that I have no idea how it works. How long do I stay? A day, two, more? And now that we're back with the stress of work and family problems, how will we balance our time together? Do I stay in his apartment alone while he goes to the office? I don't even have a job for heaven's sake and he's some real estate magnate. I remind myself that I have my own apartment waiting. It may only be a studio, but it is all mine. Also, I'm guessing that with Sammy on the watch this living arrangement will initially make everything easier to monitor. Then I remember that the "everything" entails watching me and the realization is unnerving. Last thing I want is to be a burden or have my freedom hampered for safety reasons. How tedious.

When the elevator doors close, Chase finally looks up from his phone, slips it into his pocket, and pulls me into his arms. It's like someone takes an eraser and wipes my worries clean. We are alone in an enclosed space for the first time in more than twelve hours and staring into each other's eyes, our libidos kick into action. He pushes back my hair and gives me a lingering kiss, stopping only to gently tug on my lower lip with his teeth. I use it as an opportunity to pull him closer, reaching up on my toes to deepen the kiss and slip my tongue into his mouth. In this cocooned space, we're a tangle of roving hands and limbs, moving with the intensity of two trapped lovers who shed layers of suppressed fear and worry with each touch. Panting with need, he takes hold of my shoulders and pushes me against the rear of the elevator then reaches back and slams the stop button with the palm of his hand without removing the lock of his mouth on my lips. I wrap my raised leg around him, sealing us together, with notions of elevator cameras and angry buzzing by impatient residents lost in a haze of desire.

Chase lifts my blouse and with it the cup of my bra, exposing my breast for the taking. His breath hitches and catching my nipple between his thumb and forefinger, he turns and tugs until the sensation is so intense I don't know whether to lean closer or push his hand away. His lips travel down my neck. I throw my head back, my hands falling limply at my sides as they course down my chest and close around my nipple, where he gently stretches it with his teeth.

Desire throbbing, I reach out to clutch his crotch, but he takes my hands and locks them against the wall above my head while he deftly lifts my skirt. Massaging my thigh, he lets his hand travel under my panties and with one swift tug, tears them free. He squeezes my bare ass and wild with desire, I gyrate toward him.

He places my panties in his pocket, pulls out a condom, and holds it in front of my mouth, where I tear it open with my teeth. Hands freed, I shakily unzip his pants and smooth it onto his hardness. He slips inside me and the sensation is bliss.

"Fuck, you're so wet." Lifting my leg, he locks it around his waist, deepening the penetration with each slow penetration so that the mounting pleasure stays maddeningly buoyed.

"Please … faster," I whimper. The words are barely out of my mouth before he's pinching my ass and thrusting with rapid, hard drives.

Wanting more, I swivel my hips, grinding into him, digging my hands into his back until we're hurled into a whirlwind of spirals that go on and on.

"Fuck," he calls out as they peak into seemingly never ending, ripples of ecstasy.

My heart is racing and when I drift back to reality, he's holding my limp body and kissing me gently. Bending his head back, he gives me a smoking-hot, gaze.

"Can you stand?"

I'm boneless, but manage to nod my head. Slowly, he lowers my leg, balancing me against the wall while he removes and knots the condom and slips it into his pants pocket. I smooth my skirt, making sure it falls evenly in both the front and back then run my fingers through my tousled hair, pulling it back into a ponytail with the hair band I mercifully had on my wrist.

The buzzing can no longer be ignored and a clipped voice vibrates through the speaker, "Hello. Hello. Are you all ok in there?

Hitting the speaker button, Chase calls out, "We're fine.

Elevator must have jammed."

"Sorry, Mr. Reardon. We didn't hear the call button or we would have responded sooner."

Shit, he knows it's us and looking up, I do a quick scan for a camera.

"Not to worry. There's no camera. You think I'd let the doormen watch you come. That's for my eyes only." And with a wicked grin he pinches my backside, making me yelp, just before the doors open and we exit.

Except for a sweep of tousled hair across his forehead, Chase looks none the worse from our tryst. In fact, he looks sexier. Mercifully, the porter bringing up our suitcases in the service elevator hasn't arrived yet and making a quick right, Chase stops and rummages through his pants pocket for his keys. An assortment of things jingle as he finally pulls out a set of keys. Inserting it, he opens the door then playfully tugs my head back by my ponytail, giving me a kiss that has my eyelids fluttering and my knees weak. The door swings open and we tumble through.

"Privet moy dorogoy," a Lauren Becall-ish voice calls out. "Is that you?"

We pull apart and turning, I see a woman—all legs, big smile, arms outstretched, walking towards Chase. Recognition hits like a steam roller flattens. It's the Countess.

CHAPTER TWENTY-FIVE

"And who is this, Casushka?" She gazes at me from languid almond-shaped eyes. A long, flowing dress, more couture than bohemian, smoothly contours her body and drapes her endless stretch of legs. Coupled with a sleek bob she projects a hip Gatsby look that I must admit is becoming.

"Casushka?" she repeats, shifting her eyes to Chase. And now I'm thinking what the fuck is that foreign sounding endearment she's spewing.

Taking my hand, Chase makes the introductions. "Devie, I'd like you to meet Alicia. Alicia, this is Devin, an old friend of mine."

"You look familiar." Her tone is desultory, bored, and I note the undercurrent of a Count Dracula accent that has me biting back a grin.

Despite her aloof demeanor, a discernible vulnerability

mars her nonchalance. The way she repeatedly brushes back her hair from her forehead with her fingers while her eyes dart from side to side, as if waiting for danger to pounce at any moment, remind me of what I know about her and my attitude softens.

"Devie, is that Casey?" A petite redhead appears from inside and spotting Chase, she runs and grabs him in a bear hug.

"Hey, Fiona." Chase returns the hug then steps back, studying her with that all too familiar flicker of eye that transforms his brain into a camera capable of retaining and evaluating images.

Fiona must understand this also because she murmurs, "It's all good." Then she ruffles his hair and gives him a peck on the cheek. The endearing exchange and Chase's goofy smile in return make me almost forget the Countess.

That is, until her mouth starts to move. "Chase has brought home a … guest."

Chase, looking slightly confused, interjects, "I didn't expect to see you all here."

To be honest, neither did I, especially with all the "we'll have plenty of alone time" spiel he gave me on the plane, but I quietly step back to take it all in. Everything is delicate about Fiona, from her oval face and tiny features to the light, wispy fringe of bangs that sweep just above her eyes. Her prettiness is flawed only by a tightness around her mouth and slight hollowness in her cheeks that gives her the look of someone who is more world weary than old for her years.

"Sorry for the ambush, but Mac thought it best if we were all in one place …" Fiona stops and finally noticing me, blinks rapidly several times before offering a wide grin of recognition. "Alicia? Right?" I nod and before I can reach out my hand, she grabs me in a hug, calling over my shoulder, "Devie, this is Massimo's little sister. My god, you've grown up." Sweeping her eyes up and down, she smiles and hugs me tighter. " She doesn't mean anything by it, but somehow here, with Countess Dracula, I'm bothered.

Chase must be uncomfortable too because he clears his throat before looking around and asking, "Where's Liam?"

"I just put him down for a nap. We were all at the park, and he hasn't stopped since breakfast."

There's an awkward silence, and I smooth back my hair, praying that any wildness has been tamed by the elastic holding it in a ponytail. Just-fucked hair coupled with airplane grime are never pretty. Mercifully, the doorbell rings and a porter stands with a cart piled with our luggage. The good-natured fellow greets everyone by name except me and easily engages the group while placing our suitcases in a neat row in the hallway.

"The little guy sure looked beat after his romp at the park. Must be nappin."

Light conversation bounces around, giving me the opportunity to notice the large vestibule that serves as an entranceway to both sides of the apartment. Straight ahead, hanging above a lovely antique table, is an abstract expressionist painting. I inch closer, fascinated by the rippling, bold sweep of color.

"You like it?" Chase comes up from behind and wraps his arms around me. The room is full, suitcases are being unloaded, and he acts like we are the only two here. I'm tickled.

"Yes, very much. I like the movement of its brush strokes, the way they maintain control yet offer slivers of repressed anger and unabashed joy."

"Very astute observation. You think it might be a subliminal representation of someone?"

Ah yeah, its purchaser, but I don't say anything. Instead, I let decorum dictate my answer, "I don't recognize the artist."

"I didn't think you would. It was done by a little known painter named Raymond Spillenger. He spent the later part of his years as a bit of a recluse. I used to meet him in a small bar in the East Village when I was on leave from the marines. He was a decorated war hero and we got to talking. Later, after I closed my first two big deals, he invited me to his studio and allowed me to purchase this for a small fortune, I might add, but I never regretted one penny of it."

"So, Casey," the Countess interrupts, "you plan to stay put for a while? We have a lot to catch up on, no?" Another sweep of her hair as she extends her hand and looks pointedly at him.

"We do. Where's Mac?" Chase glances toward the living room then toward what appears to be a den, looking tense for the first time since we landed, and I immediately know what they need to discuss.

"On his way back from the parking garage. We were at The Central Park Zoo and he drove us back here," Fiona adds. "I hope you don't mind?"

"It's fine. Glad Mac was here to escort you safely."

More stilted silence, and I really don't know what I'm supposed to do or where I should go. I've never been here before, have no idea where the bedroom or bathroom are, and I'm tired, hungry, and in need of a shower.

"Are you planning to go home and get ready for school in the morning?" the Countess asks, looking straight at me without so much as a blink.

Is she kidding? It's summer, I've just returned from three weeks in Europe, and damn it I don't look like a kid! *Take the high road, take the high road*, a voice inside repeats, but my mouth has other ideas and voice dripping with saccharin, I ignore her question for the moment and purr, "Chase, darling, would you please show me to the bedroom?" He narrows his eyes as I lean so close our lips nearly touch. "I'd like to unpack my … toys." And pausing millimeters from his mouth I go for the home stretch. "That way we'll be all set later to play." Pulling him to me by his shirt collar, I plant a kiss on his lips, complete with tongue.

Breaking contact, I glance over my shoulder adding tonelessly, "Schools out, Devie, unless of course…" I look up coyly "…Chase wants to take me to the principal's office where we—"

Before I can finish, Chase grasps my hand and pulls me from the room, calling out in a louder than necessary voice, "Alicia, you've never seen my place. Why don't I give you a tour, show you where the bedroom and bathroom are so you can unpack and shower."

I have to almost jog to keep pace with his retreat. I do manage to call back one last, "Nice to meet you," before my arm is given another sharp tug and I'm pulled out of the room.

"She'll do just fine." Fiona remarks, her giggle traveling down the hallway with us. And from the Countess: nothing, nothing at all.

Chase walks me to the master suite, which is huge. There's a king-sized bed with a large mounted flat screen TV on the opposing wall. It's all done tastefully in grays and tans and splashes of red.

"Wait here, I'll be right back. Just going to grab your suitcases."

"Need any help?" I call out sweetly.

"No."

He's back in seconds, placing my suitcase on top of a low chest that sits in front of his bed and my carry-on on top of a dresser. "Toys?" He cocks a brow. "Is there something you're holding back, because I'm game."

"Is that so, Cashuska?" I add and his smile evaporates.

"I told you, she's just a friend."

"Who was once a lover. Listen, you have a full house. Why don't I grab a cab and we'll catch up later." I really don't want to go, but I'm tired and overwhelmed, and I want some space to think.

"That was a long time ago. We were young. Please…" he moves closer, wraps his arms around me, and gives me one of his award winning smiles that turns me to putty in his arms "…stay with me." He knows he has me and quips, "Besides, I'm ready for the games to begin once you unpack."

"Sorry to disappoint. No naughty accoutrements." He puckers his lips in a childlike pout, and I laugh as I run a finger across them and whisper, "I do have a newly purchased Hermes silk scarf that would serve nicely as a gag for when your dear friend likens me to a child."

"You held your own. I'm sure she got the message." His lips move closer, almost but not quite touching mine, and I inhale the fresh scent of his mouth. "Now, about that silk scarf." His grin is lascivious but his eyes are soft. "I could use it to tie you up, and I do have a ruler that would do nicely for a spanking during that visit to the principal's office you suggested."

An involuntary shiver travels up my spine and I look up at him, letting my gaze lock first on the beautiful curve of his lips then travel up to meet his eyes. Inside a voice hammers out, *How are you going to touch him if you're tied?* Followed by an even louder, *Another spanking. Are you crazy?*

"Mmm, yeah, well as appealing as those all sound …" I'm shooting for dry humor, but my voice is all raspy, and I have to swallow to moisten it so I can finish. "I think I'll just opt for a shower and shampoo."

Nibbling my ear lobe, he gradually moves and plants small kisses across my cheek then back behind my ear, reaching that sweet spot that makes my breath catch.

"Why so skeptical? I assure you, you'd enjoy, but a shower works too." I feel his breath against my ear—hot—and his mouth moist on my earlobe when he takes it and gently tugs it with his teeth. "I can wash you here …" He slowly massages my breast with his fingertips through my blouse while softly nibbling my neck then lowers his mouth to graze my collarbone with feathery kisses. "And here …" His hand slides down my body and rests between my legs where he massages it back and forth. I nervously glance toward the closed door, because I know at this rate I'm a goner.

"Don't worry. They're upstairs in the kitchen." He returns to his nibbling, stopping only to add, "They can't hear a thing."

I bend my head back, giving his lips further access, and bury my hands in his hair, tugging him closer. He undoes the two top buttons of my blouse and deftly lifts it over my head as if it's a T-shirt then cups my breast with his hand.

"I love how perfectly your breasts fit in my hands." He lifts one side of my bra, exposing my breast, then reaches down to tug on my nipple with his thumb and forefinger. I moan. His hands slide under my skirt and he grips my backside and pulls me closer. "We mustn't forget this." Lowering his hands, he begins massaging my ass as if washing it, allowing one hand to drift toward the opening.

My breathing freezes in fearful anticipation, and I almost

use my hands to tug his away—almost—but then uncertainty succumbs to desire when he tugs at my nipple with his mouth while his finger continues to do a dance near my opening. I'm lost in myriad sensations until a familiar jingling lifts me from the grip of my desire into the here and now. It takes me a while to realize it's my phone ringing. I ignore it, but it persists.

"I think I should see who that is," I whisper, all languorous and breathy.

His voice is thick. "Leave it. Whoever it is will call back."

I want to ignore it but with several upcoming interviews and having been gone three weeks, it's proving to be a challenge. His advances continue relentlessly, and I lock back into our embrace, wrapping my leg around his waist as he hoists me up against the bedroom wall. Oh hell, what's fifteen more minutes? We melt into a fast-moving tangle of mouths and hands, banging into walls as I tear open and remove his shirt and he attempts to unclasp my bra.

I make another attempt to succumb, but something keeps tugging me back. I'm so cloaked in want, I can't fathom what it is. Then I hear it, the distinct melody of my phone.

I delve into the far reaches of my sexual self-control that, thank heavens, is only hiding and not completely lost, and manage to remove my mouth from his to pant, "I should get this."

He looks disappointed. His breathing is as ragged as mine, but he steps aside, freeing me to locate and rummage through my bag for my phone. For once, both are in easy reach.

"Hello?" I automatically firm my tone when I hear an official sounding voice.

"Hello, is this Alicia Cesare?"

"Yes."

"This is Kim Wagner from human resources at Estelle Designs. I'm calling to arrange a meeting between you and our international design team. Are you free on Monday morning, say 10:00?"

"Could you give me a moment, please? I just have to check my schedule." I know I have other interviews next week, but I can't recall exactly when. A scan of my phone calendar reveals that my first interview isn't until Wednesday. I quickly get back to the line.

"Ms. Wagner?"

"Yes." Her voice is clipped, but not unfriendly, and I'm glad I don't have to change the designated time. Estelle Designs still remains my first choice, that is, if I am given a choice. I rein in my flutter of forward thinking. Best to remain confident but not too cocky during this process.

"That works."

"Then we are confirmed for Monday at 10:00 am. We're located at 1400 Broadway, suite 2403."

"Yes, thank you. I look forward to meeting you then." I whirl around and notice Chase standing patiently near the far wall, beaming.

"Estelle Designs?" he asks.

"The one and only. That was someone from human

resources calling. I have another interview on Monday."

"Well done, baby." I walk into his arms and he swings me around. "Let's celebrate over dinner later. But first …" He stops, crinkles his nose, and sniffs. "What's that smell?"

I sniff too and shrug my shoulders. "I don't know. I don't smell anything."

He sniffs again and baffled I do the same, until we look like two versions of Bugs Bunny on the scent for Elmer Fudd.

"I don't know what you smell because—"

Cutting me off, he steps closer, mischief plastered all over his face.

I take a step back. "I don't like that look, Reardon."

He sniffs again, moving closer, and I move away, raising my palm up. "Don't even think it."

I take another quick step back before turning and making a run for it. I'm fast, but he's faster, and catching me by the back of my skirt, he clucks, "I do think, Miss Cesare that you are in sore need of a shower."

With one fell swoop, he throws me over his shoulder, flipping off my shoes, as he strides into the bathroom.

"Let me down!" I pummel his back with my fists, but his grasp is firm and without much effort, he reaches into the shower and turns on the faucets. Kicking off his shoes, he steps inside and lowers me screaming and laughing under the teaming water.

"You're incorrigible." I frown and he raises his eyebrows and widens his eyes all innocent as if to ask, *who me?*

I love this playful side of him. His wet silky hair hangs over his forehead, and he sweeps it back with his hand while his other traps me against the shower wall. Eyes dancing with mirth, he bends his mouth to my lips and we ignite as if the phone call hadn't interrupted. Sodden clothes are shed by shaking fingers as water rains over us and still we don't break contact. It's as if we're rediscovering ourselves in these new surroundings, and our arms and hands can't entwine fast enough. I'm awash in myriad sensations of touch and taste as our mouths lock and our hands rove. This mutual exploration of feel becomes a race to see who can touch whom more. He raises and wraps my leg around his hip, while I graze my fingernail across his shoulders and up into his hair where I tug him even closer. I hear his husky hum of arousal and quicken, and when his member thrusts and pulses inside me, I readily respond to his rhythm.

"I love how you tighten around me."

And it's like I'm soaring to the heavens to hover among the stars. Yes, it's that good.

It isn't until I find myself wet and sated atop Chase's silk comforter that I realize he must have carried me there. I hear his measured breathing at my side and I see he's lying next to me, arms and legs outstretched like he just ran a record-setting sprint. Turning to my side, I wrap my arm around him and feel my eyes flutter closed. I want to say that's the last thing I remember, but it's not. My last thought is that I don't remember the tear of a condom wrapper.

CHAPTER TWENTY-SIX

I wake to a slice of light penetrating the room from a slit in the blinds. The silk coverlet is wrapped around my legs, my hair is a mass of tangled waves, and my body feels a bit clammy. I'd obviously been drenched and fucked, but not washed or shampooed. Time for the real thing. Chase is nowhere to be found, so I pop into the bathroom and set the faucets for a warm shower, noticing for the first time that there's a bidet sitting next to the toilet. How European civilized. The spray of warm water from the shower hits like a wake-up balm and the mounted dispenser of cleansing gel gives off this wonderfully citrus woodsy fragrance. Rubbing it into my body, I melt into my massaging hand, relaxing and waking simultaneously. Closing my eyes, my mind niggles. Recollection hits like a moving bolder crashing down from a cliff. Shit. I don't think he remembered to use a condom. Nor did I remind him for that matter.

My mind rewinds then shifts into fast forward. Last period: Santa Margharita about ten days ago. Shit. Shit. Shit. Appointment made with gynecologist for exam and birth control: this Friday at 10:00. Not a help now. Possibility a condom was actually used: 0%. I may suffer mind numbness during sex, but I'm not comatose. My hands automatically shampoo my hair, rinse, then apply conditioner while my heart palpitates and my mind continues to trip over itself. I remember going to the pharmacy with Beth for some morning after contraception when she was in a similar predicament. That's what I'll have to do. I'm out of the shower, dried and dressed in the cleanest pair of shorts and T-shirt I can pilfer from my suitcase. Wet hair hanging, I grab my purse, slip on a pair of flip-flops, and go in search of Chase. I don't know the layout of his apartment, but a quick walk-through shows me he is not on this level. To my right there's a floating staircase that's quite beautiful, and when I begin climbing, I see it leads to a spacious sun-lit living area. Straight ahead in the kitchen is Chase, standing ramrod straight, an empty cup of espresso resting on the counter in front. He turns when I appear and there's no mistaking that his look mirrors my panic. We stand frozen as if we both just stole a peek at Medusa and were petrified into stone.

"I'm sorry, I—"

I'm interrupted before I can complete the sentence. "No, I'm the one who's sorry. I hate those damn things, but…" he rakes his hand through his hair and massages his neck, telltale signs that he's agitated "…I should know better than to lose my self-control like that."

I don't know what to say. He's taking all the blame, and for some reason I find it troubling. I know I'm inexperienced—well, I was anyway—but I'm not gullible.

"It's just as much my fault. I didn't exactly put the brakes on or remind you to wear protection."

"I know but you're just …"

My jaw tightens and my hands clench into fists. He must see because he catches himself and adds, "I'm older, more experienced. I should have remembered. Besides you're not even asking if I've been tested. Not wise."

Now I hear reproof, and if I wasn't so damn worried, I'd haul off and sock him one. Show him exactly how unwise I can be.

Instead, I rein in my temper and with an inquisitive lift of my brow ask, "Should I run for a shot of penicillin when I'm out buying emergency contraception?"

He seems to have realized that he put his foot in his mouth one too many times, so after a beat he offers a simple, "no."

"No?"

"I mean you don't need to go out. I…" he stops, hesitant, looking down at his feet then up at me before continuing "…I have some contraception you can take."

What?

Seeing my confusion, he adds, "I went to the pharmacy and purchased some while you were sleeping. And for the record, I am up to date with the doctor. All is well."

I should have known he would take control the instant he realized what happened. I don't know whether to be relieved by his quick action or outraged at his lack of faith in my ability to take care of it myself. Now he's definitely unnerved by my silence and, keeping his distance, stares at me, waiting. But truthfully, I don't know what to say.

"Listen, I would rather you see a gynecologist before taking any of this stuff, but with an accident like this, time is of the essence. The sooner the better. Besides, the pharmacist assured me it's safe. The dosages are different so after you read the instructions you can decide which you want to take."

Looking at the bag on the table, I begin to wonder if I have the right to be angry. After it happened, I fell asleep while he spun into action. It's just that I want him to understand that I'm as culpable as he is. He can't be the one shouldering all the responsibilities while thinking I need to be kept from meandering from one mishap to another. A perception like that would fold this relationship in no time.

He's still standing there, quietly watching me, afraid to add anything more for fear of offending. Walking toward him, I take him in my arms, and he loosens with relief in my embrace.

"Thank you."

"For what?"

"Thinking ahead, buying what I needed. Being there for me."

"What we needed."

"You're right about the 'we' part. I'm just as much to blame as you are. I could have stopped at any time and reminded you to slip on a condom. In fact, I should be carrying them with me." His face darkens at that suggestion, and I quickly add, "I do have an appointment with the doctor on Friday and I plan to discuss birth control options. It was the earliest I could get after emailing the office before we boarded."

"That's a relief because…" he pulls me closer and rests his chin on top of my head "…you drive me wild."

"Mmm, for a guy your age, you're not so bad yourself."

"Oh, Miss Cesare, your acerbic tongue seems to be getting a workout, but I suppose I deserved that. Listen, I was thinking—"

"You still can?" I deadpan. I'm on a roll and can't seem to stop.

Ignoring me, he continues. "How about if we stay here tonight. I'll grill us some steaks on the terrace, open a bottle of wine, we can eat under the smog. Does that work for you?"

"Sure, but what about your other guests?"

"They've left."

Images of us banging around the bathroom spring to mind, and although I'm happy we're alone, I'm hoping it wasn't all our carrying on that drove them away.

"I have some work to do and then I'll give you a tour of the place and tell you about my goals."

"You mean like your life's ambitions." I'm taken aback. That sounds deep for a first look and see.

"Yep, because…" he tightens his hold around me, lifting my chin to meet his earnest gaze "…it's important for me to determine exactly how…" he brushes my lips with a kiss "…and when…" his lips graze mine and my eyelids flutter with his whispered wisps of words "…I'm going to fuck you in each and every room."

"I'm intrigued, Reardon. Even the terrace?"

"Especially the terrace."

"Nosy neighbors?" My questions are hushed from his feathery kisses.

"Completely private."

"The kitchen?"

"Yes. Great stretch of table in there."

"The bathroom?" I know from firsthand experience it works, but I ask anyway. His kisses between each question feel too good for me to stop.

"Jacuzzi tub, ready and waiting."

"Den?"

"Oh yeah, huge sofa opens into a queen-sized bed."

He's so close I taste the mint in his mouth. My eyes gradually open and as I lean to take another kiss, I spot the bag from Duane Reade standing like a screech owl on its perch. I lengthen my proximity and switch to conversation.

"Well, I haven't had the tour yet, but how many other rooms do you have?"

"There's the office/library."

"Ok, how would that work?" I step back another two steps

for safe measure.

"Great desk, sofa, and some racy books to get us going."

"Don't tell me you have porn here." Now I'm starting to think about all the other women he must have taken "on the tour."

"It's not what you think. I think you'd enjoy them."

"Like all the others you entertained here?" Good-bye brain filter. Hello green-eyed goddess.

He pauses, then says, "I've never had anyone here. I mean I never brought anyone here to sleep with."

"Not even once?" In marches skepticism to hover with my narrow, disbelieving eyes.

"No."

I'm confused. I know he's slept around, and he's not the type to wait for an invite to a date's place. "If you don't mind my asking, where did you … you know, go for your … um … trysts?" I deliberately use past tense because contemplating the alternative is painful.

"I keep a suite at the Carlyle."

"You mean ready and waiting just in case?" And I immediately remember that it's where he wanted to originally take me, but I don't mention it.

He squirms. "I guess you could say that."

Chase Reardon fidgeting with unease. This is too good to let go just yet. "Well how else would you put it?" I query, a tad too innocently. He hesitates, twitches some more, and in the widening silence I take pity and murmur, "Oh my, it seems I'm trespassing on virgin territory."

I don't wait for a response. I step closer, pull him by his shirt collar, and lock us into a searing kiss. Before he can raise his arms to pull me closer, I push him away and snatch the bag from the table. "Does eighteen hundred hours work?"

He's caught off guard, confused. I love it. "Dinner? On the terrace?' His face opens into a wide heart stopping grin.

"18:00 hours is good."

"Dress?"

A naughty smirk replaces any former confusion, but I interrupt before he answers. "I'll assume casual."

Then, bag in hand, I head downstairs to the bedroom to take care of things. Humph, it's not so bad being in the driver's seat, especially when you have one helluva teacher.

The terrace is enchanting. Stretching the width and partial side of the building, it offers seclusion while showcasing a panorama view of skyscrapers in the distance. Sun-kissed flower beds filled with fragrant blossoms, ornamental grasses, and just the right blend of trees and shrubs for added privacy dot the perimeter. Dainty alyssum, black-eyed Susans, and knockout Roses add color, and to the right of a red Japanese maple tree is an outdoor sofa with plush gray cushions.

Ok, that will work.

Instrumental music quietly carries from a mounted

speaker. I turn to see Chase standing by an impressive electric grill, wearing cargo shorts, T-shirt, and a Mets baseball cap worn backwards. There's enough smoke billowing to signal a three-alarm fire response.

"Hey there, need any help?"

He throws another hunk of marinated meat on the grill. Heat singes my skin and I take a step back.

"That's some blaze you've got going there," I shout through the deafening hiss.

He finally takes notice and gives me a peck on the cheek, waving a cooking implement the size of a pitchfork.

"Only way to do it. There's a Chablis chilling on the table and next to it a bottle of pinot noir if you want red. Help yourself."

Stepping cautiously away from the grill, I walk over to a small table and pour myself a glass of the white, relishing the view and enjoying the light breeze that gentles the afternoon heat. A warm hand touches my arm, and I turn to see Chase standing at my side. His presence is quieting, and I lean my head on his shoulder just as he kisses me on the forehead.

"It's beautiful up here," I comment, more relaxed and at ease than I've felt in a while.

"I know. I often come up here to think, gather my wits …" He wraps his arm around my shoulder and pulls me closer.

"Wits?" I look up and smile because I still can't let it go.

"I've been known to use them on occasion." Bending me toward him, he knuckles my head. What is it with guys and head knuckles? With three older brothers it's no wonder I don't have a crater on top of my head.

"What made you decide on Park Avenue?" I don't want to say that he doesn't strike me as the Park Avenue type, but quite frankly he doesn't. I'd have pegged him more for SoHo or Tribeca.

"The deal was right. I was able to purchase and combine three apartments to create a duplex with great outdoor space. It also struck me as a good place to raise kids."

Well, this is a surprise. Mr. Always in Control wants a family. The idea makes me so elated I almost laugh out loud. There's the muffled sound of a phone ringing, and he buries his hand into his pocket and pulls out his blackberry.

"Chase Reardon." His voice is business abrupt then quiets for about a heartbeat of a second, and I figure that's how long the caller is given to speak. Sure enough Chase brusquely adds, "Seventy million is a damn good offer so do your due diligence." *Split second silence.* "Yeah, EB-5 program so get Jack on board. Those are questions an attorney needs to answer and remind him he's being paid hourly, not for ten-minute intervals. Get back to me when you hear." No thank you. No good-bye. Just a one finger hit.

"Now, woman," he grumbles. "Pour me a glass of wine while I tend to the fire."

As if seventy million dollars is the normal part of everyone's conversation, he heads back to a grill that now resembles a malfunctioning smokestack. When he lifts the lid, flames shoot out, making me wonder if I'm going to have to shove him into a drop and roll. Before I can make a move, he spikes the meat onto a large platter, pierces two or three pieces of something wrapped in aluminum foil placing them on the platter as well, slams the lid down on the licking flames, and cheerfully announces, "Chow time."

It would be funny if I wasn't discreetly checking whether he turned that damn inferno off. Holding the platter, he leads the way to the other side of the terrace. One look and my mouth falls open. Straight ahead is a beautifully set carved table resplendent with china, crystal glasses, linen napkins, and two small pewter pitchers filled with pink and orange roses from the terrace garden. In the center is a large mixed green and cucumber salad peppered with small heirloom tomatoes. He sets down the platter in the center and pulls back a chair for me.

"This is stunning. Is this table hand crafted"?

"Yeah, my father built it. It's made of salvaged teak he picked up from demolished buildings or just discarded in a junk heap."

"Your father's talented." I rub my hand along the smooth as glass surface.

"It's been his passion ever since he stopped drinking. Said it was about time he constructed instead of devastated. I think he was referring to lives, including his own. He carries a lot of guilt from his drinking days so puts all his effort and energy in each design, and when it's done he feels complete—whole—

like a form of therapy that helps him rebuild his life, one plank of wood at a time."

I nod in agreement because I understand how creating can be a salve for pain.

"And all the rest?" I point to the elegantly set table, chilled wine, cooked food. "When did you find the time to get it done?"

"I didn't. Sunny agreed to come by even though it's his day off to help get things ready."

"Sunny?"

"Yeah. He helps out with household chores, errands, laundry. Keeps everything spiffy."

He. "You mean you have a butler?"

He leans his head to the side and puckers out his lower lip, as if he never thought of it like that before. "I guess that's what you could call Sunny. We met in Afghanistan near the Pakistan border. Let's eat before it gets cold." He begins sharpening a carving knife.

"You met your butler in Afghanistan?"

"Yeah, he and his brother were medics in the Pakistani army, heading with other health care workers to a remote area suffering from a polio outbreak. We were doing reconnaissance work when—" He stops sharpening the knife in mid-motion. "God, it happened so fast. Sammy yells out 'IED!' Sammy had this sixth sense when it came to spotting them. Anyway, I manage to push Sunny with me to the side of the road and down a ravine, split seconds before the explosive device detonated."

Chase quiets, eyes staring ahead, body still. I'm barely breathing because he never reveals much about his life, and I want him to continue. He blinks once, twice, looks directly at me, and I know he has come back.

"After Sunny immigrated to the US, he looked me up determined to repay his debt for saving his life. I offered him this job and he's been with me ever since."

"It must have been hard, being in a war zone, having your life on the line like that." I'm thinking that his connections to Mac and Sammy and now Sunny are not like ordinary friendships developed between frat brothers or college roommates. These are alliances cemented by life-death experiences and driven by an I-got-your-back philosophy no matter the cost.

"Mostly it was tedious work, sitting around waiting for orders, conducting research, reconnaissance, until that one day, that one hour, that one minute when it isn't and you're left wondering how in the hell it all unfolded." His face closes like a blind shuttering a glaring sun, and he reaches for my hand, raises it to his lips, and plants a tender kiss in my palm. "Makes having you in my life even more sweet." The man is a conglomerate of surprises and contradictions.

I watch as he cuts the steak on a clean, uniform bias, each slice pink and tender and surprisingly cooked to perfection. He peels pack the aluminum foil and inside are plump ears of summer corn oozing melted butter. It all looks delicious and we dig in. There's everything relaxing about sharing time together eating a home-cooked meal. It's extraordinarily ordinary and for us unique.

"Fiona looks well," I add, forking a juicy piece of steak into my mouth and waiting patiently for his reply, hoping that he is relaxed enough to continue opening up about what's important to him. He pauses, chewing and mulling over my question.

"You never know with Fiona. She works hard to stay clean, but like most addicts she struggles with ups and downs."

I'm a little bit shocked by his free use of the word addict, and I'm finding it difficult to reconcile it with the lovely red-haired woman I just saw.

"I have to say Fiona's a wonderful mother. Liam's turning four next month, and she's already planning a picnic celebration at the beach for family and friends."

"That sounds wonderful. Will Liam's father be there?" The words slip out and I quickly think I may have intruded into something that's none of my business, but before I can add anything more, Chase looks at me and shrugs.

"Fiona won't talk about him, so we don't know who he is. I tried to convince her to tell me so we could at least be prepared to answer any questions Liam might have later on, especially about heredity and health issues, but she got so agitated I let it drop. After a while it didn't matter. Liam's a great kid and now it's all about being a part of his life and sharing in the fun of raising him."

"He must be excited about his upcoming birthday. I

remember living for my birthdays. It became like a countdown. I would tell anyone who would listen, in one month it will be my birthday, in three weeks it's my birthday, and on and on until the day finally arrived."

"That's exactly what he does." Chase looks at me like I'm clairvoyant. It's a painful reminder that his birthdays mustn't have been eventful.

"Before, when he woke up from his nap, first thing he did was raise all his fingers, whirling and chanting, 'In these many days it's my birthday and I'll be four,' over and over again until my head throbbed."

I'm smiling but I know the real reason for that headache. While I was peacefully sleeping, he was ushering out guests and sprinting to the pharmacy. I place the palm of my hand to his face and reach over and brush his lips with a kiss.

When I sit back down, he adds, "What's strange is how difficult it is for Fiona around this time. I mean she organizes a big birthday bash, puts on a happy face, but she has the tendency to get melancholy, even relapsed last year. That's why I thought she was having a problem when we were away. She needs to be watched. Otherwise, the party will be fun, a barbecue and bonfire on the beach, swimming, activities for the kids. Would you like to come?"

I'm delighted. "Sure." I can't help but wonder if the Countess is invited, but I don't have time to dwell because Chase looks across the table and says, "Your turn," then takes a big bite out of his ear of corn.

I eat another morsel of steak.—it really does melt in my mouth, chew, swallow—then spoon salad into a plate, doing everything possible to stall because the last thing I want to do is talk about myself. I mean, what do I have to talk about? All the things I haven't yet accomplished?

"There's not much to say?"

"Well for starters, how's your mother feeling?"

I feel my brow furrow with guilt. I really should have said something sooner. "I'm sorry I haven't thanked you. My mother is up and about because of your help. Dr. Leonard's treatment plan is proving invaluable."

He offers a simple, "Anytime," then continues to nibble and wait, nibble and wait, and I know he's adamant about my sharing.

I decide to stick with the already open topic of my mother. "I think about talking to her about my concerns, my guilt and blame. It's just that the time never seems right. When she's feeling well, I don't want to upset her by bringing up the stillbirth, and when she's depressed I don't want to make her condition worse. So there never seems to be a good time to talk about it."

"So don't. I know your mother from all the times she helped my family when my mother was sick. Even now, she keeps in touch with Fiona and my father. She would want to see you happy, untouched by her illness."

"You're right and it's probably another reason I never brought it up. Funny thing is I don't feel the need to talk about it as strongly as before. Thank you for that also. Talking to you helped unload the burden."

"I appreciate the credit, but you're coming to grips with it on your own. It's like when I enlisted in the marines or enrolled in Yale, each new experience helped me see myself in a different way. For you, it could be your trip, your award, a job interview, and these are just the beginning of a path that will change how you see life and your part in it."

Wise words to ponder, and I'm suddenly curious as to how he made his leap from soldier and student to real estate developer. It's not like it's easy to make your mark in such a competitive arena. I can well imagine the amount of capital that was needed.

"What about you, how did you become vested in real estate?"

He nods his head to the side as if he hadn't given it much thought for a while but is now reminded of its significance. "I made my first purchase with Sammy in DUMBO, the area known as Down Under the Manhattan Bridge in Brooklyn. At the time, it was mostly undeveloped … abandoned warehouses, once held Jehovah Witness Headquarters, sparsely rented artists' outposts, and a good share of drug-related crime. It really didn't look like it had much to offer, but I always felt follow the path of the artists, the writers, those who immersed themselves in the arts and that would be the next area to have the most potential. My father had been sober for a while and was as excited as I was about the area's potential. He took money from my mother's life insurance policy, cashed in some bonds from his accounting days, and took out a second mortgage and the three of us purchased a small abandoned building. We slowly converted it into condos and by then the real estate market in that section started to boom. We sold the building at a substantial profit. My father sold our house in Rockville Centre and bought a two family home in Long Beach for himself and Fiona and Liam to live. Sammy and I continued to parlay the profits into other real estate purchases. We're fortunate the market continues to do well in New York City."

His history continues to impress. I know he's deliberately underestimating his ability to glean and locate just the right area as well as select the building with the most value. I've heard him speaking to potential investors and landlords and noticed how he continuously researches online and canvasses neighborhoods, lots, airspace, and prospective buildings for purchase. He is an inveterate calculator of profitable opportunities with a keen understanding of how to select properties with both long and short-term potential for financial gain. I want to tell him how fascinated I am in his achievements, but there's no time because as soon as we finish eating, he asks me if I'd like to dance. Although our reasons may be different, my guess is that he's as uneasy as I am about discussing the past.

Nora Jones croons "Come Away with Me" and in his arms, I notice his steps are light and easy as we move to the ballad.

"You dance well. Where did you learn?" His movements are too smooth, too accurate not to have had lessons.

"Ballroom dance instruction."

I nearly stop dead in my tracks and gliding me in his arms without missing a beat, he adds, "Yes, in all that madness my mother made me and Fiona take formal dance lessons. It was the only thing that brought a smile to her face during her treatments. She would clear the living room, play something by Anita Baker and we would show her what we learned while she sat on the sofa and watched. My father would whistle and clap when we were done, wiping tears from his eyes. It was so embarrassing."

Sharing this moment from his past tells me more about his life than any nightmarish experience with a deranged thug ever would. He pulls me closer and still moving with easy rhythm adds, "I brought more kids down dressed in that damn vested suit and tie on my way to dance class than during wrestling season."

I throw back my head and laugh and he leads me in a flawless one-two-three step.

"You're not bad yourself. Don't tell me you took ballroom dance lessons too. I was convinced we were the only two kids on all of Long Island to do so."

"No, not ballroom dancing. Ballet." The music has shifted, and we sway gently to Miles Davis playing "When I Fall in Love."

"Was that your choice?"

"More or less. My parents encouraged me to participate in an afterschool activity and when they asked what I would like to do, I didn't have to think twice before insisting on sword fighting or wrestling." Now it's his turn to toss his head back and laugh.

"You may think that's funny, but I had to deal with three older brothers and I was desperate to best one of them at something."

"And … what did they say?"

You mean after they picked themselves up from laughing so hard?" He nods and a grin spread across his face. "Massimo explained that it's called fencing, and since I was only eight years old with sticks for arms, there was no way I could wield a sword. My mother said it was something we would revisit when I was older, which translated into never going to happen. Ditto for wrestling because as they put it, my body looked like a twig that would snap with one takedown. So my parents gave me a choice of either ballet or soccer and I chose ballet."

"And why was that?"

One of the things I love most about Chase is how he's interested enough in my life to want more details.

"Have you seen the soccer uniforms for our town?

"Yeah, Orange and black striped T-shirt, matching shorts. So?"

"Yeah, the most hideous orange and black stripe imaginable. Maybe if it was Halloween and I was dressing as a pumpkin I'd wear it."

"So you didn't choose soccer because the uniforms made a bad fashion statement?"

I nod and he pauses, his forehead crinkling a bit before adding, "Wait a minute. I seem to remember a photo of you in your living room holding a trophy and sporting that same ugly uniform just described."

Another thing I love about Chase is his ability to remember the most trivial details of my life and make them appear significant.

"That is correct. About two years into ballet, when I grew taller but hadn't gained any weight, it was decided that running in the fresh air would increase my appetite and fatten me up. In an Italian household, if you're not eating for two, you're sick and *dying*. I kicked up a fuss until Benny Shuster, this kid in my class, promised he'd show me wrestling moves during recess if I joined the team."

We've moved to the lounge sofa and I'm lying with my head in Chase's lap as he strokes my hair. I look up and see his eyes narrow.

"Is that the Benny Shuster you got sent to the principal's office for giving a black eye." See what I mean? He remembers it all, but his open curiosity is more caring than prying.

"The one and only. It seems that once I joined the team, little Benny's wrestling moves involved pinning me against a playground tree and kissing me."

His hand stills. "I always knew that kid had a twisted side. When I was coaching, I'd see him standing under the bleachers peeking under girls' skirts and dresses."

Oh good heavens he's actually tense and a little bit angry. "Relax, we were ten."

"Yeah, but unless someone continues to blacken his eyes, he's probably one of those perverts who uses his phone to photograph under women's dresses as they go up and down subway steps."

"Or it could be he's become a gynecologist and doesn't have to go through all that trouble to take a sneak peek." I hope I'm making him see how ridiculous he's being.

Without missing a beat, he drolly adds, "Then, let's hope that's not who you're scheduled to see on Friday."

Like I said, no detail in my life is too small for him not to remember. He also sticks to his word because that night under the small white lights winking like fairy dust along the sides of his terrace, he makes the most tender, sweet love to me on the lounge sofa. Problem is, even in fairytales there's evil.

CHAPTER
TWENTY-SEVEN

"You don't understand. Putting it off any longer is like trying to ward off a herd of charging rhinos."

Chase is massaging my foot and in between groans of pleasure, I'm trying to explain what it's like dealing with my family. My mother continues to phone to complain about how they have not seen me since my return from Europe, each of my brothers take turns phoning and texting to ask if I need help with my move, which translates into why haven't you moved yet, and my father emailed the other day asking if I required a moving van because if that was a problem he was willing to foot the bill.

Moving van? It was common knowledge that my clothes and bedding were all I was taking from my current cramped living space that was more dorm than apartment. The only reason I kept it was that my new lease didn't begin until the 15th and I didn't want to move twice. I did have a number of boxes, but no way, no how did I need a moving van. In fact, with Sammy and Chase's help, I had already started dropping off boxes.

So … today was the day the move into my small stretch of Manhattan real estate was being made official. Massimo and Antonio were coming to hang my flat screen TV. Fiona was going to be on hand to help with the unpacking, and my mother was going to take Liam to Central Park so we could all work unencumbered by the demands of a three-year-old. It seems that while I went about my life with my own high school and college friends, she had remained in touch with Chase's family, often helping Fiona out with Liam. This doesn't surprise me. My mother was often on hand to help others and kept what she did quiet, never gossiping about other families' problems or worries.

"Ahh, a little more to the left," I purr as the pressure of his fingers on my foot continue their circling.

"It's just that we have to tread carefully."

"Mmm …" His massaging feels like mini foot orgasms, and I barely register what he's saying. That is until he stops.

I look up and catch him rubbing under his chin with the back of his hand and staring ahead as if he's contemplating ways to mediate world conflicts.

"Hello, Earth to Chase." I sit up on my elbows pretending to look just as grave. "We have a problem."

"Yeah, I know."

"Damn straight, you know and you better do something

about it."

He stares at me and swallows. "I'm trying to think of the best way to handle it."

"It's very simple. Essential foot ministrations have ceased, causing a phenomenal pleasure withdrawal. Therefore the only solution is to continue massaging. " I lean back and wait, but he's too caught up in his dilemma.

"Your brothers and I, we … ah … swore this oath about dating sisters, and it may not be so easy."

Ever since I mentioned we should announce that we have been seeing each other over "thank you" pizza and drinks after move in, he's been nervous. Frankly, all this oath stuff sounds like a lot of unnecessary and antiquated drama. I am already up to my ears in change.

These past few weeks, it's like my life has been wrapped in a flood of firsts. First flurry of job interviews, first job offer and acceptance at Estelle Designs, first successful completion of two weeks at said job, first day at new apartment, and last but not least, first living with boyfriend—which wasn't as awkward as I originally thought. We melded into an easy rhythm of everyday activity. Wake up, breakfast, work, arrive home, dinner, and bed, not immediately followed by sleep due to various nocturnal shenanigans that never cease to amaze me, especially since there's no need for condoms now that I'm on the pill.

Chase gave me a key to his place, actually insisted I take it, but the truth is I'm still unsure about this living together arrangement. My whole life I've had people hovering over me, doting parents who saw to my every need, older brothers who shepherded me places, loving relatives who put me up when I was studying abroad.

Now it's time to stand on my own two feet, even though I have been swept off them. How else can I possibly maintain a relationship with an Ivy League graduate, now high-powered and successful real estate magnate who also served in combat as an officer in the United States Marines? The man is a veritable mountain of achievement. And what do I have to my credit? A 4.0 graduating cum from Parsons and an international award for best design. Not shabby but not exceptionally varied. No, I had to be more than little Alicia shuffling through life without worry or want.

"My brothers will just have to deal. I don't meddle in their private lives. They've no business poking around in mine. Besides, they're probably going to figure it out when they see you helping."

"When are they getting there?"

"I gave Antonio the key to be sure he's there if the TV arrives earlier than the warehouse indicated. Massimo says he's coming after he finishes rounds at the hospital, and my mother is bringing Liam after the park. I don't know about Fiona. Antonio seems to be ignoring my texts, so I better hurry if I want to be sure Fiona can get in."

He glances at me, worried look still plastered in place, until he wipes it clean and throws me that gorgeous, full-toothed, don't-you-worry smile.

"Yeah, ok. I have some work to do first. I'll meet you there."

He resumes massaging, and I throw my head back onto the sofa, all thoughts erased. What I didn't realize is that I should have been sharing his concern because what eventually unfolded can only be described as a Murphy's Law debacle of untold proportions.

"Excuse me," I mutter, bending to retrieve my purse that's just been knocked off my shoulder by some burly guy with a nose as wide as his barreled chest. The earphones from my iPhone pop out, and my favorite music is replaced with honking horns and screaming sirens.

I look up to meet him eye to eye, but all I see is scurrying New Yorkers wilted from the heat, looking to be anywhere but walking on streets cooked by car, bus, and truck exhausts. It's hot, the kind of New York City hot that makes it seem as if you're bending over a pot of boiling water instead of walking in the open air.

New Yorkers, always in a rush. Mildly annoyed, I push into Starbucks, wanting nothing more than to be nursing an ice coffee and enjoying a good dose of air conditioning.

Once inside, I'm surrounded by busyness. People hunker over laptops, chat on their cells, or cluster together, studying graphs and spread sheets while employees call out memorized order combos that would challenge a summa cum laude linguist. It's like an office masquerading as a coffee shop. No matter. I need this break. It's only six blocks from Chase's apartment to mine, but in today's heat and humidity the walk feels like sixty.

I'm damp with perspiration when I finally reach my apartment building even though I'm only wearing cutoffs and a flimsy sleeveless blouse. I lift my hair off my back and twist it into a bun, holding it in place with hair pins I have stashed in my pocket.

Ahh, the relief is immediate and wiping my forehead with the back of my hand, I look up and spot Chase walking up First Avenue on his way to meet me. He looks carefree in khaki shorts falling slightly below his narrow waist and a slate blue T-shirt that tugs smoothly across his broad shoulders. I could admire that view all day. He reaches me and I put my arms around him and give him a quick kiss then step back and fan myself with my hand.

"Ugh, I'm hot and sweaty."

"I'm all hot and bothered too … for you." He discreetly rests his hand on my breast. I hit it away.

"Behave. There's work to be done and I'm late enough as it is." I really shouldn't have lingered so long over coffee.

"Your wish is my command. Lead the way." He pulls my head back and gives me another kiss.

Elliot, the portly doorman, opens the door and waves us through with a big hello. Once in the elevator, Chase takes me in his arms and plants a slow, deep kiss. This time I can't resist, and I reach up and fold myself into his arms, my hands twisting in his hair, my lips pressed onto his. He lets out a low groan and deepens the kiss, his tongue doing a slow dance in my mouth, his hand gently massaging my breast through the sheer fabric of my blouse. It's not as if we've been apart but last night and this morning were mostly about my move. Now, like polar opposites caught in a magnetic field, this alone elevator time gives us the opportunity to attract. But all too soon, the elevator reaches the sixth floor and reluctantly we separate.

It's amazing how quickly Chase regains his composure, but looks can be deceiving because just as I unlock the apartment door, he pushes me against the outside wall and continues his kiss, opening the top buttons of my blouse and fondling my breast. I moan and he deepens the kiss, raising my hands above my head and pressing me into the wall. I can't touch, but I can feel and the combined sensations of mouth and breast send my need soaring.

Neither of us hear the elevator doors open or the footsteps approaching and before we can process that there is another person in the hallway, Massimo is standing in front of us in stunned silence. We separate, all of us caught in an odd stillness that's like being trapped in the calm before a storm, and for a split second I'm lulled into believing this is no big deal.

I'm wrong.

With rocket quick reflexes, Chase pushes me out of the way as Massimo charges head first into him, throwing him against the apartment door. It swings open and they tumble through, a tangle of spins and tosses.

There's muffled grunts of "you bastard" and "sworn oath" from Massimo as they wrestle around the entranceway. Chase locks Massimo in a defensive hold but Massimo, wild with anger, keeps lashing out fists in a move that looks more like he's groping in the dark than landing punches.

"Watch your hands, Massimo. You're studying to be a surgeon, for God's sake," Chase shouts as he dodges a left.

"Damn you, you womanizing, sister-stealing bastard."

What?

"Stop it, both of you," I holler into empty space because neither are listening.

I edge closer, trying to make some attempt to separate their locked bodies when Massimo spins and knocks me right onto my keister. Shimmying away from their roiling bodies, I wonder if it's possible to be evicted even before you move in. There's another loud crash and some more groaning and shuffling as I turn and hoist myself up. That's when I see it or I should say them, and I freeze in my spot, disbelief widening my eyes and muting my mouth. Blindfolded and tied to my new cinnamon colored upholstered chair, clad only in her bra and panties, and wearing a look of surprise and fear is Fiona, and standing right next to her is a flabbergasted Antonio wearing nothing but his boxer shorts.

Oh god, we've been hit by a home invasion! I start to shout for help when realization dawns and pressing my hand to my mouth, I gasp. So much for sworn oaths and my cheeks start to heat.

Chase, locked in rapid wrestling rolls with Massimo, looks up, squints, and immediately registers the scene.

This is not good.

He quickly throws a left hook and Massimo falls limp. Springing up in that quick as a panther motion I know all too well, he lunges at Antonio.

Down they both go with Chase grabbing Antonio by the throat and shouting, "We swore an oath, you kinky S and M bastard." Antonio doesn't say anything, basically because he's just trying to breathe.

"Again with this oath. What is this, the middle ages?" I call out, frustration making me seethe. I let out a disgusted *humph*. If they were actual medieval knights sworn to sexual abstinence oaths, the lot of them would be rotting in a dungeon.

I make another vain attempt to separate them as they knock over boxes and furniture impervious to my shouts. Antonio lands a jab, but Chase pushes him back down, and they both tumble into a table, causing a lamp to totter. It's the exquisite antique brass lamp I found at a local estate sale, and I lunge for the save, grabbing it with both hands as I slide on my stomach, catching it in the nick of time. Vase in hand, I look up, blowing a lock of unruly hair from my eyes only to see my mother standing in the doorway, holding the hand of a red-headed, freckled moppet I can only assume must be Liam. Terrific.

She takes one look at the scene, gasps hand to mouth (easy to tell we're mother and daughter) at the sight of you know who tied to you know where, and immediately places her hand over Liam's eyes, leading him out of the apartment.

It isn't until we hear Liam's high-pitched voice asking, "Are we playing hide and seek?" that everyone regains their sanity and spins into action.

I untie Fiona's wrists. Chase releases Antonio then stands and walks towards Massimo to help him up. We set about righting chairs and pillows and other assorted items that have been tossed about. Fiona, her face mirroring the color of her hair, quickly dresses then stuffs the rope and blindfold into a kitchen drawer.

Fuming, I walk over to Antonio and between clenched teeth utter louder than I mean to, "What the FUCK were you thinking?"

"Watch your mouth," three male voices call out in unison.

They have got to be kidding. My apartment looks like it's been trashed in a frat party gone bad. There's toppled furniture, broken glass, and over turned boxes strewn about. All that's missing are trashed liquor bottles and empty beer kegs, and I'm the one being corrected.

Antonio ignores my comment and slips on his pants and shirt, then quietly grabs a broom and begins sweeping up the mess. By the time my mother and Liam return, some semblance of order has been restored.

"Mommy, Mommy." Liam runs in and throws his arms

around Fiona who takes him in a hug. Wiggling away from her hold, he quickly turns and runs, shouting, "Uncle Casey, Uncle Casey," and jumps into Chase's arms.

Chase lifts him in the air and swings him around. "Hey, buddy, how's it going?"

It's heartening to see this side of Chase, big smile, wide, animated eyes as he lifts Liam onto his shoulders. My eyes shift to my mother standing frozen in the entranceway. Despite her calm demeanor, she's crackling with anger. Her lips are pursed and standing at attention, she glares at all of us.

Giving Liam a quick smile, she holds out an FAO Schwarz bag, and he swings his leg over Chase's head and slides down to take it. Inside is a new set of Legos, and he shifts his attention to opening and assembling them on the far side of the room.

In a small voice Fiona asks, "Liam did you say thank you to Mrs. Cesare?"

Liam turns and runs into Mamma's arms, reaching up to give her a kiss and a hug. "Thank you, Mrs. Cesare." Mamma hugs him back then ruffles his hair.

As soon as Liam is absorbed in his building, she pins us with an accusing glare. "What is going on here?" Before anyone can answer, she looks at me and adds, "For heaven's sake, Alicia, button your blouse."

Yep, wide open. Could this be any more embarrassing? Antonio, uses my distraction, to jump in first. He always did have loose lips.

"Alicia and Chase have been … er … dating, and Massimo

found out and got angry."

"Alicia, this is true?"

Shit. I'm now in the hot seat on two, no actually three counts, since I haven't visited since my return. I should have known Antonio would incriminate me first. I never seem to remember that the person to speak first in these situations has the power to divert attention to whomever he wants. I narrow my eyes and glare at him before facing my mother and answering, "Yes."

"How long have the two of you been dating?"

This is not going to be easy. I pause.

"Um, only for about eight weeks."

"I don't understand. You've just spent the last month in Europe."

I shrug, answering nonchalantly, "We met up there."

"You just happened to coincidently bump into each other while touring another continent," she scoffs disbelievingly.

"No, I … we …" I'm at a loss of words. I've never been good at masking guilt and now all the excuses I gave for not moving into my apartment sooner and not visiting … *too busy at work, need more time to pack, jet lag,* seem like lies. Some know how to go on the offense and act outraged when confronted. I stammer.

Chase clears his throat and mercifully intervenes. "Excuse me, ma'am."

Ma'am?

My mother shifts her attention to him. "It wasn't by

accident. Beth posted their Monte Carlo travel photos on Facebook and Instagram. Fiona saw them, knew I was also there for the Grand Prix and texted me their travel info in case we wanted to meet. I was able to … uh … find Alicia, and we met for lunch then drove to the Ligurian coast. Later, I accompanied Alicia to her awards ceremony in Lake Como."

Welcome to the PG-rated version of events. Impressive. My mother nods satisfied for the moment, and I think I hear Chase breathe a sigh of relief. It helped that he mentioned escorting me to the fashion awards. Well played, Mr. Reardon.

"And you, Antonio? How long have you been seeing Fiona?'

Ha! See how he likes being the one under fire, and I smile smugly at him. He glares back and it's like we're eleven all over again.

Antonio pauses then answers, "For about a year now."

All heads spin toward him except for Chase. He frostily stares at Fiona who looks the other way. Poor Fiona. I know that look, and I'm relieved that for once it's not directed at me.

"The problem with your generation…" my mother takes us in an all-encompassing gaze "…is that you're all so busy communicating with…" her hand sweeps the air "…the rest of the world with this, this …" Confused, she looks at Massimo and asks, "Come si fa a chaim?"

"Social media," he sheepishly answers, no doubt still embarrassed about the brawl.

"Social media," she repeats for emphasis then marches

on with angry vigor, "that you forget to tell your family who you are dating so that maybe he…" she looks pointedly at me and I look away "…or she…" she stares at Antonio, who wishes he could disappear "…can be invited to a nice family dinner where everyone can talk and get acquainted instead of experiencing the shock of finding out by accident."

She gives Chase a quick glance before turning to me and adds, "I see what has been keeping you so busy you couldn't visit your parents even though it's been almost two months since we've last seen you." I think of my last "talk" with my mother when she was so depressed she could barely lift herself off the bed and guilt gets an open invitation to visit. The change from then to now is so considerable that I feel tears welling. Dressed in a sleeveless ivory cotton dress, with her light brown hair swept back in soft waves, she looks elegant and happy.

Vivid green eyes shifting from annoyance to pleasure, she flaps her hand in the air in a manner that says "*what does it really matter*," walks over, and takes me in a hug.

"It makes me happy to see how well you look." It feels good to be in her arms, like being wrapped in a soft quilt scented with Channel.

Thoroughly guilt tripped, we remain silent except for Massimo who apologetically says he's glad no one was hurt. Mamma turns from me and smiles at him. It figures he would be the one to get off easy. As the oldest, "precious" Massimo is always right, even though he was the one who triggered this fiasco. Antonio must be thinking the same thing because I catch him scowling at Massimo too. To his credit, Massimo goes over to Chase and they both shake hands. Antonio might not be as easily off the hook. For starters he ratted me out when he, too, was a major cause of this chain of events and he used *my* chair in *my* apartment to do heaven knows what with Fiona.

"Really," I whisper to him so no one can hear. "Rope and a blindfold and in my apartment no less. What other lewd carrying on have you been up to?"

"You can't afford to criticize," he whisper-mouths, giving a nervous glance behind him to make sure no one is listening. "Did they let you design your uniform in the big house?" He stops and starts softly humming, "Look Down, look down."

Oh god, he knows about my arrest, but it's too late to worry who else knows. Besides, I'm too angry now to care. "Very funny, Marquis de Sade. And nice underwear. What? Too warm for leather and chainmail?"

Chase, catching the exchange which is now well above a whisper, casually wraps his arm around me and pulls me away, giving Antonio a curt nod that given the circumstances is the best peace token he has to offer.

My mother hands Massimo a wet cloth for his cut lip and takes the lead again, suggesting that me and Fiona go to lunch with her while the "boys" start the unpacking process. The idea is fine by me. I suggest JG Mellon, a nearby restaurant that serves the best burgers and I offer to bring them back lunch.

As I'm looking through all the clutter for my purse, Liam

tired of his building, runs toward Chase and pointing at me, asks, "Who is she?"

Chase takes him by the hand and formerly makes the introduction. "Alicia, allow me to introduce you to my nephew, Liam Reardon. Liam this is Alicia Cesare."

I bend down to meet him at eye level and shake his hand. "It's nice to meet you, Liam."

"You're pretty." Giggling, he takes my hand, leans in, and gives me a kiss on the cheek. Oh my, he has his uncle's charm.

Then, like a whirlwind of packed energy, he turns toward Chase, asking, "What are we going to do next, Uncle Casey?"

Lifting a heavy box to unpack, Chase drolly answers, "Atoning, Liam. We're going to atone."

I give Chase a sympathetic nod and kiss him chastely on the cheek. "Thank you."

With that drop-dead gorgeous smile of his, he counters with a simple, "You're welcome."

"Uncle Casey, when we play *tatoning,* can I tie you up like when mommy and Antonio were playing pirates? Mrs. Cesare said that's what you do when you play pirates."

I don't hear Chase's answer because a heartbeat later my mother asks me, "Qual e il significato this …" She pauses, forehead wrinkling as she tries to retrieve the right English words before finishing with, "Kinky S … M?"

Terrific. Massimo gets to clarify social media while I get stuck defining sadomasochism. She looks at me waiting for an answer.

"I'm not sure." I hesitate, biting the inside of my mouth. "I think it means strange man."

There's snickering from inside the apartment, and I give the door a firm tug on my way out. My mother looks at me, skeptically shaking her head.

"All that money spent on scouting dues and summer camp and this is how he applies those learned skills."

I close my eyes, wishing I was anywhere but here, then walk briskly toward the elevator, noticing Fiona's face and hair again blend into one flaming mass.

On the street I'm surprised to see Sammy double parked and waiting. He pokes his head out the window and shouts, "Need a ride?"

This is not an accidental encounter. It's the first time I've seen him since we arrived back in the city and now that I'm moving into my own place, I'm thinking I will be seeing more of him.

"Sure, but we're only going a few blocks."

"No problem. Hop in. It's too hot to be walking."

Too hot and too dangerous, I think, fear coursing through me as we get in the car, Mamma taking the front seat and Fiona sitting in back with me.

Turning to look at me, she worriedly remarks, "Are you alright? You look a bit pale."

"I'm fine." I immediately shift the focus away from me and introduce Sammy.

"It's nice to meet you, Sammy. You must know Chase from

the marines," Mamma intones smoothly, then quickly adds, "You look like a military man."

"Yes, ma'am."

"Please, call me Elvira." Sammy nods but doesn't answer.

"Did you serve together in Afghanistan?"

"Yes, ma'am." Extra information is never offered but that doesn't deter my mother.

"This air-conditioning feels wonderful. Lucky for us you happened to be in the area."

"Happy I could help out."

There's a slight pause, but before I can change the subject, she swoops down with another question. "What is it you do now, Sammy?"

I think I actually stop breathing, uneasiness creeping in to replace my former anxiety. I know my mother and this line of questioning is leading somewhere. Trying to deflect the course of conversation, I turn my attention to Fiona. "What a stunning ring you're wearing."

It's a large domed turquoise, clear blue with slight veins of a matrix resembling an upside down Y running across the center. Very beautiful and very unusual. She looks up surprised, relieved that something other than her involvement with Antonio is being recognized.

"Thank you. It was my mother's." She gives me a warm smile as she tenderly fingers the stone.

"I'm sorry," Mamma continues. "What were you saying Sammy?"

Damn. Interception foiled. She's really starting to irritate me.

"Real estate," Sammy smoothly answers. "I've partnered with Chase on two of his buildings."

I exhale and stare out the window, feigning disinterest yet hanging onto every word. I want to tell her to stop with all the questions, but I don't want to make it seem like there's a problem, so I keep my mouth shut and strain to listen.

"War buddies and business associates." I can only see the back of her head, but I can imagine her pursing her lips as she lets out a wow burst of air before remarking, "You two must be close?"

"Yes, ma'am."

Blissful silence follows and breathing a sigh of relief, I spot the restaurant ahead. The car is blowing air-conditioning at a cool comfort level of 72 degrees and it must be at least 98 degrees outside, but I can't wait to jump out of the car and away from the litany of questions. The last thing I need is for my mother to piece together Sammy's role in protecting me or my near mishaps in Europe. Sammy pulls into a rare open spot on the corner and before any of us can make a move to open the doors, Mamma quietly but firmly looks him straight in the eye.

"Then, Sammy, I'm sure you'll take good care of my daughter."

"Yes, ma'am."

She knows.

CHAPTER TWENTY-EIGHT

y apartment is comfortable in a cozy, close kind of way, and although it's a bungalow compared to Chase's palace, I like the ease of stretching my legs and curling my toes in my own space while watching some inane reality TV show.

Mornings I'm up by six and two or three times a week, I jog the course around the reservoir in Central Park. Traveling to work on Broadway between 38th and 39th has become routine: walk to the six train on 77th and Lex, take it to 59th, change to the N or the R and take that to 42nd, then walk the remaining three blocks. This mundane bit of every man's travel cost me a hefty battle. Initially Chase insisted Sammy drive me to work, but I wouldn't budge and to prove my point, I slipped out the service entrance of my building and walked to the subway.

Even though I won the battle, I wondered if I might lose the war. I mean how effective was my security if I was able to shake them so easily. Chase explained "the slip" was enabled by the element of surprise. They simply weren't expecting my deceit. And I thought my parents were masters of guilt.

Mostly, though, I see his worry. With Liam's birthday approaching, fears of a relapse from Fiona are compounded because, for some unknown reason, that period of time triggers an internal Armageddon for her. Chase has Mac watching Fiona, and I'm sure the Countess as well, so the last thing anyone needs is a pain-in-the-ass whining about wanting independence. I promise to follow the rules, but I want to travel to work like an ordinary person, sliding the bright yellow metro card I paid for, walking through the turnstile and getting on the train or hailing a taxi if I work late or meet colleagues for drinks at the end of the work week.

By the start of my forth week, I breeze past security and up to the 24th floor without that new job angst.

Today, when the doors slide open the receptionist, Kim, greets me with a flat, "Freak-out on four. RVM sees sagging instead of draping. Wants you ASAP."

"Got it." I lean forward, making sure to throw out a pointed, "Good morning, Kim."

"Yeah, you too." *Tap, tap, tap*. Her fingers dance across the keys as I about face back to the elevator to the fourth floor to find Virgil. Since my start at Estelle Designs, Virgil has afforded me every opportunity to extend my reach as a newcomer by allowing me to help out with an assortment of projects.

"Thank heavens you're here. Just look at this." Virgil

reaches out his hand, head cocked to the side, elbow snug to his hip as he points to a fully-clothed display mannequin. "Tell me, is this designer fashion or something a pioneer woman would head west wearing?" He turns, and before I can answer, adds, "Good god you look like a blanched tomato. Don't tell me you won that battle to ride the subway instead of being driven in a new, top-of-the-line Mercedes SUV or are we going to have another episode of a spiked haired ex-marine barreling into the office demanding …" Here Virgil pinches his lips and says, "'May I have a word with Miss Alicia Cesare?'" with Chase's exact intonation. "You came out of that conference room white as a ghost. I even noticed your hand shaking, but when he took it in his and kissed it before leaving, I knew you had him…" Virgil holds up his finger and twirls "…wrapped around your finger. That man will do anything for you."

I clear my throat because I'm thinking what Chase really wanted to do was wrap his hand around my backside, landing several sharp slaps, but I don't want to discuss my relationship issues with my boss even if that boundary line was crossed when Chase showed up. True, it was before office hours and the place was mostly empty, but Virgil was here and so was Charlotte Henry, who's not my biggest fan.

Not so with Chase, though. Charlotte took one look at him and I knew he had yet another groupie. Her lips actually pulled back into a smile baring perfectly aligned teeth when Chase reached out his hand and formerly introduced himself. He may have wanted to throttle me but here, at my work place his demeanor was all business courtesy. "Sorry for any inconvenience," he said before leaving.

"No problem," Charlotte answered in a sultry voice, wooden smile intact until looking at me, it transformed into its usual cold stare. Heading to her office, her final, "However did *you* manage to snare him?" nearly caused me to tackle her from behind.

I drag my focus back to Virgil. "Yes, we worked it out, and I have my reasons for wanting to take public transportation."

"One of them must be insanity," he mutters before shifting to the problem at hand. "Can you help with this ensemble? The scarf is supposed to drape over the long jacket, not hang like some housecoat."

Normally after only four weeks into a starter job all I'd be doing is printing copies and fetching coffee, but shortly after my second week I corrected a Janet Jackson type wardrobe malfunction that occurred when a model's breast popped out of her top as she was being photographed. I happened to be back from a coffee run and was able to perform emergency stitching and nipping in enough of the right places so the shoot could continue and, I might add, look spiffier. *Thank you, Mamma for sharing your sewing expertise.*

I go to my purse and pull out a pair of sewing scissors that I always carry just in case. I remove the scarf and spread it out on the large table, pushing back the dozens of dresses that line the walls and open a small slit for a button hole. The opening will have to be finished, but for now it will do. Using a tape measure, I pinpoint where the button should be sewn so it's hidden but offers just the right amount of tapering. Rifling through the bars of hanging clothes, I nip a matching extra button from a sweater and sew it onto the scarf, lengthening the slit the tiniest bit to hold the button.

"This will due for the time being bu—" Just as I'm about to add what else needs to be done, Charlotte appears, her face expressionless except for the tiniest sweep of blue eyes across the shaped scarf.

"Is it Dr. Draper to the rescue again?" she queries, head to one side, one corner of her mouth lifted into what is supposed to be a grin but looks more like a snarl. When Virgil refers to me as Dr. Draper, it's spoken with humor and appreciation. With Charlotte, it's with deprecation and malice, but I say nothing. She is a respected part of the team and her eye for detail and form is impeccable.

"I still think it droops like an oversized sack."

Virgil places it back on the mannequin, smoothing it here, lifting another side slightly before stepping back and studying the overall result and shaking his head.

"I disagree. This works, the scarf complements the skirt and turtleneck and adds a natural elegance that offers more than warmth. It says, 'come enjoy my carefree lifestyle, take a stroll with me along this rocky bluff, or let's grab a cup of espresso on our shopping stroll down Madison Avenue.'" Charlotte rolls her eyes but Virgil just continues. "That is the beauty and power of fashion, Charlotte, but I'm afraid that for all your technical genius it escapes you. It's a good thing we're here to remind you."

We? Did he just include me in his description? Charlotte remains stock-still, like some garden party ice statue that shows no signs of melting even though the temperature is hitting 100.

Virgil shifts his attention to an assortment of outfits in the back and walking toward them, gives Charlotte one final glance. "I want Alicia to be part of our team for the production." To me his only comment is, "Don't disappoint."

I let the words percolate, but I really want to jump and hoot except Ms. Iceberg is standing right across from me. I walk to the table return my scissors to my purse, grab my coffee, and start toward the elevators, leaving her to seethe in silence. My escape is not fast enough. She thrusts her blood red polished finger in front of my face, indicating I should wait. It's like being held in place by a witch from some Grimm fairytale.

Calling out to a cluster of her team that's milling around dozens of outfits slotted for the show, she brusquely announces, "Meeting in five, my office. The logistics of this show are unraveling and time is running out." They scatter like rodents fleeing an exterminator. She returns to the stock of hanging dresses rifling through them one at a time, pausing every now and again to select the one she wants, leaving me to stand and wait. When she finally turns, it's as if she's noticing me for the first time. "Grab me a coffee, milk no sugar. I'll be at my desk."

What a bitch.

The next several weeks are a whirlwind of activity. Selecting, sewing, clipping, fitting, and for me ... coffee runs. You can never climb that ladder of success too quickly. I don't mind. The atmosphere sizzles. Charlotte has shed her animosity and blends with the group for the benefit of a stellar result. She even covers for me when I accidently tear a tulle skirt then shows her expertise in repairing it and combining it with a delicate cashmere pullover. Her talent for blending color and texture is second to none, and I continue to learn from her expertise. Other than work, I have no life. I'm up at six, at the office by seven-thirty, and home at nine where I collapse into bed often too tired to eat dinner. I let myself into Chase's apartment on Friday nights, but it's usually just to collapse exhausted in his bed where I'm asleep within seconds. I love feeling his arms around me, and I have to say I sleep my soundest when I'm with him. On working Saturdays, he insists on driving me, and I'm too tired to argue. It's a welcome relief to sit in his air-conditioned car, and Sunny is always there to hand me a container of homemade yogurt with fresh fruit and an iced espresso in a covered paper cup as I dash out.

The show is in two weeks and all nerves are frayed. Virgil is convinced the catwalk is too passive. "Mannequins meandering down a carpet," is how he describes the models. "Where's the excitement, the creative communication and interaction with the audience?"

"You're confusing theater with fashion," Charlotte interrupts.

Virgil shoots her a withering look and the rest of us disappear into stationery silence. This could turn into a King Kong-Godzilla fight. The quiet stretches. Charlotte is the first to break it.

"Let me see what I can come up with to jazz it up," she conciliates.

This gives me an idea, but I don't know if I should offer it. My heart begins to pump, and I feel my palms start to sweat. My mouth opens and I'm surprised to hear my voice sound so clear and articulate.

"How about if jazz band performers become part of the catwalk." The silence turns comatose. I swallow and turn my gaze directly to Virgil adding, "Some of the musicians could even serve as models wearing the outfits that suit their physiques. We could intersperse them with the professional models."

Charlotte looks like she swallowed a spoiled scallop. "What an outré idea."

"What the F***?" I search my brain for some meaning or Italian equivalent and come up blank.

"Oh for heaven's sake, Charlie, speak English so the rest of us can understand what you mean," her skinny right-hand man who heads men's wear remarks. Except for Virgil, he's the only other person who can get away with standing up to her and calling her Charlie.

"It's over the top, to the point of being ridiculous. What do we possibly know about music? This is a fashion show, not a musical theater performance." At this point, she's actually snorting.

Virgil waits, his face expressionless. I've seen him look like this before and it's usually when he's contemplating something. At least my idea merits consideration.

"Why can't fashion be theater? What people wear expresses their feelings, what they want to communicate to others. It should be interactive and what better way to accomplish this than by combining it with another art form. How do we find a decent jazz band this late in the game?" he throws out to all of us. Mimi, who I first met during my interview in Lake Como, answers first, her soft voice a balm to my jittery nerves. "Clark may be able to help."

I remember Mimi telling me that her husband is a musical director of a small downtown theater. "I can see if he can make some calls."

Charlotte shoots her a disdainful look. At least I'm not the only one on her to-scorn list.

Virgil barely waits for her to finish. "See what you can do to make it happen."

When I finally escape at nine o'clock, I spot Chase up the street, waiting in his pride and joy: a Porsche 911 Carrera. Black, with a sleek design, it's fast and smooth on the highway and good in stop and go traffic in the city. When I initially asked about it, Chase proudly rattled off a list of details: rear engine, rear wheel drive, seven-speed dual clutch gearbox. Curious, I had asked what other colors it came in, and he threw his head back and laughed, saying he didn't know but should have realized that's what would interest me.

"Hop in, I'm taking you to dinner." I hesitate because I'm thinking that all I want is to collapse in his bed and fall asleep nestled in his arms. "Give me a hard time and so help me, I'll drag you in by the hair and force feed you."

"Well now, how can I resist such a romantic invite?" I get in and he pulls me into an embrace kissing me soundly then uses his thumbs to stroke under my eyes. "I know, I know. Dark circles, little sleep, no food. Feed me and I should look human again."

"This show can't happen fast enough," he admonishes. "How about Platoon. We'll shoot across to the east side and be there in no time."

"Sounds delicious."

My stomach rumbles with my mouth watering at the thought of their roasted halibut. Chase briefly looks my way and asks, "What did you eat for lunch?"

"I had a banana." I lean back and close my eyes, relaxing my body, and he reaches over and takes my hand.

"You won't be effective if you don't eat." And he lifts and

kisses my palm. Several points south of my waist jump to attention as his lips linger on my hand.

I lean my head on his shoulder and he wraps his arm around me and pulls me closer, helping my limbs loosen and my mind slow. I let out a relaxed sigh. "I know I'm not performing brain surgery, but the amount of creative and physical energy this show demands is daunting." I look up and kiss his cheek. Then mouth turned up in a satisfied grin add, "I think I may have sold an idea to Virgil and the team to use during the show."

"Kudos to the beginner. What is it?"

"I suggested we have a jazz band perform with some of the musicians mixing with the models to liven up the catwalk. Virgil liked the concept." I pause thinking of Charlotte's disapproval, the downward turn of her mouth in reproach, her refusal to look at or speak to me for the remainder of the day and the barrier of silence she erected between me and her staff. Her plan was simple and ingenious. Once Virgil left for an on-site meeting, she gave me every menial task imaginable. If I wasn't on a coffee run, I was matching threads and sweeping up scraps and sorting and lifting boxes. It didn't take long for the others to get the message. Talk to me and they could be scrubbing the restrooms.

Chase removes his arm from around my shoulder and caresses the furrowed area between my brows with his thumb.

"And Charlotte?" he asks softly.

I aim my forefinger and shoot with my thumb. "PUKH."

"Is she good at what she does?" he asks, annoyance saturating his question.

"Very talented. Her technical and design expertise is unqualified. I just don't know why she doesn't respect my work. I follow her direction, piece items together based on her input, and still my work is not good enough."

"Maybe it's time to stop seeking her endorsement. If you wait for approval before taking any risks, you'll stagnate. Take it from me. I lived with contempt."

This I find surprising given his success and overall who-gives-a-fuck attitude. "From whom? Your family?"

"No. Not my family, but from just about everyone else. Friends, parents of friends, teachers, neighbors, anyone who knew my family circumstances. For a while I disappeared into myself. Didn't talk much or interact with others, just went for long jogs and lifted weights alone in my room. Then, as my mother became sicker all that self-loathing turned to anger, I was like a feral animal, picking fights and hurling insults with anyone I even thought was looking at me the wrong way, forget if they said something derogatory. It wasn't until Mr. Holden, the football coach, convinced me to try out for the team that I found an outlet for my frustration. I threw myself into sports and turned the fear and anger into competitiveness. Now I really don't give a shit what other people think. Except for those I love of course." He gives me another peck on my cheek. His sharing moves me, helps me open up.

"I just don't want to get too ahead of myself. And … well

what if the idea fails?"

"I don't believe it will. I can't think of anyone who will work harder than you to ensure that it takes off. Fashion is not something I know about, but it sounds like it will give Estelle Designs the press they want. It's about profit as much as pretty."

"I disagree."

He turns briefly to study me, then shifts his eyes back to the road. "Believe me, fashion is about selling and money making."

"I know. I mean I don't believe that you don't understand fashion. Just look at you. You're like some GQ model. The dark suit you're wearing fits you perfectly, and the vest, shirt, and tie all come together to spell power and know-how. You know how to use fashion to your advantage."

"That's only because I've abandoned the grab and sniff method from my past."

"How in heavens name did that work?"

"Very simply." He looks at me and grins. "Grab an item of clothing from the heap of tossed clothes on your bedroom floor, smell, and if you don't retch, it becomes your fashion statement of the day."

"Well, you weren't the only boy to have that particular method. Remember Mrs. Calderone?"

"The health teacher at school?"

"Yep. She had to pull all the boys aside to teach them good hygiene, deodorant use, laundering gym clothing, basically anything and everything that had to do with cleanliness. I was inside the boys' locker room once and did they ever need that lecture."

His grin evaporates. "And what, pray tell, were you doing there?"

This could be a problem. "It was no big deal."

"I'm all ears."

He wasn't going to let me dodge it. "Beth dared me to hide in the boys' locker room and I accepted."

"Just like I said before, there's a streak of ubiquitous recklessness in you that I hope has abated as you've matured."

Oh, Mr. Webster, it still hovers, but I say add nothing to this most recent *Chasism*.

"So what happened?" See, always interested in details and outcomes.

"I was caught by Coach Holden and my parents were notified." I leave out the part about seeing some of the boys undress as they headed for the showers and how Beth later created problems in algebra based on my observations.

Jasper's P measures 6.2 inches. If Logan's P is 15% larger than Jaspers P, how long is Logan's P? Beth even recorded our "data" on a bar graph. We screamed with laughter for days.

"There is a wicked smile on your face, making me believe there's more to the story."

Why rile him with what was really only harmless adolescent curiosity and humor. "Not really. I won the dare but was grounded for a month."

"Well-deserved punishment. Your parents cared enough

to set limits."

"Oh, they set limits alright and without any application of the American justice system, I might add. In the Cesare household, you were guilty until proven innocent, and in the case of Boys Locker Room vs. Alicia Cesare, the evidence was overwhelmingly against the defendant. Even made me meet with my Aunt Anna, who was a nurse, for lessons on the male anatomy in case I had questions I was too embarrassed to ask my mother." I leave out that Beth was invited also since she was part of the scheme. "*So what time is cock class this afternoon?*" she would ask then arrive right on time with her *notes*.

"Will Virgil be conducting auditions?"

His shift back to the present is sudden, and it takes me a moment to follow. "You mean for the musicians?"

"Yeah."

"I don't know. Tryouts weren't mentioned, but it makes sense. We're concerned it's going to be difficult to find a band on such short notice."

"Shouldn't be a problem. Musicians are hungry for work. I'll check with Sammy. See if he has any recommendations from the club."

I had forgotten that one of the buildings they co-owned housed a nightclub, and Chase loves jazz so it stands to reason that some of the shows feature live jazz music.

"Ok. I'll give you Virgil's email and any prospective bands can funnel their information through him."

"Sounds like a plan. Now enough talk of work. It's time for

food and some R&R."

So dictatorial but he's right. I do need a break.

We reach the restaurant and Chase pulls into a nearby parking garage. I open my door, climb out, and begin my ascent up the ramp while he hands over his keys and takes a ticket from the attendant. Late August is a big vacation time for the city, so traffic is light and there aren't the usual number of pedestrians clogging the streets. The evening is sultry tempered by an occasional breeze, and I lift my face to let it ruffle my hair. My body unwinds and I let my mind drift, calm and unencumbered for the first time today.

It happens so fast I almost don't notice, but a second glance tells me I'm right. It's him. My stomach sinks to my feet, and when I look at Chase he's immediately alarmed.

"What's wrong?"

The words catch in my throat, and I have to take several breaths to help get them out. When I finally do utter them, they sound faraway, as if someone else is speaking.

"I think I'm being followed."

CHAPTER TWENTY-NINE

hstttt!

His whistle assaults my ears, making me jump and the attendant abruptly stops the car. Chase grasps my hand and in brisk wide strides pulls me in its direction. The attendant jumps out of the car and Chase slips him a twenty.

"Change of plans, bud." He scoops back the keys.

He opens my door, slamming it as soon as I'm inside. Then, in a swift, single motion runs to the driver's side, slides in, and revs the ignition. Hurtling like some NASCAR driver, he backs into the street and heads west. I don't even notice he's phoned Sammy until I hear his voice.

"We have a problem. Alicia says she's being followed." *Pause.* Yeah, at my place in ten."

I stare at him, my mind muddled and panicked. I don't want to have to deal with this. I thought that now we were home we were safe, but this isn't what concerns me most. I realize I'm more scared of Chase leaving me again than I am of Walnut Nose.

"What does he look like?" Chase interrupts, forcing me to focus on the problem.

"Very definitive features, wide face, flat bulbous nose, and he walks with an unusual gait. I'm wondering if he has some kind of deformity because, I'm not one hundred percent sure, but I thought I also noticed disfigured fingers on one of his hands. "

He stills. His eyes darken, like deep pools of water concealing all kinds of dreadfulness. He turns, scrunches his lips together, and adds, "That's some comprehensive description. Where have you seen him?"

"First time was at a Starbucks, near my apartment when I just moved in. Next was when I went to lunch with some co-workers. That was about a week ago, and just now across the street from the parking garage. At least, I think it was him. It's too dark to see his face, but I recognized that slower, shorter gait he has, almost as if he's sliding on the sides of his feet. Maybe it's just a coincidence." I doubt my wishful thinking as soon as it's out of my mouth. Chase looks at me, disbelief marring his face.

"Three coincidences. I don't think so. Sammy has some photos for you to look through when we get home. See if you can identify him." He stares at the road ahead, hands gripping the steering wheel, mouth tight with a slight quick tick to the right.

"What aren't you telling me?" I query, panic gripping my voice.

At first he says nothing, just continues to stare at the road ahead, stopping when necessary, passing a turning vehicle with precision, continuing as if we're on a leisurely drive. I have come to understand this part of him when he pulls back to piece things together, decides what to and what not to reveal. I also know it doesn't help to rush it. He will say what he wants to when he's ready. I lean back and close my eyes, and once again he takes my hand and gives it a squeeze.

"His name is Borysko, aka The Ukrainian. We'll confirm it after you look at the photos."

Terrific. Another thug with a nickname and my mind swims with different scenarios, each more horrific than the other except for one. It jumps to the forefront like a rainbow that appears during a storm. Did he just say we were going *home*?

When we reach the apartment Sunny is waiting at the door sporting his usual white Nehru jacket, creased black pants, and white indoor slippers.

"Hello, Mr. Chase, Miss Alicia." He gives me a once-over and shakes his head. "I will have some food prepared in fifteen minutes. Mr. Sammy is in the office." And he disappears into the kitchen.

Chase's hand stops me when I attempt to follow him into his office, and he gently turns me toward the kitchen. "Go eat. Fifteen minutes more or less will not make a difference in identifying this bastard." He wraps his arms around me and I hold onto him tightly. "You're safe now. Please go have something to eat. I'll join you in a few minutes." I nod my head and he releases me and heads toward his office.

Enticing aromas of blended herbs and spices waft toward me, making my mouth water. I am starving. In the kitchen, Sunny is warming a combination of dishes and when he sees me he pulls out a chair for me to sit, then places serving dishes heaped with a variety of different foods within arm's reach. "Eat."

There's chicken peppered with diced tomatoes that, as soon as I take a bite, makes me salivate for more, and platters of rice with green peas and chick peas that pack a kick but blend perfectly with the rice. Mouth full, I grab a piece of pita bread. "This is delicious, Sunny. Thank you."

"*Humph*. Eat. Thank me when you're done." He heaps a fragrant medley of fresh vegetables and lentils onto my plate.

When I can't eat another morsel, I lean back, take a sip of ice water and wipe my mouth on a linen napkin. Sunny spared nothing and even though it must be after ten, he's attired as if serving a formal dinner party. Chase never struck me as being the type of boss who requires serving attire, so when I asked he told me that Sunny insists on a specific dress code, said it gave him "a purpose, a function in life," and except for his days off when he visits an old friend, he stays at the apartment, sleeping in an extra room adjacent to the kitchen. Chase offered him one of the larger guest rooms, but Sunny refused so Chase had Sunny's preferred room enlarged and added a bathroom and galley kitchen for his private use.

"Everything was delicious, Sunny." He beams, his lips widen in a grin, making his usual serious expression livelier, more youthful, and I realize for the first time that he mustn't be much older than Chase.

"Who taught you how to cook?" I ask, suddenly curious about his past. There's a flicker of pain that shudders his eyes, and he briefly looks away, making me regret I asked. When he finally turns to face me, his expression has changed back.

"My mother. My mother had the gift of goodness inside. She saw beauty in a world when it was at its ugliest and turned all she felt into aromatic dishes." His use of past tense lends a somber note to his description, and I remain quiet giving him room to share more if he wants, but he just looks at my empty plate and smiles. "Good. You are too skinny. How can you turn the beauty you hold inside into your lovely designs if you do not eat?"

The comparison to the memory of his mother warms my heart and my first instinct is to give him a light kiss on the cheek, but I don't know cultural protocol so instead I offer a warm smile.

"Thanks to you I just ate for an army." I take my dish to the sink, but he uses both hands to shoo me away.

"Go. Go. They are waiting in the study for you."

I head toward Chase's office where he and Sammy stand hunched over a laptop. When they see me they straighten, allowing their tight, stiff demeanors to evaporate into a cavalier "we're not worried" stance. Do they think I don't notice?

"Did you eat?" Chase queries.

"Eat? I'm amazed I fit through the doorway." I decide levity mediates gravity in situations like this, especially since Chase is ready to keep me under house arrest until Dimitri is caught.

"We're going to start by showing you five different photos," Chase informs me, shifting the computer in my direction. "See if you recognize him."

I lean over the laptop, click through the first three, and shake my head.

"No, he's bulkier than these men. When I reach the fourth I say, "That's Walnut Nose."

Chase and Sammy look at each other and break into wide grins. "Walnut Nose?" Chase quips.

"What? Only they can assign nicknames," I answer testily, annoyed at the relentless scare tactics of these thugs.

"It does fit," Sammy pipes in. "Looks a bit squashed too, if you ask me."

"Right? I have called him Squashed Walnut Nose, but it's a bit of a mouthful." Now we're all laughing and it feels good.

"Well, you were right…" Sammy nods toward Chase "… it's Borysko."

"But why the hell does Dimitri have him following Alicia without making any attempt to be discreet?"

Sammy doesn't even have to think before answering. "It's more about getting to you than actually hurting Alicia."

He's right. Already Chase is rifling his hand through his hair and rubbing the back of his neck as he paces the study.

"So what do I do? Remain relaxed while he terrorizes her." I go over to him and wrap my arms around his waist, hoping to calm his frazzled nerves,

"Terrorized is a bit of an exaggeration. I mean, I'm concerned, but he hasn't threatened me or hurt me in any way. I think Sammy is right. If we overreact or disrupt our lives because of his scare tactics, it's like we're accepting defeat."

The soldier inside Chase knows this and he leans back and looks at me with a flicker of surprise, as if he hadn't fathomed I could grasp it. I comprehend perfectly but also know this is not the time for taking unnecessary chances.

"I promise I'll be careful." I pull back because Sammy is in the room and getting this close to Chase's mouth without taking it to the next level has never been my strong point.

He gives me a hard stare. "You realize your subway commuting is over."

"I'll have Sammy drive me to and from work, and I'll keep him informed of my whereabouts." Chase seems mollified.

"Good. Sammy and I are going to wrap this up. You best get some sleep. You have to wake up early tomorrow for another one of your marathon work weekends."

"Last one. Virgil gave me Friday off, so I have lots of time to spend at the beach to celebrate Liam's birthday bash."

"Isn't the show the following week?"

"It is, but by Monday the prep work will be finished and all that I'll need to survive will be the actual days of the show." It's going to feel good to have my life back again.

"You can get some rest on Friday, and we can head out early Saturday morning. My dad has a guest room. If it's ok with you, we can spend the night there and go to the beach on Sunday before we have to head back."

"Sounds like a vacation after the hours I've been working. Maybe we can leave on Friday and have lunch at my parents' house before my father has to be at the restaurant?"

"Sure. I'll clear my schedule for Friday." He pulls me closer, kissing me lightly, tenderly, then deeply.

We separate and I smooth my hair back, mostly to give me time to catch my breath. He has that power over me and no matter I'm bone tired and, I admit, a bit frightened, desire has kicked in and all I want is to feel his touch. Not about to happen with all that's going on, so I give Sammy a good night peck on the cheek. His help is invaluable and a real source of comfort to both me and Chase.

"Thanks, Sammy."

"G'night, Alicia. See you in the morning."

I shut the door but my foot catches on a piece of carpet, causing me to drop onto all fours like some tottering toddler. God, this fatigue is making me clumsy. As I'm righting myself,

Chase's voice carries through the closed door, "Don't let her out of your sight."

I straighten and stare ahead. Seems like I was given the censored version of the gangster flick. Well, no use speculating possibilities I couldn't fathom.

Bone tired, I don't get into bed. I collapse, barely taking the time to strip, slip into one of Chase's T-shirts, and drag myself into the bathroom to brush my teeth. I grope in my purse, grab one of my facial wipes, and smooth it over my face so I don't sleep with a whole day of makeup and grime caked on. Pulling the sheet and coverlet up, I drift for what seems like only minutes but must have been longer because I feel two arms wrap around me and pull me closer. I settle into Chase's embrace, letting fatigue succumb to relaxation and slumber.

I wake to Chase's phone's lively wake-up tune. I quickly turn it off. He's still asleep, arm thrown over his head, soft billows of breath just shy of a snore rhythmically flow from his parted lips. He looks young, unencumbered. I reach over and lightly brush his hair back. An arm snakes up, grasps me by the wrist, and pulls me on top.

Looking up through sleepy eyes, he takes my other wrist and tugs, bringing us face to face.

"You look fetching as ever this morning."

"You were just snoring half of a second ago. Now you're

all wide awake and frisky." I move my eyes downward because there's no mistaking what else is up. I feel his hard swollen member pressing into my stomach.

"No."

I raise my knee and gently massage his penis to prove him wrong.

"Snore. I. Don't. Snore." He's looking up at me, rumpled wake-up hair spiked at odd angles and a crooked grin tugging his mouth.

"Oh yes you do. Big loud gusts that sound like a locomotive." I sweep my free hand across the air with a deep churning in my voice imitating a motor.

He tugs my wrist and quickly turns me onto my back and begins tickling me, first under my arms then along my sides. "Take it back."

The tickling is merciless, but I won't give in. "Your snores are so loud," I sputter through gasping breaths of laughter, "they sound like sonic booms."

He finally stops and grinning, begins nibbling my ear before traveling his mouth down my neck, kissing each of my tattooed stars. Slowly. My blood heats and I raise my neck to meet his caressing kisses as a heavy, steady throbbing begins below. He lifts the T-shirt I'm wearing up over my head and the touch of his fingertips slowly moving up my sides sends shivers down my spine. He tosses it aside.

"I'm going to be late for work."

"Then we'll be quick."

His mouth and tongue linger, traveling across my collarbone and down to my breast. When he takes my nipple in his mouth and gently sucks, my hips arch and I push his head downward. My body is on fire, quivering with anticipation. He moves his mouth lower, slowly leaving a trail of kisses down to my navel and below until he reaches just that right spot where he lets his tongue work its magic, and I think I've died and gone to heaven. My pleasure mounts with throbbing intensity, but just before release, he stops. I almost weep from frustration but say nothing because with him it's all about control. His mouth continues down my thigh until he reaches my big toe where it stops and sucks. My mind is numb, my body thrumming with need. I lift my head and peek up through heavy lidded eyes to see his need matches mine. I want nothing more than to feel him inside. Through panting breaths I plead, only to throw my head back when his mouth moves upward to settle to where it was before. The mounting starts again, slow and steady. I moan. He stops, but this time he grasps my ankles and slides me to the end of the bed, then standing, he glides inside me, raising my legs over his shoulders and filling me with deep thrusts. The rippling escalation goes on and on with each penetrating lunge until I scream out his name.

His loud groan follows as he calls out, "Fuck, Alicia," in a raspy whisper that tells me the sensations are as overwhelming for him as they are for me. His movements slow and the last one makes him quiver before he collapses on the bed, taking me to lie on top of him. I want nothing more than to linger and laze, but one look at the clock has me jumping out of bed and racing into the shower.

Dried and rubbed with scented lotion in record time, I step into a subtly patterned black silk slip dress with a sheer black on black geometric overlay then quickly put on a pair of strappy high heeled black sandals. Easy to wear now that I have a ride to work. My hair is damp so I pull it back into a braided bun at the nape of my neck and put on lipstick that's a deeper red than I usually wear.

"Aren't you getting dressed for work?"

Sitting up in bed, head bent over his phone messages, he answers, "My first appointment isn't until 11:00 today." He looks up and pauses, his eyes raking my body from head to toe.

"Woman you are all kinds of sexy in that dress." He's up in no time and reaching for me.

My hand shoots out, palm up. "Oh no you don't. I'm late enough as it is." There is no way I'm letting him touch me. Even this distance is dangerous.

"How late can you be? It's Saturday." He moves closer. I back away.

"I'll see you tonight."

"Call as you're finishing up. I'll come get you."

"Ok." I trot into the kitchen where Sunny hands me a packed lunch large enough to feed a trek through the Himalayas.

"Thank you, Sunny." I grab the bag and head out the door

and into the elevator. Thank heavens Sammy is already waiting in front of the building.

I'm late. But not by much. Still, everyone is busy working, bustling through the offices and hallway, lugging clothing and mannequins or plugging away on computers.

"I thought you may have gotten stuck on a subway, but one look at that radiant face tells me you were probably stuck somewhere more … pleasant.

"Good morning, Virgil." He smiles and nods.

"You're needed in Charlotte's office. Some logistical problem with the timing in the show. Oh and by the way, we found an excellent band, thanks to Reardon Realty. Someone you know?"

"You know I do. Glad he could help."

"I'm sure he was thrilled with your thank you."

I look around to make sure no one else is listening. "His 'you're welcome' wasn't half bad either." Virgil throws his head back and laughs as only Virgil can, and it's so infectious that I lower my head and laugh also. I walk away with the sinking realization that I'm moving from bawdy innuendo to simmering wrath.

My knock is tentative. The answering voice is not. "Come in."

I walk in expecting to see a room full of people but it's only Charlotte sitting at her desk, rifling through a stack of photos and diagrams. "Nice dress."

I almost turn to make sure she's not talking to someone

else.

"Thanks. Virgil said you needed me."

"I did, about half an hour ago."

And she's back.

"How can I help?" I'll be damned if I'll apologize for being late after working back-breaking non-stop hours this past week.

"The sequence of these models seem stilted, out of order. I need you to situate them differently. Give them a more timely flow. Also, the red dress hangs too much in the front. It needs tapering."

"Certainly." I take the stack she holds out and turn to leave.

"Oh and …" My hand freezes just shy of the doorknob.

"Email me Chase Reardon's cell number. I want to call on behalf of Estelle Designs to thank him personally for his help with signing on such a notable Jazz combo."

For a split second I'm not sure I heard correctly. Did my boss just ask me for my boyfriend's cell phone number? Her head remains bent over a pile of documents on her desk where she methodically signs one before flicking to the next. It's like I don't exist. I remain silent while my mind screams, *Holy fuck, your nemesis is crushing on your boyfriend.* Throwing her a curt nod, I give the door a quick tug on my way out.

Awesome.

CHAPTER THIRTY

The week whizzes by as I'm caught in a flurry of alterations, fashion matching, scheduling problems, soundtrack issues ... the list is endless. I stick to my schedule though, sleeping at my apartment during the week and at Chase's on weekends. Chase continues to pick me up after my late nights and often sleeps at my place, making sure there's something for me to eat before I crawl into bed. When Thursday rolls around, I'm counting the minutes until the end of the day, each one seeming like an hour. I'm already packed for the weekend and have my bag with me. Finally the hands of the clock hit five, and I sprint for my purse and travel bag. The day dragged but went smoothly, with the pieces of the show seamlessly falling into place. All that remained was meeting the models and musicians on Monday and having a run through on Tuesday. I'm at the elevator when Charlotte appears.

"A word please," she says, standing in front of Kim's desk, the cold, pale perfection of her face offsetting the crackling ice of her blue eyes.

"Yes." I step away from the elevator and turn to meet her gaze.

"You never did give me the phone number I requested. I'm tying all the loose ends together before the show and this is next on my list."

I bet it is, you ice queen.

She takes out her phone and looks expectantly at me. I had previously discussed this with Chase, joking that he had yet another groupie I might be forced to fend off. He suggested I give her his personal assistant's number, but I purposely didn't offer it earlier taking secret delight in making her ask again.

"Sure. Everything has been so busy here it must have slipped my mind," I lie. Her red-polished nails click against her phone as she efficiently adds the number I give her to her list of contacts, then turns and heads back to her office without so much as a thank you. No matter. There is no way she's spoiling my good mood.

The early start we planned does not happen. Chase tries gently waking me, but I burrow into my pillow. "Five more minutes."

I don't know how long this went on for but I assume he eventually gave in and let me sleep. By the time I do wake, it's after ten. I sit up in bed and stare ahead, focusing on nothing but remaining awake. Without saying a word, Chase hands me a cup of espresso that I finish before my feet are able to hit the floor. I groggily mumble a thank you and stumble into the shower. I don't want to waste the day so I move as fast as my body allows. Chase, as usual, is packed and ready, working in his study while he waits. I quickly dry my hair, pulling it into a ponytail and slip into my blue sundress. Lunch at my parents' house is at two then we're off to Chase's dad's house in Long Beach to help Fiona prepare for Liam's party tomorrow. We'll sleep there since his Dad, unlike my parents, will not quibble about who sleeps where.

When we arrive my father is waiting on the front porch to greet us. I haven't seen him since I left for my trip and he takes me in a big hug. "I missed you. Did you forget your old papa?"

"I missed you too."

He holds me at arm's length, smiling. "I said good-bye to a young girl and a beautiful woman has returned." He turns and shakes Chase's hand, offering a curt hello.

This is not going to be easy. Chase clears his throat, a nervous habit I have noticed before and shakes hands. "Hello, sir, it's good to see you."

Sir? Have we time traveled back to the 1950s?

"Come. Come inside," and Papa wraps his arm around me and leads me into the hallway as Chase is forced to grab the closing door before it slams in his face.

The table is spread with a lunch that would have fed

Napoleon's army. There's a platter of aged cheeses and cured meats, like salami and prosciutto, and homemade stuffed peppers, olives, and artichoke hearts. Another dish holds jumbo shrimp hung over a dish of cocktail sauce and lemon wedges chilling on ice in the center. There's fresh baked focaccia, bruschetta, and yard-long grissini, and these are just the appetizers. I'm starving and swipe a shrimp, dipping it in the sauce and taking a bite, then hand another up to Chase's mouth for him to enjoy. He immediately takes it from my hand and gives me a formal thank you. Marine Corporal Chase Reardon is going to be on his best behavior today.

Antonio comes out of the kitchen where he is busy preparing our meal and looks sheepishly at me and then Chase. I take him in a hug and he playfully knuckles my head and grabs Chase in a bear hug. Of all my brothers, he is the most affectionate, and I do believe he cares deeply for Fiona. He's finally made peace with Papa, who understands that his youngest son wants to be a chef and not an accountant. He'll start his training at the Culinary Institute this fall. Meanwhile, he helps at the restaurant and unfortunately has to work tomorrow.

"Helooo." Mamma comes out of the kitchen all smiles, offering kisses and hugs to first me and then Chase. "We are so happy to see you both." Chase visibly relaxes, and I see a soft, warm look replace his former reserved countenance. He likes my mother, says he remembers her visits as a child, and the delicious meals she would bring when his mother was too ill to cook. Says he also remembers a green-eyed, pig-tailed little minx who would wait for her outside playing hopscotch. God, I thought he was beautiful even then.

Massimo comes straight from the hospital looking a bit tired from his long shift, but takes me in a hug, then shakes Chase's hand. He steps back and takes another look at me and asks, "Something's different. Did you change your hair?"

"No," Mamma interrupts. "She lost weight. Have you been eating?" Here we go again.

My yes comes at the same time as Chase's no, and I toss him a fish-eyed stare. "I am eating. In fact, I've been introduced to a wide assortment of new foods from someone who works for Chase. Antonio you would love his dishes. I'll get the recipes for you." Chase narrows his eyes at me because he knows my acumen for shifting attention away from myself.

Francesco arrives with a loud "I'm starving, what's for lunch?" greeting. When he spots me he breaks into a smile. "Look who's back," he announces and lifts and spins me before giving me a big hug and asking if I'd managed to bring him back a beautiful Italian woman. Francesco continues to date extensively and his debonair looks make him a hot item with women. I once had to physically shut Beth's gaping mouth and drag her by the arm away from Francesco playing basketball in our side yard. Then again, she had to do the same to me when Chase was here playing.

So far so good. Everyone is playing nicely in the sandbox. The doorbell rings and I raise an eyebrow in question. "Are we expecting anyone else?"

"Oh I forgot to mention I invited Thomas," Francisco adds. "Bumped into him on the street and he said he hasn't seen you since Nice. Wanted to know how you were doing, so I told him to come and see for himself." There's a beat of awkward silence. "What?" Francisco asks through a mouthful of bruschetta. Don Juan is clueless.

Chase's eyes harden. He knows Thomas and I dated briefly. He also knows it was Thomas who slipped me the hash in Nice. I didn't tell him, but he told me he heard Thomas mention it at the pub that night. He just figured I would be smart enough to resist. Yeah, well we know how that went down.

"Is someone going to get the door?" Papa asks, coming in from kitchen.

"I'll get it," I offer. Thomas is an old friend and I haven't seen him in a while. Chase will just have to deal. Oh god, who am I kidding? This is a recipe for disaster. I open the door and Thomas is holding a bouquet of flowers and a box of chocolates.

"Hey, stranger..." he wraps his arms around me "...where have you been hiding?" His eyes sweep from my face to my toes. "You look beautiful." He hands me the flowers and candy.

I scoff, waving my hand. "You don't look half bad yourself." His rugged lifeguard tan coupled with his light hair and eyes give him an appealing healthy look. I lead him inside and go find a vase for the flowers.

There are hellos and back slapping from the guys as

Thomas shakes everyone's hand and kisses my mother. From the corner of my eye, I see Chase watching me place the flowers in a vase. I walk over to him and he wraps his arm around my waist and possessively pulls me closer.

"Thomas, you remember Chase." Thomas warily extends his hand for the handshake, his eyes flicking across Chase's arm around me. "Yeah. How are you?"

"Good." They shake hands, but there's something about the way they stare at each other that's unsettling, like flashes of lightening indicating an impending storm.

"Um, I'm going to see if they need my help in the kitchen." Chase lets go of my waist. I give him a peck on the lips before turning and heading toward the kitchen. Scrubbing pots would be better than withstanding that tension. This is going to be some long meal.

Francisco is munching on a shrimp when I crook my arm through his and lead him into the kitchen. "Why are you giving me that accusatory look," he queries then both hands raised, says, "I did not hide Mr. Moo, swear to God." I laugh because when we were younger I had this stuffed monkey named Mr. Moo that I carried everywhere. Francisco used to take pleasure in hiding it and then pretending he had no idea where it was. After stomping through the house in search of him, I might find Mr. Moo sitting on top of a bowl of fruit or standing on his head against the kitchen chair. One time, I found him in the bathtub with a bar of soap taped to one hand and a scrub brush in the other. Each time I would break into fits of giggles.

Antonio interrupts with, "He didn't get the memo about your seeing Chase" and then lowers his head and whispers, "and he wasn't part of the apartment fiasco."

Francisco looks from Antonio to me then back to Antonio. "When did this all come about?"

"It started in Monte Carlo when Alicia was arrested." Now I think Francisco's eyes are going to bulge out of his head.

"Shut up, Antonio." He can't help but flap that mouth. He shrugs and continues to stir the coq au vin he's cooking, as if he hadn't just ratted me out. Again.

"It's obvious I've missed a lot of family action studying for the bar this summer. What were you arrested for?"

"Not a big deal. The thing is that Chase and I have been seeing each other and, well having Thomas here is awkward."

"I thought Thomas was just an old friend."

"A friend who's smitten with Alicia," Antonio interrupts, turning from the pot while pretending to lift a joint between thumb and forefinger to his mouth.

"You were arrested for smoking pot in a foreign country? What were you thinking?" Francisco is annoyed, and I'm in no mood for another lecture about this. Dealing with Chase afterward was punishment enough.

"Can you ever keep your mouth shut?" I flick the back Antonio's head with my fingers. He reaches for a small piece of bread and shoots it in my direction. It hits its mark and clings to my hair and lifting it out, I pop it into my mouth.

"Obviously, I wasn't thinking, but it's over and done with."

"We still have to talk about this thing you have going with Chase."

"There's nothing to talk about. We're seeing each other. End of story." We hear someone walk toward the kitchen and pretend to busy ourselves with trivial tasks, but it's only Chase so the argument resumes.

"I didn't know you were seeing Alicia." A soft menace clings to Francesco's words and Chase stiffens when he sees Francisco's eyes narrow and his lips tighten.

"Stop right there." I step between them after stomping first on Antonio's foot for his big mouth.

"This whole medieval oath you all swore is over." I stare pointedly at Francisco. "I don't tell you who you should or shouldn't date, and if memory serves I think some of my former classmates are part of your ever growing harem." I thrust my hands out from my chest. "Remember Pammy Anderson?"

Francisco looks confused and more than a bit surprised. "When did you develop such a sharp tongue?" Antonio inclines his head toward Chase with a quick nod. I swear he needs a hit in the head to remind him to keep things to himself.

The tension in the room is palpable, but Chase is the first to hold out an olive branch. "Hey, buddy, I hope you're ok with this." Then he wraps his arm around me and gives me a kiss on the forehead, keeping it deliberately light.

Francisco breaks into a grin and shakes his head. "If Alicia is happy, I'm happy." He always was the easiest of my brothers to reason with and the most adaptable.

"Trust me, Alicia is happy," Antonio says, leaning back from the stove, "She's been crushing on Chase for years." And he makes kissing sounds with his mouth. I rummage through a kitchen drawer looking for tape for his mouth, come up empty, and console myself with elbowing him in the ribs on my way out of the kitchen.

Lunch goes smoothly … at first. When the conversation shifts to cars, my father warms toward Chase. Chase is a veritable source of knowledge on all different makes, models, speeds. You name it, he knows it.

"The boxer-type six-cylinder of the Porsche is like no other," Massimo throws out before taking a heaping forkful of food into his mouth.

"Yeah, but the TVR Sagaris can hit 185 MPH with its 406 horsepower and a 4.0-liter straight-six engine. It's lightning fast." My eyes glaze over. Chase wears the expression of a kid on Christmas morning. Thomas, though, is quiet, too quiet.

"When do you leave for school?" I ask, trying to nudge him into conversation. He is my friend and I don't like seeing him like this.

"Next week. I found an apartment so I'll be driving there on Tuesday."

I nod. "You must be excited. You worked hard to get to this point. I hear the Physician Assistant's program at Rutgers is one of the best in the country."

I feel compelled to keep him engaged, even though he

refuses to meet my eye.

"Have you packed?"

For the longest time he says nothing, just continues to look down at his plate. When he finally looks up, it's to offer a blunt, "Do you have feelings for this guy?"

There is no easy way to let Thomas down, and even though I haven't led him on, I feel badly. Still, he needs to know the truth and best to hear it from me.

"Yes, I really care about him."

He looks crestfallen. I don't know what else to say, so I just stare at him in silence.

"How long?"

"What?"

"How long have you been seeing him?"

This is really none of his business, but he's raising his voice so I answer to help tone down his upset.

"A little more than two months, but that's not important. You are. You are such a great guy, kind, sensitive, caring and…" I don't have a chance to finish because, grinding back his chair, he stands, leans across the table, and before I can react, pulls my head toward him and kisses me on the lips. Hard. I'm speechless as he pulls away, offering a curt, "Excuse me," to no one in particular and leaves, the slam of the front door resonating throughout the dining room.

Everyone has stopped talking but the only person I'm thinking about is Chase. I peek in his direction through lowered eyes and no surprise there, he's fuming. Probably using every ounce of self-control no to go after Thomas and knock him out. I'll have some explaining to do too, although I don't believe I encouraged the kiss in the slightest. It didn't even feel like anything much, sort of like kissing a relative or good friend, only on the lips instead of the cheek.

Papa breaks the silence and shaking his head offers, "A man hopelessly in love is a sorry sight to behold," and then he reaches over, leans my mother back, and kisses her hard and long. I roll my eyes and my cheeks heat, but I must admit it eases the awkward moment because Chase reaches over and holding my chin, places a tender kiss on my lips suggesting the incident is over.

It's a five minute walk from Chase's dad's house to the beach. When we arrive, there's a tangle of four-year-olds slathered in sunblock, running helter-skelter, while harried parents struggle to keep them from jumping into the water or getting lost on the other side of the beach. A curly, dark-haired toddler summersaults into an umbrella, overturning it just as we arrive, forcing Chase to sprint for the save before it spun into someone's head. I don't even have time to take off my sundress. I just whip out my face paints, purchased especially for the occasion with Fiona's explicit instructions that they be FDA-approved, non-allergenic with organic ingredients and easy to remove. I make a large sign that says 'Paint Your Face Here' and another that says 'Tattoos' and tape them onto an umbrella. A line of excited four-year-olds jumping and squealing, "Me, me, me," immediately forms. The racket is deafening, but at least they're all in one place. I think the parents are ready to sign over their homes in gratitude.

An exhausted looking Fiona jogs over and gives me, then Chase, a big hug. "You guys are the best. Thanks for coming. Antonio is working so he won't be able to make it."

"I know," I reply. Antonio just began overseeing brunch at the restaurant.

Liam stands in front of the line, a big Mets baseball cap covering half his face, skinny arms hanging down at his sides.

"Alicia, I want a pirate tattoo."

"One pirate tattoo coming up." He jumps up and down, laughing and squealing "thank you" then gets all quiet and serious when I press it onto his arm.

While I paint faces and press on washable tattoos, Chase organizes groups for relay races and ball tosses. When it's time for lunch, sandwiches and juice are whipped out of a large cooler and placed into small sand-riddled hands. One bite gives meaning to the word *sand*wich. I chew gritty cheese and bologna that really don't taste like either, making me believe they must be some kind of organic plant substitute.

"Christ, this is awful. Tastes like gritty sh—"

I put my hand across Chase's mouth, just as a precocious girl with a mop of ringlets pipes, "Tastes like gritty *what*?"

Chase hands me his sandwich and lets her jump on his back for a ride, mumbling to me, "They're like gnomes with superpower hearing," before he gallops off with her laughing and shouting orders for where he should run.

One talkative, bob-haired mom introduces herself, ironically as Barb, then immediately tells me that her son, Jonathan, has already started to read. "That's Jonathan," her accountant looking husband points out. My eyes travel to a small towheaded boy attempting to stand on his head on the shoreline just as the water ripples over his face. He falls down, sputters, sneezes, and coughs out salt water, then does it again. And again. And again. "Way to go, Jonathan. You can do it," they both shout in unison.

Did they just encourage their son to swallow half an ocean?

"We find his determination remarkable." Accountant dad remarks, pushing up his glasses with his forefinger, "And can you believe the little guy has a Twitter account with over ten thousand followers."

Chase is back from being a human horse and is standing next to me, a chunk of fake cheese dangling from his hair and a smattering of sand stuck to his perspiring forehead. I discreetly remove it and brush away the sand. He hardly notices because he's staring at this father like he just stepped off an alien spaceship.

When the couple moves on, he mumbles, "What could a four-year-old possibly be tweeting? #peedmypants #vegansucks." He stops and glances furtively around, as if expecting to see some small body suddenly materialize.

"Little demons are everywhere," he mutters before trotting

back to help organize a soccer game.

I look up and notice a tiny girl, two long blond pigtails fastened with huge pink and white pompoms that perfectly match her pink and white ruffled bathing suit. She asks for a tattoo, and I immediately reach for the hearts and rainbow.

"No, thank you. I will take the skull and crossbones." She turns and bares her forearm for me to press it on.

"Are you sure?"

"Yes," and then "can you please paint my lips dark brown."

"Excuse me?"

"Dark brown, unless you have black."

"Face painting does not include lips," I tell her, quickly realizing her parents would have my head if I turned their princess into a Goth-looking cheerleader. She looks as if she's about to cry.

"How about if I outline a heart in black on your cheek?"

She smiles. "Could you put some blood dripping from it?"

"No."

She shrugs, waits for me to finish, then skips off making me realize that sometimes a simple no is all that's necessary.

When my line finally empties, I collapse into a chaise lounge and slip off my sundress. It's a cloudless late summer day and the shade from the umbrella and light breeze feel wonderful. I lean my head back and close my eyes.

"Little monsters will wipe you out."

At first I think it's Chase that's how similar the voice is to his, but when I look up I see an older man offering me a cold can of diet soda. I sit up and take it.

"You're Elvira's youngest, right?

"Yes." Except for being a bit stouter, his resemblance to Chase is remarkable.

He extends his hand. "Bill Reardon. I'm Chase's dad. Didn't get a chance to see you last night. Fiona had us running around to prepare for this shindig."

I sit up. "Mr. Reardon, hello." His handshake is firm and warm.

I pop open the can and take a long sip as he takes the chair next to mine.

"Call me, Bill. Mr. Reardon makes me feel old." He stares at the crew of kids running here and there, some playing soccer others swimming with arm floats the size of motorcycle tires, and of course Jonathan who's still attempting headstands.

"Know why they don't ever stop moving?"

I have no idea what he's getting at so I say nothing.

"Meat."

If I thought I was confused before he answered his own question, I'm even more baffled now.

"They're craving some burgers and hotdogs fired up on a grill. Used to have a big barbecue at these parties. Now parents demand this new wave food. Never could understand all this tofu crap… and he stops, nervously looking around, making the resemblance to Chase so pronounced that I chuckle.

He smiles and takes a sip of soda. "Chase says you're a fashion designer."

"Just an assistant, but I love what I do."

He pauses, staring ahead at the sea that's amazingly calm except for an occasional frothy white rise and fall.

"That's the key to success. Gotta love what you do." He takes another sip.

"You must love woodworking. I saw the table you made on Chase's terrace. The craftsmanship is beautiful."

"So you've been there, eh?" There's something about the way he phrases the question that makes me wonder what's so significant about being on Chase's terrace, and then I remember the no women rule.

"Yes."

"That's good. Glad you appreciated the table. Took me a while to get it right, to smooth and finish it to my liking."

He's a perfectionist, much like Chase, but somewhere must have lost his way before turning his life around again. His honesty is refreshing. It's like he's looking at you and saying "I've seen it all so don't waste my time with gibberish or foolishness." Chase jogs over and falls into a chair. He pops open a soda and takes a long gulp.

"I see you met my father."

"We've been talkin' it up. No need for formal introductions. I remember Alicia when she was this high." He holds out his hand palm down about three feet off the ground. Terrific. I'm etched in everyone's mind as a child. As if reading my mind he adds, "Who I must say has grown into a beautiful woman." He gets up groaning a bit as he stands. "I have to go carve up the watermelon. God forbid there should be a cake. They might all drop from sugar poisoning." He throws a last glance at his son, pauses, then bends his mouth toward Chase's ear. Why I'll never know, because clean as a whistle I hear, "She's a keeper. Don't fuck this one up."

Then he walks toward the cluster of parents readying a table with assorted fruits. I snort out a quiet laugh. The man is beyond blunt. Chase raises his eyebrows and rolls his eyes back in his head. The gesture is so unlike him that I throw my head back and laugh.

Dusk drapes the beach, signaling the hovering fall season. Chase has lit a large bonfire where we are melting s'mores, any guilt dissipating with the last of the guests. Liam shifts from sleepiness to rapture every time he takes a bite. Eventually sleep prevails and he nestles his head in the crook of Chase's arm. The jingle of Chase's phone startles, and I take Liam from his arms so he can take the call.

"Reardon." His voice has a clipped resonance indicating it's a business matter.

"When did this happen?" Concern etches his serious expression and after a minimal pause, he adds, "So they're still on the premises?"

"I understand. No, don't call Sammy. He's off the radar now."

I know that Sammy is spending the weekend visiting his mom who suffers from Alzheimer's, hoping to give his sister a welcome break from caregiving.

"I'll be there in less than an hour."

He clicks off and looks at me. I can't hide my concern. "What's wrong?"

"Seems there may be a carbon monoxide leak in one of our new buildings. I have to head to Brooklyn now."

"Ok." My response is automatic, almost matter of fact, but I'm worried and a moment later, I add, "Please be careful."

"It'll be fine. I should be back in a few hours." Then as if that's not enough to have to worry about, he leans over and quietly adds, "Keep an eye out for Fiona. This is not a good time for her. She seems ok, but I'd feel better if you didn't let her out of your sight. When you get back, stay in and lock up for the night. My father retires early. Call me or Mac if there's a problem." He has this team of helpers and still, they're stretched thin because of all the problems.

"Sure. Don't worry about us. We'll be fine." I shift Liam in my arms to give Chase a kiss good-bye.

Fiona walks over from packing up and looks questioningly at Chase. "Leaving?"

"I have to go for a bit. I'll see you later. Alicia is going back with you."

"Alright." She gives him a wide smile.

At the time it's reassuring, but in hindsight I realize it was all pretense. It's difficult to determine why or how the subsequent sequence of events unfolded. All I know is that one minute everything was fine and the next all hell broke loose.

CHAPTER THIRTY-ONE

I carry a sleeping Liam out of the car and into the house, Fiona dragging in the cooler behind me. Chase's father left earlier with a trunk full of beach toys, gifts, and other sundries from the party.

"Why don't you give him to me? You must be exhausted." Fiona holds out her hands, but Liam just nuzzles further into my arms.

"It's ok. I'll put him down then come help you unpack." But when I place a sleeping Liam in bed, he rouses and clutches onto my neck, not wanting to let me go. I lie down next to him, determined to help him fall back to sleep before getting up to help Fiona, but he's restless. The excitement of his party coupled with sun and swimming has left him overtired.

"Read me a story," he begs and sleepily hands me *Hop on Pop*. I ruffle his hair and prop up the pillows, lying next to him and begin reading. Fiona looks in and gives me a thumbs-up, and then I hear her thumping around in the kitchen, unpacking the cooler. A slight breeze wafts through the bedroom window cooling my exhausted, overheated body. Liam's eyes flutter closed, a smile plastered on his face, as I read, "WHERE IS BROWN? THERE IS BROWN! Mr. Brown is out of town."

Somewhere between Mr. Brown and WILL HILL, I lose all sense of time. It isn't until I sit up with a start that I realize I must have fallen asleep. Liam, his thumb in his mouth, is nestled snuggly in his bed. I rub my face with my hands to help me wake and tiptoe out of the room. My first realization is the silence. It's deafening. The next is how dark the rooms are. I flick on the lights, still treading softly, thinking Fiona must be asleep. I check the clock and see that it's 9:00. I must have fallen asleep for a good two hours. I still had not caught up after all the long work hours, and today was exhausting. I peek into Fiona's bedroom. Empty. A quick look through all the rooms reveals that they are dark and empty. A faint unease surfaces, but it's quelled when I think I hear her in the garage. I open the door to the garage but it's empty. In a panic, I run toward the front door, flinging it open only to find that the driveway, too, is empty. The car is gone. My palms begin to sweat and my heart starts to race. Chase's words, "Don't let her out of your sight," reverberate in my mind and my fear intensifies. Locking and bolting the door, I check again on Liam, who remains fast asleep. I don't know if I should wake Chase's dad or call Chase. He told me to let him know of any problem, so I make the call. He picks up immediately.

"Hey, how's it going?"

I don't know exactly how to begin. I know he's going to become agitated and it's my fault.

"I-I think Fiona is gone."

"What?"

"I put Liam to sleep and must have fallen asleep myself. When I woke the house was empty."

There's a deep intake of breath that sounds like a cooking pot beginning to boil and closing my eyes, I brace myself for what's to follow.

"I tell you to keep an eye on her and you fall asleep." He's enraged, and I feel myself start to shake from fear and concern for Fiona.

"I'm sorry. She seemed fine. Last I remember she was in the kitchen unpacking and now she's gone."

"How long?

"I don't know. An hour, maybe longer."

He lets out a gust of air.

"What can I do to help?" I'm thinking I can borrow his father's car and go and look for Fiona while his dad stays and babysits Liam.

"Help? I'd say you've done enough damage trying to help." He raises his voice, derision clinging to each word. "I should have known better than to leave you in charge. How can you possibly understand? Born with a silver spoon in your mouth … you're clueless."

I recoil from his words, each one like a punch in my gut,

and I have to swallow past the lump in my throat before I can speak. "I'm so sorry."

"God damn it." I hear him punching something and I think it might be the steering wheel. He must already be on his way back. "Do you think you can manage to wake my father and then sit tight until Sammy gets there to drive you home?" Now he's replaced rage with sarcasm and my guilt morphs into anger.

"I can manage that." Refusing to give him any more of an opportunity to insult, I offer a quick good-bye and hang up then immediately start pacing, stopping every now and then to wipe the tears from my face. Thoughts ranging from righteous indignation to self-recrimination ping pong in my mind. I keep coming back to the same thought. Chase is right. I have no first-hand experience with drug addiction and it's this ignorance that prevented me from seeing the denial and deceit inherent in a drug user. If I had been aware I wouldn't have fallen asleep so easily. I hear a rustling by the door and look up to see Chase's dad standing in the living room. His hair has that just woken bedhead look, and he squints his eyes to adjust to the light.

One look at me and he says, "It's Fiona, right?"

I nod quickly, swiping the tears from my face, hoping to keep him from seeing how upset I am.

He plods to the kitchen, rummages until he produces a coffee pot, and gets it brewing before I turn to finish pacing the length of the room. Rubbing his face, he sits down at the kitchen table and stares straight ahead in silence. When the coffee maker beeps, signaling the coffee is done, he gets up and pours himself a cup.

"Want some?" I shake my head. I think if anything passes my lips I might throw up.

He takes a sip and looks up at me. "Not your fault," he says. I take a deep breath in some vain attempt to calm my shaking because I do blame myself.

"He gave you a hard time, didn't he?"

I don't answer. Chase is his son and really what is there to say.

"This must have thrown him. Casey has this need to be in control.

"Mmm, I noticed," I murmur.

"I'm afraid that's my fault."

I stop pacing. I want to hear what he has to say. He looks at me with eyes the same piercing blue as his son's. "You're good for him. He's happier than I have ever seen him. He's become a whole different person. Whistles while he runs errands, completes odd jobs around here with a smile plastered on his face. Never did that before."

Whadya know, Grumpy whistles while he works, and I almost laugh out loud at the understatement. My hurt reaches so much deeper. Chase's angry words weren't really about my falling asleep on the job. They reflect his deep-seated belief that I am incapable of understanding the depth of his problems. In his mind, my ineffectiveness echoes my upbringing, which places me on the inside while he remains, how did he put it, "the commoner outside." A bone-numbing sadness seeps into my core, strangling until I feel I can't breathe. Chase's father must have gotten up because I feel his hand on my shoulder. When I turn, I see a sorrow so laced with guilt and grief that I rest my cheek against his hand in an attempt to offer as well as receive solace.

Looking at me, he clears his throat and quietly says, "He needs a strong woman. Don't give up on him."

A pair of headlights pierce through the front window, garishly brightening the room, and I know Sammy's here to drive me home. I only hope he had the time to properly visit with his mother. I don't need more guilt heaped on top of what I already carry.

"Mr. Rear—" I stop, correcting myself. "Bill, I have to go. I hope Fiona is alright."

He nods, his hands lying limp at his sides. I give him a hug and then a kiss on the cheek before grabbing my bags and leaving. I throw them and myself in the backseat. One look at me and Sammy hands me the box of tissues he leaves resting on the front seat. I try not to sob, but my shoulders shake and my tears are relentless. Once I do stop, I lean back on the seat and cave in to exhaustion. I don't wake until Sammy has pulled into a spot in front of my building. Mercifully, he realized that I would want to come here instead of Chase's place.

"Hang tight." His only words as I leave the car and walk into the building, not giving a second thought to bulbous nose

Ukrainians, mobsters, rapists, or an angry boyfriend. I just want to curl into a ball and sleep.

When I check my phone the following morning there are at least a dozen messages some I don't recognize because they appear to come from outside the US, but most from work, begging me to please come in to deal with before-show glitches that continue to crop up. Why not, I think. What good is it to sit at home and dwell. I drag myself out of bed and into the shower, not bothering to dry my shampooed hair. I pull it back into a braided bun, slip on black leggings and a black silk tunic, then slide into my black heeled strappy sandals. I add no jewelry.

"Who died?" Virgil remarks as soon as I walk into the office.

I don't answer, but inside a voice screams, *The relationship with the only love of my life.* Wisely, Virgil says nothing more. By the end of Sunday, when I have not heard anything, I text Chase.

How is everything?

He immediately responds. *Still looking.*

My concern mounts. Where could she be? I think about phoning Antonio, but I don't want to worry him. He's busy working at the restaurant and will find out soon enough. Another concern slips to the forefront. With all the worry over

Fiona's disappearance, I never asked Chase about the carbon monoxide leak. I'm hoping no news is good news.

Sunday rolls into Monday and everyone is bustling to prepare for a fashion show that now seems inane. I care, but worry for Fiona's well-being trumps work. When my cell rings at the end of the day, I quickly answer expecting to hear Chase with news. Beth's voice offers a cheerful hello and I can't hide my disappointment.

"Well a fine hello to you too," she adds. When I don't answer, she immediately offers a worried, "What's wrong?"

I hadn't seen Beth but once or twice since our return from Europe and still we could fall into the rhythm of good friends who know and understand each other well.

Choking back tears, I can't speak.

"I'm on my way," she answers. "I'll meet you at your office in half an hour."

I really don't want nosy colleagues listening to my problems. "No, not here."

"Ok. Then at the rooftop at Patroon. You sound like you can use a drink."

"Yes, that works."

Sammy is waiting to drive me and when I get in the car, he's grinning.

"Any word?" I ask breathlessly.

"Fiona's been found and the good news is she wasn't high." I let out a cry of relief and bury my face in my hands.

"It's ok, Alicia."

I push back my hair with both hands and let them rest on my head. "Where is she now?"

"At the hospital undergoing some tests. She's a bit banged up. She won't say what happened and everyone is respecting her privacy. We're just happy she's been found."

I wipe my tears and my initial relief is replaced with sadness when the realization that Chase hadn't bothered to call and tell me the news himself empties me of emotion. Tonelessly and with dry eyes, I tell Sammy where I'm going. I ask about the carbon monoxide leak and Sammy assures me it was a false alarm. With so much happening it slipped my mind, resurfacing now that I know Fiona is alright.

Sammy heads east and says nothing more, and I welcome the silence. With my relationship with Chase frayed, I have no idea why he's still chauffeuring me around and make a mental note to take a cab home tonight. Chase and his demands be damned.

Beth is already waiting at one of the few available tables with seats. She throws her arms around me then steps back and sets me down, taking a seat in the chair next to me. Summoning a server, she looks at me expectantly waiting for me to order so we can start talking.

"Sapphire martini, stirred, three olives, please."

"So now you're hitting the gin. Tell me what happened?"

It's hard to know where to begin, everything unraveled so quickly. I explain how the weekend started wonderfully with lunch at my parents and how it ended miserably when Fiona disappeared. As I rehash the events out loud, the stress Chase is under crystalizes. I know he worries about me, especially with the appearance of Walnut Nose (this I do not share with Beth). Then there is the disappearance of Fiona, and on top of that a poisonous gas scare in one of his buildings. Still, he could have called. And his harsh words were uncalled for. I am not some spoiled diva who can't withstand hardship.

"He had no right to say those things to you," Beth interrupts. "You're a good person."

"Yes, but he is under so much pressure. I just don't know why he's still so mad at me."

Beth is unconvinced. "That's taking empathy to new heights, even for you, and what makes you think he's still angry."

"He hasn't called or answered my text, and when I call it goes right to voice mail … and, well …" I'm hesitating because it's painful to explain.

Beth waits patiently, eyes wide with concern.

"It's more than just that. It's how he looks at me sometimes, like I'm some kid who's incapable of understanding his real life problems."

Beth reaches out her hand and grasps mine. "He's probably up to his ears with worry and stress, but that doesn't make him any less of an AA with those bastard tendencies I told you about."

Now there's a mouthful that only Beth can deliver with aplomb.

"What?" I'm confused and shaking my head, attempt to clarify. "Chase's never been to alcoholics anonymous. His family had some problems, but I don't think …"

"An AA," she interrupts to clarify, "is simply an aggravating asshole, and this particular AA needs to realize what he's tossing away."

"What are you getting at?"

"Did you know Marcel is in town? He's been trying to reach you."

I shake my head, but that would explain the unknown number popping up on my phone.

"So let's all go out dancing tomorrow night. You can't just mope around waiting for the AA to call."

I smirk because the quick application of acronyms is so Beth. She doesn't even have to think. They just spill out of her mouth. "It sounds like fun, but I don't know. There's work and the show to think about," I offer feebly.

Inside, I'm thinking how I just want to devour a gallon of mint chocolate chip ice cream then crawl inside myself and fall asleep listening to Adele croon lost love lyrics.

Beth is insistent. "We'll make it an early night. I'm telling you he needs to be flushed out, and the only way to do that is to go out and enjoy yourself without him."

I'm thinking it'll be more like sticking my finger in a hornet's nest, but shrugging my shoulders, agree.

"Sure, why not?" It has to be better than hanging around a lonely apartment, waiting for a text or phone call. We finalize a plan for meeting at a club in the meatpacking district and when we reach the street, Sammy is waiting.

"Hop in," he says cheerfully. "You too, Beth. I'll drive you home."

"But I live all the way downtown."

"No problem. You mind taking a ride, Alicia?"

"Not at all." And we both get in the car. Tomorrow's time enough to begin cabbing it. No need to share the details of our plans with Sammy, and I give Beth a nudge when she starts to mention a meeting time. She nods, says she'll call, and shouts out a "Thanks. See you tomorrow night."

In bed, when I rest my head on my pillow, the sadness is suffocating, the longing like a fog of grief that presses. I miss that AA.

The time at work crawls, although the countdown to show time is accelerating. Everything needs to be done yesterday. My usual efficiency has taken a hit, and I hear Virgil shout, "Alicia, remove yourself from whatever funeral your mind is attending and help us out here."

For the remainder of the day, I make a special effort to remain on task. There's the final run-through with the models at 1:00, and I work through lunch to make sure everything is ready for them. What was formerly thought to be perfect can look mediocre under the lights or on the body of a particular model, so I make sure to keep extra fabric on hand, lots of straight pins, and my sewing scissors which I safeguard in the back pocket of the pant suit I wore especially for easy access to them. I step off the elevator and into a flurry of frenetic movement. I head for the dressing area and inch my way past a multitude of clothing racks, musical instruments, workers, and models. Virgil is flustered which is a contrast to his usual gently mocking demeanor.

He rushes over to me. "Go introduce yourself to the models. I want you on sight before any of them step in front of the lights. Make sure the fit and color of what they're wearing looks right. There's a wine-colored jacket that appears purple in front of the lights. See if there's any way to dim them when she steps out tomorrow."

I immediately head toward the bustle of activity in the rear of the room. A large group of semi-clad men and women cluster near mirrors, slipping on a medley of skirts, pants, coats, jackets, dresses, spraying the room with different colors and textures. I spot the wine-colored jacket on a young woman who stands towering over the other models. Blond and at least six-two with no hips, she is a striking example of a Viking bloodline. I maneuver her and the jacket toward Bailey, who's in charge of lighting, introducing myself as we walk. Her name is Sonya and she's in the city hoping to become an actress. Everyone here seems to be on the path to another career.

"Hey, Alicia, it's crazy today and this is only the rehearsal. I may stay home the next two days," Bailey shouts down from a stepladder when I summon him.

I get right to the point. "We have a problem with the hue of this jacket under these lights. Any way they can be toned down when Sonya steps out?"

"No problem. I know exactly what I can do."

Everything should be that easy, but I don't have time for a problem solved breather because when I turn around my eyes widen in disbelief. No, it can't be. But it is. In the corner of the room, stepping into a Marsala wine colored evening dress is none other but the Countess. As if connected by internal radar, we lock eyes. I'm sure my expression is one of shock and surprise, but hers is unforgettable. It is the look of a panther eying its prey.

The rest of the day is a blur, and we don't have the opportunity to speak. I still haven't heard from Chase, making these last two days stretch to forever. When the last of the musicians, models, carpenters, seamstresses, managers, and whoever else is involved in this production leave, a dim quiet settles on the office. A quick check at the wall clock shows it's 8:00, and I think it's the right time to get ready for tonight. Beth said there's a strict cocktail dress code and I didn't want to have to bother to go back to my apartment to change, so I packed my black slip dress. I figure I'll sneak out the service entrance to ditch Sammy and cab it. What good did it do to continue to depend on Chase's buddies? Besides, I haven't seen Walnut Nose in quite some time and Sammy indicated that the carbon monoxide leak was a false alarm.

I slip into the restroom and quickly dress, taking time to brush my teeth and freshen my makeup. I put my pants suit in a carry bag and bring it back to my desk to leave at the office. Slipping into the T-strap shoes Chase bought me for the awards ceremony, I can't help but wonder why I'm wearing them since they're such a painful reminder of him. I figure I enjoy wearing them because they bring back memories of a happier time when I felt at home and in love.

I really don't want to go, but it's too late to back out. Besides there's that hole inside that keeps widening and maybe a drink and some dancing will help close it for a bit. Sometimes I think I should call him, just to see how he is, but then I think of what he said and my fingers falter on my phone. If he really believes I can't understand what he needs, then why prolong the inevitable breakup. It must be what he wants or he would have reached out by now.

I will not cry, I will not cry, I inwardly repeat, but before long I feel my cheeks are wet and my nose running. The pain is gut wrenching. It's as if my soul is bared to a relentless stabbing pain that makes me want to curl into a ball and disappear. I brush away my tears and grab my purse, ready to head down in the elevator. When I look up I spot Virgil, pensively studying me from across the room. I wave a good-bye but he holds up his hand asking for a moment then heads in my direction.

"Are you ok?" Concern etches his eyes

"I'm fine. Just tired," I lie.

"Problems with the Chaser?" He's been calling Chase that

ever since he remarked on his good looks when we all met in Italy.

I don't want to talk about my problems at the office, but the disquiet in his expression encourages me open up. "We had a disagreement and…" I feel that familiar lump form in my throat "…we haven't spoken in a few days. I really don't know where the relationship is going."

He puts his arm around me, and I cover my face with my hands to hide my tears. Virgil takes out a crisp white handkerchief and hands it to me. I hesitate even though I really need to blow my nose. It's of such fine quality and monogramed no less.

"Thank you," I croak, too upset to say anything more.

He waits patiently. Then in a soft, even voice offers, "That man loves you."

I shake my head because I don't believe it's true.

"It's the way he looks at you. The way he holds his hand in the small of your back, the way he fended off all those leeches at the awards ceremony. If you don't see it, then you must be blind."

"You don't understand. We have differences."

He guffaws. "Who doesn't? My guess is he did something stupid." Then Virgil gives me a good once-over, obviously surmising that I'm going out for the evening and snorts, "Just remember, two stupids never made a smart."

I really don't want to continue to discuss my personal problems with him being my boss and all, so I straighten up, pull myself together, and give him another heartfelt thank you before slipping his handkerchief into my purse, making a mental note to be sure to hand-wash, iron, and return it. He nods and heads toward his office and slinging my purse over my shoulder, I make my way towards the elevators.

I spot Sammy parked near the corner and head toward the car, thinking what's there to hide? I'm only going out for a cocktail and some dancing with friends. There's time enough to sever these ties. The thought makes me queasy, but I shake it off, get in the car, and tell Sammy where I'm going. He says nothing, just drives in the direction of the meatpacking district. I give no further information and when we arrive, I offer a simple thank you before getting out of the car. I don't expect Sammy to be waiting at the end of the evening, especially now that Chase hasn't bothered to call or show up.

The hotel lobby is a sparse room with one attendant standing behind a sleek desk. The elevator is hidden toward the back and once inside I hit the button for the rooftop. A burly, square-jawed bouncer stands in front of a set of heavy doors that I assume must open to the club. He sweeps his eyes up and down my body, nods approvingly, but doesn't step aside to allow me access.

"ID," he states and when I hand him my driver's license, he studies it, looks back at me, then down and up again, before querying with a hint of disbelief, "Alicia Cesare?" It's like being checked out by some beefy version of the Swiss Guard.

"Yes, that's me," I offer, but he's more interested in what

the chic attendant standing to his far right has to say when, heels clicking against a floor so waxed you could see yourself in it, she walks over and whispers in his ear. Nodding his eyes swivel back to me.

"You're familiar with Reardon Realty?"

It's so random I'm confused. "Excuse me?"

He speaks slower as if addressing someone mentally challenged.

"You know Rear-don Real-ty, yes?

Oh for heaven's sake, it's like being stalked by a ghost, and I stifle the urge to roll my eyes. "Yes, I know Chase Reardon." With the magic words spoken, the double doors are opened and I'm allowed entry. I step into a space flanked by floor-to-ceiling windows offering panoramic views of Manhattan. A massive circular bar carved into a column that reaches the vaulted ceiling holds hundreds of different brands of liquor. Every beautiful person in the city appears to be in this room, no doubt invited to attract big spenders. Chase told me that a successful nightclub can make 15 to 20 million a year, but I shake the thought from my head because I don't want to think about him tonight. I spot some of the models from our show drinking at the bar and catch the distinguishable profile of the Nordic beauty, Sonya, sipping a pink cocktail from an oversized Martini glass. People dance to loud techno music and as I make my way through the crowd, I hear someone calling my name and following the direction of the voice, see Beth standing next to Marcel at the bar. I had only met him once, but his dark wavy hair and aquiline profile separate him from the crowd.

"You made it." Beth grabs me in a hug then adds softly, "I thought you wouldn't come." I smile and Marcel takes my hands in his and kisses both cheeks. Very French.

"Aleesha, it is so good to see you again."

Mmm, also very French. "It's nice to see you too, Marcel."

"Here, sit." And he offers me his seat.

Beth thrusts a cocktail menu in my hand and points to a specific cocktail. I look down and read: *Chase, the Dragon.* She doesn't even wait for me to respond, "I already ordered you one. Even if you hate it, it's too apropos to ignore."

"Sure. Why not."

She hesitates for a moment then, flashing her thumb in the direction of the entrance remarks, "Did you have a problem getting in? That beef-head bouncer took one look at my name on my ID and asked if I knew anyone at Reardon Realty. Hope you don't mind that I mentioned the AA's name."

Marcel furrows his brow, flummoxed by Beth's coded English.

"It's fine. I had to do the same." I don't say anything, but I'm wondering how the hell this club was able to associate my name and Beth's with Chase. Beth arrived before I did, and I didn't tell Sammy where I was going until I got in the car. Unless … I narrow my eyes and sigh in disgust. Sammy, Mac, and the AA must communicate about my whereabouts. Mac may have even followed Beth here, knowing it's where I'd be because we were meeting tonight. I have no idea what ties Reardon Realty has with this establishment. Maybe there's some secret organization for high-end club owners that gives them and their friends priority. *Humph*, go figure. So much fuss about a simple night out. Now more than ever, I realize how I need to sever these ties. He's mistaken if he thinks he can break it off while still having me followed like some pesky appendage.

The drink is some concoction of rum, vermouth, and fruit and as it turns out, I don't hate it at all. In fact several *Chase, the Dragons* later, I'm rocking on the dance floor like I own the place. Marcel is a decent dancer, light on his feet and Beth is swinging, hands lifted, hips swaying with some hipster she just met. I stop dancing, walk to the bar and order a *Good Girl Alone* vodka cocktail which goes down as easily as the *Chase, the Dragons*. The metaphors are too rich to ignore, and when I tell Beth, she laughingly orders me another. By this time, Marcel has gotten us a table and a waiter sporting a long ponytail and dark sunglasses even though it must be close to midnight brings it to our table.

What I don't immediately grasp but will realize later, is that not eating, being depressed, and interchanging sweet alcoholic beverages do not mix well for a long evening out. By the time I finish the champagne Marcel orders, I am on top of one of the leather sofas, dancing to a techno version of "Feel this Moment." Ah yes, Pitbull, Christina Aguilera and I are all in the moment. Two days of pent up frustration and gloom are released with each shimmy and shake of my body to the beat. Somewhere in the distance I hear Beth call out, "You go, girl," and I raise my arms to move to the revved up tempo of the music. Never have I felt so in touch with my body, each swivel of my hips and glide of my feet, move for him.

The people in the room evaporate and in my mind Chase's eyes are watching. It's as if only he and I are here and it's cathartic, energizing, mesmerizing all at the same time, until … It happens so fast, I'm baffled. One minute I'm dancing alone, shoes kicked off, feet jumping, hips swaying, and the next Marcel is bending me back and kissing me as people cheer and clap in the background. I hadn't even noticed he was dancing with me on the sofa. When he finally releases me, I'm stunned and well, curious. How surprisingly titillating and … soft. Very soft. And a bit squishy. I lick my lips and rub them gently with the tips of my fingers, not realizing the song has ended until Marcel extends his hand and helps me down from the sofa. Once my feet hit the floor, the room spins. He catches me and continues to hold me while I slip on my shoes. Those shoes. The shoes Chase gave me before the awards ceremony and immediately the familiar pangs of loss and loneliness return with a vengeance until swaying and dizzy, I excuse myself to go to the restroom.

Blundering my way through a long curving hallway, I reach a cluster of closed, unmarked doors I assume must be the restrooms. I open one and step inside. Amazing. I can actually pee while viewing the Empire State Building in the distance. I finish, wash my hands, then clutch the sink to wait for the room to stop spinning. It doesn't. Fresh air is what I need and I walk back through the hallway, out the large doors, and straight past the bouncer, who doesn't even glance my way. Apparently leaving is a hell of a lot easier than getting in. After three misses to the elevator button, I get it right, and once inside I'm engulfed in a kaleidoscopic mural of what looks to be Maria from *The Sound of Music*. Am I trapped in some cinematic hallucination? I pull my head back and study the wall, nearly toppling with the effort. Yup, it's Julie Andrews. The doors eventually open and I stagger through the lobby and into the cool evening. Taking deep breaths, I head to the corner and continue walking, hoping the exercise and fresh air will straighten my unsteadiness. My mind's numb. In fact my whole body feels anesthetized, but still memories of Chase permeate. I think of how solicitous he behaved when I told him about having had a twin and my mother's depression after his death. But mostly I'm thinking about how it feels to be wrapped in his arms, how enrapturing and safe, as if I'm caught and lost only in him.

The tears blur my vision and I lower my head, shielding my eyes with my hand and let them fall, increasing my pace in some vain attempt to escape the sadness that permeates my core. Panting from exertion, I finally stop and clutching my knees, bend to catch my breath. It's when I look up again that I realize that somewhere in my wandering, I must have taken a wrong turn. All that surrounds me is darkness and deserted sidewalks and streets. No traffic. No people. No well-lit bustling bars or restaurants. Empty. I turn, attempting to backtrack toward where I think the club is, but the area only seems to get more desolate.

I decide the best return route is a shortcut through an alley that leads back to the main avenue. That's when I see them. Three guys nonchalantly leaning against the wall of a building smoking a joint. I quickly turn to walk in the opposite direction but they see me.

Whistling and calling out, "Come to Daddy, baby," and "Aren't you a hot piece of ass," they saunter toward me.

I break into a run, turning to see how close they are, but when I spin my head back, the ground sways, and I stagger, falling onto my hands and knees. One of them is already on me and snickering, straddles me, while grabbing and tugging the back of my dress.

I don't even have time to shout for help because next thing I know he's being lifted and tossed onto the sidewalk like a sack of discarded potatoes. A pair of strong hands help me up, and when I turn, I'm looking straight into Sammy's face.

"Pfff, am I glad to see you," I slur with the rest of my "I think those guys are up to no good," being swallowed by a lazy tongue. Even I can hear my drunken speech.

My knees buckle when I attempt to stand on my own, and Sammy swiftly scoops me into his arms not saying a word. Ahead, there's a tussle with several grunts and groans and a spinning motion of head butts and body punches, until the three are scattering like bowling pins hit in a strike. Squinting at the only figure to remain standing, recognition dawns.

"Hey, wait a minute. Is that Mac?" And without waiting for an answer, I break into a lopsided grin and shout out, waving, "Hi, Mac." Boy, am I glad to see them. Sammy says nothing, just keeps walking until we reach the car where he adeptly opens the door and places me in the backseat. It doesn't take me long to figure out that Sammy and Mac are here for me. Dropping my head in my hands, I groan. Even in my drunken haze, I know this is not good.

Sammy gets in the driver's seat, slams the door, then turns and hands me a bottled water. "Drink."

I take it, a rush of embarrassment and guilt surfacing, because I've wreaked havoc tonight and it was never my intent. Between sips I lean my head back wincing when I think of the evening. Did I just jump and dance on top of a sofa at some swanky club? I start to feel nauseous. Was I kissed by Marcel while people whistled and clapped in the background? Yes and Yes. Then on top of everything I leave and get lost. I immediately reach for my phone only to realize it's in my purse back at the club. The evening just keeps getting worse.

"Sammy, I'm sorry to be such a bother, but I have to go back and get my purse and tell the others I'm leaving."

"No worries, Alicia. Mac is taking care of it."

Tears prickle. He's being so nice and I've been so irresponsible. Besides, I miss Chase. I hate that we're not talking. Before I know it I'm leaning back in the seat and blubbering like some two-year-old. Sammy says nothing, just reaches back and hands me a handkerchief, making me think how strange it is that for a second time in one day a man has given me a handkerchief. Have tissues become obsolete? My brain's inebriated meandering stops dead in its tracks when I hear Sammy's "hello" spoken toward the mounted phone screen being answered by a deep voice I recognize all too well. I bolt upright. It's him.

"Is she in the car?"

Chase's words are clipped. Annoyed and thinking of all the *Chase, the Dragons* I drank, I giggle and blurt, "Well hello, Mr. Chase the Dragon."

There's a pause and for a moment I think he's hung up.

"Are you drunk?"

Nope, he's back. I look up and squint toward the voice screen as if at any moment the live Chase will emerge. "Little bit."

Sammy interjects smoothly, "I see you both realize you're on speaker."

"That works for me because she needs to know she's behaving like some inexorable nexus of mayhem and trouble," Chase sputters enraged.

The nerve of him to insult me, disappear and then reappear as a voice that continues to ridicule by tossing out one of his weird *Chasisms*, and to think I was just missing him. Well enough is enough.

"Just shelve that Yale degree for a moment, buddy. I'm a

nexus of mayhem and trouble? You can't afford to talk, Mister *Wizard*."

"What did you call me?"

I lean forward, "The W.I.Z.A.R.D." I spell slowly and loudly, without the hint of a slur which I consider quite an achievement given the circumstances. "I can hear you and you're controlling things as always, because I *am* in this damn car, but as usual, I CAN'T SEE YOU, so why don't you pull back your curtain and show your face."

"You have the nerve to call me that after all I had to do to keep you from harm tonight. You're like some out of control adolescent who needs to be protected from herself."

"Did you just call me an adolescent?" I shout, reaching for the door handle. "I will not stand for another insult from you. Sammy, let me out of this car."

"Don't you dare leave that car or you'll regret it for a month of Sundays every time you try to sit."

"Now you're threatening me?" I boldly shout but slide my hand away from the door. A month of Sundays. What does that even mean? He's really hurling those *Chasisms* at me tonight, which could only mean he's extra exasperated. Good, so am I, but my palms begin to sweat and my heart pounds like I just ran a sprint.

"Oh that's no threat, sweetheart. That's a promise." His voice is deceptively low.

Gasping at his audacity, I forget my fear and again reach for the handle determined to jump out of the moving car rather than listen to one more thing he has to say.

Sammy must have had enough because without so much as a nod, flinch or fluster, he activates the child safety locks, hits *end call,* and turns on the radio—loud. I rest my head against the seat and sip some water trying to relax. No one can rile me like that man. Closing my eyes, I lie back and instantly feel like I'm on a ship caught in a squall. The music is reverberating in my skull, and I realize I've just catapulted from considerably buzzed—ok drunk—to hung over in the few minutes it took to have that argument.

"Sammy, could you please lower the music." I take another sip of water, rubbing my temples to ease the beginning of a throbbing headache. He does and only when we reach my building does he release the safety locks, but I wait before getting out. I owe this man an apology and a big thank you for being there for me. That's the first thing I realized, once I calmed down. The second is that Chase and I have to do some serious talking. I can't go on like this.

"Thank you, Sammy. I'm sorry for the trouble I caused tonight." He reaches out his hand and helps me out of the car nodding a *"you're welcome."* As I start to walk towards the building, he calls out, "Please tell me you're remaining in your apartment for the night so I can put The Wizard at ease when I speak to him later."

I throw him a rueful glance. "I'm sorry you were caught in the middle of that argument and, yes, I am going straight to bed. Tomorrow is a big day. It wasn't wise of me to drink so much and stay out so late. I have to leave by seven-thirty tomorrow morning. Does that work for you?"

"Take two Advils and you should be fine," he says as I stagger from the car to the entrance of the building. "See you at 7:30," he adds, watching me walk through the revolving doors.

Waving, I think how lucky I was to have Sammy and Mac tonight. God only knows what would have happened in that alleyway. Chase is right. I behaved like an out of control teenager. Remorse and guilt vie for control as I undress then collapse into bed too tired to wash up. I do manage to down two Advils with another large glass of water. I can't afford to be anything but stellar tomorrow. Turns out it's not only work that's going to demand my undivided attention.

CHAPTER THIRTY-TWO

*I*t's Defcon 2 and counting down. Workers scurry over draped wires while half clothed models dash about looking for their designated dressing area.

"Wardrobe, now," Virgil calls out the second he spots me.

Surprisingly, I feel ok. I was up and dressed before the alarm went off and out the door by 7:25. Although my stomach balked at the thought of food, I did manage to pop down a vitamin with a glass of orange juice before leaving.

I head immediately to that area and step into a sea of clothes, makeup, and needy people. The morning wizzes in a frenzied blur of activity, but the pieces gradually fall into place for what seems to be a seamless pre-opener.

Desperately needing coffee, I head to a kitchen area and pour myself a cup from a large aluminum urn that looks like a discarded remnant from some soup kitchen. A powdered chemical version of milk sits on a Formica counter, and I spoon some into the tepid coffee. I need this caffeine jolt.

"Hey, didn't you get the memo?" Bailey calls down from a stepladder as I sip the awful brew.

"What do you mean?"

"There's a complete spread of food and beverages in the back room."

"For all of us?"

"That's what I'm told."

I toss the coffee in the sink and head in that direction, calling out a quick, "Thanks for the tip," to Bailey. I don't get far. Blocking my way is Virgil, who, arms crossed, eyes me with a what-are-you-hiding expression that makes me uneasy.

I walk past, offering a causal, "Just going to grab a quick cup of coffee."

"Word has it you were out celebrating last night."

I freeze and when I turn he's staring at me with a Grinch Who Stole Christmas grin. Hands on hips, he waits in silence for me to respond. I keep it nonchalant. "Um, for a bit."

"Don't be all coy. I want the scoop. Who's the kisser?"

"What?"

"A few of the models said you really let loose at the club with some guy who bent you back and planted a smooch smack on your lips. From their description he wasn't the Chaser."

I should have known Virgil would find out about last night. The office gossip grapevine is relentless, and he's its leader.

Shrugging a shoulder, I answer, "Just a night out with some friends."

"And the guy?"

"Someone I met in Paris."

"So …"

"So what?"

"The kiss … how was it?"

Oh for heaven's sake. Is nothing private today? I opt for brevity, hoping he'll get the hint.

"It was ok."

He nods, waving his hand and widening his eyes. "And …"

"I don't know." I pause, remembering. "I guess a bit soppy."

Puckering out his lower lip, he grabs his chin as if deep in thought. "How disappointing. I guess the French aren't always the best lovers."

Lovers? Is he for real? "Virgil, that never entered my mind. So curb those X-rated thoughts. Marcel and I are just friends."

"*Humph*, tell that to Marcel."

I'm thinking enough chitchat about a night I want to forget. "I hear there's food and coffee." I point to the room ahead. "Has Lincoln Center become generous?"

"Doubtful and Estelle Designs didn't foot the bill. We're hemorrhaging money with this show. My guess is one of the sponsors sent it."

"Can I bring you anything?"

"No thanks. I'm off to check on fittings. Some of the participating musicians have unique body shapes, and I need to see everything looks as it should. I'll meet you in the dressing area. We're scheduled to start promptly at one."

"Got it."

The door to the food area is closed and when I turn the doorknob it's locked. I give a light knock and try the door again. This time it opens. The windowless room is dimly lit, but I can see that there are two long tables spread with platters of cold meats, cheeses, and salads. My mouth waters and my stomach gives a loud rumble. Obviously, my appetite has returned with a vengeance. The roast beef peeking out from fresh rolls looks delicious, lean, and sliced thin, and I head right for it.

I sense him before I see him. There's a light wisp of breath on my neck and my eyes flutter closed as I lean back to give his mouth access.

"I've been waiting for you." He reaches back and I hear the click of the door lock. He pulls me back toward him and continues nibbling on my neck. "So … I see Dorothy got home safely last night." He places a kiss for every star down my neck. My breathing quickens and my "yes" comes out soft and wispy, but when I try to turn to face him, he holds me tightly in place. I feel his lengthening member pushing into my back and I want him. I've never wanted anyone like I've desired Chase, and now after three days of yearning, the feeling is stronger than ever.

"So, you're the Secret Santa," I manage to get out.

"Yeah, when I can spare time from being The Wizard."

That comment hit its mark. "Why are you here?" My voice is again breathy as he continues to lean into my neck.

"For a multitude of reasons." His voice against my ear is

searing, soft. "A complaint was filed, actually shouted, followed by a threat to do something dangerous, all after a drunken meander through deserted downtown streets. I'd say that warrants my coming maybe even calls for a visit from strange man. What do you think?"

Hmm, flushed out and a bit peeved. "I like your visit," I murmur.

"And strange man?"

I swallow because I remember the term I used with my mother as an acronym to explain Antonio's shenanigans with Fiona. I also have a vivid recollection of Chase's threat in the car. "Depends on how it feels."

"I assure you it will feel good while reminding you of how you should behave."

This time he lets me turn, and I look up into his face. He looks tired, worn from worry and unshaven, but even so he's sexy as hell. I trace my finger across his lips and he groans and pulls me toward him, wrapping my hair around his hand then tugging my head back and kissing me roughly. Before I can catch my breath, he pushes me back against the wall, and capturing my hands above my head, deepens the kiss, his mouth and tongue claiming mine. It is a kiss that ends too soon but will be remembered for a lifetime. Every bit of passion, longing, yearning, and need meld into his touch. Anger dissipates and when we disengage, we're both breathless. My hands fall limply at my sides, and I slowly open my eyes. He lowers his hands to my waist.

"Your skirt doesn't leave much to the imagination." Pausing, he stares into my eyes then slides his hands down to my thighs, moving them slowly up my short bandage skirt, letting one rest on my thigh while the other begins a slow and methodic massage of my backside. "It and your thong will make it very easy for strange man's visit."

Every muscle below my waist clenches, and I'm torn between lust and a *"this is your workplace"* warning. In the end there is no decision to be made because he lets his hand slide out from under my skirt and looking at me regretfully announces, "To be continued when you're more available."

I'm at work with a huge event about to start momentarily, and all I can think about is how I want his hand to continue to work its magic.

He steps back and gently pushes a stray piece of hair behind my ear. "Come with me to my cabin upstate this weekend. It'll just be the two of us. No families, no kids, no interruptions. We can talk and … catch up."

I don't have to think twice. I want to be with him. When I'm with him, there's a need that's fulfilled, a chasm that closes. I nod a yes. He shuts his eyes and I catch a faint, clipped sigh of relief.

"I'm off to Chicago for business tonight. I'll be back on Friday and we'll drive straight to Summit. You'll love it there. We can hike, horseback ride–"

I don't let him finish. I reach up and pull his head down to mine in a kiss. He pulls me closer, deepens the kiss, and my legs buckle, but he holds me by my waist in a firm grasp. I don't care what we do as long as we're together. When we part he gives me a smile that makes me want to throw myself into his arms again. There are approaching footsteps outside the door. It's lunchtime and by now, others must have heard about the spread of food.

"I don't want to let you go, but you need to get back to work, and I have a plane to catch. Sammy will drive you to and from work for the rest of the week. I imagine they'll be late nights. Don't give me cause for worry." He becomes very still, scrunches up his nose, and lets out a huge sneeze before unlocking and slipping out the door, giving me no opportunity to answer. The man is infuriatingly consistent, but I couldn't care less. We're going to spend the weekend together and that's all that matters. Walking purposely to the table, I grab a roast beef on a roll and take a bite. Delicious.

Nibbling as I walk to wardrobe, I stop short when standing in the distance, Virgil calls out, "Over here."

He looks at me hard. "Good god, the Chaser's back." Then adds a clipped, "Oh don't look so shocked. You're a dead giveaway. Swollen lips, smudged lipstick, mussed hair. That is not the handiwork of some mush-mouth Frenchman."

The man is equipped with gossip radar.

"I'm in no mood to share, Virgil. Believe what you want." I take another bite of my sandwich and walk down the hallway.

"I don't need confirmation, young lady."

I continue as if I don't hear. "You take that walk of shame, with that ponytail swinging with your hips … and at work no less." I raise my hand in the air to get him to stop, but my face is the color of the Countess's dress. Thank god he's staring at my back. Still, I can envision him throwing his head back when I hear his usual raucous laugh.

I make a beeline for my desk, grab my purse, and head to the restroom. One look in the mirror confirms Virgil's observation. My lips are swollen, my lip gloss smudged, and more of my hair hangs outside the clasp than in the ponytail. I undo the band, run a brush through it, and catch it back up into a ponytail. Then I dip a paper towel in cold water, hold it to my lips and smooth on some lip gloss before heading to wardrobe. It's countdown.

Day one of the show is a huge success. The spring line is a hit. The musicians put the audience in a good mood and in a last minute touch we put Virgil's Panama Jack hat on the lead trumpet player to accent the Khaki vested suit he wears on the catwalk. The Countess struts in her dress with the confidence of an open feathered peacock. By the time day one is over, I'm ready to sleep for a week. Part two is tomorrow and then thank heavens it's over.

I'm in bed by nine, up again at five, and at the office by seven. Part two is a remake of part one but offers a show of fashion that is trendy and classy. I love the line. Virgil looks peaked. I know he joined the others for celebratory drinks last night and is paying the price this morning. I wag my finger and tsk.

"I know, I know. Too much fun. Now I have to pay the price is what the kisser is thinking."

I roll my eyes. By 12:00 there are the same pre-show jitters as yesterday and Virgil is beside himself with worry. Seems like the same draping issues have resurfaced. I'm directed to behind the scenes where I hear him in a heated argument with one of the seamstresses.

"This needs to drape, not hang like a sheet thrown over her shoulders."

I look and see he's referring to the top of a dress Devie is wearing. It's no wonder it hangs. She's all angles, without the hint of a curve. Anywhere.

"Alicia, tweak these proportions so there's some form." Virgil moves his hand in a circle around her chest area. Oh good heavens, he wants me to give her boobs. I head toward the large table where there's a basket of bust cups and choose a pair I deem to be the right fit. Devie is wearing a silk organza empire waistline dress that flows to her knees. I almost need a stepladder to reach her chest and I'm five-six. Holding a needle and thread and some pins, I extend my hand beneath her dress in the general area of where there should be breasts, but for the life of me I can't find them. I grope around a bit and finally find what feels like a small welt. Except for an occasional hello or wave good-bye, we've hardly spoken, so it's no surprise that the Countess stares ahead as if I'm not there, chatting every now and then with another model while I sew the cup into the dress in exactly the right spot. I can't get in and out of her chest fast enough.

The other model is sitting across from us waiting for her fitting. She casually asks the Countess if she has any plans for the weekend.

"I do not know," she answers, her d is accentuated and the slight upward slant of her eyes assume the sly look of a fox as she continues to peer ahead oblivious to my stitching. "Last weekend was long and tiring and I am exhausted from this show."

"So you were out partying and neglected to invite me?" she thrusts out her bottom lip in an exaggerated pout.

"No, definitely not at a party," Devie glibly answers. "I was with a guy I've known a long time."

My hand stills, the needle poised to hit its spot for the next stitch.

The other model raises her brows in surprise. "Do tell more."

"We spent a great deal of time looking for his sister who went missing, then he crashed at my place afterward."

"Ow," she screeches when I accidently prick her with the needle. My hand is shaking so badly I have to pause before continuing. "Bitch," she mumbles under her breath.

I don't answer because all I want to do is get away from her. I can't confront her here at work with everyone milling about.

My heart is racing so fast it seems to sink into my stomach. I finish the stitching, knot, and cut the thread and turn and walk away, not giving her the satisfaction of commenting or looking back.

"Are you alright?" Bailey asks, looking down from his stepladder as he finishes the last bit of lighting. "You look like you've just seen a ghost."

"I'm fine," I answer. Anything more would have turned the lump in my throat into a well of tears. Shock turns to anger with each step I take away from the Countess.

That bastard. He insults me, sends me packing, and then searches out Devie to help. And ... they spend the night together. And ... he has the nerve to show up here to invite me away for the weekend after paying for a banquet spread of food ... like some gigolo bearing buy off gifts. My mind stutters with negative thoughts. Go away with him for the weekend? Like hell I will. He can rot in hell before I share his bed again. And his rules, right out the window with him.

"Don't give me cause to worry. Sammy will drive you to and from work," I mimic.

A few passing technicians give me strange looks. I couldn't care less. I storm to the stage to prepare for the show, taking deep breaths along the way in an attempt to calm down. It's like spraying a burning house with a water gun.

"Alicia." I hear my name being called.

"What?" I snap. Then immediately regret it when I see the soft spoken intern, Wendy, hesitate with uncertainty.

"Charlotte says to be at stage three ASAP," she stammers.

"Got it. Thanks." I soften my tone and she gives me a relieved smile. The asshole is now turning me into a shrew. Somewhere in the far reaches of my mind a voice tells me it's unfair to place so much blame on Chase without giving him a chance to explain, but anger wins, and I feel justified in holding him accountable.

Putting myself in cruise control, I get through the rest of the day. The thorough pre-planning and well-received spring line help the show proceed seamlessly. By the end of the evening I'm exhausted, stressed, and depressed. I sneak out the service entrance and grab a cab back to my apartment, not bothering to call Sammy. To hell with all of them and that includes Walnut Nose. Let him try to approach me and see how he likes the quick kick in the balls he gets for the aggravation he's causing. I'm spewing anger everywhere.

When I get home I pull down the shades, throw myself into bed, and fall into a restless sleep. I stagger awake around two, remove my clothes, and drag myself into the bathroom to wash up and slip into a T-shirt. It's one of his. I yank it off, but not before I breath in its scent, saturating my senses with the smell of sandalwood and sage that's all him. I slide under the sheet and pull it and the coverlet over my head.

At eight I wake with a pounding headache and decide to take the day off. It's scheduled as a half-day and will be really nothing more than a celebratory champagne breakfast, and I'm in no mood to party. That done, I turn off my phone, call down to Elliot the doorman and tell him I do not want to see anyone, slip into oversized sweat pants and a T-shirt, and get back into bed. It's easy to sleep away my misery. There doesn't seem to be anything to stay awake for and I'm exhausted from the long work days. The few times I do wake, Chase's comments about my inability to understand his past surface to haunt me, and I convince myself he's right. I can't offer the same depth of knowledge and experience that Devie can. No wonder he needs her and not me. They lived through the same childhood problems that bond people for life. There isn't any way I can be for him what she is. Chase has it all wrong. When it comes to past lives, I'm the outsider looking in. Miserable, I cry myself back to sleep, burying the hurt in the far reaches of my mind.

CHAPTER THIRTY-THREE

Somewhere during the course of my self-induced stupor, I think I hear my lobby phone buzzing, but instead of answering, I turn over and fall back to sleep, nestling into my soft comforter. I'm roused by a gentle touch to my forehead and the blinds slowly being pulled back. Sunlight streams in and my eyes slowly open. It's as if they've been sealed shut for days. I look up and see of all people my mother.

"Mamma? What are you doing here? No one called up that you were here."

She sits on the edge of my bed and looks straight at me. "A mamma does not need permission from a stranger in a uniform to visit her daughter." But then her eyes soften and she looks at me with concern. "I tried knocking, but you didn't answer so I used one of the keys given when we signed the lease. I'm sorry to surprise you like this, but when I called your cell it went straight to voice mail and your office said you called in sick. I was worried."

"I'm sorry," I manage to sputter, my throat parched and my eyes refusing to open more than slits against the glare of the sunlight.

All I want to do is crawl back under the covers. She continues stroking my forehead and if feels so comforting that I let the tears come. For the first time since my brush with the Countess, I let my feelings out and it isn't long before I am crying in my mother's arms. She says nothing for the longest time, just strokes back my hair until the last tear is wrenched from me and I stop sobbing. When she finally does speak, her voice is tinged with regret.

"I think I have taken to my bed enough for the both of us. Yes?"

I don't answer. I don't want my sadness to remind her of her past depressions, so when she pulls back the covers and calls out, "It's enough moping. Time for you to get on with your life."

I feel I owe her some shred of an explanation. "I don't know what to do. Chase and I ... we've been arguing, and, well, I'm afraid I can't undo what I've done."

"Nonsense. At your age nothing is so wrong that it can't be made right with a good meal and a heart-to-heart conversation."

She obviously doesn't know how Mr. Rules operates. This is not going to be easy to correct. I try to explain without going into too much detail. "He did something that made me so angry, and then I did something awful too." I think about how I stood him up today and how worried he must be that he's been unable to reach me. On top of it all, I ditched Sammy.

"Nonsense." My mother shrugs, waving her hand dismissively. It was nothing more than a playful kiss during a harmless night out on the town."

I still, every bone and muscle freezing. "What?" I manage to sputter, sure I must have heard incorrectly before her all too knowing look has me adding, "How do you know about that?"

"Facesbook." She gazes at me, shaking her head as if to say, how ridiculous that you even have to ask the question. "Antonio signed me up as part of PR for the restaurant, and well, this morning there it was."

Shit. I dive back under the covers. Nothing, absolutely nothing is private today. I am going to kill Beth. She pulls them back.

"Do you love this man?

I don't have to even think about my answer. I just raise my head and pause.

"That's what I thought. Then go to him."

"You don't understand. He's going to be so mad. I don't think I can face him."

"Gentle and fierce. You have to be both when dealing with a man."

I sit up, contemplating my options. Fierce. I better be because this getting together, if it does happen, is not going to be pleasant. I am in so much trouble.

My mother gives me no time to dwell. "He's waiting for you and he's concerned. He doesn't understand why you won't take his calls."

I throw up my hands in disbelief. "How do you know all of this?"

"I spoke to Bill. He called asking if I knew if you were ok. Said Chase was beside himself with worry."

I take in a deep breath realizing again how unfair I've been. I should have given him a chance to explain. Instead I believed everything that witch of a countess had to say.

"I don't even know where he is. We were supposed to go to his cabin in Summit for the weekend."

"His father said that's where he is. Went up there to, how do you say, lick his sores."

I can't help but smile. "Wounds, lick his wounds." My mother's English is impeccable, but idioms still give her a hard time. She throws me a lopsided smile happy that I seem to be crawling out of my funk.

"I have to figure out a way to get to Summit. I don't know if there's train transportation."

"No need. I will speak to Massimo and have him loan you his car. He's working the weekend shift at the hospital, and I can't see why he'll require it.

I shake my head skeptically. "I don't know about that. He's awfully protective of that car."

Mamma is already tapping the buttons on her phone. "I

would like to speak to Massimo Cesare. This is his mother calling." Her tone is polite and insistent. Obviously not needing permission pertains to sons at work as well as daughters at home.

"Hello, Massimo."

"Yes, Yes I am well. Everyone is fine. I have a small favor to ask. Alicia needs to borrow your car for the weekend to meet someone upstate. It's rather important."

My mother is silent for some time, and I can only imagine what Massimo is saying. I don't have long to wait because she mouths that he is worried I can't handle driving a car with a shift.

"Tell him I know how. I drove one in Europe," I whisper. If she's surprised she doesn't say anything, just nods.

"You have nothing to worry about. It appears she learned how to drive a standard automobile in Europe. She is quite proficient now."

More silence, shorter this time. She must be winning the battle.

"No, she is not able to come to the phone. She is preparing for the trip. Mamma winks at me. "Expect her in half an hour."

I'm in and out of the shower and dressed in a pair of jeans and blouse within ten minutes. I slip into my boots, give my hair a thorough brushing, and grab my purse and travel bag with clothing I quickly throw in for an overnight stay. I'm thinking optimistically.

"Take a sweater. It gets cold in the mountains at night." I

run back and grab my fisherman sweater before giving her a kiss. "You may want to pick up a chicken to cook, maybe some potatoes and carrots to roast, and a bottle of cabernet. There's not much better than a home-cooked meal and a good bottle of wine to help clear up a misunderstanding," she adds.

Yeah, well in theory that all sounds good, but what I'm really thinking is that the only chicken in this suggested menu is going to be me when I have to deal with his temper, although he also has some explaining to do too.

I stop on my way out, realizing my mother came into the city explicitly to see me and now I'm leaving. "How about you? How are you getting home?" I ask.

"Antonio is running the restaurant tonight so your father is meeting me here for dinner. Don't worry about me. Now go." She shoos me out the door. "You don't want to be driving unknown country roads in the dark."

I give her another kiss and take the elevator to the lobby, thinking how she and my father must have plotted and planned this entire scenario. I can hear them now.

"Elvira, that girl has your stubbornness."

And Mamma would furrow her brow in worry. "Yes, but she usually answers or texts me back. Something is wrong."

"The only thing wrong is her disposition. On the outside, all soft and sweet, but inside..." I see him making a fist as if he's standing right in front of me "...a will of iron, like her mamma."

"I know, I know, probably lost her temper and now regrets

it."

Papa nodding, then agreeing, "Go see. Make sure she's alright. I'll meet you later." And their concern turns to action.

Sammy is waiting in the car at the corner, and I wonder how long he's been there. I thought for sure he would have left when I didn't show up. I should have known that he would never do that. He and Chase have this ironclad pact that doesn't vacillate or break once agreed to. He waves and honks when he spots me. Technically, he could drive me to Summit, but it's a long way to travel to and from in one night, and Chase and I need this alone time. He'll simply have to drive me to the hospital and then be assured I'll be ok with GPS.

Once in the car, there's no questions asked. Sammy never delves, just drops me at the hospital and says, "Safe travels. Call if you need anything."

Dealing with Massimo is not as easy. He's waiting for me outside the hospital parking garage, the Porsche beauty already parked in its driveway.

"I don't know what you pulled to convince Mamma you needed this car, but I swear, Alicia, if there's so much as a dimple—"

I don't give him a chance to finish before throwing my arms around him and giving him a big thank you hug. I knew it would work. He stops his tirade and lets out a deep, cleansing breath in an attempt to grab a Zen moment to help him deal.

"I promise I'll be careful." And sliding into the driver's seat, I start the car, stalling only twice before reaching the street. A quick look in the rearview mirror shows me Massimo gripping his head with both hands and cringing.

I reach my hand out the window and give him a thumbs-up only to hear him shout, "Two hands on the wheel." The rest is lost because I'm off.

Shifting becomes smoother with each mile, and once I'm on the thruway it's easy. I listen and sing along to my favorite music and then rehearse in my mind what I'm going to say when I see Chase. I think of calling him but dismiss the idea. Better we meet face to face.

When I reach the main street of the town closest to Chase's house, I spot a market and pull into the lot to take my mother's advice. I pick up a fresh chicken, fingerling potatoes, a bunch of carrots and mixed greens and celery for a salad. I'm feeling confident so I add a dozen eggs, bacon, orange juice, espresso coffee beans, and a loaf of bread for the morning. Hopefully he won't slam the door in my face after I traveled all this way. Next to the market is a liquor store, and I buy two bottles of pinot noir, suggested by a sommelier who's onsite conducting a wine tasting. By the time I pull into the long private road leading up to Chase's house, it's dark. My headlights help guide me up a gravel driveway, and I park the car outside a four-car garage and make my way up to the well-lit house.

This is no cabin.

Wicker chairs and cushioned sofas sit on a well-lit wrap around porch that overlooks a pond on one side and a forest of trees on the other. Deer nibble at berries and bushes in the distance, and eyes glowing in the blackness, they look up then scurry off when they spot me. A canoe tied to a large weeping birch tree floats in the pond. I stop, lower my bags, and wipe my sweaty palms on my jeans. I'm nervous.

There's no bell so I knock, timidly at first then louder when he doesn't answer. I have a moment of panic when I think that he may have left leaving me no recourse but to drive all the way back tonight. But then I hear feet shuffling and the door opens. Staring at me from glassy eyes is Chase hunched over with an afghan wrapped around his shoulders. He looks up at me, and blinks his eyes slowly.

"I think I'm dying."

What? I anticipated many different scenarios from this encounter, but this was never part of the repertoire. He opens the door wider and walks inside, and I follow, dragging the packages with me and quickly closing the door to keep out the draft.

"What's wrong?" I stare at his flushed and perspiring face, hoping I don't have to call 911. He makes some circle around his head and throat with his hand then lets it travel down his legs.

"You're throat and head hurt and your legs ache? Is that it?" It's like cuing a toddler.

He nods his head and moans. I feel his forehead. He's burning with fever. Guiding him through the kitchen and living area and into a bedroom at the far end of the hallway, I pull down the covers on a majestic four-poster cherry wood bed and settle him beneath them then check the closet and find a wool blanket that I quickly toss on top of him to help get his shivering body warm.

"Have you taken anything for your fever?"

Through chattering teeth and a flushed feverish face, he mutters, "I popped some aspirins with a couple of chugs of beer a few hours ago, but they didn't go down well."

Mother of god, the man is a self-induced wrecking ball. I rummage in my purse, find some Advil, then remove the orange juice from the grocery bag and pour him a glass. He swallows the pills, no questions asked, and falls back onto the pillow. In the kitchen I find a clean cloth and wet it with cool water to place it on his forehead. His eyes flutter closed, but he's still shivering. The temperature outside must be dropping because there is a damp chill in the house, a clear indication of what winters must be like up here. I can't locate the thermostat to turn up the heat, but I see wood already set for a fire in a massive stone fireplace along the far wall in the living area. Newspapers, kindling, and large matches sit in a bin next to the fireplace, and I use them to help light a fire. It's comforting to hear the crackle of the wood burning, and at least it's giving off some heat.

Chase seems to be breathing easy and relieved, I return to the kitchen to put away the groceries. It's a large and well-equipped country kitchen done in red and white with a pot-bellied wood burning stove on the far side. It's lit but the wood is nearly gone. I go back to the wood bin and place several of the smaller pieces into the stove and they immediately ignite, sending some warmth into the kitchen. Chilled, I reach into my overnight bag and put on my sweater thinking I can always help Chase onto the sofa in the living room to keep him warm if the bedroom remains too chilly.

In the kitchen I'm surprised to find a coffee grinder and an espresso pot. I get it going and while waiting for the coffee to brew, I pull out my phone and text my parents and Massimo that I made it without mishap.

That done, I reluctantly decide to check Facebook. My finger nervously poised toward the screen, I take in a deep breath and force my eyes to look. There's several photos of me, Beth, and Marcel toasting and downing *Chase, the Dragons* and whatever the hell else we were all drinking. Then there's a few of me and Marcel dancing on the dance floor. Not optimum but all relatively harmless. I shrug, thinking … hoping … praying that Beth took down the photo my mother referred to because so far there's not much he can hold me accountable for except maybe having one too many drinks.

Then I see it. A close-up of Marcel bending me back over his arm and kissing me. This is not good. The still photo makes it seem as if the kiss lingered when I actually ended it quickly. Nervously, I get up to check on the patient and see that he's sleeping. Maybe he hasn't seen it. He has been too sick to do much of anything. There might be time to have it removed. I reach out to Beth and text *What the F*** Take it down*, knowing she'll realize exactly what I'm referring to. Her reply is immediate which doesn't surprise me.

AA flushed out AND pissed off. Luv it. Will remove but it's out there.

Now I'm in a panic. *Where else did u post?*

Waiting for her response, I contemplate scratching the coffee and opening the wine.

I hear a text come in.

Vined it. Don't be mad. It worked.

Shit! She made and posted a video of me and Marcel. No use responding. The damage is done. Besides Chase has to answer for a few things too, like why he ran to Devin after chewing me out and shipping me off. But I'm uneasy. Something tells me I was set up by Devie and that Chase only needed her to help navigate the underbelly of the drug scene so he could find Fiona. With Devie's mother's drug problems, I imagine she'd have some knowledge of them.

I decide to tell Chase what happened. I'll explain it was one kiss that meant nothing. I nix the wine, pour myself a cup of coffee, and take it with me to keep vigil by his bed. First order of business is to help him recover. There's a pillowed rocking chair so huge I melt into its cushioned depth and then cover myself with the patchwork quilt resting over its back. This is going to be a long night. From Chase's symptoms, I figure he has the flu and make a mental note to keep him hydrated with Advils administered at the right intervals to reduce his fever. Changing the recipe from roast chicken to chicken soup will also help. He's strong and should be fine.

Several times he wakes calling out my name and when I hold his hand and wipe his head with a cool cloth, he nods off again but it's a restless, feverish sleep.

A few times he mumbles waving his hand, "No, don't get too close. I don't want you to catch this," and makes feeble attempts to face away from me. I shush him, wipe his forehead with a cool cloth, and assure him I'm fine.

Eventually, I must doze in the chair because when I open my eyes there's a faint stream of sunlight peeking through the window shade. Standing, I stretch out the kinks in my back and neck. Chase is sleeping, but he's drenched in perspiration. His fever must have broken during the night. Gently, I kiss his forehead and he opens his eyes.

"You're here." he whispers, his voice dry and raspy. I hold out a glass of water for him that I had resting on the night table, and he sits up and sips, taking another and another until the glass is empty.

"It's good that you're drinking, but you have to change your pajamas. They're soaking and so are these sheets. I have to change them or you'll get chilled."

He attempts to get up, looks at me sideways, and falls back holding his head, moaning. Panicked, I feel his forehead but it's cool. "What's the matter?"

"I'm so weak. It hurts when I move my hands."

"Here, let me help you." I hold him under his arms and slide him back into a sitting position, then pull his T-shirt up over his head and place it on the bed. I untie the top of his pajama bottoms and gingerly slide them down and off, placing them on the bed as well.

That's when I see it. Rock hard and standing tall.

I look up, catch his lopsided grin, bedhead hair spiked in all directions, and laugh.

"A few hours ago you were dying. Absolutely not. You're still too sick. Tell Private Johnson he's dismissed."

"I love it when you play bossy nurse. Later, you can examine Private Johnson, feel and stroke his head, make sure he's up and about. He might even need some mouth to mouth."

I push his hand away as he reaches for me. "You're incorrigible."

I find a pair of pajamas in the chest across from the bed and hand them to him. He's a bit wobbly and I have to help him slip them on but he looks much better. His cheeks have color and his eyes are no longer glassy and unfocused. For all his sexual bravado a minute ago, he sits dozing in the rocking chair while I rummage in a closet outside the bathroom for a clean set of sheets. I swiftly make up the bed and guide him back under the covers. He's asleep within seconds.

I scoot into the bathroom to wash up and change into leggings and a hoodie. I brush out my hair and fasten it in a braid that's more tousle than weave, but at least it's out of my face. Heading into the kitchen, I start preparing the chicken soup. The cupboard is practically empty, but I do find an onion, a can of mushrooms, and a box of rice which will all add flavor. Forty five minutes later, the soup is simmering, the wine is breathing, the table is set, and I'm exhausted. I plod back to the bedroom, lift the covers, and snuggle next to Chase's now cool body, telling myself I'll just rest for a few minutes. Somewhere during the course of this nap, he reaches out his arm and pulls me toward him. I nestle close and fall back to sleep.

When I first open my eyes, I have to think about where I am. Strange bed in an unfamiliar room with a crisp chill hovering. It's only when I see Chase sitting in the rocking chair, freshly showered, with a pair of pants hanging low on his hips that I recollect where I am and smile.

"Hey you. How are you feeling?"

"Much better. Thank you."

His voice is polite almost formal and a wave of unease flickers through me. I shake it off when he looks at me and grins.

"The soup you made smells delicious."

I rub the sleep from my eyes and swing my legs off the side of the bed. "Let me get you some. You must be hungry."

His hand snakes out and grasps my arm. "No, stay where you are. I'm going to join you."

He gets up from the rocker and slides into bed. There's something about his demeanor that's off, too stiff, too cordial but his face is inscrutable. I lie down and turn to face him, stroking my hand down his cheek placing feathery kisses on his lips. He puts both hands on either side of my face and gently but firmly disengages. I look into his eyes and swallowing, think this is as good a time as any to tell him about a kiss with an acquaintance during an inebriated night on the town that meant nothing.

"Chase, we need to talk."

"Yeah, but not now."

He's so close we're a hair's breadth away from touching, and he's smokin' hot, hair mussed, pants low enough for me to glance down and glimpse his happy trail. "Let's spend time together in bed." The measured cadence of his voice is barely a whisper. "Shall I dare you to a visit from strange man?"

I swallow then nervously bite the inside of my cheek when I remember the meaning behind the acronym. Uncertainty prickles the nerve endings up and down my spine, but the challenge sounds exciting. I splay my hand across his chest and slide it down, tracing his line of hair that trickles from his navel to below his waist. His stomach muscles tighten. They're firm and wondering what else might be hard, I search lower, but he stops my hand and holds it to his mouth, first kissing my fingers then sucking each with a slow, moist raking of his lips. I close my eyes and relish his touch.

"So?"

I don't easily refuse a dare, especially one that sounds so enticing. "Alright." But I am quick to add, "What do I have to do?"

"Do? You do nothing but agree to remain in this bed. I do it all." Those words should signal a warning, but my body is already aligning with his as need replaces caution, although I do also ask, "What will you do?"

He replies without a moment's hesitation. "Offer you unremitting pleasure."

The ache in my belly deepens with his words, and I nod in agreement. His move toward me is lazy. He lies me on my back and lifts the bottom of my hoodie over my head and slides it off then uses the sleeves to tie my wrists together before fastening them to one of the spindles in the headboard. Slowly, he rests the hood over my eyes. The sweatshirt offers little give and with the press of his body on mine, my hands are securely trapped.

"Everything ok?" he asks.

I shake my head, wondering what in heaven's name he's planning next. He takes his time, pushing down one cup of my bra to palm my breast and then the other where he does the same. With my eyes covered and my breasts exposed, my body strums with anticipation.

The first flick of his tongue across my nipple is so sudden and intense that I gasp. He slowly circles it until that familiar ache begins below. Stopping, he plumps my breast with his hand before taking it in his mouth and sucking, gradually then firmly and deliberately, until I arch from the bed moaning. The incessant heat of his mouth pulling and nipping releases a need below that shouts for attention. Leaving his mouth on my breast, he slides his hand under my pants, letting it rest on my stomach while his mouth switches to my other breast. Desire mounts and I exhale a deep breath of want. His warm hand slides beneath my panties, where it pauses on my stomach waiting, resting, until anticipation drives me wild with need. Then, with a slow even rhythm, he circles his thumb lightly across my clit, pausing for just that fraction of a moment to press. The throbbing ache between my legs intensifies, and I have to bite my lip to keep from begging him to insert it.

He doesn't. Instead, with a measured movement of two fingers, he teases my swollen folds and when my hips arch up toward him, he inserts first one, then the other, flickering and pressing, then releasing just as that special spot is about to be triggered.

I groan with frustration offering a pleading, husky, "Please."

His only response is a soothing croon. "Not yet but soon."

He slips off my leggings, making sure to brush his hands down my thighs before gliding them back up to take off my panties. The hood slides off my eyes and I watch as he spreads my legs, opening me further to the whim of his touch. His gaze reveres but he quickly shutters and replaces it with an unflappable, impenetrable look. Gradually he bends to let his teasing tongue torment my opening. My skin is hot and flushed, and between my legs I'm heavy and slick. I have this pulsating frenetic need to climax, but when I reach the pinnacle he abruptly stops, moving his lips to leave small kisses up my inner thigh and across my stomach until they lock onto my breast where again, he begins the gentle tugging and sucking.

I try to detach, anesthetize those parts of my body enflamed by his touch, but his mouth and hands are everywhere and my body begs for release. When he does stop, it's only to move his mouth lower, and I fight back tears of frustration because I know what's to follow. This time he inserts two fingers, sliding them in and out in rapid pulsating motions until I'm panting with need. He releases and again lets his tongue relentlessly work its magic, ceasing split seconds before I climax. The agonizing sensation of building only to have it cease before culmination ignites such intense feelings of frustration and rejection that I crumble.

"Please. Don't do this. Why won't you love me?" My voice is hushed and needy, and I wrap my legs around his torso to pull him toward me.

Tightening his forearms, he raises his body from mine and forces my legs to unclench from him.

His tone, devoid of modulation demands. "Tell me, Alicia. Do you want to feel this moment, this time … for you to come?" I close my eyes, dread coursing through me because I know he's referring to the song I danced to on the sofa just before Marcel kissed me. His play on words sound cold and cruel, and I attempt to express my remorse between hushed breaths of want.

"That peck with Marcel, it meant nothing to me."

His body stiffens, his jaw tightens. "Mention that boy's name in my bed again and my threat of not being able to sit for a month of Sundays will feel very real."

He's furious and I'm afraid to think what more is in store for me.

"You were curious though, about the feel of that kiss on your lips." He switches tone, his voice low, almost gentle.

I'm not fooled and shaking my head, offer a soft denial. He deftly lifts and bends my legs at the knees and gives a hard slap to my backside. It stings but fuck, this would be hot if he wasn't so detached. He waits and all I want is to have him hold me and kiss me and penetrate me.

Hoping the truth will make them happen, I softly murmur, "A little bit."

If I thought my assent would make him see reason, I was mistaken, because after that, time becomes trapped in tormenting tremors of building and stopping that keep me on the edge of unfulfilled need. I had no idea the extent my body could be used against me and no amount of pleading or coaxing convince him to stop his agonizing torment.

Eventually it ends, because hands freed, I'm crying into my pillow. I don't know how much time passes between the agony of his relentless withholding and my wracking sobs, but I feel his hand lightly touch my shoulder. I jerk it away.

"Don't touch me. How can you possibly think I want your hands anywhere near my body?" I'm angry but mostly I don't trust my traitorous body anywhere near his touch.

His hand freezes and he rests it back on the bed. "I'm sorry. I may have taken it too far."

I catch my breath in two rapid sobs before managing to get out, "You think? You made your point ten minutes into your, your ..." I stammer searching for the words, can't think of any and hurl out, "Whatever the hell that torment is called."

He reaches out his hand again. I feel it graze my back before it rests so close to my body, I feel its heat. "Erotic sexual denial. It heightens pleasure and teaches control." I sense his eyes boring into my back, but he makes no other attempt to touch me.

My temper whips into a fury and, making sure to keep some distance, I turn to face him, "Well thanks for sharing that NOW." I don't see how knowing it earlier would have helped, except to possibly temper some of the feelings of rejection but shouting is better than giving in to my urge to pummel him since that would involve touching. In some warped need to assign meaning to his explanation, I attempt to wrap my head abound his words, *heighten pleasure, erotic sexual denial,* but the more I think about them, the more they sound like sugar-coated bullshit.

Narrowing my eyes, I add, "Do you know what I think?" He remains quiet, too quiet. "I think you meant to punish me. Is that right?"

He doesn't answer, which is tantamount to a yes. My sobs have stopped and emotionally spent, I dejectedly whisper, "I begged you."

His silence clings to the air, and I sit up taking the sheet with me wincing as it grazes my breasts. The room is lit by a moon so full it mocks us with its glow. I loosely wrap the sheet around my body and plod to the kitchen to make sure the stove is turned off. I don't want to burn the bastard's house down, but I sure as hell am getting out of it. When I turn, he's standing in front of me, hands limp at his sides, probably paralyzed from overuse. I walk past him without so much as grazing a hair on his arm and head back to the bedroom to dress and pack.

Recognizing my intent, he offers a tattered, "Don't leave."

Furious, I spit out, "Give me one good reason why I shouldn't."

His reply gets right to the point. "Role Reversal."

I stop and once again it's so quiet, I hear my own breathing. Without looking at him I ask, "You mean strange man visits you this time."

"Yes."

He stands in front of me, pale from being sick and from the sex starve and a quick glance down, reveals he's as needy as I am. I want to pull him toward me in a carnal kiss, surrender my mouth, my tongue, my need for him. But I don't. This is too good a proposition to ignore and shamelessly, I don't have to think twice about my decision.

"Ok, I accept. Same rules, opposite roles. Agreed?"

If he became any whiter, he'd pass for a ghost. "Yeah."

Oh my. Where to begin? My imagination conjures dozens of ideas, and I sift through them like someone let loose on a buying spree with free money. Why hadn't I thought of this sooner? Gone is the dejected, frustrated damsel in distress.

I point to the bed. "Get naked. I'll be right back."

I run to the kitchen drawer for a necessary prop, back into

the mud room to get a piece of rope I spotted earlier when looking for the laundry room, and into Chase's closet where I grab one of his white collared shirts. Dropping the sheet, I put on the shirt, slip the kitchen utensil into its pocket, and slide into my black lace panties. Perfect. In my overnight bag are the high heeled shoes Chase bought when I was in Italy, which I seem to want to wear everywhere these days. I have no idea what I was thinking when I packed them on a trip to a ranch upstate. Romantic dinner out … clubbing at a place in town … or maybe I just anticipated hot make-up sex. Whatever the reason, they're perfect for my striptease and I carefully slide into them. They really are beautiful.

Chase is lying on the bed watching my every move and sauntering toward him, I take the rope and tie his hands using one of Antonio's famous knots then wrap the rope around the same bedpost he used for my hands. I stare at his prone, nude body that waits for me, and suddenly it's both Christmas and the Fourth of July. Taking my iPhone I tap Michael Bublé's "Feeling Good" and hearing his slow, soft croon start, I place one foot in front of the other and slowly strut into the room, stopping to stand with my back to Chase. Slipping the shirt off one shoulder and turning to look coquettishly at him, I slide the silver spoon into my mouth and suck … slowly, eventually leaving it to hang from my mouth as I gyrate to the beat. I fold my hand around the bedpost, and roll my shoulder forward and back to the beat, then wrap both hands around the top of the bedpost, and shimmy down, straddling the post while sucking the silver spoon.

Mmm hmm, I am feeling good. He never takes his eyes off me, but I do think I hear the label *wiseass* cross his lips. One at a time, I slowly unfasten the shirt buttons until the top of my breasts are only just revealed. Then raising my hands, I rock my head back and forth to the music, never taking the spoon from my mouth. I slide the shirt back and forth across my back until I finally let it slip off my shoulders and slide to the floor. Facing away from the bed, I bend over and leisurely lower one side, then the other of my underpants, exposing parts of my ass as I shimmy up and down to the music again and again. I take them off, twirl them around my index finger, and toss them in his direction. When the music reaches its crescendo, I bend over and, dignity be damned, take the spoon out of my mouth and use it as a riding crop while continuing to move to the rapid beat of the music. One sly, backwards glance shows me Marine Reardon's Private Johnson saluting at attention without so much as even a commanding touch from my hand. That is going to change. Keeping on my shoes, I saunter over to the bed and on bent knees, I straddle his prone body. Slowly, I graze my fingernails down his sculpted chest, lingering at his trail of hair before continuing to the middle of his V, where I stop when he leans toward me and let them graze the underside of his extended cock. I hear a hiss of breath and reaching up, I sear my slips to his, making sure to pull back every time his mouth attempts to take control of mine. Finally, I lower my mouth to greet the private.

"Alicia," he warns, his voice is taut, his expression tense. But I'm not done. I take the tip of his swollen member into my mouth and lick its surface. Private Johnson is now reaching for the stars. I suck, savor, stop, suck, savor, stop, and in my mind the captured alliteration makes me want to laugh out loud. I don't, but I do continue. I trace my fingers around and around his lengthened penis, tug more and more as I reach the top, then recognizing he's at the cusp of his pleasure, cease. He groans, and I think life's a bitch when you've shown your student all the ropes, and I stop to look at his tied hands and grin.

"That impish smirk is as unsettling as your actions," he grumbles. "Either get on with it or stop."

Problem is, after a marathon of foreplay, my body is primed for some direct action. I kick off my shoes and tumble on top of him in bed. He looks at me suspiciously not sure what my next move will be. Even I'm uncertain, but I do lean in to kiss those beautiful lips, slowly at first, then moving my tongue inside and deepen the contact. I'm so turned on, I have to fight the urge to impale myself on him for relief. I stop and he closes his eyes and takes a deep breath to help manage his control. I look away and do the same. I'm going to have to exercise caution or this could implode. What if he comes and I'm left without satisfaction?

The thought unsettles, and in that moment of hesitation, he throws out, "Are we done now?" impatience clinging to each word.

His eyes are pleading and poor Private Johnson remains at attention, not moving a muscle. What a waste if he should suddenly spurt and collapse. The moment I nod my head yes, he spins into action, freeing his tied hands—I should have assumed he could do this—wrapping his legs around mine and flipping me onto my back. He uses his forearms to straddle on top and easily penetrates my all too ready opening. Let's face it, we've both had enough foreplay to last a decade. Thrusting hard, he stops only to lean back and lift my legs onto his shoulders deepening the penetration. Again he plunges, each thrust a signal to urges that have been begging to unwind. This time there is no wait, no stopping, and I scream out when an intense, relentless release shudders my body, tossing me into wave after wave of incessant undulations. His follows and he shouts out my name which sounds so thrilling I lower my legs and wrap my hands around his head and pull his lips to mine, creating even more ripples of ongoing pleasure as our mouths lock. We stay entwined for a long while, neither wanting to break contact first, until he slowly pulls out and falls onto his back. Sated and out of breath we lie side by side unable to move. Eventually I calm and turn onto my side and he reaches out his arm and pulls me closer.

I tenderly run my finger down the side of his face across his dark, sexy stubble and slowly around his lips. "Do you forgive me?"

He lazily runs his finger across my jaw to my lips and leaning in, he gently grazes them with his teeth. "It seems these lips have been very busy."

I swallow and my breath hitches when his finger again travels across my lips then down my chin and across my neck. "Just remember where they belong and we'll be fine." I breathe out a sigh of relief, thinking the worst is over, but his eyes darken and narrow. "That Frenchman better stay away from you. Don't think I didn't notice his sneak attack."

He must have seen the video as well as the photos, and it's not going to be easy for him to forget. I look at him and circle my forefinger across his lips. "Only you. They're only for you." I kiss him lightly.

We stay quiet, each of us reflecting on what to say next, not wanting to jeopardize the closeness. Surprisingly, he breaks the silence first and his question takes me by surprise.

"Why didn't you show up or answer my calls?"

I take my time answering because I realize my hasty decision was more foolish than justified. I was jealous and worse, I felt inferior, like some naive child responsible for causing a disastrous chain of events to unfold.

"I found out you sought out Devi to look for Fiona. It made me feel that I didn't, well actually, that I would never be able to live up to your expectations. I realized after Fiona went missing that you were right. I didn't fully grasp the problems from your past because if I did …" My voice is so low from swallowing back tears, that I only just manage to whisper, "I would never have allowed Fiona to leave."

His arms tighten around me and his expression softens.

"I'm sorry I said those things to you. You didn't deserve them. Why should you have to know how to deal with these problems? No one should have to understand the pain of addiction and ..." He pauses, trying to swallow the ache of the memory and finally adds, "Rape. You're not knowing is what I love about you. And yet you still want me. That's what I don't understand. Why you're still here with me."

His words simultaneously unsettle and perplex, making me wonder when the grip of his past will loosen enough for him to live free from its clutches? It's like some contagion that affects anyone who reaches out to its victims, and I ache for the burden he carries and the feelings of unworthiness it unleashes. I answer, explaining what I see in him. It's easy because it's what I've always seen.

"I'm here because you're worth it and basically what's there not to love? You're gorgeous, smart, hardworking, caring, honest, the list goes on."

He's uncomfortable with the accolades because he looks at me and smirks. "Even when I'm being a pain in the ass?"

"Since that's most of the time, I would have to say yes."

"You think I'm difficult to deal with, eh?" We're still face to face and suddenly serious, he gently strokes my hair away from my forehead. "I thought you left me. I don't know what I would do without you."

"I didn't leave you. After Fiona was found, when you didn't call or text, I figured you thought I couldn't handle the situation. That hurt, not hearing it from you."

He continues stroking my hair and I close my eyes relishing the ease of his touch. "When Fiona went missing, I knew it was bad. It's always big trouble when she drops off the grid. Once I knew you were on your way back with Sammy, I started my search. Antonio also set out, hoping to find her. He was worried sick. That first night, I drove around for hours, going to her friends' houses, local bars, junkie joints, any place she had a history of frequenting. No one had seen her. I called Devie as a last resort. Devin knows new, out of the way places where drugs are peddled." He pauses and stares moodily in the distance, and I look up into his face waiting for him to continue.

"We drove around the rest of the weekend, got a few tips but didn't find Fiona until she showed up battered and bruised at a local hospital, refusing to say what happened. By that time I was so wired one doctor insisted I leave and get some sleep, even gave me a prescription for, as he put it, 'a mild sedative.'"

I raise a wry brow. "Was that before or after you punched the wall?"

He stops and gives me a sheepish smirk. "I believe it was shortly after."

"Well you were concerned, but that is a nasty habit you have. Keep it up and one of these days you're going to break your hand."

"See, that's why I need you. You civilize my darker side." He raises my hand and kisses it. "Antonio never left her side and once I knew he was staying, I took one of those pills and slept for fourteen straight hours, which is another reason why you didn't hear from me. Mild my ass." He shakes his head.

I don't answer because I'm thinking he's lucky he didn't get a tranquilizing shot in his ass and a hospital cot to fall into to quiet his temper. His mood shifts and he's quiet for a long while. I know he's still thinking about Fiona.

"The thing is she would never leave Liam for that long, and with her history the first test the hospital administered was for drug use and it came up clean. I don't know why she won't say what happened to her."

"Maybe she's scared."

"Of what?"

"I don't know. Possibly someone from her past, you know, from when she was taking drugs."

He stills, mulling over my words. "As far as I know, she severed those ties long ago."

Shrugging, I ask, "Does she owe anyone money? Maybe someone in the past she bought drugs from."

I have no idea where this theory springs from. Possibly from one of the dozens of detective shows jamming prime time I may have watched, but it sounds viable.

"You know Fiona was the sweetest kid, a bit bookish with a creative bent and a love for nature and photography. But she had it hard. After my mother died, my father went on bender after bender, sometimes disappearing for days. I tried holding it together but was unraveling myself. When I enlisted, my aunt moved in for a while, but then her son was in a serious car accident and she had to leave to tend to him. Fiona was pretty much on her own after that. She says she first started using in eighth grade when she smoked pot with some friends. She eventually graduated to cocaine a year later. Seems like some slick bastard peddled the stuff cheaply near her school, luring kids into getting high and eventually hooked. Then, when he owned them, he raised the prices forcing them to come up with huge sums of money, god knows how, to feed their habit. Thing is I never understood where Fiona got the money to buy. She held minimum-wage jobs, never was arrested for stealing, and used the money I sent home to pay as many bills as she could. She never even liked drinking."

It's easy now to imagine the lonely child grieving the death of her mother, the loss of her father to alcohol and her brother to the marines. Her retreat into drugs, while foolish and self-destructive, is understandable.

"Any idea who this dealer is or if he was ever arrested?"

"Who the fuck knows and little good it does even if he was arrested. There's hundreds more to take his place. People who think street thugs are primarily responsible are only seeing miniscule parts of the whole. The street dealers are merely puppets in a game of kingpins and foot soldiers. The ones pulling the strings are the drug lords who bask in their millions in mansions tucked behind gates guarded by armed criminals. They're responsible for the family members, friends, neighbors, children—the list is endless of those who become addicted. That guy could be anywhere by now. We have definitely lost the war on drugs. Only way to win that war is not to use."

I know who he's referring to, but I don't mention Dimitri Ostopenko or The Finger or any of the other toxic pseudonyms he and his notorious gang are referred as. What's apparent is that Chase holds him and those like him accountable for rampant drug abuse in this country, and I don't disagree.

He's quiet but still continues stroking, his long fingers gliding through my hair, massaging and circling. It's as if he's getting as much comfort giving as I am in receiving, making the gesture a gift, and we lie together, enjoying this quiet intimacy.

I'm surprised when in a ragged whisper, he adds, "And then there's the shame, the fear ... the strong need to see that you're not dragged into that ugly side of my past. I think those are the real reasons I sent you away."

His eyes glaze with intensity and in their depths I see his ghosts. A conglomeration of hurt and fear, loneliness and anger. And for the first time I understand, truly understand, that there is no clear and easy path away from the clutches of a past. And although alcoholism, illness, drug abuse may have been the tipping points, the domino effect triggered by their toxicity created even worse problems until there weren't any safe havens, there weren't any people or places where the victims could unburden themselves, where they could feel worthy to live a life that offered hope and love and understanding. And yet ... in so many ways, Chase moved on from that trap. He succeeded, and even now continues to help others, but inside … inside a part of that defenseless child remains and still holds an intense need to protect himself and all those he loves from past demons that haunt his present. I see now that only with time and love, and acceptance and patience, can the burden be lightened. And even then there's no guarantee. But no matter the difficulties, I know there will be problems, I love this man. I believe in this man. I know that together we can paint happiness into our lives. I don't say any of this to him because I've learned that words do not hold the same weight as actions. It will be our behavior toward each other that will determine the success of our union, and so far we've more than proved that our love can survive. In fact, we've made it blossom, nurtured it to new heights and depths with lots more vibrancy remaining. We lie in compatible silence, relishing the comfort of the others proximity.

Eventually Chase's stomach gives a loud rumble.

"You must be hungry. When did you last eat?

"I don't know. Sometime before I got sick."

I reach for my cashmere hoodie that is now a twisted stretch of fabric, frayed and pulled along the seams, and opt for my sweater instead. It's a shame. I really liked that sweatshirt.

As if reading my mind, Chase offers, "I'll buy you another. C'mon let's eat."

His mood lightens and he quickly slips on his jeans and reaches for the white shirt I tossed aside during my dance. He sniffs. "Mmm, smells like you."

Buttoning it, he stops to remove the teaspoon that peeks out from its pocket and uses it to swat me on the backside when I bend to slip on my jeans. I turn my head and give him a narrow-eyed steamy look that says there's more where that came from if necessary, and he throws up his hands in surrender.

"Truce, Gypsy Rose Lee."

Who? But I'm too hungry to ask for specifics, and he's already in the bathroom washing up for supper. I join him, washing my hands and face and generally freshening up. Chase puts more wood on the fire and we move into the living area to sip wine while the soup heats. His cheeks have color for the first time since I arrived and except for a bit of a raspy voice, he looks healthy.

Putting his arm around me, he pulls me closer. "If you don't have to leave first thing tomorrow, let's go for a morning horseback ride. We can watch the sunrise."

"You own horses?"

"Yeah, three of them. They're stabled around the far end of the driveway path. Have you ridden before?"

"A couple of times. No lessons or anything, just a sunset ride when I was in Arizona and another along the beach on Long Island."

"You can ride Mae. She's gentle except when provoked.

Then she rears up and takes off, will even take a bite out of you." He raises his brows and smirks.

"Then best not to aggravate her." I reach over and nip his ear, quickly pulling away before he gets any other ideas.

He has to eat and so do I. We putter around the kitchen, he pours us some more wine, I ladle the soup into bowls, and we sit around the table falling into easy conversation. He tells me he bought the ranch from a contractor who built it for private use but was selling because his wife did not like how cold it got in winter and that it was located in the Snow Belt, getting so much snow they had to wear snow skis to navigate the long driveway/road that led down to the road.

"Brand-new custom kitchen, top of the line furnace, Fieldstone fireplace made from stone brought from a Pennsylvanian quarry, cherry wood cabinets and furniture."

"You bought it furnished?"

"Yeah. A good deal too. Once he decided he was going to build in Florida he was anxious to sell. Most likely understood, happy wife, happy life." He digs his spoon into the soup, blows lightly, and swallows. "This is delicious."

What he's telling me makes sense because with Chase, it's about quality but at the best price, and he's an expert at seeking, finding, acquiring and then when and if it deems prudent, selling. That's how he succeeds in real estate. He knows how to find just the right deal whether for himself or for developing, renting or selling.

"Well, this house is beautiful. Who helps you maintain it?"

I blow on my spoon, cooling the soup before raising it to my mouth. It is good, warming, soothing.

He must be hungry because he doesn't answer until he's spooned two or three more times. "I have great neighbors who I pay to take care of the horses, keep the snow shoveled, the house clean..." he shrugs "...stuff like that."

That's another strength, his ability to build relationships and maintain loyalty with people he trusts. He may not be the easiest person to work for, but I'm sure he pays well and his demands are reasonable.

We finish eating and he insists on cleaning up.

"You cooked and took care of me." He reaches over and gives me a kiss. "Thank you. Now it's my turn to help." And this is yet another of his strong suits. Chase is not one to take advantage of people. In that way we are alike.

The evening sky spills and scatters stars, and we sit cuddling under a blanket on the porch sofa, admiring its vastness. A part of me wishes it could always be like this, where we're removed, free from worry and the problems we now share.

As often occurs, he reaches over with his thumb and massages that space on my forehead between my eyes. "No worrying. It's all going to be fine." I nod and nestle into his arms, his presence offering comfort. He stares into the darkness, before clearing his throat and adding, "There is something I want you to do." I immediately look up and he pulls me closer, holding my head to him. The gravity of his tone is unsettling. I wait for him to find the words and when he does, my heart does a flip. "If anything happens that strikes you as threatening or even a bit unusual, promise you'll tell me or Sammy and above all else don't go running out by yourself trying to fix things. I don't want you to think you can take matters in your own hands. " I turn this over in my mind trying to decipher what constitutes odd enough to warrant alarming people, and when I don't immediately answer, he firmly tugs me up by my chin, "Do I have your word?" He's back to looking stiff and somber with an 'I will not take anything but your complete cooperation expression' that never ceases to unnerve.

"Yes, I promise." But I'm still confused. His request, actually his order, sounds like the baffling, *'if you see something, say something,'* slogan papering subways, buses, and other transportation hubs throughout the city, making me contemplate, exactly what am I to be on the lookout for: a suicide bomber, a remote-controlled explosive device like the ones Chase spoke about, and if I've never seen one how can I recognize and report the danger. Same with this situation, although I did eventually realize I was being followed. It's all perplexing and my head spins with the subsequent what ifs.

In bed, later that night, I spoon into him and we drift off, cocooned in the black stillness of the deceptively peaceful and silent country night.

CHAPTER THIRTY-FOUR

ae and I hit it off immediately. I feed her an apple and she nuzzles under my arm. Chase raises his brows in an '*I told you so manner*' that makes me chortle and Mae neigh. He adeptly saddles both horses, gives me a boost onto Mae, and we're trotting on our morning ride in no time. Chase is riding a large stallion with a sleek rum-colored coat who's aptly named Bacardi. Mae is gentle and the motion of the easy ride soothes any lingering frayed nerves from the past week. It's cloudy but even so a panorama of mountain, trees, and wildlife lies before us. Deer, birds, beavers and even a skunk that, thank heavens we manage to avoid, add beauty and tranquility to the surroundings. Some of the leaves are beginning to golden and crimson, suggesting the flame of color they would be in a few weeks. His parcel of land includes about two hundred acres, and he points out the boundaries as we ride down the path. We missed the sunrise but not on my account. This time, Chase needed the rest, and I let him sleep in. It doesn't matter, though, because this is one of those moments that you wish could be bottled like a fine, aged bourbon to be poured and enjoyed again and again.

"Up ahead and to the west there's a dense cluster of trees that offer no easy path or view. A lumber company offered good money for several acres of them, assured me they would plant replacements, but I figured that's no substitute for hundreds of years of life that would be destroyed in minutes. Some things are just worth keeping as is."

Chase may be a developer, but he has an appreciation for land and the wildlife it serves.

A tall, lanky older man with a weathered face and prickly white beard meets us outside the barn after our ride. Chase introduces me to Clyde Peterson, who tips his hat, mutters a "ma'am," then guides Mae and Bacardi into the barn without uttering another word. The nice to meet you on the tip of my tongue evaporates with him.

Chase is already heading toward the house, halting his long quick strides to shout back, "Let's make breakfast. I'm starving."

I jog toward him, thinking how peculiar it is to meet yet another quiet man seemingly held in by the constraints of his temperament and most likely military training. Was he yet another marine friend? But Clyde looks too old to have been in Afghanistan with Chase, yet still has that military bearing with eyes so fathomless, it's easy to gauge he's seen battle. Then it hits me, Clyde must have served in Viet Nam. How Chase remains connected to these military types is an enigma. Perhaps he belongs to some veteran's organization or more likely is a contributor for those who've served and are less fortunate. How like him to be there to help by offering employment in addition to contributions.

Sliding off my boots in the mud room, I can't help but grin when I notice the leftover rope from before. Chase's head is already buried in the refrigerator pulling out the butter, eggs, and bacon I bought yesterday and scattering them across the counter.

"I think I'll fry these up?" He picks up the carton of eggs.

I take them from him and he turns to rummage in a drawer, clattering pots and pulling out an assortment of frying pans and lids.

"Doesn't your grill work?" I'm referring to his top of the line freestanding stove with built in griddle and grill that looks like it could cook food for all the customers at Patroon.

"I don't know. He shrugs, poking out his lower lip. "Never tried it."

Mismatched pots and covers now clutter the far counter and leaving the drawer hanging open, he moves back toward the refrigerator and grabs the orange juice.

"Want some juice?"

The kitchen looks like a tornado hit, and we haven't even begun cooking. "No, not right now, thanks. Why don't you jump in the shower and I'll cook us breakfast."

"Sure you don't mind?

I shake my head. "No, it's fine." There's no way I want to clean up the mess after he cooks.

"Ok."

I wash up, put away the pots and covers, then study the stove to see how it works. I turn on the griddle, place the strips of bacon in a neat row once it's hot enough, then lower it as the bacon starts to sizzle. I put on a pot of coffee, set the table, pour us orange juice, and go back to cooking the bacon, stopping to pop bread into the toaster. By the time he's out of the shower and dressed, everything is just about ready except for the eggs, which I wait to fry so they won't get cold. Sitting companionably over breakfast is well, nice, and very normal given the bumpy starts and finishes of our relationship.

"Mmm, delicious," he offers between mouthfuls of toast and eggs.

I shrug. "Thanks. I would have made omelets but didn't have the right ingredients."

"This is perfect." He continues eating, relishing each mouthful and his appreciation of even the simplest home-cooked meal makes cooking for him a pleasure.

He finishes before I do, leans back, coffee mug in hand. I can read his body language well by now, his calculating gaze, erect demeanor, mouth pulled taut, all indicate he's waiting to share something he's not sure I'm going to accept. Well that won't be anything new and appetite waning, I almost stop eating but I don't want him to comment so I finish then meet his eye, hoping to prompt him to share what's on his mind.

He looks at me evenly. "This was good." And I don't know if he's still referring to the meal or something more, so I just nod silently. He reaches over, taking my hand in his and lightly brushes his finger across my knuckle.

"I love you, Alicia Grace Cesare."

And I don't know what stuns me more, the love admission or the fact that he knows my middle name. Definitely the love part. I get up and sit on his lap, taking the time to trace my forefinger around his beautiful mouth and across the rough, sexy stubble on his face, and that's when I feel my cheeks moisten. He gently wipes away my tears with his thumb and rests both hands on the side of my face.

"When we return to the city, I want you to stay with me." His eyes lock on mine, holding me captive, while inside a cacophony of thoughts and feelings scatter then try to assemble in some conglomeration of comprehension. Before I can answer, he places his finger across my lips. "I don't need your answer now. Take time to think it over."

He rests my head against his shoulder and gives my forehead an endearing kiss before lifting my chin and capturing my lips in a passionate hold with his, awakening those parts of my body that crave his touch. Without warning he stands, lifting me in his arms and carries me into the bedroom toward the giant rocker resting near the bed.

"I had visions of fucking you in this rocker every time I woke and saw you curled into it asleep."

This is so like him to catch me by surprise by dropping a bomb for me to contemplate then sweep me off my feet, literally, with a more immediate proposition too inviting to ignore. Will I ever be able to keep up with the twists and turns of his mind? "I thought you were too sick to see anything."

"I always notice you." He lowers me in front of it, letting my legs slowly slide down his torso and once I'm steady, places his hands under my sweater and gradually raises it over my head.

Our eyes never waver. We're locked in each other's spell, waiting, revering, and absorbing the other until he slides his hands down my sides and slowly unbuttons and removes my jeans, stopping to kiss my navel and lower his mouth down each leg as he slips them off. I close my eyes and lean into his caresses.

"We're going to take this nice and slow."

Caught in his web of passion, I silently offer a prayer that I've sufficiently paid my dues for that kiss. When I attempt to unbuckle his belt, he removes my hands and kissing each, lowers them to my sides then undoes it himself. He slides off his pants and boxer shorts, sits in the chair, and straddles me on top, maneuvering my legs around his waist so they hang from both sides of the chair.

"This one's all yours."

Raking his teeth gently across my bra, he tugs at my breast. I moan and arch toward him. He moves his hand up my side and around to the front, slowly lifting my bra and massaging my exposed breast, tweaking my nipple before tugging it gently between his teeth and sucking. My need jumps a notch and then another when he switches to the other breast. He's rock hard against me and I lower my hand to guide him inside.

"You're so wet," he rasps and pushes in deeper, the chair leaning with his plunge.

I moan and swivel my hips and the chair rocks with the momentum. Gyrating in slow, even circles, I take the time to react to building sensations increasing the force to match a need that mounts and coils with an intensity unlike any other. The chair moves with me, increasing my forward and backward glide and he cups and raises my backside, allowing me to push deeper until I feel as if I'm flying, tumbling over and over again into a rapture of sweet nothingness. I scream out his name as I spiral yet again when he reaches his climax. Thoroughly spent, we remain interlocked, the creaking and rocking of the chair moving with our pounding hearts and heavy breathing until eventually both slow and we are lulled into a soothing forward and backward motion. I don't want this moment, this union of physical and emotional perfection, to end.

I rest my head on his shoulder and whisper in his ear, "I love you too, Chase Richard Reardon." How about that. I know his full name. Love has that effect, that ability to expand your mind, allowing you to recall details you never thought you knew. Unfortunately it also drives you to attempt things you'd never dream of doing with no amount of warning or precaution sufficient to alter the course.

The remainder of morning and afternoon blurs into packing, showering, cleaning up, and loading the car. It surprises me that he puts it all in Massimo's car and reading my questioning look, he simply says, "I'll drive you back to the City."

"What about your car? You're leaving it here?" This I can't believe.

"Uh …" He pauses awkwardly. "No. Sammy's driving it back."

"Sammy?" Yet again, I'm confused. "What is he doing here?"

"He's fishing and camping with a friend, who drove him up."

Funny, he never mentioned that to me when he dropped me off at the hospital. Then it hits. Sammy never intended to let me drive up here alone. Probably followed the entire time in a friend's car, leaving his in the parking garage.

"Well, no need to drive me then. You can ride back with him." I really want his company, but I don't like the idea that plans were arranged without any input from me.

"That might be hard. He's with someone he really wants to

be with. I'd just be a third wheel."

"You mean, Sammy has a girlfriend?"

"Yes, Sammy has a girlfriend. Why so surprised? He's not celibate or gay. Her name's Sandy and she lives here in Summit," Chase explains, reading my questioning silence. "She breeds Labrador retrievers and delivered one to a couple on the Upper West Side before picking Sammy up and driving them here for some hiking and fishing. They both love the outdoors. She's driving back with him to spend some time in the city. Visit a museum, see a show."

"Sandy and Sammy, it's cute. What's she like?"

"You'll find out soon enough. I think that's them now."

Sammy pulls into the gravel driveway and peering out the windshield is a set of large brown eyes above a small snout of the cutest fur ball of a puppy imaginable. Sandy holds him to her when she gets out of the car, and he stretches his head and nuzzles into her neck much like a baby would. Introductions are offered and Sandy reaches out her free hand to shake mine. Her eyes are kind and down her back a glossy black braid extends all the way to her bottom.

"Nice to meet you, and this is Rupert." She turns so I can see Rupert and as I gently pet his head, he looks up and licks my hand before burying it back into Sandy's neck. "Rupert has a new home in Carroll Gardens. We're dropping him off there on our way to Manhattan. Right little guy?" She looks down at him and Rupert lets out a little whine as if to say, "yes but I don't want to leave you." We agree to meet back in the city for cocktails sometime during the week before Sandy returns to Summit and with swift efficiency, Sammy starts unpacking Sandy's car as Chase pulls his car out of the garage. He watches Sammy load pet paraphernalia, including doggie blankets, towels, pads, puppy chow, biscuits, and a small cage into it with the same expression Massimo had when I drove away in his prized Porsche. Chase then gets into Massimo's car and maneuvers it to the side while Sandy places Rupert in the cage then drives her car into the garage. There's more shuffling of automobiles than cards in a poker hand. I'm suspect.

Walking back toward me Chase is all smiles until, narrowing my eyes, I look him straight in the face and ask, "Did Massimo put you up to this?

"What do you mean?"

"Don't be deliberately obtuse. Ask you to drive me back?"

He wags he's head back and forth, as if contemplating the right way to answer then blurts, "It was more like begging."

Sammy interrupts my retort. "Hey, Alicia, it's your first time up here. How'd you enjoy the mountains and country air?"

Annoyed for being played and deliberately kept out of the loop, I'm possessed by the urge to needle.

"Amazing. We relaxed, went riding and well … I was just so relieved I was able to come."

I'm discreet with pauses in all the right places. Sammy nods smiling, but Chase, holding the car door open for me, studies my face. Sliding into the passenger seat, I throw a deadpan look borrowed from him and add my own brand of wide-eyed innocence.

He shakes his head and mumbles, "A real wiseass," before getting in the driver's seat and shifting seamlessly into gear. We're both a bit quiet on the car ride back to the city, listening to the soft jazz playing and thinking about our busy work week ahead. Rain pelts against the windows as the gray, drizzly day finally succumbs to a downpour. Chase says nothing more about my moving in with him, and I know he's giving me space to think about it. My feelings are mixed. First inclination would be to say yes, simply because when I'm with him I'm simultaneously more alive and at peace, like being part of a conglomeration of hope and joy and creative energy. But in this fray there's also doubt. So much has happened so fast and I don't know if I can keep up. I've barely had time to establish myself in my career, haven't solidified my independence where I can boast of an impressive 401K or a respectable savings account or even living independently. How can I possibly hold my own in this relationship? Chase reaches out his hand and with his forefinger, rubs the furrowed space on my forehead, then lifts my hand and kisses it. He says nothing, just continues to hold my hand, and I look at him and think this brave and beautiful man who has seen so much of life wants me. How is that possible? And it's not that I don't think enough of myself. I do. I'm self-motivated and self-assured ... well, most of the time. It's just that I may need more life experiences to prove myself to me. The phone interrupts. He talks with hands free but we're not on speaker so I can't hear the other party. It's business though. His voice is terse, official.

"When was this?"

Pause.

"There was a carbon monoxide alert but it was a false alarm. Any smoke?"

I sit straighter.

"Ok, I'll be there in about a half hour. Could be a wiring short, but let's not take a chance."

I look at him for clarification but his face is blank as if smoke and carbon monoxide alerts are nothing out of the ordinary.

"What's happened?"

"I need to take care of some business in Brooklyn. Seems like several smoke alarms have been triggered. I'm sure it's nothing. The building is vacant, but even so I want to be on site when the fire trucks arrive. Sammy's on his way back. Call if you need anything and remember what we spoke about?"

"You mean the 'If I see something say something spiel.'" I regret my words the second they're out of my mouth.

"Don't be flippant. Do I have your word?"

He's mad and I'm feeling guilty for causing us to leave off on this note after having just spent a wonderful time together.

"I'm sorry and yes of course I'll let you know if anything out of the ordinary happens."

I think he's appeased until he adds, "I have you're word that you'll stay in the apartment for the night, just lock and bolt your door. Sammy will let you know when he's back. I don't like leaving with this overlap, but if I have your assurances …"

I cover his lips with my finger. "I promise. Go take care of business. I'll be fine."

Without another word, he pulls into a spot in front of my building, and I know it's because he's giving me space to think about his proposal. *No pressure*, he had said and he meant it, but after this last conversation I also know that he would like nothing more than to see that I am safely tucked away in his apartment with Sunny on the lookout and Sammy on the way. Not a valid enough reason to extend an invitation for me to move in, but I don't dwell on it because I need to get out of the car and he needs to be on his way.

Herman, the night porter, opens my door then hops back toward the opened trunk to carry in my bag.

"You be safe too," I whisper just before Chase leans in, pulls me to him, and gives me a kiss good-bye. "Call me when you are on your way back."

He nods and as soon as I walk through the entrance, he pulls away. As always, there's an empty feeling when we part, like a small part of me has gone missing. It's different from my usual. This has an added layer that tugs at the heart instead of just leaving a void.

My text message pings. *Are u in your apartment?* Attached is a smiley face sending off a kiss in the shape of a heart.

It seems he's learning how to sweeten his orders.

I text back immediately, *Yes. Here all alone. Miss u.* And

add a frown face. It's fun to act corny—trite and helps lighten the heavily weighted burden of problems we've begun to share.

His response is automatic. *Then I'll have to spend the night. Ok?*

The missing piece falls back into place as I text back YES, adding a heart-eyed emoji. You have to wonder who thinks of these lame picture characters that just seem to bring out a smile.

One good look around my apartment and my smile evaporates. Clothes are scattered on my unmade bed, makeup, soap, gels, and perfume bottles clutter the bathroom and coffee cups and saucers litter the kitchen sink. God I was in a funk before this weekend. I break into some cleaning, making sure to chill a bottle of white wine for later. So much for maintaining space to think about living arrangements and unpacking my bag, I can't help but grin when I remove the shoes and panties I wore during my strip tease. I carefully box the shoes to store in my closet and start sorting clothes for the laundry when the buzzer catches me by surprise. That was fast. Reaching for the intercom, I hear the crackly voice of the porter Herman.

"Miss Cesare, there's a package here for you marked urgent. We're a little short staffed at the moment. Do you mind coming down to pick it up."

I've gotten used to being referred to as Miss Cesare by the staff here without feeling like I'm at least thirty like I use to.

"Sure, Herman. Do you know who it's from?"

"It's labeled to Alicia, from Sammy."

"I'll be right down."

Maybe the package has something to do with the emergency at their building and not wasting a spare moment, I grab my keys, lock the door, and scurry into the elevator. Herman, a wisp of a Filipino with thin black hair combed across a receding forehead and weary brown eyes, immediately reaches for the envelope when he spots me.

"Hello, Miss Cesare." He gives me a nod that's almost a bow, then hands over a manila envelope.

"Hi, Herman. Thanks for letting me know this was waiting for me." I take the envelope and do a quick scan for Sammy, but the lobby is empty. I start prying open the metal fasteners on my way back to the elevator and fishing at the bottom, I feel something cold and stiff. When I pull it out my stomach retches and I grab onto the side of the wall for support. In the palm of my hand is a severed finger sporting a thinly veined and beautifully set turquoise ring.

CHAPTER THIRTY-FIVE

y scream is stifled by a hand wrapping around my mouth and tugging me back with the force of a hail wind. I drop the envelope and kicking and squirming, throw my fists back, but I'm held tightly, my neck twisted at an angle that makes it hard to resist. Lifted by thick, muscled arms, I'm dragged into the empty stairwell. Something sharp pierces below my breast, and the more I resist the more it penetrates. I can't see what it is because when I try and move my head, the hand tightens across my mouth and nose and I can't breathe. The back of my heels bang against the steps and pain shoots up my legs as I'm dragged down the stairs and into a storage area in the basement. Dank wisps of breath curl around my neck and ear and I shiver.

"Say nothing, do nothing. If you so much as whisper a cry for help, your finger will be the next to turn up in a package.

Do you understand?" He thrusts a blade that still has blood clinging to its edges close to my face, hurls his foot back, and slams the door of the storage room shut.

My heart feels like it's pounding through my chest, but I nod an assent. Slowly he removes his hand from my mouth, making sure to keep the knife pressed against my back. I remain rooted, too afraid of what this madman might do if I move.

"Good girl. Now turn around slowly." I do as I'm told and find myself staring into a pair of eyes so gray they look colorless. The business-like suit and tie he's wearing doesn't fool me, and I quickly deduce that I'm face to face with Dimitri Ostopenko.

He glances into the envelope that he's managed to reclaim, and shakes his head. "Tsk tsk. Such a pity she did not follow orders. She so enjoyed playing itsy bitsy spider with her little boy." He moves the knife to my hand, sliding the flat part of the blade across my knuckles in repeated slow motions.

I want to scream, make a run for it, do anything possible to escape from this sadistic maniac, but he's wielding a knife and blocking the doorway.

Mustering courage, I yank my hand away. "What do you want?" My voice is cold, hard.

He shrugs, his thin lips pulling back into a twisted grin. "Why, Alicia, I want what any man longs for: a wife, children, a ... how do you Americans say, a place to hang my hat. I am a simple man. And you?" he asks matter of fact, but his deadened eyes mirror the brutality of a killer. "Do you want to marry your lover, Have children with him? I understand he's quite successful now. Nothing like the straggly urchin I once knew."

It's unsettling how much he knows about us. Chase was right. The man oozes vengeance.

"What do you mean Fiona didn't follow orders? Where is she?" I stare him in the face, wanting him to see I'm not intimidated by his brand of terrorizing.

"So many questions you have." He raises the knife and presses the tip against the corner of my lips, and I feel I slight prick before something wet drips down the side of my chin.

He wipes the blood away, letting his finger trail across my cheek then down my neck, stopping just above my breast where he lets it rest before finally lowering his hand. "I think I am tired of hearing your voice." And before I know what's happening he takes a soiled rag from his pocket and stuffs it into my mouth. Turning me, he holds the knife to my back and marches me to a cardboard box where an assortment of extension cords, thick wires, and electrical tape fill its contents. "Now slowly bend and hand me that tape." The blade's point pinches my back and follows me down as I pick up the reel of tape and slowly turn around and hand it to him. Still holding the knife to me, he tears off a piece with his teeth and places it across my mouth with his free hand. He continues talking as if we're having a nice chat while strolling in the park.

"I had all those once. A wife, children, a house, even a dog."

He becomes still, his hollow cheeks and lank hair offsetting those feral eyes. "Then poof…" he waves the knife in the air, forcing me to take a step back "…gone. Just as if a magician waved a magic wand and made them disappear. So now…" he lifts my hair with the edge of the knife and pushes a wisp back then lets the point rest against my neck "…I use my own style of magic to get what I want."

Too afraid to make any sudden moves, I use every ounce of effort to remain calm and not appear to be begging for my life.

"Do you know what maskirovka is, Alicia?" He leans close, his stale breath comingling with the sweet scent of cologne, and I have to fight the urge to heave into my gag.

I have no clue where he's going with this, but the longer he talks the more chance I have of staying alive. Someone must be moving in several floors up, because there's scraping of furniture and some hammering against the walls where they're probably hanging pictures. Maybe someone will come down to add or pick up something from storage, but for now the room is deserted.

I shake my head and force my mind to focus on a plan of escape. Locked storage bins holding discarded furniture, boxes of Christmas decorations, bikes, empty suitcases, and old photo albums line the walls on either side of the room. Replacement windows and shower doors lean against the far wall and in front of them, there's a wooden box of tools and a discarded pile of rags. In the toolbox I spot a hammer and different types of screwdrivers, all potential weapons if I can reach them. To my left, there's a door that I assume leads to an outside alley.

"So quiet. Has the cat got your tongue? Maybe you are just confused, so I explain better." He eyes me like a teacher would a pupil, except he's wielding a knife instead of a pen.

"Maskirovka is something masked, like a hoax or a pretense." He looks up and closes his eyes as if deep in thought but keeps the knife poised at my throat. "It is a very effective ploy in defeating an enemy. First, a masquerade is created to keep your adversary from learning your true intent. A person may be tricked into believing an emergency exists somewhere, perhaps a gas leak or fire. He goes off running to see what's wrong... " he jogs in place, his face twisted in mock concern before stopping to study me "...and leaves the real target unguarded, vulnerable to attack. We Russians are masters at this. Used it to win battles even wars and you know what? It even works on an Ivy League hotshot and a pretty little nothing like you."

His gaze moves to my neckline then lower, lingering on my breasts. I eye the toolbox again, but he's holding the knife too close to my throat for me to make even the slightest movement. "You are shaking. Maybe you think I am going to kill you? Stick my blade in you over and over until you rasp out your last breath? That I would never do. I am a lover, not a murderer. Besides, why kill when you can achieve reprisal in so many more effective ways." He reaches out and grabs my breast, pulling me toward him and I double over in pain. "When I am through with you..." he holds the knife to my other breast "...you will be alive, but there will not be much left worth wanting." Lowering the knife, he slips one arm from his suit jacket and then the other and places it neatly on top of a box. "No need to stain a good suit."

There's a scraping sound of footsteps immediately above us and startled, he glances up, lowering the knife just enough for me to jerk to the side and slam my knee into his crotch. He doubles over in pain, and I hear the knife drop onto the concrete floor. I scramble for the toolbox, scrabbling for the hammer, but he grabs a handful of my hair and yanks me back, hurling me against the stacked shower doors. One topples and shatters, and as I struggle to my feet, he slaps my face with the back of his hand, and I tumble back into the shards of glass.

Flashes of light jump in front of my eyes and I thrust down my hands to try to propel myself up again. Pain sears across my left palm where a jagged piece of glass pierces and I close my fingers around it, flattening it so it's no longer slicing my palm. He grabs hold of my foot and drags me away from the broken glass. I try kicking, but the force of his slap is making the room spin and soon he's on top of me, lowering his mouth to mine and forcing my lips open. I move my head from side to side but the weight of his body keeps me pinned.

"You fucking cunt. When I get through with you, you'll be nothing more than a discarded piece of meat." Trapped under his weight, I can't move and he uses his free hand to open and tug down my pants. My mind races, my eyes dart in terror looking for any means of escape. He lowers his hand to undo his belt and I manage to shimmy my hand free. He slows his momentum for a bit because basically nothing seems to be happening for him. His press against me remains flat and flaccid, and lips curled in anger, he makes a fist, raises and swings back his arm. I force myself not to flinch and maneuvering the shard of glass between my thumb and fingers, strike it across the underpart of his upper arm. I hear the thin fabric of his shirt tear and feel the glass slice flesh. I turn my face ready for the blow, and when I open them again I see him recoiling in pain, shock mirrored in his eyes as deep red blood spurts and gushes. I shove him off me and drenched in his blood, boost myself up. With shaking hands I pull up my pants, tear off the tape and spit out the gag. Adrenalin coursing through me, I bound through the door and race up the stairs two at a time, believing that at any moment I'll be forced back into his snare. When I burst into the lobby, my ear is still ringing from the slap and my eyes have trouble focusing. In the distance, I spot Sammy talking to Herman who's holding the phone and shaking his head shrugging. I try to move, to call out and tell them I'm not in my apartment, but my legs lock and then buckle. The rest is a blur.

CHAPTER THIRTY-SIX

"It's not my blood," are the first words I gasp as Sammy holds me up. The next to tumble out of my mouth are, "Oh god, we have to try and find Fiona … He … He …" I can't finish because my heart feels like it's going to pound through my chest and I can't catch my breath.

"Take it easy, Alicia. Fiona is ok. She's at home with Liam."

"Her finger, he has her finger." I'm crying and panting, trying to break free from Sammy's grasp and run back for the envelope, but Sammy holds me in a tight grasp and forces me to make eye contact.

"You say this isn't your blood." He checks me from head to toe, gently looking over my neck, my arms, the back of my head, and stopping when he sees my hand. There's a gash that I hadn't noticed before dripping blood on the lobby floor.

"Hold your hand up like this." Taking my hand he raises it, keeping my arm bent at the elbow and to my side, then wraps a handkerchief around it. It immediately soaks with blood and, as if caught in a surreal moment, I gaze questioningly at the bright red soaking into the stark white. My breathing is still rapid and I feel as if I'm trapped in a fog that mars sights and sounds, keeping them distant and fuzzy. Sammy takes off his jacket and wraps it around my shoulders, then without saying a word reaches down and buttons and zips my jeans. He pulls out his phone, hits the 9, but I clutch his arm before he gets any further.

"No, not an ambulance. Please, drive me to the hospital."

Giving me a curt nod, he returns his phone to his pocket, gently takes my elbow, and guides me to his car, which is illegally parked in front of the building. Mercifully, it wasn't booted by some overzealous city official.

We drive to Lenox Hill Hospital on 77th between Lex and Park, its bright blue awning jutting out as if welcoming you into a hotel, except for the red letters spelling: Emergency Entrance. As soon as we reach curbside, Sammy throws his keys to a valet parking attendant for hospital patients and visitors and escorts me through the emergency entrance. The room is packed, but one look at my blood-soaked blouse and sliced hand and I'm led into a small enclosed room toward the entrance. Sammy stays by my side, his quiet calm reassuring, but the musty metallic smell from my blood-soaked blouse mixes with the compressed air from the small room, and I press the back of my hand against my nose to keep it at bay, but it continues its assault until every breath I take exhumes its toxic fume. An official looking woman in a white blouse and dark pant suit tells me to take a seat, but her voice sounds muted. The overhead light dims and the patterned floor spins closer and closer to my face. The last thing I remember before passing out is the blood bubbling from his arm like rushing water in a flood.

"I think I killed him." The tall, dark-skinned gentleman who introduces himself as Detective James Wilson listens but says nothing.

I've been crying since I came to and found myself lying on a bed surrounded by a curtain with the bustle of doctors and nurses scurrying to treat an array of patients lining the perimeter of the large room. Through a part in the curtain, I see that every so often one walks to a computer and taps in information before moving to examine another patient. Detective Wilson looks down at me with compassionate eyes that contradict his firm, "I'm going to need to get a statement from you," expression. Exhausted from my sobs, I nod weakly but before he can get any further, he's interrupted by a petite nurse, hair pulled into a blond ponytail with wisps escaping on each side and a no nonsense expression that meets his head on.

"Detective, you're going to have to put that on hold. We need to take this patient for an MRI. Then her hand is going to need to be seen to."

My wound has been wrapped in a temporary bandage, but blood continues to seep out from its white cover. I look for Sammy but he's nowhere to be found and my guess is he was asked to leave for the benefit of my medical privacy and questioning.

"I'm looking for Alicia Cesare. Can anyone here tell me where I can find Alicia Cesare?" I recognize Chase's voice before I can see him through the drawn curtain. There's a soft voice of someone, no doubt a nurse attempting to calm him down.

"Sir, please, lower your voice. Let me take you to her." The curtain is pulled aside and Chase takes one look at my blood-soaked blouse and shouts, "Dear god, where's the doctor. She needs to see a doctor now."

And for the umpteenth time, I find myself saying, "It's not my blood."

He's wild with worry, not listening to my assurances that I'm fine, and making such a ruckus that two nurses and a doctor scurry to my side. I take his hand in my good hand and squeeze and, as I expected, the warmth of my touch calms him. He raises it to his lips and kisses it, then turns to the doctor who continues to speak only to me.

"We have to remove your clothes and slip you into a hospital gown for your MRI. You fainted when you arrived and your eye is bruised. Everything appears fine but best to make sure."

"Alright." My voice is low, but inside I'm shaking with alarm.

"I'm not leaving you," Chase intercedes.

"And how do you know the patient?" Bristling with protective efficiency, he looks at Chase.

"I'm her boyfriend."

"I want him to stay." My response is decisive.

The doctor nods then adds to Chase, "You can come along with her for the test, but she's going to be brought right back here so why not just take a seat and wait. It won't be long."

Chase is forced to let go of my hand when a gloved nurse appears and stands by my side. She takes my clothes as I remove them and places them in plastic bags. Thank heavens I can leave my underwear on because the large opening at the back of the gown removes whatever shreds of modesty and privacy I still had. It turns out my bed is also a gurney and I'm wheeled to the elevators and into a chilly stark white room.

When I'm wheeled back, I see Chase waiting, head in his hands. He looks up when he sees me and instantly reaches out to hold my hand. We don't have long to wait before another doctor with a flurry of dark curls framing his face just like Marcel's introduces himself.

"Hello, I'm Dr. Argant." He reaches out and shakes Chase's hand. "And you're?" His smile is filled with calm assurance.

Mollified, Chase takes his hand. "Chase Reardon. How is she?"

Dr. Argant looks at me, I assume needing my permission,

before he speaks to Chase about my condition and when I nod, he looks back at Chase and officially adds, "Her MRI shows no signs of concussion, her eye is bruised, and her hand is not broken but needs suturing. We're waiting for the plastic surgeon because the cut is deep and we want to avoid damage to any nerves."

"How long is that going to take?"

"The doctor's in the hospital. We've paged her, so it shouldn't be long. In the meantime…" he turns and looks at me "…there's a Detective Wilson who wants to speak with you."

"Can't it wait? She's in no condition to speak to anyone now." Chase is abrupt and protectively squeezes my good hand.

"I'm afraid it can't." Detective Wilson materializes through the curtain as if on cue. With him is a gentle-looking woman dressed conservatively in a dark skirt, blazer, and pumps, looking like she morphed from courtroom to hospital room to compliment the stage.

"Hello, Alicia. My name is Lauren Mercer and I'm from the district attorney's office. I often work with Detective Wilson who's a lead investigator from the Special Victims Unit. We would like to ask you some questions. I know you're hurting, but it's important we speak to you while the details of the attack are still fresh in your mind."

"Special Victims Unit?" Chase interrupts. "Why is that necessary?"

"With certain types of assaults, we prefer to be the ones

to gather information from the victim," Ms. Mercer answers, looking directly at me, her soothing professionalism easing my tension. I like her manner.

"That won't be necessary," Chase interjects, rapidly shaking his head, denial and fear marring his usual on-target judgement. "A sex crime wasn't committed. This was an attempted abduction by someone who is out to get me."

I look down at my fingers, at my sliced hand, then graze my eyes toward the side window—anywhere but at him because grabbing breasts and tearing down someone's pants while trying to penetrate constitutes a sexual assault in my book.

Stretched silence slices the air and Chase's whole body stills. Studying my movements, his shoulders tighten and his hands clench as storms rivaling Katrina and Sandy whip across his face. A heartbeat later, he folds his fingers into a fist and pounds it into the wall, making me wince and jump. He doesn't even grimace just stares ahead as if he hadn't just punched a hole into a hospital wall.

Some surly nurse with hairy arms and matching facial mole barrels through the curtain, surveys the damage, and turns on Chase with the force of a dragon protecting its lair.

"That's hospital property you've damaged." Then, without waiting for an answer, she turns on her heels and marches out to attend to a wailing patient.

Detective Wilson throws a quick glance at Ms. Mercer, who barely flickers her eyes in response before he wraps his arm around Chase and casually steers him away from us.

"Why don't we let these women chat for a bit while you and I grab a cup of coffee?" It's delivered as a question but shifts to a command with the firm flick of his thumb in the direction of the exit.

Chase quiets and returns to my side, bending down to stroke my hair. "Are you sure you're good with this?"

Reaching out my good hand, my fingers lock into his. "I'm fine. He mostly groped and bullied me." Which is basically true. Why let him worry more about the course of this private conversation than is necessary. Then, before I forget add, "But please bring me a change of clothes. I couldn't bare putting those back on again." He nods and just as he's leaving the same burly nurse appears, glaring pointedly at the hole then at Chase. Staring straight ahead, he jerks his hand toward the damaged wall.

"Send me a damn bill for the damages. I'll forward my information." Then he disappears with the detective.

Ms. Mercer focuses all her attention on me as I sit on the hospital cot and gaze ahead at the blank wall. "I know this isn't going to be easy, but your statement is crucial in apprehending whomever it was that assaulted you."

My voice is low, more monotone than whisper, and my mouth is so dry, I have to swallow several times before answering. "I think I know who his is."

I don't want to relive those moments, but I want Dimitri stopped. His streak of terror has gone on for too long. I'm going to be questioned about a sexual attack because that's what his guilty verdict involved. I can only imagine how many drug related attacks and murders he committed. The man is a monster who repeatedly has hoodwinked the criminal justice system. I'm determined to help bring him down any way I can.

"Good, but let's start with what happened shortly before you went down to the lobby when you were still in your apartment?" As if reading my mind she hands me a cold cup of water that an attendant brings in from outside my cubicle. It's as if there's another world on the other side of this curtain. Chunks of time seem muted and although I'm sitting on my hospital cot, I feel faraway, as if I can see myself from a distance.

I explain how I was buzzed by Herman and told that a package was left for me and how I said I would come down and pick it up, assuming it involved the emergency occurring in Chase's building. I start talking about the contents of the envelope and Fiona, but my tightening throat traps the words and it's hard to finish. Ms. Mercer waits patiently and when I'm finally done, hands me a tissue before continuing.

"What was he wearing?"

It still amazes me how he was dressed, and I shake my head to clear it before continuing. "A three-piece gray suit, impeccably tailored to his thin, tall physique, with matching shirt and tie. He looked like a CEO heading to work."

She seems unfazed, as if thugs and rapists dressed like they're heading for the office is nothing out of the ordinary. She seamlessly shifts to the next question. "You said he used a knife. When was the first time you saw it."

Just remembering the blade makes me tremble, but I muster the courage to answer, highlighting details as best as I can.

When she asks, "Did he talk during his attack?" I tell her how he threatened to maim me.

I sob into the tissues she continues to hand me. It's as if a flood of fear is unleashed, and I only stop when she asks if he penetrated any part of my body. Blowing my nose and wiping my eyes, I am spent but calmer.

"No," I answer, my voice level for the first time. "He attempted but when nothing seemed to be happening for him, he became angry and raised his fist to punch me. That's when I used the piece of glass to slice at his arm. I never imagined there'd be so much blood. Is he …"My voice is a strangled whisper. "Is he dead?" I let out a shuttered sob, dreading the answer and she remains silent for the longest time.

"You may have given him an arterial wound, but he hasn't been found so I doubt you killed him if that's what you're worried about. You did what you had to do to survive. If he's who you say he is, then it's possible he had the urge but the lingering residual effects of the drug he received prevented him from executing it. Add revenge and rage to that agitation and, well, let's just say you didn't overreact when you struck out at him."

"Let's hope that bastard's lying in some city morgue with a toe tag." Chase is back looking worn but calmer. He walks over to me and brushes the hair off my perspiring forehead.

"You ok?"

I lean my head into his hand and nod. I have a headache, my hand throbs, and I still can't seem to get the scent of blood from my nostrils, but nestled here with him close, every nerve and muscle relaxes, and I feel safe.

"It's a good idea to write down any flashbacks you may have. We'll need you to go to the precinct to ID photos and …" Ms. Mercer doesn't get the chance to finish because a smartly dressed doctor pushes back the curtain and steps inside the cubicle. The room just continues to ooze doctors, nurses, and aides.

"I'm afraid your time is up with my patient." She curtly nods at Ms. Mercer and Detective Wilson then shifts her attention to me. "I'm Doctor Stitcher, and I'm going to tend to your hand."

There's a wave of muffled snickers that she deftly ignores as she moves to my side and unwraps the bandage. The cut looks deep, but it's a neat slice and I appraise it with cool detachment. It's as if I'm floating in this bubble with everything and everyone around me figments of my imagination.

Dr. Stitcher shoots another pointed look at both Mercer and Wilson and, taking the hint, they hand their cards to Chase with a quick reminder to me to meet them at the precinct house on 67th between third and Lex tomorrow at noon.

"If she's feeling up to it, we'll be there."

I lie back at the doctor's orders and wait for the numbing injections to my hand to take hold, relieved that Chase plans to come with me tomorrow. Who needs to relive a treacherous time, scanning for photos of your assailant, alone. My eyes meet Chase's as he holds my good hand and waits for Dr. Stitcher to finish stitching.

CHAPTER THIRTY-SEVEN

"Slip your hand through here." Chase widens the sleeve of a new white hooded sweater, and I wince more from his stretching such beautiful cashmere than any pain from my hand when I push it through the opening. I breathe in its newness, hoping it will squelch the stench that continues to singe my nostrils. I have no idea where my clothes from earlier are and it's a good thing. I never want to see them again.

"Sit down. Let me help you put on your jeans." Chase is insistent. I sit. My mind and body are numb yet jumpy, and it feels strange to have such contrasting emotions warring inside. One thing is for sure, though. I want nothing more than to get out of this hospital cubicle and into a long, hot shower.

Perky blond pony tailed nurse, who walks like she has springs in her shoes, tells me her name is Jackie then hands me a pill that I assume is a painkiller and a cup of water. I toss it back and drink thinking Dr. Stitcher suturing and Nurse Jackie dispensing drugs. Humor can sprout anywhere.

Chase has the car pulled to the front of the hospital and after tucking me safely inside and buckling my seat belt, he gets in and heads in the direction of his apartment, no questions asked. I'm relieved. I have this need, this want to just feel him near. Leaning my head on his shoulder, I rest my bandaged hand on my lap and close my eyes, praying the wolves remain at bay.

The spray of the steamy shower cleanses my tired muscles … or so I think. I soap and rinse, soap and rinse, wash then rewash my hair, until I feel I've sufficiently removed any lingering residue from that maniac's touch. I reach for a towel, only to drop it and return to the shower to repeat the process. The third time around Chase appears with a plastic bag and wordlessly wraps it around my bandaged hand, making sure to secure it with bandage tape before leaving.

I was assured by the doctor that my bandage is waterproof but not meant to be immersed in water and find myself thinking how many showers constitute a soaking.

"Are you sure you don't need any help?" I hear through the rush of water.

"No, I'm fine." My voice sounds shaky, and I clear my throat and continue to stand under the spray. Each time I'm sure I'm done and the smell is finally gone, I'm assaulted yet again by its pungency.

Exhaustion finally renders my body washed enough to

stop and after drying off, I wrap myself in Chase's long, white terry cloth robe that hangs on a hook on the wall. I breathe in its scent and thank god it smells of him.

When I open the door, he makes it seem as if he's just appeared, but I know he's been hovering there since I first entered. I heard the light scrape of his shoes as he paced. It's a good thing too. My arms are limp, my legs leaden, and I can barely keep my eyes open. Nurse Jackie's pill has kicked into action.

Chase scoops me off my feet and carries me into his bedroom where the bedcovers have already been pulled down. I sink into a plush pillow and feel a slight tugging on my arm as he removes the wet plastic bag from my hand (I had forgotten it was even there) then removes the waterproof bandage and replaces it with a dry one. Rubbing a towel under my head, he dries my soaking hair as best he can before replacing the wet towel with a heated dry towel that he leaves in place. The warmth of his touch and that towel lull me into soothing nothingness, and I close my eyes and begin to drift. A heartbeat of a moment later they fly open again when, as if right in front of me, I see that the turquoise ring on the severed finger had the same upside down Y that I noticed the first time I saw it on Fiona. I've no time to ponder the consequences of this memory because a deep and dreamless sleep assaults and pulls me under.

I wake up with cotton mouth, a throbbing hand and a serious case of bedhead. The smell of bacon and pancakes makes me forget them all and tightening the tie on Chase's robe follow my nose into the kitchen. Chase, fully aproned, wields a spatula, flipping pancakes and poking sizzling bacon in the middle of a kitchen that looks like it's been hit by a tsunami. "Hey, Sleeping Beauty..." he looks up and gives me an ear-splitting grin "...I was just coming to check on you." Standing next to him is Sammy, bags and dark circles under his glassy eyes and looking like he hasn't slept in days.

"Hi, Sammy." I shuffle toward the table then stop short when the reality that it's a work day hits.

"What time is it? I think I slept in and never bothered to call work." I peer at Chase from eyes that refuse to fully open.

Spatula in hand, he stops what he's doing and wraps his arms around me. "No need to worry. I phoned in sick for you, made sure to keep it vague."

Sunny, head shaking, grabs the spatula from him like it's a fire extinguisher needed to douse a blaze. "It's after ten and well past the time for a first meal for you." Sunny chastises, surveying the kitchen and shaking his head again. "Now sit down and let me take care of this." He ends with a curt "please" that's more command than polite request then hands me a double expresso on ice with one hand while he flips a pancake with the other.

Chase guides me to the kitchen table like someone might an elderly invalid, but it's sweet, then lifts my bandaged hand and kisses it gently. His worried eyes peruse its surface then shift to mine.

"I'm so sorry. God, what if it had been your right hand? You wouldn't be able ..."

"Sorry for what?" I cut him off. "Some maniac's fumbled attempt to harm. I'm fine. Nothing hurts, I feel strong. " All bald-faced lies as my bandaged hand, swollen eye, and quaking insides can attest to, but why upset him more than he already is. In fact, why make them all more concerned than they already are.

Sammy continues to watch me through narrow, worried eyes, Chase is unusually twitchy, and Sunny remains a bit grumpy toward the both of them. I straighten my shoulders, sweep my hair out of my eyes. It really is sticking out in all different directions.

Looking pointedly at Sammy, I exclaim, "Yeah, well you should see the other guy." Then when his eyes widen in surprise, I quickly add, "What are we waiting for? Let's eat. I'm starving."

As expected, they all break into wide grins and Sunny starts bringing platters of food to the table.

"What time do you have to be at the office today?" It's Monday and with the long day stretching ahead with only a visit to the precinct to look forward to, I don't want to be left alone to dwell.

"I've taken the day. Thought we could just settle in and relax."

Sunny bangs a pan onto the stove and shaking his head, places more bacon on the sizzling grill. He seems a bit out of sorts this morning, which is very unusual for him and I hope it's not on my account. Maybe Chase and I can go out after I get a change of clothes, and Sunny can go back to his weekday work routine.

"I'm going to need to pick up some clothes from my apartment. I've nothing to wear today other than the clothes I came home in last night," I manage to get out between mouthfuls of pancakes and scrambled eggs.

Sunny's "*humph*" aimed at Chase swings my attention away from the food and toward Chase who says nothing, just continues eating looking a tad too innocent for my liking. In fact all three are quiet. Too quiet. I don't want to ask if anything's wrong because that would only shift the focus to me and concern for my injuries, but something's up that's for sure.

"I'm also going to need my blow dryer. My hair is a mess." I ignore their obvious uneasiness and lift stray strands of wavy hair up and out, knowing that this need is foreign to Chase who just washes, combs, and lightly gels his hair into place.

Chase clears his throat and grabs another pancake from the platter, never making eye contact. I look first at him, then at Sunny who, grumpy face intact, continues whipping up stacks of pancakes as if a party of eight is about to arrive. The only sounds are the scrapping of forks against plates and the sizzle of the grill.

My almost spoken "Ok, what's happening you guys?" is interrupted by Chase who casually throws out, "That won't be necessary. I took the liberty of having some necessities from your apartment brought here last night so you're all set."

"Thanks," but another, even louder "*humph!*" from Sunny prompts me to add, "Specifically what necessities are you referring to?"

"Oh, just your clothes, shoes, underwear, pocketbooks, sweaters, some coats stuff like that. Not your furniture though. I didn't think you'd mind if it was left behind for the time being." He bites into a piece of pancake dripping with syrup as if he hadn't just told me he moved me into his apartment without my consent or the benefit of a discussion.

All three nervously watch me until Sunny decides on the most prudent course possible and flees to his room. Sammy clears his throat mumbles something about having to get the car washed and also bolts. Tearing my locked gaze from Chase, I decide to check for myself exactly how many *necessities* he had hauled here last night.

In the alcove, my entire wardrobe is hung, folded, stacked, and neatly organized on one side of Chase's enormous walk in closet. A closer look shows me they're ordered according to color and season. I don't even bother to open any of the built-in drawers, that's how sure I am that inside is my lingerie, stockings, and socks probably ironed and color coordinated.

Still speechless, I can only wonder how he managed to pull this off while I slept. Even with his scrupulous efficiency he had to have had help. Heaven knows what buddies he drummed up to work through the night. No doubt Sammy and Mac were involved with Sunny operating as an irritable third. He must have opposed, his conservative bent believing that Chase should talk to me or good god, probably marry me first.

He mentioned that to me once when I was staying with Chase. "You are both in love. Why not marry and make lots of babies."

The thought is sobering and once again, looking at my belongings, I open my mouth, shut it, and open it again, attempting to say something, anything, but nothing comes out. For the first time in my life, I am shock-rendered mute.

Chase hovers in the alcove, eyeing me like someone might a circling tiger and all of a sudden, the whole preposterous scenario hits. Three meticulous marine minds and a military medic moving, managing, and consolidating just about everything I own, and I realize that my muddled mind is now spinning out of control alliterations. A hysterical-like giggle surfaces that I find hard to control, and Chase takes it as an opportunity to plead his case.

"Will you try it out, just for the time being? If it doesn't work I'll move it all back." His tone is tentative, and while not pleading, it's peppered with wistful need. I remain rooted in place, looking from the closet to the wardrobe then back to Chase. Confused thoughts swarm my mind and laughing, I try shaking my head to clear them. What am I going to do with this man?

It's only when he holds out his arms that my mind quiets, and using my heart as a guide, I step into them. His sigh of relief is audible and he pulls me closer, tightening his arms around me. Relishing a touch I never could resist, I wrap my arms around his neck and look up into his eyes. Green sparks confronting blue stormy seas. Fire and water. Opposites in so many ways but the same where it really counts. Love. Empathy. Concern. And knowing that we're home when in each other's arms. I feel it. He feels it. Doubts, differences, maniac mobsters, severed fingers with recognizable turquoise stone rings, (surely there can't be two of them), and hardened memories of a trying past, melt into a haze of nothingness, and replacing them is a sun-drenched clarity that encompasses joy, understanding, and acceptance. It's in that awareness, that I see my destiny and I have my answer.

"Yes, I'll live with you."

For a minute he looks confused, like he never thought I would agree so easily and then he laughs out loud and spins me in a wild circle. "But …" I continue when he finally stops. "I'm not happy about a live-in relationship that's based on fear for my safety."

He becomes still, reflective, a sadness tugging at eyes that had been just smiling into mine, and I know he's pondering yet again the events of my ordeal. A man, burdened by a past that continues to chase him into the future.

"I'm concerned. I won't deny it. But you also showed me that, while you are incapable of obeying an order, you are able to take care of yourself. By the way do you ever do as you're told?"

He's grinning and I'm happy that the former heavy moment has passed, recognizing that this is how it's going to be with him. One instant lighthearted and free-spirited and the next sad and struggling. But I can do this, I can handle this, and opting for humor as the best solution, I shrug, a smirk tugging my mouth to the side.

"Yes, but only when I'm not in the mood to irk you." He gets this "what the fuck" perplexed look plastered on his face, so I figure I better elaborate. "I didn't leave the apartment to purposely 'disobey an order.'" I'm really going to have to help him lose this military verbiage. "I thought Sammy left a message that you needed my help. In hindsight, I should have realized that if that were the case, he would have phoned or texted."

"Well, you made a mistake and now you're hurting because of it. Just know that next time you foolishly dart off after agreeing to stay put, I will make sure you can't sit for a month of Sundays." And in steps over-controlling, fear-propelled inflexibility.

I don't know if it's the relief of realizing I'm safe, the heady feeling of moving in with him, or some masochistic wish fulfillment fantasy, but I trace my finger across his beautiful mouth and whisper, "If it's anything like being fucked seven ways from Sunday, do you promise?"

He looks at me, surprise etching his face, then breaks into a raucous laugh that reminds me of Virgil, and still holding me in his arms, exclaims, "That reckless nature rears up yet again. What am I going to do with you?"

I don't have to think twice before answering. "Love me."

And nodding he guides me to the bed, where ever mindful of my sore hand, he lays me down and gently removes my robe. We meld into an embrace, two forming one, a singularity that's strong, and kind and patient, a distinctive oneness that drives away differences, dangers, and doubts and signals that together, we are undefeatable.

ACKNOWLEDGMENTS

When a story begins to unfold in the imagination, there are so many involved in the process of helping it evolve so that characters spring to life, events intrigue, and momentum is maintained. Thank you to family and friends who didn't cease to encourage my efforts even when I had doubts.

Thank you, L.G., for being my first reader when CAPTIVE OF A COMMONER was in its infancy. You were my inspiration to continue writing, even when I seemed to have hit a brick wall.

Thank you, M.G., for helping me share the story of Chase and Alicia with others. Your enthusiasm encouraged me to believe that others would enjoy reading their story.

Special thanks to my husband for his patience and gentle reminders that I should get some rest when I was pounding the keyboard at 2:00 A.M. His help answering questions about the development and sale of real estate in Manhattan were crucial to making Chase's career experiences accurate.

To my late mom who read the first several chapters and told me all the people in her life Chase and Alicia reminded her of. She affirmed that I had made them real.

I can't forget Alice whose remarks about the prologue helped me rewrite Chase's past so that it was so much more genuine and applicable than the original. She was a fan even before I finished and was quick to suggest that I continue writing.

Heartfelt thanks to Max Dobson of the Polished Pen who not only revised and edited but thanked me for letting her share Alicia and Chase's world and complimented my "beautiful prose." As a debut author those words were like being gifted with wings to soar.

Thanks also to Paul Copello who could double as a mind reader. He designed a cover that exceeded my visual and artistic expectations and didn't stop until he felt it reflected the characters' lives and met his creative demands.

Thanks to Google and AA for providing information about alcoholism. Thanks also to all the beautiful fashion magazines that helped clarify design trends and ideas.

And last but not least … thank you, readers, for taking a chance on a new author's work. Without you a book is nothing more than empty words. I hope you were able to escape into the lives of Chase and Alicia and enjoy reading about them as much as I enjoyed writing their story.

CPSIA information can be obtained
at www.ICGtesting.com
Printed in the USA
FSHW01n0924220618
49401FS